I0593480

Viper's Fate is a standalone reverse harem novel with multiple love interests. Intended for mature readers, 18+, it contains dark fantasy elements regarding graphic violence, murder, several high heat MM romance scenes, and ABO sexual content that some readers may find offensive. Please proceed with caution.

VIPER'S FATE

JADE BONES

For my cat, Mowgli, who at eleven years old still firmly believes he's a lion. Don't worry, bug, we all know you're the real alpha of the family.

CONTENTS

BLURB

When I turned my back on the most brutal gang of alpha a-holes this side of the bridge—my family—I also gave up my claim as their Alpha.

No one knows my secret. But a killer from my old life has returned, and Fate decides to bond me to the one man with the key to my past, even if he doesn't realize it: the lone survivor of my family's most unforgivable rampage.

Oh, and two other alphas, just in case I thought I could get out of this alive.

All I have to do is keep my head down and make sure my past stays buried until our bond fades—and takes the rut building between us with it. But the killer's twisted game ensnares me, and the only way I can fight is if I admit who I am.

Luc, Theo, and Jace have no idea who they're bonded to... but the rut is coming, and my alpha soul is breaking free.

For better or worse, they're going to find out.

Warning: Viper's Fate is a standalone reverse harem novel with multiple love interests. Intended for mature readers, it contains dark fantasy elements regarding graphic violence, murder, several high heat MM romance scenes, and ABO sexual content that some readers may find offensive. Please proceed with caution.

1

JEL

Tonight is pure shit on a stick already, and that's not even counting the asshole stalking me.

"You had to choose the alley, Jel," I mutter, glancing up at the security mirror angled to show the lane behind me, along with the glimpse of a shadowy figure walking at an unhurried pace. Five hundred slasher films not enough for you to learn the lesson? Never take the alley at night.

I know how this goes: idiotic girl makes hubristic and sinful errors, chooses the road where no one will hear her screams until far too late, and dies. Painfully. Maybe she puts up a good fight—I for damn sure would—but it's futile, unless she ticks all the boxes to become a final girl.

I'm not final girl material. Trust me.

Tonight's mission should be enough proof for that. The final girl is the good girl, the innocent one, the virgin. I'm no fucking innocent, and something tells me that gatecrashing your TA's party, breaking into their house, and stealing from them isn't the kind of thing a good girl does, no matter how valid her reasons are.

Seriously, the asshole had to pick tonight to paint a target on my back? I have priorities. I do not have time for this.

A footstep falls somewhere in the distance, closer than I expected. There's a weakened streetlamp about two meters ahead; if I can make it to the light, I can pause there, fake a conversation on my phone, and hopefully scare this creep off.

I ignore the rising need within my blood to do something else entirely, but that doesn't mean it isn't there. It's always there, especially in moments of danger, like this. If I were to look in a mirror, my eyes would already be glowing—an eerie shifter gold that marks the moment before the change. I can taste venom on my tongue, feel the sharp prick of fangs elongating.

A voice inside me—my soul—whispers for me to turn, to throw my phone and the weak distraction it represents away and fight. Or better yet, use my innocence as bait. He'd fall for it. I know he would. They always do.

But I vowed not to be that person. Not anymore.

Steeling my expression into a *don't fuck with me* look, but silently promising not to start anything, I pull out my phone and turn around to lean against the streetlight.

There's no one there.

I hold myself deathly still, scanning the shadows back and forth. I'm technically in viper territory, which means if someone is after me, I'm *technically* in deep shit. I don't think this stalker is a viper, though. Those guys are six feet of testosterone and aggression; they'd never trail someone in silence for so long.

Besides, I can handle a viper. I've been handling them since I was four.

Shadows flicker along the street as I leave the alley. I'm nearly at my TA's house, and the eerie silence of my lonely walk over here has disappeared. Now, I'm surrounded by the eerie, hushed noise of other people. Someone is definitely getting sucked off behind that trash can, and those trees are giggling. Trees shouldn't giggle after dark. It's just unfair.

A prickling sensation, like someone's watching me, crawls up my spine. I shiver and turn, hair whipping as I narrow my eyes at the shadows on the other side of the street. Is there someone in there? It looks like there is... someone with strange, round ears on top of their head.

What the fuck?

Has someone shifted and hidden in the shadows? They look too human for that, though. I don't know any shifter vitality with a tall, human body and round ears on top of their head.

I blink rapidly, fists curling into a protective stance, but then the shadows shudder and flare. Two boys appear around the corner, their phones blaring with music and bright, artificial light. There's no one hiding in the shadows.

They cross the street, and the nearest one bumps into me.

For a second, my body's instincts offer me a sharp, blazing sense of fear. Like this was the guy following me in the alley.

Then my shifter senses kick in, and I glare at the asshole as he makes an obscene gesture at me for getting in his way. It's just a college boy. I think I even recognize him from campus. I could take him down in three seconds flat.

Why am I so jumpy?

Shaking my head, I follow them through a cobblestone arch and into the house.

Immediately, I wrinkle my nose. I know I don't get out much these days, but this is something else. Even with the truly nuclear levels of perfume and cologne people are wearing, you can't drown out the alpha pheromones and unbridled shifter notes stinking out this place.

Seriously, do parties always smell like this, or have I picked the one where everyone decided to eat ass before they came?

Holding my breath, I accept the red solo cup shoved in my

direction and follow the crowd up the front steps and into the center of one of the larger rooms. It's loud here, too, the vibrations of the bass thudding through my body in a way that isn't exactly unpleasant, just unfamiliar. The beer tastes like piss.

Piss and ass, what a combo.

People wander around me, the crowd undulating like water as I scan the scene for a junk room or large closet. It's too dark to see clearly. I'll just have to check every door.

I wonder how long before an alpha accuses me of being suspicious. I don't fit in here. There are others like me; I can see them through the gaps in the crowd, despite the low lighting. But they don't stay visible for long. They either pair off with other awkward loners, or they find somewhere better to hide.

Sink or swim for us losers, that sounds about right. My experience at Sawlefire Academy has been pretty much sinking for a year now, socially speaking. The fact that I'm choosing this life doesn't make it any easier to bear.

I have the bizarre urge to paint this scene, like some kind of obscure *Géricault* with neon tones. Even if we're still technically afloat, we're fucking starving for more than this life, am I right?

My skin prickles. The lingering sense of someone watching me has followed me all the way inside. Did the stalker really stick around? That's not just stalking, that's... weirdly aggressive. It doesn't fit the profile, because I'm clearly not alone and vulnerable anymore. So unless he's going to stab me in the middle of a crowded party, what is he trying to do?

I tell myself the mystery stalker has long gone—vanished as soon as he saw me pull out my phone. But it's no use. I can still feel him.

Maybe I should try stealing the painting another day.

No, there won't be another day. There are so many people here, and it's such a stupid thing to steal, no one will suspect it. No one will be paying attention to the stack of paintings at all.

No one except a very embarrassed artist who hadn't realized exactly which portrait the TA was going to take for the exhibition.

God, why that one?

That one was a mistake. It wasn't even meant to be in the pile. It's like some trickster god interfered at the last second, purely to watch me shit bricks trying to fix this before it's too late.

"Where has he kept it?" I mutter to myself, searching in and out of the rooms at random.

A strange figure captures my attention, distracting me for a second as I stare at him. His face is covered by a mask—leather crafted into the shape of a rat—and the red-tinged smoke from the dance floor writhes around his feet.

The ears on top of his head... They're very... round...

My heart kicks up, thudding in my chest. Then someone bumps into me and I turn to see two drunk guys wearing similar masks—leather, but plain design this time, like Jason's hockey mask.

They giggle like idiots, shushing each other and adjusting the masks' straps, and I shake my head and look away. It's obviously some party prank they're going to trot out soon. More reason for me to get the hell out of here now.

Reflexively, I look back for the rat, but he's gone.

Whatever. I have other things on my mind. And I need to stop being so damn jumpy. It's embarrassing.

"Jel," a voice says behind me, making me jump.

"Cameron," I say, turning around and smiling up at my TA in a gesture that's barely off feral. "Cool party."

Holy demon testicles, did I really just say *cool party*?

But Cameron only grins and hands me a new cup, taking my empty one and throwing it in a trash can behind the hall table. "I'm surprised you came," he says, taking a sip of his own drink and leaning his hip against the table behind him. "I didn't think you were the partying type."

"Says you," I scoff, deliberately looking him over.

Cameron looks like someone crossed an accountant with Yoko Ono. You can tell he's an art student, and you can tell he's a TA... and the mixture is very strange. Really, you can't think about it too much at one time or it will make you dizzy. The snake tooth necklace he always wears sets my hackles up, but that's not his fault. It's just a snake's tooth, not a shifter tooth. And I assume the thing was already dead before it became jewelry.

Despite the necklace, I've always kind of liked him, in that way a sixteen year old girl has a crush on the guy that smokes behind the bike shed. Even now, knowing that he's the source of all my problems and currently cockblocking my attempts to fix things, my heart pounds just a little.

He reaches forward, taking a strand of my bright red hair between his fingers and plucking something from it—a leaf, I think. Probably from the alley.

"Well, I should let you... mingle," I say, trying to twist my face into something bright and friendly. It's not a common expression for me.

The way he bites his lip makes me think I've missed the mark. Dammit.

"You should try the little chocolate cakes," he says, pushing away from the table. "They're good."

"I will do that," I grit out, still smiling. God, please just leave. I need to rob you, already.

"Oh," he says, just before he goes. "I liked your painting, by the way."

His eyes glint, and I wish, firmly, for the house to swallow me whole. Just wrap me up and bury me alive, please. Thank you.

"Thanks." My smile is firmly fixed to my face now. If anyone could look at this expression and not see it as a declaration of war, they need some kind of medal for reading things in good faith. "I do my best."

"This definitely was your best," he agrees. "I liked its energy." His eyes fix on me then with a deliberate steadiness that makes my heart flutter—not altogether in a good way, this time.

Someone kicks the smoke machine over in the room beside us, and the spluttering waft of red smoke whirls in our direction. It casts a strange glow to his face, which mixes with the oddly deliberate way he said that. Unease prickles along my spine.

Does he mean energy as in, the subject that I painted? Or does he mean *energy*? As in, power. Magic.

Because if he knows...

I shake my head. He can't know.

"Well, you know me," I force out. "Full of energy."

He watches me for a second longer, before lifting his hand and walking off. "Enjoy the party."

Oh, so long as you're providing for your guests' every need, including B&E, I will.

As soon as he's out of sight, I escape, resuming my search. The third bedroom upstairs doesn't hold anything either, and I'm beginning to get a little frantic by this point. Goddammit. I'm looking for a stack of thirty paintings or so; it should be easy to find. It should be so fucking easy—

The basement.

As soon as I think it, I freeze, tilting my nose subtly toward the crowd. There's a scent I don't recognize filtering from the sweaty dance floor. That shouldn't be unusual in and of itself, except... it's kind of familiar, too. Like I *should* know it. Like it's from my dreams.

I turn another half step and find two golden eyes staring back at me from across the room. A shiver races through me, the sheer shock of it bringing me to a complete standstill. For a moment, the thought hits me: is this the man who was stalking me?

No, of course not. There's no way someone like him could disappear without me noticing.

He's... shit, he's huge. Even in the shadowed corner, I can make out that much. Strobing colours flick across his face, making it difficult to read his expression; all except for his eyes, that is. The flash of gold tells me his instincts are flaring. Something is making him want to shift, right now. For me.

The feline slant to his posture makes me think wolf, or tiger perhaps. I don't know any tigers, and certainly no wolves. But the way he looks at me... It's like he knows me. Like he's been waiting his whole life for me.

Then the light hits him properly and I recognize him.

Oh, God. He's the man from my painting.

Well, one of them.

But that's impossible. Those men don't exist. It was a fantasy, a foolish dream that I stupidly included in my submission pile because—clearly—the aforementioned trickster god possessed me. And then the TA went and picked it for the annual exhibition, and I had to come and steal it back before anyone saw it.

I can't let people see that painting. It isn't just the subject matter, which will make our practically-a-convent university expel me on sight. It's what I did to the painting. The magic I tied to it. If that magic is ever revealed, it will reveal everything else about me, too. Like who I am, and the secret I'm hiding.

The painting itself is simple enough, just three men standing with me in the center, looking like a fucking idiot. We're buck naked, the lot of us, not a shred of clothing to be found, and their fierce positions make it clear just how much they care about me.

Like anyone has ever cared about me. Even when they pretend they do, they're only ever protecting themselves and their own interests.

Swallowing, I turn aside, putting the whole thing down to coincidence, and that's when I see the other two.

Fuck, they're all here. The men from my painting exist.

And they've seen me, too.

2

JEL

OH BOY.

The men prowl toward me as if compelled, and suddenly I know exactly what this is. What's happening.

A shiver of fear and longing runs through me, making my nerve endings tingle and my soul burn with need. Bloody hell, no wonder that painting seemed to pour out of me, like I was possessed. They're my *mates*.

Shit, I really have to get that painting back now. It was bad enough when it was just an erotic painting with my biggest secret tied to it. Now? The university will probably see it as some kind of link to their precious gods.

Which makes me either a saint or a heretic, and as a woman I don't like my chances.

The first guy reaches me. He's easily six foot, with effort-lessly spiked hair that shines kind of iridescent in the light. It's that casual kind of hairstyle that all the fuckboys love, making it look both soft and sharp at the same time. I keep catching notes of golden orange in the strands, even though I'd swear his hair is black.

He leans against the wall beside me, eyes narrowed, and says, "Tell me why I already know you."

"If you say I've been running through your dreams, I'll castrate you," I say before I can control myself, fear guiding my tongue because, holy shit, this is my *mate*.

Then my brain catches up.

Crap. That's not what a beta would say. And I'd never pass as an omega, so I don't even bother trying. See, this is why I don't talk to people at all. It just makes it so much easier when I don't have to control my runaway mouth.

A spark of interest flashes in his eyes. "Sorry, babe, I keep it above the waist until the third date at least."

He winks at me, his smile softening the fuckboy attitude. Despite my churning stomach and dry mouth, it sends a little shiver through me. His lines are corny as shit, and he's got that typical alpha machismo that I hate, but there's also something strangely charming about the way he looks at me and waits, like I'm an intriguing puzzle he wants to solve, and he doesn't want to rush the experience.

Then the other two arrive, and my head finally overrides my weak, romantic, lonely-ass heart.

Three mates. Three *alpha* mates, fighting over me before they even know my name.

I stand up straighter. "Okay, I think we need some ground rules before we even start this conversation," I begin, but they aren't listening to me.

The second guy gives me a crooked smile, soft brown hair falling into his eyes and ending just above his shoulders. There are faint blond streaks through it, from the sun rather than a bottle, and a fading tan that no one else from this city possesses. I wonder if he's a surfer and spends all his holidays at the coast. I know I imagined a surfer when I painted him.

At the thought of my painting, I subconsciously lean in closer to him. Now that he's close enough to read, he's got this faintly himbo energy that immediately gets me on side, but then I get a whiff of his scent and nearly slam back into the wall trying to get away.

Alpha. Fucking hell, *alpha*.

There's something about his vitality that's even stronger than the first. Maybe not stronger... but more agitated. Like his soul is bottled up and the pressure is about to blow the cork right into my skull.

"She's your mate, dickhead." He answers the first guy's earlier question, still smiling that crooked, disarming smile. His eyes flash golden. "And she's mine, too."

The first guy growls, and the change that comes over the second is immediate. The laid back surfer vibes fade as a shadow passes across his face, but it isn't like a normal alpha challenge; it's quieter. There's a predatory stillness to him that makes my fangs want to slide free and plunge venom into his neck, so I can escape.

They begin to subtly square off, like I'm completely forgotten.

"Rein it in, *Theodore*," the new guy hisses, trying to brush Theodore away like he's an annoying fly. "The lady isn't impressed."

"It's Theo, you fucking tool, and you know it." Theo shoves him back, and the growls shift into snarls.

The third guy clears his throat, coming to a halt before me. My breath leaves me in a rush. If the first guy looked at me like I was a puzzle, this one looks at me like I'm some kind of rare treasure.

He's wary... Unlike the first two, he holds back, staking a claim with his eyes and the fierce slant of his mouth, rather than the almost visceral energy bouncing off the others. It's infuriating, that calm sense of simply having. Of not needing to fight for me; of already having me, without ever having won.

Like I'm some kind of prize.

He smiles, sending a shiver down my spine. "I've been looking for you, sweetheart," he says, voice low and clipped. "Shall we get out of here?"

Wow. His eyes are so blue, I actually take a second to realize the sheer asshole that's just come out of his mouth. But damn, those eyes. They're like gems, and there's a hint of smoke curling at his lips.

Dragon. He has to be a dragon. I didn't think there were any dragons left after—oh, *fuck*.

No.

My eyes widen, and I stare in horror between the three of them. This can't be happening.

The first guy—Theo—frowns. "Do you two know each other?"

They've practically got me crowded into a corner now. All three are paying me attention again, but it's in completely the wrong way.

Do we know each other? You could say that—if a history linked by blood and violence counts. If my guilt counts. But surely not... it can't be him, can it? What would *he* be doing here? In this city? He should have run far away from here.

I peer closer at him, trying to match the face of a boy I once knew, if only from the distorted print of a newspaper, to this hulking man before me. He smells of ash and fire, his scent singeing the back of my throat as he leans in and studies me. Cool blue eyes carry far too much ice for a man like this, and the soft fall of black hair over his face softens him in a way that screams of danger. Of a predator pretending they aren't a threat.

It can't be him... there's no way that boy became this man.

Or maybe I'm just telling myself that because, if he did, it would make the guilt easier to handle. It would mean we didn't break him after all, and maybe my sins could be forgiven.

"No," I snap, convincing myself it's true.

As if in answer, a strange sensation wells up inside me. It's like... heat. A twisting, turning sensation that's trying to reach out through my chest to the world beyond.

"Never met," the guy agrees, but he's frowning now. They all are.

He shifts, rubbing his chest, and the motion is mirrored by the others. It's like they can sense the same thing I can, like this weird sensation is flowing through them, too.

Oh. This is our bond.

I place my hand on my sternum, willing my face into a mask of perfect control as I lock the sensation away. It's just my body. Just a feeling.

But then it hits me properly. My eyes roll back in my head, and I fall against the wall, unable to move. One of the others grunts, and there's a scuffle like they've been knocked around too, but I can't focus on it. I can't take in anything but the warm, golden sunlight that's filling me from head to toe.

Horribly, my eyes grow wet at the corners. I squeeze them tighter together, biting my lip so hard I taste blood. I've never felt anything like this before, and it's scrubbing me raw from inside out.

I know what love is, what it feels like, just as I know how to lock it away so it can never hurt you. This is... something else. This is every golden summer of childhood wrapped up in one. This is late nights at the beach, festival fireworks, and a sense of safety so strong it regresses me to an age too young to remember.

This bond feels like something I'd lost years ago, and had

been told I would never find again. But now I have, and my entire body aches with the pain of wanting it.

"What the hell is this?" one of them hisses, on the other side of darkness. I still don't open my eyes.

"Bond," another grits out. He's closer now, his breath hitting my cheek.

A shiver runs through me, and I nearly reach for him. Nearly drag his warmth into mine and bury my nose in his neck, just to smell him. Just to know he's there.

"This is a bond?!" I think it's the dragon speaking. "I thought they were sweet."

Someone laughs, the sound a low, lazy drawl that makes me think of the surfer. "Bonds aren't sweet. They're electric."

"High voltage," one of them murmurs, almost sounding awed. "Pure electricity running through my veins."

They're right. That's how it feels—it feels like the lights have been out for twenty years, and someone's just switched them on.

How is this even possible? How can I have a fated mate —*mates*—with everything I've done to my soul?

It isn't possible. That's the answer. I don't have time to form a pack, and I *can't* form a pack with three alphas. The idea is... ludicrous. We have no omega, and everyone knows a pack needs an omega to balance out the alphas' instincts.

These men are meant to bond to an omega. Not to me.

I snap my eyes open, and see all three of them steadying themselves against the wall and each other. They look like they've been knocked around in a violent storm, eyes wide, lips swollen and red from where they've bitten down in shock. When they see me looking, their expressions transform, heat and desire mingling in a way that doesn't feel like lust anymore. It's beyond lust.

It feels like longing. Like destiny.

My soul shivers inside me, and I can't make my mouth form the word 'no'. Even with their macho bullshit, even with my intense need to finish my little theft tonight and get out of here, I don't know how to walk away.

How do you walk away from a happily ever after you thought you'd lost?

Maybe we can rain check. Talk this out. They might have an omega already.

"Look," I begin.

Before I can work out how to finish that sentence, my instincts slam into high alert, and everything freezes.

It happens in slow motion.

I see that guy from the alley again. The jock who bumped me. He slips on his mask—a bear this time—grinning as his face disappears. His friend beside him puts on a matching one, and together they tip their heads back and howl.

It's a prank—my brain tells me they're doing some kind of hazing thing, like I predicted earlier, but the scent in the room is off. My instincts are screaming that something else is happening, something that doesn't match what I'm seeing.

There's an undercurrent of danger.

The air shifts, and for a second I'm thrown back to that night, with the dragons. I hear screams, smell violence twisting the air, and wonder if my mind has finally cracked under the weight of my guilt. But then I realize—no—this is real. It's happening right now.

Again.

I shake off my unease, locking it deep inside me so I can become who I need to survive. I shut the bond away too, a dozen padlocks clicking into place in my mind, because I can't afford that weakness.

Somewhere, somehow, this party has gone wrong.

I back up into the wall, using the pressure to ground myself and to make sure no one can get me from behind. The three men before me have clued into the danger as well, but they look as uncertain as I am about where it's coming from.

The smoke machine splutters in the corner, choking violent streams of red smoke across the dance floor. It's still kicked over from earlier, and the effect means the smoke is distorted. No longer streaming smoothly or controlled, it spits and sputters until the room is hazy and confusing.

A flash of a leather-covered face next to me makes me spin around—it's one of the smooth-faced masks from earlier.

Another flash, from the other direction: a second.

Face after face appears through the smoke, covered in leather masks and howling like wolves. Some are smooth masks revealing nothing, but most are animals. Wolves, bears, tigers...

It's the Hunt. Adrenaline kicks in, mixed with the sharp edge of fear. What the hell is the Hunt doing here? Why didn't I hear about it?

Then my brain takes over. No—they're acting like the Hunt. It isn't real. There's too much laughter. This is the prank; I haven't found the danger yet.

What I'm sensing is happening beneath the laughter.

I force down the instincts that tell me to shift and attack, to bite through someone's throat until their blood spills out between us. My shifter soul knows exactly what she wants, but the human part of me needs to focus.

It's taken years for me to learn how to quieten her desires and let my logic lead the way. I won't lose that now.

After a second, I breathe in the air again, focused and deliberate. I smell joy and laughter, giddy excitement, sweat that doesn't reek of terror.

No malice. No fear. Not in this room.

My shoulders turn rigid as I let my senses roam further.

I hear the sound again, closer than before: a bloodcurdling

scream. It's nothing like the excited screams of the party, who've quickly realized what this bizarre parade is and are already cheering them along. The parade is just a bit of Halloween fun. It's safe.

Whatever is causing those screams is not, and in the chaos of the masked figures, no one else has realized. If this is my stalker—and my instincts tell me it is—then he's timed his attack perfectly. The alphas are distracted, their senses locked onto their temporary pack with the faux Hunt.

Fuck.

A new scent appears, far sharper and more vivid than the scent of emotion. It's the smell of blood.

3

JEL

"What's happening? Is it a hazing prank?" I grab the nearest one—the surfer with the eerie alpha stillness—by the chin and turn him to face me. "What's going on?"

"Halloween prank," he says through smooshed lips. "A bunch of the alphas thought it'd be funny. But—"

"I know," I snap. "I can smell it."

The Hunt might be innocent, but that blood is real.

Someone is using the Hunt to conceal a far more sinister crime than stupid university pranks. It's smart. And insulting.

And really fucking dangerous.

I back up to the wall again, since I still can't see properly through the smoke. I need to know my back is covered, since I've got no one to cover it for me. Carefully, I let my sight shift a little, my eyes glowing through the fog as I use my extra senses to build a stronger picture.

The alphas are taking too long to notice something's wrong. They're caught up in the jubilation of their little stunt, running among the party and through the house. From what I can tell, our little corner contains the only alphas in this room who aren't actively participating, which means the only people to have noticed the scent of blood are us.

But it won't take long before they do, and then this hunt will turn real. Real, uncoordinated, and violent. Whoever this assailant is, he's planned his attack perfectly, because in about three seconds, no one will be able to hunt him through the chaos.

What's his aim? Is he trying to rob Cameron, and someone got in the way?

My mind turns back to the rat I saw before, but I let the thought go when the nearest leather-masked figure comes to a sudden halt. Her eyes glow brighter, a snarl erupting from her mouth as her hands shift into claws.

Time's up. The alphas have caught on, and if we don't get out of their way, we're fucked. Whatever this guy's original plans, he'll have ignited the killing instinct of twenty drunken alphas.

It's about to become a bloodbath.

As if on cue, the same alpha I've been watching turns on the man next to her, her friend, and slashes her claws across his chest. He howls, blood splattering across her face, its acrid scent filling my nostrils. They turn on one another, previous bonds forgotten as the worst in us takes over.

"Stay behind me," Theo says, stepping between me and the rest of the room.

I almost roll my eyes, despite the urgency.

"I can look after myself," I snap, trying to shove past him so I can continue to see what the hell is going on.

More of them are shifting. Attacking. It's confusing the scent. Obscuring the trail.

I'd bet everything I own it's exactly what he wants.

"I said stay!" Theo growls, holding me back without effort. "Jace—get here."

So the surfer is Jace.

"What's your name?" Jace asks Blue Eyes in a low drawl.

He spares a moment to stare at him, then says "Luc," in a tight voice, and steps into line.

I'm flanked on all sides as these men back each other up without argument, wordlessly deciding to appoint themselves my protectors.

Hissing, I whirl around, ignoring the screams of terror from the rest of the party. They're no longer tinged with exhilaration and hilarity—willing victims to a harmless prank celebrating the year's spookiest night. The party is tainted, the fear spreading and contaminating everything it touches. The stench of blood overwhelms me, but I can't trace it. I can't tell if someone cut themselves trying to escape a robber, or if it's something far worse.

I don't know which way to go to help.

Man, tonight really was fucked from the beginning, wasn't it? The stalker in the alley, the men from my painting, and now this...

It's almost too messed up. I mean, what are the odds? I decide to hunt down my painting, and I find the men from it instead. A stalker targets me and then apparently unleashes hell onto the party I'm going to. I stumble onto a fated mate bond with a *dragon*, of all people.

For the first time, I wonder if my joke about being possessed by a trickster god when I submitted my paintings isn't too far off the mark. That or Fate herself.

They say our academy is built on the blood of gods. I always thought it was stupid academy legend, but the prickling along my spine tells a different story. The chaos of tonight is no coincidence; it's intentional. And foreboding as hell.

Whatever Fate's plans are for us all, if she's bringing us together on a night like this, it can't be good.

I've just decided to make a break for it, through into the kitchen, when the world whirls. After a moment, it culminates in darkness and the echoing slam of a door. Blinking, I fight the racing of my heart to work out where I am. Who threw me in here? Was it—?

Of course. The flicker of a phone light breaks through my thoughts, and I see three familiar faces.

My would-be mates appear to have locked us in a closet.

"You really know how to show a girl a good time, don't you?" I ask, my tone riding the knife-edge of fury.

How dare they lock me in here?

"Ssh." A hand covers my mouth, suspiciously accurate in the darkness. "Listen."

I fight down the rising tide of fury and turn my attention outward. Fuck. He's right. The screams are louder now, more chaotic. The alphas are going after the danger, but everything is too twisted. It's pure instinct and violence, with no logic in sight.

I hate to admit it, but I might not even last out there. In fact, I'm almost one hundred percent sure I won't. Not against twenty adrenaline-filled alphas.

That's no excuse not to try, though.

The hand over my mouth eases, and I slowly step sideways until I hit a wall. It doesn't take long. As my eyes adjust to the darkness, I confirm all three of my— no. I'm not calling them that. All three of them are here, though. Wanting to protect me.

Something stirs in my chest, a gentle unfurling of a thread, and heat spreads through me.

I begin to laugh, the sound low and tinged with hysteria. Not now. Fate, you have to be kidding me, you horrible old witch. I bite my cheek and will the familiar feeling away, to a more suitable time, but it's no use. Our bond doesn't like being ignored, and now it's using the deadliest tool in its arsenal to try and get us to reconnect.

It's trying to use the rut.

At a time like this, it might even work. Close quarters. Dark space. Adrenaline from the chaotic nightmare outside the door pulsing through my veins.

It's a potent mix, and both my shifter soul and my human desire rise to the challenge.

"Breathe," I whisper to myself.

If only I hadn't been raised to thrive in this madness. If only my blood didn't sing at the first drop of violence. But it does—it's instinctive. Inevitable.

Two sides of the same coin.

A soft growl echoes from the other side of the closet, followed by another and another. I'm not the only one overrun by my instincts, but at least I have the darkness to hide that.

They can't see the claws emerging from my hands—claws a snake shifter like me shouldn't have, but an alpha certainly does, no matter their vitality.

I squeeze my eyes tightly shut, hiding the unearthly glow that I can no longer control. Even in the darkness behind my eyelids, I can see their eyes light up, blinking into existence as golden, metal claws unsheathe from their hands.

I hide mine behind my back.

They can't know this about me. No one does.

"You can't be serious," Theo murmurs, his voice rasping, thick with desire. "Now?"

Someone—sounds like Jace—groans, his body thumping back against the wall as he slides down it to the floor.

A low chuckle comes from Luc. It sounds just a little mad. "When else? Since when is the rut ever sane?"

A hand lands beside my head, against the wall. My pulse

races, and I keep my eyes completely shut, my hands clenched into fists.

My lack of sight only heightens my other senses.

Luc leans closer to me, studying me. His breath hits my cheek, and I can smell the curiosity falling off him in waves. "I thought you were a beta," he says quietly. "But maybe you're an omega, if you're overriding our protection instincts like this."

I nearly burst into hysterical laughter. If only he knew.

"I'm not an omega," I snap. "This isn't a heat; this is pure alpha testosterone. You just don't know how to control your rut. Keep it in your pants, for fuck's sake."

He huffs an amused breath, his nose sliding along my cheek as he breathes in my scent. The magic I've woven holds, because he doesn't stiffen in alarm. If anything, the desire rolling off him rises. With a growing flush of heat in my cheeks, I realize I can smell the clean, sharp scent of arousal as his dick hardens in his jeans.

"The rut isn't made to be controlled," he says in a voice that's verging on unhinged. "It's made to be enjoyed. Pure release."

Pure violence, you mean.

Still, his words speak to the instinct in me, to the roiling sea of my shifter vitality—the nature of my beast—that begs to coil around a warm body, to bask in the sunlit warmth of our bed.

And to fuck, long and hard, into the night.

"Shit," I whisper.

He laughs properly this time, and I sense two other bodies coming in close. Desire rolls over the tiny space between us, charged with energy and need. "We have to pass the time in here somehow," he says, voice rough. "I'm not letting you out there until it's safe, sweetheart."

The hand that isn't beside my head appears at my waist,

Luc's fingers trailing down until he reaches the hem of my leather skirt.

A moan escapes me, and three snarls echo in response.

He lifts the fabric inch by inch, sliding beneath it and flicking his thumb over my panties.

This is unhinged. This is worse than the parts of me I've been trying to outrun—the pieces of my soul that bring me shame. Who the hell has sex in a closet while someone outside is hurt? My protective instincts are screaming within me, demanding I put my safety last.

But there's one flaw with that. The people I most need to protect are my pack. And Fate tells me they're right here. My bondmates are right where they're meant to be if I want to keep them safe.

In fact, doing exactly this would be the safest, most soul-pleasing option no matter which way you look at it.

"Do you like that?" Luc asks, beginning to stroke me through my panties. "Fuck, you're already wet."

Of course I'm wet, you giant asshole. An insanely hot dragon shifter is fingering me in a closet while my suppressed soul screams from the rut she hasn't felt in years.

"Right there," I breathe, angling my hips up into his fingers.

Luc groans, the sound tinged with incredulous laughter as I begin to thrust against him.

"By the way," he murmurs casually. "What's your name?"

I start to laugh, the sound becoming a moan as he glides his thumb perfectly over me. "Jel," I tell him.

He repeats it back to me with heat, desire.

This is insane. The metallic stench of blood is all I can smell, and yet I've never wanted to fuck someone more.

The rut is tearing at the edges of my sanity, begging me to let loose. But without an omega, this is...

Dangerous.

My shifter soul hisses with pleasure; she loves danger. She misses it.

"Don't get her too revved up," Theo says, his voice thick with desire. My eyes have almost adjusted to the darkness, and I can sense him leaning against the wall beside me, his arms folded. "Trust me, you want her to come with Jace's tongue on her at least once." His voice lowers. "And then I want to fuck her."

Jace kneels beside me, his breath warm on my thigh. He flicks his long hair out of his eyes and looks up at me from beneath dark, thick lashes, his lips parting with desire.

Luc slips his fingers into my panties, and doesn't even wait before sliding two inside me. His thumb brushes my clit in slow circles while he fucks me slowly. "She can come more than once," he says easily. "Maybe I'll even leave my fingers in her while you lick her, Jace." I can hear the smile in his voice—smell the faint tinge of smoke in the air. "Not even moving them. Just filling her up."

He's beginning to lose that James Dean wannabe edge to his demeanor. Now the rut is taking over, instinct is dominating the need to be cool. To be wary.

I'm about ten seconds from a gang bang in a closet. And almost every part of me is screaming *go for it, girl, it's been way too long.*

But one, tiny, rational part of me is loud enough to make up for it.

Low growls come as a response to Luc's promise, and I sense them shuffling in closer to each other. But they aren't quite in sync. These men aren't friends, no matter that they temporarily share a goal. Any minute now, they'll turn on each other, just like the alphas outside. Without an omega to soften them, there'll be nothing to guide them away from the violence in their souls as they fight to claim me.

Not to mention, someone out there is in trouble, even though that's getting really hard to remember.

"Luc," I whisper, tasting his name on my tongue. He moans in answer, his fingers sliding faster, obscenely wet as he fucks me close, so close to the edge. "No," I grit out. "Stop. Not now."

His eyes snap open, burning with the shift, the change. He's seconds away from the rut, the claws on his fingers just barely concealed as I ride them.

"What?" he snarls, voice low as his fingers still.

"Not. Now," I hiss through clenched teeth. "Just—stop."

He curses and pulls his fingers away, stepping back. The wet sound of him withdrawing makes me bite my lip to stop from moaning again. Three sets of glowing eyes fix to me in the darkness, and I force myself to breathe. On the plus side, being able to pull back from the edge like that really supports my cover that I'm a beta, and not subject to a rut myself.

On the other hand, I'm not a beta, and this is torture.

It's torture that won't be over for a while, either. The rut has started now, and it will build over the next few days until it explodes, one way or another. Goddammit.

Breathing heavily, my chest heaving in long ragged breaths, I struggle to regain normality. One breath, then another. I need my wits about me—not this terribly timed, aggressively insistent mate bond and the rut it's trying to ignite to bind us together.

I need to get back out there and chase this chaos to its source, before my stalker can become the killer I'm certain he's dying to be.

That's when I realize how quiet it's become on the other side of the door.

4
JEL

"THE HUNT HAS LEFT," I WHISPER, MY CLAWS RETRACTING AS THE urgent focus of my instincts switches from desire to protection. Outside the door, the room has gone terrifyingly quiet. "The alphas must all be outside now. Ssh—listen."

I press my nose to the crack in the door and breathe in the scent on the other side. Luc mirrors me at the hinges, and Jace and Theo prowl back and forth as if they can guard us from attack in a three by three space.

Blood. Sharp and acrid. It's the same scent as before, and this time it overwhelms the energy of the Halloween prank. There is only malice now, only violence.

I take another breath and reel back, retching, as the rest of it hits me.

Death.

This wasn't just a random attack, or a burglary gone wrong. This was murder. My stalker has got what he came for, and I hid in a closet and let it happen.

Guilt and rage course through me until I'm shaking, burning with the need to get my hands on this creep.

I can almost picture the scene—party abandoned, masked

men chasing an impossible trail into the street. Dead girl lying in a pool of her own blood.

Has anyone checked if she's okay? I mean, I know she's not *okay*, but maybe there's still a chance to save her.

The quiet of outside shatters, but only with one voice.

"Get off me," the girl demands, her voice shaking with pain and adrenaline.

She's putting up a fight, but she's hurt. Probably close to unconscious, judging by the disorientation in her voice.

Prickles of anger and loathing flood me.

I sniff the air. I can definitely scent death, which means this is victim number two. A possible survivor.

"We have to help her," I say, pushing past Luc, reaching for the handle. "Let me out."

"No chance," Theo growls.

He moves in front of the door, arms folded. "We'll go."

Luc nods sharply. Before I've even realized what's happening, he's through the door and out into the room.

Which leaves me with two self righteous bodyguards.

The anger in me burns. Fuck these assholes. I don't even know them—they're *strangers*—and they've decided they're in charge of me? That they have a claim to me? I don't fucking think so.

Light bleeds in from under the door; it's one of those knock-together jobs. A shitty fitout with little attention to detail. There's a good two inch gap below the door.

In the dim lighting, they don't see me shift. My clothing falls to the floor, a heavy thud of leather followed by the slither of slinkier fabric.

No one notices the slide of scales over floorboards, but I can taste their confusion on the air. Jace starts forward, hands swiping cautiously through the space, but I'm under the door and into the room before they work it out.

It smells like death out here. Death and the disease of rotten power. Ambition fueled by hatred. It makes me recoil, belly sliding over jagged mortar and crumbs from the party, but I press on. Luc is nowhere in sight.

The tangy scent of testosterone overwhelms me for a minute —alpha squaring off against alpha. The Hunt is just outside the house, on the lawn. The rest of the guests are nowhere in sight.

The alphas are turning on themselves, like the killer no doubt relied on them to do. I change direction, away from the fighting. There are masks on the ground, covered in blood, but I'd bet good money none of them are His. Whoever these alphas think they've caught, they haven't.

The killer is too good for that.

His scent lingers on the air—I can taste him. Definitely a 'him', but... apart from that, I can't sense anything about him. No distinctive vitality, no hierarchy. Nothing. It's almost like his scent is a void. A nothingness.

The trail goes lower, below me, through the floor. Tongue flicking, I race to the basement; my goal in every way tonight, it seems.

Before I can reach it, a warm hand scoops me from just below the head, and I'm lifted into the air.

That hand... Oh, God. It's—it's like a touch I've craved all my life. Warm and soft, tingling with power, with fire. In my shifter form, it's even more overwhelming than when we were in the closet together.

Luc holds me before him, piercing blue eyes freezing me like a spotlight. His lip curls into a small smile, and I'm struck by the sparkling crystal of his eyes. Like two gems. I thought I was meant to be the hypnotizing one, with what my venom can do to people, but trust me to find the one shifter who apparently moonlights as a snake charmer.

"So," he says softly, his expression unreadable. "You're a snake."

My tongue flicks out, tasting triumph and an odd spike of tension coming from him. Probably because the killer is still loose, and without a target these alphas are already turning feral. Dangerous.

The thought of what my three lovely guardians might do to trap me further—for my own *safety*, of course—leaves me with little choice. I shift back, relishing the shock on his face as the snake he was holding suddenly becomes a five foot four naked woman.

"Now who's smirking, asshole?" I ask with a grin. "Out of my way, please. I'm a little on the cold side, for obvious reasons. And my name is Jel West, so don't go getting any ideas about my vitality."

The fake surname rolls off my tongue with ease. It's the same name I give everyone when they learn my vitality is a snake, before they can start getting shifty about exactly how close I might be to the vipers.

The name 'West' comes with its own genealogy, if anyone bothers to check. We're distant cousins to the main house, diluted down through more than five generations. Close enough that Marcus would be offended on our behalf if anyone crossed us, but not enough that the vipers give a shit about us otherwise.

The name 'Vario' comes with a very different genealogy.

The look of stunned incredulity on Luc's face fades, replaced for half a second by heat and something else, something I can't read. Then he steps back, just as the other two come racing over.

"She shifted!" Jace says, the words choking halfway as he catches sight of me. A second of stunned silence passes before his brain connects and he shoves my clothing at me. "Here," he says, breathless.

He turns away and smacks Theo on the shoulder so he follows suit. Despite all my reservations, my heart softens. Three minutes ago, he was dropping to his knees to eat me out in front of two strangers, and now he's all modest because I'm showing a little skin.

"Alright," I say, slipping my skirt and lacy black top on, unhurried. I have no issue with nakedness; I've done too many life drawing classes, both as artist and model, to care about that, and something about these guys feels safe, no matter how they annoy me. "He's in the basement."

Instantly, the mood shifts. Three heads swivel toward the door with single minded focus.

We hurry down the steps, soon coming to stand at the bottom, nothing but the filtered moonlight through dirty glass to guide us. The basement isn't finished, and there's a faint scent of damp creeping in.

The quiet whimpers of his second victim have faded now, and it's eerily quiet. Too quiet. Every nerve in my body is on fire. Where has he taken her? What is he doing to her?

"Jace," Theo says quietly. "Take the perimeter."

Jace melds into the shadows, all trace of their argument gone. I'm reluctantly impressed. I get the impression these two don't normally get along, and it wouldn't be unheard of for two alphas to jeopardize everything for the chance to butt heads instead of accepting the other's authority. But there's no sign of that here.

Theo steps in close to me, one hand on my shoulder. His touch burns, just like Luc's did. I feel a sharp rush of anger— they're trying to control me *again*—but now isn't the time. This isn't about me. So, I firmly shrug off his hand but allow him to take point close by. Boundaries, buddy. When we get out of here, we're going to talk about them.

Together, we follow Luc forward.

The scent lingers, but it's faint—overtaken by the girl's fear. At least she's still alive; dead girls can't be scared. Take it as a win.

Movement rustles, and suddenly she's there, unconscious on the ground, appearing as if out of nowhere.

The movement must have been the killer dropping her.

With a snarl, Luc lunges for the corner while I rush to the girl, checking her pulse and searching for signs of injury.

"I know her," Jace says quietly. "Her name's Greta. She lives on my street."

A scuffle sounds from the corner, but when Luc turns around, he's empty-handed.

"He's not here," he snarls, kicking over a pile of paint tins in fury.

Then he freezes.

I sense what's happened before I see it. There's actually a light emanating from the bloody thing. It's so bright that we all turn, as one, to what his temper tantrum has revealed: a stack of paintings tucked into the corner.

Mine's at the front, and it's even worse than I remember. The expression on my face is euphoric. My hands possessively clasp around the necks of the two beside me—Jace and Theo—while Luc kneels before them, crouched to spring. In their eyes, a fierce light shines, golden and bright. They yearn for something we, as the audience, can't define. Except I'm not just the audience—I'm the artist. I know what they yearn for.

Me.

This is the most embarrassing fucking moment of my life.

I open my mouth to speak, but I'm cut off by three rumbling snarls, low in their throats, as they turn one by one to face me.

For a second, I see it: that same yearning from the painting. It's real. *They're* real.

The knowledge hits me, slamming through the adrenaline, and before I can stop myself, I imagine what it would be like if I let it be real. If I said yes to the mate bond between us, said yes to whatever fucked up destiny has led us here.

The light grows brighter. It's all around us, within us. God, I want this.

It's as if Fate herself hears my moment of weakness, because in that instant, the light shatters into a thousand glittering pieces. The sparks dazzle me, drifting without purpose for several seconds before honing in on the painting like it's magnetic.

I want to reach for the painting, too. No—it's like the painting is reaching for me. There's an energy in it, a vibrating, magnetic pulse that stretches further and further, past me, past the room, past everything and onward to persons unknown.

I don't know what this energy is doing, who it's calling to, but I know what the source is. It's power—raw and dangerous. And it's mine.

It's the power I've been concealing in the painting. Anchoring your power to an external source works better than blockers, stronger, and without the unpleasant side effects. I've been siphoning my shifter soul into this painting for months.

No, not my shifter soul. My alpha soul. The part of me I can never let free, because if she's free then I have to claim everything that comes with her.

I have to claim the vipers—my family.

I have to be the person my father raised me to be. The person I swore was dead.

"No," I mutter, the word coming out strangely broken. "I can't, I—"

But I do. I can feel it; the bond courses through me, filling me with Fate's design. Has my body betrayed me yet again?

"Jel," Theo murmurs, his eyes wide as he stares at me from across the basement floor.

He was the first to notice me tonight, and he's the first to answer Fate's call now. My eyes fall to his chest as he prowls slowly across the basement floor. The looping, low cuffs of his sleeveless shirt slip to the side, revealing the tanned skin over his ribs. The sight does stupid things to my insides as my own shifter soul rises to the call—giving into what Fate has created between us.

I wet my lips, my heart racing at the triumphant smile this elicits from him. His movements become eerily graceful. Like a predator. Orange and black fur ripples over his knuckles—definitely tiger.

All I can think of is the closet. Their hot breath against my skin. Jace on his knees before me. Luc's fingers stroking me higher and higher.

Theo comes to a halt in front of me.

Two muffled sounds appear from either side, and I realize Luc and Jace have followed. They're surrounding me now, seemingly unaware of the competition.

Their vitalities aren't, though. Theo growls, a low rumble in his chest, without ever taking his eyes off me. One of the others snarls, and I can feel the tension heightening, feel the rapid swell of testosterone and aggression that can only end in blood.

I have to get them to back down. It's the only answer.

"Is this really what you want?" I hiss, my heart stammering as Theo's jaw clenches. "A fated mate bond challenged by f—" No, Jel. "Three alphas?"

He freezes, looking around at the two behind him as if he's seeing them for the first time. The snarls grow louder.

And part of me screams in joy.

This fight, this energy—it fuels me. Feeds me. I want this more than I've ever wanted anything. It's my painting come to life; three alphas surrounding me in fierce, protective ecstasy.

Gritting my teeth, I hold onto my human brain and force the words out around every instinct screaming against them. Maybe if I say them out loud, it will stick. "We need to reject this call."

Immediately, pain like I've never felt before rips through me. I don't understand; I thought the pain of a rejected mate only came when you were the one *being* rejected. I'm not being rejected, Fate, you nosy shit. I'm the one rejecting them!

I clutch my chest, fighting not to double over. It's a battle I lose in seconds, but at least I can take grim satisfaction that the winces on the boys' faces mean they're going through it, too.

"A challenged mate bond isn't something I want," Jace says after a beat, steadying himself against the wall with one arm. A thin band of sweat beads along his forehead. He's still so close, I can feel the warmth radiating off him.

"Can't handle the competition?" Theo snarls, but his words are a little too slow. Too hesitant.

"Mate bonds aren't meant to be competition," Jace throws back, not rising to the bait. His mouth twists into a pained grimace. "They're meant to be fate."

I turn to Luc, the only one who hasn't spoken. "And you?" I ask.

His eyes flick to mine, so piercingly blue it stuns me for a moment. He pauses, and then the corner of his lip twitches—smug and defiant. "I don't need to chase a girl who doesn't want me." He watches me for a beat, and then adds, "but I'm curious to know if you still don't want me when you're all alone."

Slowly, deliberately, he lifts his right hand to his mouth and sucks two fingers between his lips, as if he's cleaning off a stray drop of chocolate. Or something else.

A scowl spreads over my face. Arrogant prick. How dare he use that moment of weakness against me?

"We agree, then," I snap, ignoring his declaration completely.

The pain still tears at me, like a thousand needles stabbing into my organs.

Looking around at their faces, I'm not sure 'agree' would be the best word for the situation. But they don't argue. They simply watch me with grim expressions that still bear an edge of pain.

Fate doesn't like to be contested, it seems.

She'll have to get used to it.

Theo's attention returns to the painting, an unreadable expression crossing his face, and I snatch it up before he can say anything. He still tries.

"Not a word," I snap, holding up one finger.

He goes quiet, but the soft rumble in his chest tells me he's amused. The sound does extremely unwelcome things to my insides. Extremely unwelcome, and extremely pleasant.

This is what I hate about our vitalities. They're bound by their instincts, ruled by a complex system of need and duty that overrides all else.

Like, for example, the poor girl slowly waking up in the corner, and the bloody body upstairs.

Abruptly, I'm disgusted with myself. Before the boys can interrupt me again, I shove through their little circle and march over to the girl. As she stirs, I kneel down beside her, murmuring softly. It's not my usual style, but there's no way in hell I'm letting these jerks assume the role of alpha protector with her. She doesn't need that macho shit right now.

"She's alright," I say quietly, glancing up at the others. "There are no serious wounds. Although..."

Frowning, I smooth her bright red hair out of the way and run my fingers across a strange puncture mark on her neck. Blood leaks out of it, droplets splashing across her neck and shoulders, and it's bruising up around the edges. The bruises and viciousness of the puncture look like some kind of brutal stabbing, but the damage is so small, like a syringe... But injecting her with something wouldn't leave this amount of blood.

"It's like someone's tried to drain her blood away," I say distantly, my mind whirring.

It couldn't be... Could it?

Luc stiffens, and my heart thuds as I once again consider that he's the only dragon I've seen in this city for years. I never knew the survivor's name, but it could have been Luc... There's no reason it couldn't be.

As I stare at him, my blood pounding in my veins, an eerie sound starts up. It's like a humming, whistling sound, but mostly tuneless. Just three single notes, back and forth. It's not electronic, but it doesn't completely sound human either.

Luc's face grows pale, like the humming means something to him, but before I can ask—before I can decide whether I want to—the door to the basement slams open and police clatter down.

The night dissolves after that, descending quickly into sirens and noise, ruining any chance for the three of us to talk privately. Thank God.

Theo tries to discreetly stop me a couple of times when I leave, and Jace doesn't even try to be discreet about getting me alone, but with police swarming the place there's no chance to deal with their concern.

Or my own, but that's the way I like it. Locked up tight like a clamshell. Nothing gets in; nothing gets out.

Besides, it doesn't matter. It's done. Hot closet sex or not, it's over. Everything about this bond screams no, and I've long since learned that the only instincts I can trust are my own.

Even if several of my other instincts are screaming yes, yes, God, yes.

Sighing, I take a second to desperately fight down the inner need burning within me—along with the stretching, preening sensation of our new bond. It doesn't seem to have accepted my rejection, which is fucking rich.

But also, it isn't overly strong, like I would think a new bond would be. Perhaps it just needs time to fade.

I'm determined to give it that time.

Satisfied, I give my new bondmates the slip, leading the paramedics to the unconscious girl. Before they wheel her away, I slip a napkin with my phone number and a quick note into her front pocket. I don't recognize her, but who knows her story? Maybe she's got thirty friends waiting for her. Maybe she's got no one. I wouldn't want to wake up alone after that.

Then I take my painting and go home to sleep.

5
THEO

THE FIRST THING I DO WHEN I GET HOME IS RIP THE COVERS OFF MY mirrors and stare at my own reflection. I still look the same, still feel the same. This bond from Fate hasn't changed my appearance.

Even though it feels like it's changed everything else about me.

I run my fingers over my face, pressing and pulling at the skin. It molds around my bones with ease. Just my skin. Nothing to be alarmed about.

Except for the simmering, burning rut that lies beneath it. I've never felt one this strong. It ignited the second we stepped into that closet, and it hasn't let up since we left.

It wants me to give into it. Normally, I would, but it's never been specifically *for* someone before, and I don't know what the hell to do with that energy. The rut is always dangerous, but now it feels unhinged.

Jel isn't here, obviously, but it still calls to me, making my thoughts fuzzy and unguarded. Unfocused.

Above all else, I need to focus.

I grit my teeth against the rising sense of urgency and start throwing the covers back on the mirrors. Maybe if I can't see the deranged look in my eyes, the rut won't burst out of me sooner than it has to. One black cloth, two, three... all the way up to six, if you count the little magnifying mirror. Which I do.

The mirrors are my mother's idea. She thinks it's motivational. If you can see your flaws, you can burn them away—her words, not mine.

She has an unusual knack for seeing my flaws.

It took me until I was eighteen years old to realize she couldn't see her own for shit, and by then, the damage was done.

When everything is covered up again, I sit on the end of my bed and stick in my earbuds, hoping the music will distract me. Rut or no rut, I need to focus and think of a plan. There's nothing to worry about so long as I have a plan.

So long as I know how to win.

I drop back onto the covers and shut my eyes, letting the music wash over me while my hand lowers onto my dick—not stroking it, just resting there. Easing the need that's already making me feel restless and edgy.

The sooner I win, the sooner I can fuck this rut away.

So, what's the plan?

Jel didn't seem the type to fall for the toughest guy in the room, which puts my usual strategy out. If anything, she wanted to fight us, which is kind of hot for a beta.

Doesn't help me, though.

A familiar, sneaky voice takes up inside my head. *Maybe this isn't a fight you can win.*

My eyes snap open, and I stare up at the ceiling as the drums kick in, blaring inside my mind. They drown out the voice at least, but now I'm agitated. Raring to hit something. I squeeze the hand covering my cock, massaging as I thrust upward.

I can win every fight. I haven't lost a single competition or fight since... before.

And I never will.

A knock at the door breaks my concentration.

"Go away," I snarl, moving my hand behind my head.

The door opens anyway, like I knew it would.

Mom comes through, peering down the stairs into my basement room with her lips pursed. Her eyes flick to the covered mirrors, and she pinches her lips tighter.

As she walks down the steps, she reaches over the rail to flick off the nearest cover, then the next and the next.

"You trying to give me an ego, there, Mom?" I ask, barely keeping the fury from my voice as I sit up on the edge of the bed.

"I'm keeping you focused," she snaps. "You can thank me later."

She wrinkles her nose and reaches forward, pinching a bit of imaginary dust from my shoulder and flicking it away. "You've put on weight."

"I've put on mass," I correct her. "Muscle."

She hums with vague disinterest. "I heard there was an altercation at that party last night."

It takes a lot of effort and training to keep my expression neutral. "If you can call murder an altercation."

Her lips curl; I've walked straight into her trap. "You let someone murder an innocent victim? While you were there to stop it?" Her frown deepens. "Were you hiding, Theodore? We've talked about this."

Flashes of memory hit me, making me tense up involuntarily: childish faces teasing me, poking me as I ran and hid in safety. Mom's voice sneering at me when she heard I didn't fight.

"I wasn't hiding," I grit out, ignoring all memory of the

closet and the sweet sounds Jel made on Luc's fingers. "And I found the survivor."

"Yes," she says tightly. "You and three others, if I hear correctly. You can't share the spotlight, Theo. If you don't seize it, someone else will."

"Well, we can't have that, can we?"

She misses my sarcasm entirely. Pausing to inspect herself in the mirror, she plucks out a persistent lone hair from between her eyebrows with two fingers and straightens. "I'm sure you can track the murderer from the scent you found last night," she says as she begins to climb the stairs, already leaving now that her judgment has been passed on. "You should be able to solve it rather quickly."

Like I couldn't think of that myself. There was no scent to track, and besides, it isn't my responsibility to solve this goddamn murder.

I don't bother telling her that, because she would only argue that I hadn't looked hard enough. Hadn't fought hard enough.

I barely hear the door shut behind her. My mind is stewing on her words. The longer I lie there, the more pissed off I get, especially because it's just occurred to me that there's some truth in what she's saying. There was one part of that situation that *was* my responsibility.

Jel.

My brain starts working.

Maybe I'm looking at this competition from the wrong angle. There must be a reason Fate chose such a messed up scenario to bring us together. Does it mean Jel needs my protection in the future?

What if it isn't about winning my mate, but proving that I'm worthy of her?

That sounds a lot harder.

The simmering rut beneath my skin flares, tugging at me. It urges me closer to the fire that my soul is desperate to burn. I drop my hand back down to my dick, stroking through the fabric of my shorts.

Maybe this competition suddenly sounds harder, but it also sounds more intriguing. More meaningful. My soul is invested in this kind of challenge, and so am I.

I grit my teeth against the overwhelming sensations and pull out my phone, searching for a distraction by scrolling TikTok. I check the views on my latest thirst trap without expression, relieved they're still climbing. Shadows and red light are the shit, I guess.

My DMs flash.

Looking fire, big guy.

My jaw clenches. It's Jace.

The rut flares again, harsher now. It grinds in my chest; a churning sea of need as I thrust up into my hand. I swallow thickly and stare at my phone like it's a lifeline.

Jace. That's right.

Of all the people to pit me against...

I've known Jace for years. His ridiculously chilled out energy has always sent me to the very edge of my competitive nature. As soon as I met him, I wanted to take him down. It's rare that he'll ever beat me, either on the track or in the ring.

Still, he keeps challenging me. Keeps betting against me.

Doesn't seem to mind paying up, either.

But this is a different kind of competition, and I know all too well that Jace has something to offer in that ring.

I slow down my movements and glance sideways, catching sight of myself in the mirror. My pupils are blown wide, dark with heat, and it makes me think of Luc. The unknown.

A dragon shifter.

I shiver as I think of his expression last night when he tried to cage Jel away from us. How his eyes had darkened as smoke curled out of his mouth.

Fuck that was cool. And kind of hot.

No doubt about it, if we're just talking about attraction, my competition is good. But *are* we just talking about attraction? Or does Fate want something more from us?

Does Jel need a mate who can protect her against a danger as awful as the one from last night?

Before I can stop myself, I'm replying. *You still going after her?*

He doesn't hesitate. He's obviously thinking about Jel, too. *Why? Are you worried?*

Yes. No.

Not exactly for the reasons he thinks I am.

Against you? Hardly.

He sees through me, like he always does. It's part of why he irritates me so much. The other part is because I almost like it.

You're a hot guy with a big dick. Stop overthinking it.

I drop my phone back on the bed. It's one thing to say don't overthink it, but if I'm meant to win by protecting Jel, then I need to know her. I need to know what she might need protecting from.

Not only that—I want to. I want to know the girl that Fate has picked for me.

My soul wants to know her, too.

At that thought, the rut I've been trying to hold back burns. Flares.

I give up.

Swallowing an instinctive grunt, I hold my free hand up above my head to study it—specifically, the golden claws hovering just below the surface. I can just see them if I tilt the angle correctly. My other hand speeds up, sliding beneath my shorts and grasping the velvet heat of my cock without restriction.

The rut is an experience unlike any other. The symptoms of an omega's heat ease with every touch. Their biology is built to be soothed, and they respond beautifully as soon as they let go.

An alpha's biology is different.

The rut is the culmination of every burning, violent instinct of devotion within us. It's meant to pair with an omega's heat, to be soothed by it. But if it doesn't, betas are taught how to receive it in a way that eases the danger. Keeps it to a low simmer, instead of a raging inferno.

We're also taught how to manage it ourselves, if we have to. Locked away, where no one can be harmed, except ourselves if we were too stupid to take the proper precautions. It's illegal to do anything less—too bad for you if you never bothered to learn how to contain it.

Problem is, now that I've got a mate around, I won't be able to ease the rut on my own. I can take the edge off, but anything more than a quick and dirty orgasm will be painful to say the least.

I've already edged myself for too long. The pleasure is turning into pain, urging me to find my mate, to hunt down the only form of true release the rut will allow me.

I pull myself off faster, no longer playing with the sensations. Just searching for the end and whatever relief it can bring.

With my other hand, I thumb the sharp points of the claws, feeling them dig into my skin from the wrong side. But I don't let them free. They're different to the claws of my tiger vitality. Golden. Metallic. Tiger claws only appear when I shift; the rut is always there, waiting to be ignited.

"What about three ruts?" I mutter to myself. "Hey Sawlefire Academy? What the fuck are we meant to do with three ruts burning from the same flame?"

They never taught us how to keep *that* safe. Probably because it can't be. It can only be fatal.

Maybe this is the danger I need to protect her from...

As if in answer, a smoky haze takes over my vision. My eyes roll back in my head, my breath coming in sharper pants. If I can't fight it back, I have about three minutes to set up the protective runes and drink a healing brew, and then... I'm gone. Twenty-four hours, at least. And without my mate: pain. So much pain.

I can't let the rut win. Not yet.

A bright green beetle scurries on the window sill, reflecting the light. I huff a laugh, but the energy surging through me makes it come out louder. Manic. It's an old wives tale, those green beetles. Tiger beetles.

I guess the gods are watching. Never knew Fate was such a horny mistress.

"I'm not giving in to you," I mutter under my breath. "Not like this."

Not when my mate isn't here, and she doesn't want to be.

My voice sounds lower. Deeper. Almost like there are two of them together.

Images flood my mind—Jel in that closet, panting wildly on Luc's fingers. Her head tipped back in pleasure. Her hands grasping at the wall behind her back as she fought to maintain control.

I spill over into my hand, fast and urgent, the cry catching in the back of my throat. It's quick and dirty, just like it needs to be. It's barely enough.

Then, before it can urge me to find more, always more, I push the rut away and collapse, languid, into the sheets. It goes reluctantly, as though it has a mind of its own. Sometimes I think it does.

But whether this shitstorm has three alphas burning in the

same fire or not, I can hold this rut off for a while longer. And I will, because it gives me an edge I can't afford to lose. Not if I'm to be the last man standing when Jel gives into Fate.

Not if I'm to be the one who protects her.

It takes several minutes before my breathing loses its ragged edge and I feel in control again, but finally I sink my earbuds back in, focus on the pounding beat of the drums, and close my eyes.

As I do, the realization of what this little episode means hits me.

The rejection didn't take.

Jel wanted us to sever this bond, but I don't think Fate's listening. It feels stronger than ever to me.

It feels like it's growing.

The corner of my mouth curls upward, and part of me delights at the thought of seeing how the little beta handles this. Whether she can deny the strength of our bond for a second time, or whether she already wants to give in.

That settles it. Fate has given me her blessing, so I'm not going to overthink it. I'm just going to win.

I'll prove I'm the best because I am the best.

6

JEL

"WHY THE FUCK IS THIS CLASS SO EARLY?"

The barista, shockingly, does not answer. He stares at me, one eyebrow raised as if to say 'you were better when you didn't talk'.

"Fair enough," I mutter, accepting my ceramic takeaway mug and escaping.

The campus is buzzing with talk of the murder on the weekend. I think we might have news vans camped out permanently here for the rest of the week, at least. The survivor—Greta—is still in hospital, but she sent me a small thank you text, so I know she's okay. Can't let any of these vultures know that, or they'll descend on me for answers I don't have.

My phone vibrates in my pocket, but I don't need to check to know who it is. Now that my exchange with Greta is over, there's only one person who contacts me. Dear little brothers; where would we be without them, am I right? Pains in the ass, for sure, but when your family reveals their true colours, nine times out of ten, it's the little brothers that stick with you.

He'll be checking in on me, now the news has hit the public, but I'm not in the mood to deal with his concerns just yet. He can come and check on me in person if he's that worried.

Something one of the nearby students says catches the attention of a blonde woman standing in front of a camera. She gestures for her crew to descend on the student in a flurry of noise and drama. Shouts carry across the quad, swirling like the falling leaves that fly around the students. It's a bizarre scene, almost like a Baroque painting, as the colors of the reporters' coats whip in the wind while they point and jab at each of the students in turn, directing their cameramen to the most profitable witness.

For a second, it almost looks like the student points in my direction, but that can't be right. No one notices me.

I pull my hoodie up further over my distinctive red hair and turn away. A familiar flash of brown catches my attention, distracting me, and I turn to find Theo watching me from across the hall. Great. Exactly what I don't need right now.

How can he even think about our bond after what happened to the victim?

Everywhere I look, I see her face plastered on photographs and articles. Tributes and amateur op-eds line the notice boards and walls, so that you can't even blink without being reminded of what happened and who died. She looks weirdly like me, in some ways. Her hair is the same bright red as mine, and we share that kind of scowling grimace as our resting bitch face.

Shared. We shared.

I cut into the center of the crowd, hoping to lose Theo. Unfortunately, this brings me closer to the Dean's office; a mistake I don't recognize until it's too late, and I notice the Dean beckoning me closer.

They're coming in from all sides this morning. It's so not my day.

It's not my week. One night outside of my comfort zone, and I end up with an unwanted mate bond to three alphas, a possible-but-God-I-hope-not link to a past I'm trying to forget, and a murder I just let happen.

I hid in a fucking closet and let it happen.

I nearly ended up in a *rut* while it was happening.

Disgust and shame swirl through me, but it's a familiar combination when it comes to my instincts, so I lock it away in a neat little box without much effort and walk close enough to hear what the Dean has to say.

"Angelica. My office, please." Dean Driscoll leans out the doorway of the little receptionist's nook that divides the hall from his office. He hasn't even asked his secretary to get me; he's come for me himself.

Lovely.

The last time he called me in here, it was to tell me a student claimed I'd stolen art supplies from campus. It was a total lie, but he somehow turned it into a second warning, and I only get one more.

Ten bucks says he's here to pin the murder on me, because theft is just like murder.

I'm still just unsettled enough from the other night to feel edgy when I step foot in his office, rather than ready to fight. It's not a good start. You need to be on your toes with this asshole.

Which is why, when I turn to shut the door and find three bodies crowding into the space, I'm almost touched. Certainly relieved.

"This is a private meeting," Dean Driscoll says stiffly as Jace shuts the door and leans back against it.

Luc gives him a look that could melt flesh from bone, and the Dean swallows. Visibly.

Fucker never got intimidated for me, even if he is terrified of my family.

Oh well. I can't complain about a cover I deliberately took. My fake surname has served its purpose here, and he has no reason to be scared of a beta who is only distantly related to the vipers.

Ha. Distantly. If only he knew.

Theo comes to stand beside me, staring at the Dean with his arms folded in a clear challenge. He glances down at me briefly, his expression unreadable as he runs his gaze deliberately across my body, checking my face and then my posture.

"You okay?" he asks roughly, startling me.

"Yeah." I answer on reflex, too shocked to do anything else.

Theo nods and turns back to the Dean, apparently satisfied and ready for an intense stare-off with the most powerful man in the room.

I frown, my mind thrown straight back to our first meeting. There's an energy about him that's pure machismo and aggression, itching for a fight, but there's something else there, too. Something more serious. I know a strategic assessment when I see one, and he just assessed me all over.

I wonder what he found.

No one has ever looked at me so closely before, like they actually cared about the answer instead of about whatever emotions or justifications they could project onto me.

I shake off the thought and the weird sense of warmth it creates in me, and turn to the Dean.

"Well?" I prompt him. "I have classes to get to."

Irritated, he turns his gaze back to me. "Your painting, Angelica. We're destroying it. Its inclusion in the show was an oversight, and it can't be known that something so vulgar was produced on campus grounds."

I swear, sometimes this place's religious roots are a bit too prominent. We might have lost touch with the old gods over the centuries, and the stories I hear tend to be more about the old shifter gods basking in orgies and sex parties than about them upholding any kind of abstinence commandment, but admin never seemed to get that memo.

The Academy has always been weirdly prudish and controlling, and the existence of my painting was like catnip to their administration team as soon as Cameron filed the exhibition paperwork. Which was like, the third item down on my list of why I needed to get the painting back from Cameron.

"Can't destroy something you don't have," I point out, watching as understanding crosses his face.

"I would highly recommend you destroy the offending article," he says tightly. "Anything that brings your placement here into question with respect to the school's reputation could be problematic, to say the least. Your distant family's protection can only extend so far before it becomes damaging."

Yeah, yeah. I'm a liability. It's been spelled out to me before. The only reason I've lasted this long is that the Dean doesn't want to give Marcus Vario any reason to take offense on behalf of his brother's wife's cousin's step daughter. Or whatever I said I was on the admissions form.

"I thought you said family wouldn't affect admission here," Luc says thoughtfully, making me jump.

Something strange crosses the Dean's face. It's almost a wince.

"Mr D'Amour, I can assure you your place is secure."

"So it's one rule for my family, another for hers?"

The wince vanishes as if it were never there, replaced for a moment by rage. But I don't notice anything beyond that. I'm caught on the surname of my mysterious mate. The one that's imprinted on my brain, making sure I never forget.

I wasn't wrong; it is him.

Luc D'Amour. The boy who escaped. The only survivor.

The one whose entire clan was murdered by the vipers.

By my family.

White noise buzzes in my ears, reaching fever pitch quicker than I'd like. In all the chaos from the other night, and the absolute exhaustion I'd still felt this morning after it all, I'd actually convinced myself I was wrong.

That's why he commented on my vitality—my snake soul.

Giving him my fake surname saved my ass in more ways than I realized. He thinks I'm just a West, and consequently have nothing to do with the main house.

If he thought otherwise, he'd have rejected our bond on sight. Right before he killed me.

A pounding starts up on the door, and it takes me a second to realize it isn't in my head.

The heated discussion between Luc and Dean Driscoll stops abruptly as the Dean frowns at the door.

"Tilda, tell them to come back later!" he yells through the door to his secretary, while ushering us toward the exit. He lowers his voice again and snaps, "This conversation is over. Angelica, you know the conditions of your admission here. Mr D'Amour, I suggest you consider where your priorities lie. With your impeccable record and grade point average, or with a student who is so close to failing, she may very well drag those in her orbit down with her."

The warning in his voice is clear, and I turn away before I can see Luc take it in. It's better if he does leave me. He should run far, far away from me before he realizes who I am—for both our sakes.

The framed degree on the wall shakes as the pounding starts up again, just as Dean Driscoll reaches for the handle. A feminine voice that sounds like Tilda's responds, but she's agitated and muffled. He bares his teeth and rips the door open.

Three reporters immediately begin yelling.

Most humans don't know about the hidden layer to their

society, but that doesn't mean we're without technology, you know? We have TV stations, radio stations, and a whole hidden network of the web they can't access.

Right now, that hidden network has exploded into the Dean's office.

"Is it true that the murder was the result of a pack of unaffiliated alphas claiming the party as territory?"

"Dean Driscoll, is the alpha affiliation clause still holding?"

"There were rumored staff on premises during the attack, Dean Driscoll, do you have a comment?"

The Dean freezes, his face twisted into pure rage. Then he combusts into motion, shoving us out the door while he tries to use our bodies as some kind of shield, herding the reporters as we go.

"Dean Driscoll, first reports of the body suggest the victim was drained of her blood in the same fashion as the murders of the D'Amour dragons in 2012. Is it true the surviving heir of the D'Amours is attending Sawlefire Academy this year?"

My heart thumps wildly in my chest, my blood turning cold. I wasn't wrong about the syringe marks, either. It's just like what happened to the dragons.

I mean, shit, everyone loves being right, but if I could just be *a little less fucking right* about all this shit going on, that would be grand.

That's two connections to my secret past in less than 48 hours: the matebond connecting me to the last remaining survivor of my family's madness, and now this.

This is no coincidence.

It takes all my strength not to look at Luc. Still, I can feel him stiffen across the tightly crowded foyer. Dean Driscoll freezes too, the atmosphere suddenly palpable. Only Theo and Jace remain confused and oblivious, trying to shoulder their way past the reporters without starting a brawl.

The Dean clears his throat. "The University will not be commenting on speculation and rumor," he says fiercely, and I'm almost impressed, even though I can't stand the prick. "Our condolences are with the victim's family, and we will send through an official statement this week."

The reporters surge, yelling over each other. Theo snarls, getting up in the face of a man that shoves his microphone at me, desperate for any kind of scoop.

"Back off her," he grunts, and the reporter drops back in fear.

Theo slams his hand against the wall, blocking them from doubling back and clearing a path for me at the same time.

When we're free of the office, Jace pulls me against his side, muttering an apology as he sweeps us through the hall and through the growing crowd of people. "I'll let you go when they're not following," he says lightly. "Cross my heart."

I don't miss the way his expression softens the second our bodies touch, his lips parting with a sigh like relief. My own body reacts the same way, my skin tingling as I lean into his warm, safe scent without meaning to. I thought I'd imagined how strong the bond felt, but I hadn't. It draws me in, begging me, promising me more than I've ever been promised before.

My heart thuds dangerously, and I pull away as soon as there's space.

He lets me go, holding up his hands in a harmless, safe gesture, despite how his eyes darken with desire.

A noise rises in my chest, a word—I don't know what. I don't let it out, I turn away and run before everything that just happened in that office can catch me.

I duck into an alcove as soon as I can, thunking my head back against the brick and rubbing my hand over my face. Now that I'm away from the bond, where I can think again, my brain whirrs, kicking into overdrive to make up for lost time.

The reporters are going to be all over this, blaming it on the vipers just like the killings back in 2012. Everyone knew the vipers did it, even though they were never charged because they own the fucking police.

But here's the thing... The murder at the party can't be the vipers. For one thing, I would have sensed if my family were there. Their style isn't exactly subtle.

And more importantly... The link between the party and the dragon murders isn't the killing itself; it's the draining of the blood. And what no one apart from my family understands is that the vipers never drained any blood. That happened after, by the same person who led the vipers to the dragons' doorstep.

Everything that happened that night... there's so much more to it than anyone knows. It wasn't a territory fight. It was revenge—revenge for kidnapping me.

The only problem is, it turned out the dragons never kidnapped me.

I didn't see my kidnapper's human face. I was too scared. But I saw enough to know the blurred photograph leading my family to the dragons had been a lie. A scapegoat. I'd seen brown fur, a flash of a tiny body scurrying away into the sewers as the vipers burst into view... A rat. Not a dragon at all.

The vipers had been duped—pitted against the dragons for an unknown person's sordid amusement. Not only amusement, but gain, too, because while they were out, someone had broken into the snake pit and stolen from my father's private vaults.

Of course, my father couldn't have anyone knowing that. Which means no one does. It's our little secret.

But the vipers never drained the bodies. That part always remained a mystery to us—what kind of sick bastard would go in after and take their blood?

And why in the name of *fuck* has it happened again?

I tug painfully on my hair, pulling myself back into my body, away from the memories—controlling my sensations so I can't feel anything else. The memories haven't consumed me yet, and they won't now. I've controlled them for too long to fail at this hurdle.

I just need to work out how to handle the press. Those idiots have no clue what they're digging around in, but now they're here, my days of anonymity and safety are definitely numbered. The campus ignored me before; they're going to hate me when this comes out. The vipers were never charged with the murder, but everyone knew they did it.

It doesn't matter if they were duped, or if someone else drained the blood. No one cares about details when vengeance is on the line.

I have to talk to Luc first, before this gets out.

Leaning my head around the corner of the alcove, I scan the corridor for a sign of him, but he's nowhere in sight. He disappeared before I was even out of the office.

That's when my brain finally starts working again, and I connect the truth of what I saw the other night to what happened all those years ago. I freeze, my heart racing, the pieces falling into one big line of dominoes in my mind.

The stalker following me in the alley. The rat mask that didn't fit with the rest of the parade of alpha vitalities—bears, wolves, panthers.

I'm the only one who knows it was a rat that led my family to the dragons. If the victim's body was drained the same way the dragons were drained, then the killer at the party is that rat. I'd swear by it.

And what's more, he knows I know, because I'd bet my stupid sexy painting he let me see him deliberately.

He was giving me a message.

7
LUC

THIS SEMESTER HAS BEEN... UNEXPECTED.

I drop my bag by the bench press and glare at the only other person in here. No one comes to this gym. This isn't the kind of space where the jocks and the gym bros work out.

When my bag hits the floor, dust plumes up from the moldy mat beneath it. Cobwebs sway from the bench press, disturbed by the motion.

I come to a stop before the punching bag. Someone has scrawled a face in the middle of it, with crude teeth and mean little eyes. My lip twitches. Oddly, it will make it easier to focus and—I hope—not lose myself to the storm swirling inside me.

If I'm hitting the face, I'm less likely to be imagining my own issues in its place. And then maybe they'll fade away.

Maybe I'll forget the sound of that humming in the basement.

I strip off my shirt and square off.

Coming to Sawlefire Academy was meant to be simple. I thought Sawlefire would give me the talents I needed to form a new dragon clan of wanderers and outcasts. It was meant to help me escape my past, but now, if my suspicions are right, my past is nipping at my heels.

The killers who took down my family are back.

I begin with a few light warm ups, getting used to the feeling of the bag beneath my knuckles. Testing my form. It's been a while since I was in here, and it's bringing back memories I wish it wouldn't.

The problem is, the memories were already coming.

Which one of them was it? Who is the killer this time?

Or is it a copycat, kissing the vipers' ass? There's too much I don't know, too much that doesn't make sense.

Warmed up now, I begin hitting the bag properly. Sharp, violent jabs until sweat pools on my arms and forehead. I shouldn't be wasting my time here. I should be following the scent of cool mint, and claiming that glittering treasure Fate promised me. I should start a new life somewhere, and leave this city to rot.

But if I don't get my shit under control, I'll no longer be the kind of man who can accept this gift at all.

Pausing, I sniff the air, worried that I'm already too far gone and the trail will have disappeared. But no, I can still smell it. Cool mint, and the sharp tang of golden treasure. It filled the party as soon as she arrived. I knew before I even laid eyes on her that my mate had entered the room.

And then she was there. Hiding on the edge of the dance floor.

Christ, did she think she's inconspicuous in that outfit? Or is she just shy? Surely she couldn't actually think that was an outfit you could hide in... half the eyes in that place were on her.

One even tried to claim her. Cameron. I saw the way he looked at her, eyes sharp with desire as he leaned in and spoke quietly, just for her.

At any other time, I would have already challenged him.

This is my mate, the answer to everything I've been searching for. A new life, away from the past that haunts me.

The only problem is, I suspect Fate is playing a game with me.

I run my hand through my hair, tugging at the ends until it hurts. My body drips with sweat, my knuckles covered in scrapes and splatters of blood. I should have put on the gloves, but I wanted to feel the burn of the punching bag.

All signs are pointing toward Jel being the answer to the gaping fucking hole in my life. But she *can't* be the answer. She can't.

Fate has to be playing.

I pause as a thought occurs to me, my fists clenched, poised to begin round three. Maybe it's time I asked Fate directly. It's one of the perks of being a dragon after all; it's about time I used it.

When the gods were still around, a few thousand years ago or so, dragons served as guardians of their treasure. As a reward, we kept a line of connection with the gods long after they'd been forgotten. Think prayer on speed dial.

I've never used it. Asking a question of the gods means getting an answer... which comes with a whole other stack of shit, because gods aren't exactly known for being fun to deal with.

But I think I might already be dealing with them.

Closing my eyes, I pull the silver charm from my pocket, where I carry it at all times even though I've never worn it, and clench it in my fist.

"Come on, Fate," I murmur. "What are you doing to me?"

A cool wind flutters across my shoulders, but there's no other sign of someone listening.

Apart from the deathly stillness in the room. And the icy fingers that toy with the hair at the nape of my neck.

Fate is here, alright.

"I've been praying for a new life," I say through gritted teeth. "And you've given me a soulmate that leads right back to my old one. A snake. A *viper*, even if she's only a West and not a Vario. And she appears on that night, of all nights?"

I don't know precisely which viper infiltrated the party. The night they came for my family, ten years ago, there were dozens of them. All the alphas, at least. But the viper betas are vicious too, so it may have been more.

And now one of them has returned for an encore, right when Fate bonds me to one of their own.

I laugh, low and humorless. "We both know that's no coincidence. So what game are you playing with me? What do you want me to do? Do I not get to have a new home, then? A new life? If that's the case, just give it to me straight."

The icy fingers trail across my neck, up my jaw, and over my lips. I grip the pendant so hard, the metal nearly slices my skin. She's toying with me.

"This city deserves to burn for what they did to my family," I hiss, snapping my eyes open. There's no one there, of course. "Why are you trying to keep me here?"

Let me leave this city behind. Let it rot.

But I want...

I shouldn't want. Not that. Not her.

It takes several minutes for me to realize the fingers have disappeared. I sigh, frustration and anger filling the soft sound, but then music starts up.

A humming, tuneless sound.

A *familiar* humming, tuneless sound.

My phone sits on the ground next to my bag. The screen is black, dead, but the phone isn't silent.

"Are you kidding me?" I mutter, staring at the phone with

my lips parted in shock. My heart races in my chest. What the hell is happening right now?

I shake my head, smacking my ears violently, but the song continues. It's definitely the same one; I haven't imagined it. The killer was humming this, somewhere in the basement, before he escaped.

And he hummed it as he prowled through my house after the carnage, finding the bodies, draining them of their blood. After the screams had gone quiet, one of the killers, one of the *vipers*, came back. I hid from him, trying not to breathe, not to get caught until my family could rescue me. I didn't realize what they'd done to my family, yet. How far they'd gone.

And I didn't know what he was doing to the bodies until much later, when the police reports came out. If I'd known, maybe I would have found the balls to stop him.

Breath heaving, I leap to my feet and pick up my phone. I swipe it unlocked, but there's nothing there, no source of the sound.

It's getting louder.

For half a second, I freeze, knowing I can't go down this path. I can't become this person again—it cost me too much.

Then, I hurl my phone against the wall, where it shatters into a dozen pieces. Clutching my hair, I sink to my knees, fighting back the memories.

I thought I'd lost my mind at the party, when I heard the humming in the basement. How can the song that's haunted my dreams for years be here? Now?

Fucking vipers. Fucking murderous bastards playing sick, twisted games with me, and now Fate and the gods are getting in on the fun.

My fist slams into the floor. Someone tries to enter the room, sees me, and turns around again immediately.

Why has Fate brought me here? There's nothing coincidental about finding my mate the same night I find the killer who took my family, who drained their blood for his own sick reasons. Absolutely nothing.

Fate led me to Jel, a snake, who led me to one of the men who took my family from me.

Jel can't be the answer to my search for a new life, not when she's dragging me backward, shoving my past in my face. She has to be a test instead—something I'm meant to overcome.

Or maybe protect, like I failed to protect my family.

And still, I want her to be the answer. I want her to be the answer to everything I'm searching for.

Bonds aren't artificial attraction; they're perfection. Destiny. A gift chosen by the only person who knows you inside out. And after only a few minutes with Jel, I felt it. I felt the possibility of a life I haven't had for years.

I slam my fist into the floor again, relishing how the broken mat tears through my skin.

I have to get a grip. I can't let these memories rule me anymore. They ruled me once, sending me into a self-destructive spiral for years.

I want more than that. I want peace. I don't want to lose myself to the same violence that nearly tore me apart once before.

That's when I hear it—the humming still rings from the phone. Or... is it the phone? Or is it someone else?

"You're fucking kidding me," I snarl, lifting my head and staring at the empty room.

There's no one in the mirror but me, and still I hear the sound.

Is it in my head?

It's like a nursery rhyme...

I have to get it to stop, but nothing ever made it stop. Only blood. Only pain. Only—

I stare down at my hand, at the broken shards of glass sticking out of the skin. Blood oozes over my knuckles, sticky and hot.

The mirror is shattered.

But the humming has stopped.

Sighing, I run my clean hand through my hair and begin to pull the shards free. I'm back in control, for now at least.

I just have to keep it that way.

8

JEL

I KNOW I NEED TO SPEAK TO LUC, BUT MY BODY HAS OTHER IDEAS. Every time I've seen him walking in my direction, I turn the other way.

There's a dark look in his eyes that worries me, and the cuts on his knuckles are fresh.

I need a drink before I speak to him, that much is certain. In fact, I think I just need a drink full stop. It's five o'clock somewhere, right?

I shove through the laneway leading back around the building to the foyer at the main entrance. It's quicker this way, and since some idiotic luddite professor has sent me on an errand, I'd rather avoid the crowds.

Seriously, why didn't they just email the schedule to me? Instead of messaging me on the clunky school app and telling me they'd left it with the administration office.

I couldn't even work out which professor it was... They'd done something to their name to screw with the characters, so it was just a bunch of letters and symbols. Not the first time I'd seen them mess up something like that, but you'd think they'd learn eventually.

A flash of long, sun-bleached hair and dark eyes at the end of the lane makes me pause. It's Jace. His eyes catch and hold mine as he pauses in the middle of crossing the quad. The connection between us is instantaneous. Electrifying.

My body remembers vividly how he feels against me, and I crave it like I've never craved anything. Just a taste isn't enough.

I crave them all, and maybe that's the real reason I'm running from Luc. Because this bond between us all is a dream. A glittering bubble of a dream with a needle poised right at the surface. It'll pop eventually, whether I push the needle in or not.

If I admit who I am, I'll lose him. No second chances. No more golden sunlight to bask in for a few stolen seconds.

I know I can never have the reality, but if I tell him the truth I won't even have the dream.

A blackheaded figure appears beside Jace, the buckles of his leather jacket glinting in the sun. I duck back into the shadows.

This is stupid. I have to tell him who I am. The reporters will dig it up soon anyway, and if I can give him time to take it in, he might not challenge me, at least.

There's no way I'd win an alpha challenge from him with my soul locked up like it is. Other alphas, sure, probably. But not him.

I don't know how that little boy in the newspaper became him.

"Why is Fate playing with us like this?" I mutter to myself, ducking through a shortcut, away from the quad completely, and up the side steps of the admin building.

It's surrounded by high stone walls on either side, giving me a few precious moments of shadowed silence before I launch into the crowded foyer.

"Why Luc? And why bring us all together that night, of all nights? It can't be a good omen." I kick a stone down the stairs, snarling when it turns out to be heavier than expected. My toe throbs.

It has to be some sick joke. To bond me with Luc, not only on a night marked by murder, but marked by *the same kind of murder* that links our pasts together so horribly?

Tweedledum and Tweedledumbell are just the cherry on top.

A delicious, juicy cherry that I'd give up anything just to taste. And they aren't anything like Tweedledum and Tweedledee. They're smoking hot, deceptively intriguing, and strangely considerate of me in ways I never expected but am dying to know more about.

Okay, so I might be lashing out at them a little in my pain. I think I'm entitled. They can handle a few shitty nicknames.

"You're watching all this with popcorn, aren't you?" I snap, pausing abruptly to stare up at the sky, like I might find Fate on a flying carpet staring down at me.

Weirdly, something does shimmer across my vision. Like a giant dragonfly, but the colors are all wrong. I've never seen a purple dragonfly.

And I've never seen one with horns.

Blinking, I shake my head and duck through the open doors. Immediately, a hustle of noise and drama hits me. A number of people are waiting for appointments, and it looks like there's a tour starting soon.

I take my place in the queue and zone out. Fate is, however, once more against me as the two women behind me immediately start gossiping about the murders. I suppose it figures. Everyone is.

I manage to ignore them, right up until they mention Luc.

"They're saying the last survivor goes here," she whispers loudly. "Can you believe it? I would've left this place and never looked back."

I snort a laugh, disguising it as a cough when the woman looks up sharply. Me too, babe. Me too.

I would have run far, far away. Away from the shifters who took out my entire pack, leaving a scared ten-year-old child as the lone survivor only because they couldn't find him.

Away from the shifters who stole everything he loved.

The vipers. My family.

My eyes squeeze tightly shut as the memories finally break free from the maelstrom of my thoughts. Around me, the buzzing foyer fades away, leaving darkness and the sour taste of blood.

I may have been saved, unlike the poor dragons, but I feel like a part of me died that night, too, because I saw my family for what they really were.

They found me outside the dragon nest—conveniently placed so as to sell the kidnapper's story—and I'd tried to tell them something wasn't right. That a rat had taken me, not a dragon.

I'd tried to tell them, but I'd seen on their faces that they didn't care, and in that moment, my family's true priorities had become horribly clear. My safety didn't matter at all—it never had.

It was the insult that mattered.

It was their reputation.

With barely a cursory check to see if I was alive, they'd leaped at the excuse to take out our rivals completely, using my name as their battle cry. They left me standing there in the rain, rope burns on my wrists, tears streaking my cheeks as they swarmed the house and took it down.

They used me, in the name of love.

And, you see, love doesn't work like that. But it's the only kind I've ever known.

Alphas are all the same.

The woman at the desk waves to me, greeting me with a bored pout.

I force my expression into a smile. "I was told there was a schedule waiting for me."

"Name?"

"Angelica West."

She flicks through a pile of envelopes. Flicks through again. Shrugs. "Not here. Check the noticeboard—they might have stuck it there if we were busy."

How confidential. I thank her and turn away, skimming the noticeboard for any paper with my name on it. My eyes land on one just as a muscled arm reaches over me and plucks it free.

I know who it is without looking. My body knows. I shudder, trying to hold back the shivers of pleasure as I melt, falling toward one of the men Fate has chosen for me.

"Looking for this?" Theo asks without looking at the paper, a sharp grin on his face. Then he tilts his head to the side, as if seeing me properly. His breath catches, his eyes flashing golden for a moment. A furrow creases his brow, and a low snarl drops from his throat. "Your scent is off. You're upset."

For the first time since I met him, he leans in too close. Too sharply. Maybe it's just because my memories are riding me today, but I remember abruptly that Theo is an alpha.

For the first time, I remember that he's dangerous. Not so much in a fight—not to me—but in so many other ways.

If I'm not careful, these men will try to use me like my family did. They'll see some rival standing in their way, and they'll make up an excuse that puts me in danger and them as my protectors, just so they can take him down.

And with the promise of my painting hooking me in—three men who care for me, want me, need me—I might fucking let them.

"You're holding my schedule up like a middle school bully," I deadpan. "Of course I'm upset."

Theo's frown deepens. "No, that's not it." He sniffs again, golden light shining from his eyes. "You're afraid."

My heart stutters. The emotions I usually keep locked tightly away rattle their cage. "So?" I snap. "Someone was murdered. I'd be stupid not to be afraid."

I reach out to grab the schedule, but he snatches it back. "It's customary to pay the messenger," he says.

There's a slow grin on his face now, but he still looks too serious. He almost looks concerned, and that's more dangerous to me than an alpha challenge.

"In what world?" I snap. "Your boss pays you. Get a better union."

He steps back and winks. "For the small price of a kiss, it's yours."

"Ha ha." I snatch for the paper again, falling short once more. "You know, you can't call yourself a messenger if you don't deliver the message."

Theo grins at me. "One kiss," he says, voice lowered as if he's sharing a secret. "Don't you want to know why Fate picked me?"

"Cruel irony?" I fold my arms and sit back on one foot, regarding him.

This time, he doesn't laugh. Theo watches me, his gaze intent. "What do you think? You're the one with the painting."

Ah, the painting.

I was hoping they'd all forgotten about that, considering how messed up the other night was.

I take a step back, but he follows, closing the space between us even more than before. The sunlight catches on his hair, wind from the open doors stirring some of the shorter wisps that have already escaped the gel. It doesn't match the shadowy, low voice when he asks, "Why did you paint us?"

Suddenly, it's like I'm back in that room. I can smell the thick, light-headed scent of the oils. The open breeze stirs through in an attempt at ventilation, ruffling the hairs on my arms. I can feel the thick paint strokes beneath my brush, and the strange haze that took over my body as those figures came to life on the canvas.

Painting that thing terrified me. It was like something took hold of me, took over me, and the picture that came out was something I'd never seen before. Usually I paint what I know. I stick to references and memories, letting my style influence the structure but never completely changing it.

I don't know where this painting came from, and when I'd finished, I wanted to destroy it. But I couldn't. Their eyes captivated me, as did my own. The way I looked so content in their arms. Content, fierce, bold.

The way I looked nothing like how I am in real life, because those qualities are alpha qualities—everything I've fought years to control and tame.

And then, of course, I realized what using my own venom in the paint had done, the magic it had woven, and I couldn't have destroyed it if I wanted to. It was my ticket to surviving here without blockers.

It was a piece of my soul, on display, and I couldn't hurt it without hurting myself.

"I don't know why I painted you. I've never even seen you before," I tell him, the truth making me feel sick. But he has to know. Otherwise, he'll keep pushing and pushing, thinking that I'd seen him around and chosen them all on purpose.

I didn't. I didn't choose them at all.

Theo shifts his weight, ignoring the sudden rise in conversation by the doors. Something is happening, but I can't drag my eyes away from Theo for long enough to pay attention to it.

The horrible thing is, now that I'm seeing him alone, without adrenaline distracting me, I realize that Fate picked well. Below the surface level cockiness, there's something in him that resonates with me. It's like looking in a mirror, but the reflection is murky and distorted.

I want to stay long enough for it to become clear.

"I don't know," I repeat, when neither of us have spoken for too long.

"Don't know, or don't want to admit?" he asks quietly, leaning down so I can hear him without straining.

I stiffen, expecting the alpha bullshit to start now. But it doesn't. He's in my space, his large body crowding me into the wall behind me, but there's a quality to his actions that counters the aggression. It's in the way his warm breath brushes my cheek, the way he doesn't force eye contact, but rather leans one shoulder against the wall as if this is just a casual conversation between friends.

I frown up at him, my body tingling and my thoughts buzzing as I try to get a proper read on him. I need to keep my defenses up around him, that much I know for sure.

"Jel," Theo says quietly. "This is about me, too."

Urgh. He's right.

Damn him for appealing to an alpha's sense of justice, even if he doesn't realize it.

"Fine." I sigh, closing my eyes and letting my head fall back against the wall. "I mean it when I say I don't know. It was like something took over my body, and when I finally came back to myself... there you all were."

When I find the courage to look at him again, I have to swallow down the heat that rises in me. His expression is too open, too full of desire. I can barely stand to look at it.

"Then you painted a call to Fate," he says quietly.

I did *what*?

The memory of how the painting reacted when we found it hits me. All that light, that energy... The painting's power lit up like the fucking sun. I thought it was calling out to someone, and I was right. It was calling to Fate.

To the gods.

"I am not taking responsibility for her poor creative choices."

He laughs, a quick huff of a thing as if he didn't mean to let it out. His eyes flick to mine, and they aren't filled with that calculated alpha strategy, like usual. They're warm. Interested. Surprised.

I wonder if it's the first real thing he's shown me.

Before I can work out what to do with the slow warmth rising in me at that, the activity behind Theo explodes into yelling. I see cameras and microphones being shoved into a hysterical girl's face, and my stomach drops.

Theo spins around, holding an arm in front of me to protect me. I bite down on a tart response; I guess I can forgive him. My senses are on high alert too, even dulled as they are.

"It's about the murder," Theo says grimly. He loops his arm around my waist and tugs me out of the way of campus staff who come rushing down the corridor.

"Yeah, no shit," I snarl vaguely in his direction, my eyes fixed to the scene.

Staff hush the crowd, herding a ton of bystanders out and shutting the door. The noise halves, so their voices carry easily now and I don't have to strain.

For a few surreal minutes my world narrows to a softer sensation than the sharp, urgent survival I'm used to. Warm fingers press into my waist, gentle words carry over the hushed heads of the reporters... I think I see that weird dragonfly again, trapped inside, hovering above us.

My eyes flutter half-closed in pleasure as, once more, my instincts ignite a burning conflict in me.

How can I dance with romance and desire when our campus has been infiltrated by a killer? I should be rising to the hunt, chasing down the threat and protecting the packs. And I feel that violent urge, I do. But the other doesn't fade, not even close.

How can these two parts of me spin so fiercely together?

I know the answer of course, because this is what it means to be an alpha: violence and desire in equal measure. Two sides of the same coin.

It's unacceptable.

I swallow, shoving Theo back and listening closer.

"We found it in the library," the girl being interviewed sobs, and the cold slap of reality hits me. This isn't just the victim's friends giving an interview; something new has happened. "Scrawled over the archives."

"Those books are *ancient*," a second girl sobs, and I let out a confused grunt until it hits me.

Books have been damaged. Not people. Books.

"And the words were written in blood? Human or animal?"

"I don't knoooow," the girl wails. "It just said the gods will pay."

The gods will pay.

Why does that sound so familiar?

The crowd surges around us, more students flooding in from behind to see the commotion. Theo reaches for me again, rigid with tension now as he tries to protect me from the wave of vultures flocking to the carcass, but I'm already stumbling off course from the jolt.

I steady myself against the nearest surface—Theo's chest,

apparently. It's rock hard and slightly damp, as if he's been lifting weights, but it doesn't gross me out. Instead, a jolt of heat courses through me, growing warmer when I look up into his warm brown eyes.

"Did I mishear her, or did she say that someone is shaking a stick at God?" Theo asks lightly, his gaze darkening as he looks down at me.

I have no idea. These vultures will latch onto whatever smells like meat, and I've never known anything less than I've known the answers to these questions.

Desperate for a distraction, anything that can take me away from those eyes, from the hand on my waist and the breath against my neck, I snatch my schedule from his hand.

A break in the crowd lets me duck to the side, flipping the paper over distractedly to make sure it's actually mine.

My blood runs cold.

This isn't a schedule.

It's disguised as a Lonely Hearts notice, but it's far from romantic.

To the sexy redhead with the killer legs in line at Barber's Coffee this morning. You looked like you could do with a friend—someone to air guilty secrets with.

I'll show you mine if you show me yours?

Fuck.

I stare back out at the crowd, barely seeing them in front of me. Theo tries to catch my eye, but the activity separates us, and I let it. As if summoned, a familiar head of long, sun-bleached hair appears in the doorway—Jace, his expression twisted in concern as he searches for me. He must be able to feel my panic through the bond. It calls us together, but I can't. *I can't.*

I back away down the corridor, as far as I can get from these people who would destroy me if they knew.

The media circus might be rabid, unethical, and bloodthirsty... but they're right. And so am I—the rat mask wasn't a coincidence. The murders are connected, and what's more, I'm the link.

The killer knows about my role in the dragons' death. And not just that—he knows what no one should know except for me.

He knows my guilty secret.

I'd tried to tell my family that the kidnapper wasn't a dragon, that the kidnapper had reeked of a very nasty, very manipulative secret. But I didn't try very hard, because I wanted revenge, too.

Alphas are all the same.

My alpha soul awakened that night, and it craved violence. It craved blood and vengeance against the people who had harmed me. And against my family, too, for letting me be taken, and for leaving me there in the rain without even caring about me.

In that moment, I made a choice: I chose to let the violence happen, because with violence came vengeance, and my bloodthirsty heart longed for the blood. It didn't care whose. My family's or theirs; they could all suffer like I had. Like I did.

So, I pointed them through the door.

I let my family take them down.

I murdered them, too.

9
JEL

I sleep restlessly that night. My dreams pass in a fucked up haze of longing and guilt, but the worst part of it is when I wake up. At least my dreams are obviously nightmares; when I wake, the first thing I feel is the bond.

That's the real dream.

It washes over me, soothing my fears, my worries. It tells me everything will be okay, I just need to find those three men. Find them and bury my nose so deep in their scents, I'm drowning in them. Their hands on my skin, their lips against mine. Pushing and aching and wanting so hard, no one can take it from us. No one can take anything from us. We're alphas. We're the top of the food chain, and we'll destroy anything that—

I shake the dream away. We're alphas, and we'll destroy each other.

I go to my classes and take the opportunity in between droning professors to build my walls back up brick by brick. To remember the facts. The logic. Forget the fucking dream.

By the end of the morning, when I've finished my work in the campus studio, I've listed out the facts. The rat from my past is back, and he's taunting me. What lengths will he go to? And what does he want?

I need answers to those questions and those questions only. Anything else is just noise. My past and my guilt are just noise.

I throw my paints back into their case, stacking everything as neatly as possible without wasting effort. There's only a certain extent you can keep these things clean anyway. If I'm not personally covered in at least three layers of paint, I don't feel like a human, you know?

Well, I don't feel like a semi rabid snake-human hybrid with a repressed soul and a burning secret, but you say tomayto, I say tomahto.

In case it wasn't obvious, I'm starting to feel a little fragile around the edges. I need a painting session at home to reset. Like, doors locked, speakers blaring, painting outfit *on* kind of paint session.

I wonder what my mates would say if they found out I paint topless...

No, it's not worth going down that road.

A timid voice clearing their throat makes my shoulders tense. Slowly, I turn to find a girl I don't know very well hovering behind me. Tegan, I think. Yeah. That's it. She looks surprisingly like me, in a lot of ways—we both have the same flaming red hair, at least.

Right now, she has terror in her eyes and a mulish, stubborn set to her jaw.

This is going to be fun.

"What?" I ask bluntly.

"You turned in a dangerous painting," Tegan says without preamble. "As head of the committee for health and safety, I'm going to need to see the painting so the committee can take the appropriate measures to rectify the situation."

She nearly makes it through without flinching. Nearly, but not quite.

Why do they always send the mice for this sort of thing? I want to like her, really I do, but she rubs every single one of my instincts the wrong way.

Keeping my expression very still—largely because, if I make her squeak too much, my blood pressure is going to rise sharply and then I don't know what I'll do—I tell her, "It's taken care of."

Then I turn away, lifting my art board and carrying it to the side of the room where it can dry on the rack.

The throat clearing comes again.

Still facing the rack, my eyebrows shoot up and I silently mouth *are you fucking kidding me?*

After a beat, when I've got my anger under control, I turn around. "You're still here."

"The committee needs to review the painting," she squeaks.

"The committee needs to take their lordly decrees and shove it up their—" I break off. "The painting is gone, Tegan. You don't need to worry about it. It was never meant to be submitted. Cameron got over-zealous and forgot this was a university, not the New York underground art scene."

The mulish expression on her face furrows deeper. "But the painting was alleged to contain hypnotic properties."

I grow very still. "Who said that?"

"The Show Director reviewed the paintings and found—"

"Bullshit, no one had seen them yet. Who said that?"

It can't have been Cameron, because he desperately wanted the painting in the show. He's the whole reason I'm in this stinking mess. So who else saw it between my studio, my private assessment with Cameron, and his house?

Tegan actually stamps her foot, and it's so ridiculous my anger almost disappears. "The Committee does not reveal anonymous tipsters, now please, hand over the painting so we can review whether or not it was laced with *hypnotic sex magic*." Her eyes widen, and she slaps a hand over her mouth.

Too late, babe.

I burst out laughing—long, loud peals of laughter that ring through the empty studio.

"So let me get this straight. Some fussy old Professor caught sight of my painting, felt a little tingly in places they weren't expecting to, and now they want to burn it in the name of protecting the children, even though everyone at this school is a legal adult?"

A fierce anger rises in me, washing away my attempts to disengage and replacing them with righteous fury.

Is she serious right now? We have a murderer on the campus—a murderer that I am almost one hundred percent sure is responsible for kidnapping me and setting my family on the dragons ten years ago—and she's worried about a painting? If she knew what it really was, I'd get it, but she doesn't.

Fuck this place.

"Look, you and I both know you're never getting your hands on that painting, so how about you just walk away now. Before one of us gets hurt."

My blood rises, the familiar, delicious ache of violence guiding me forward. Alarmed, I force myself back from the edge, but not before Tegan goes running from the room.

I came closer than I'd like to revealing myself there, but at least it served a purpose.

I can't believe they're targeting my painting and they don't even have it anymore... Whichever professor saw it wouldn't have even known what they were looking at. Thank God.

I'd be in a lot more trouble if they did.

There was no sex magic in my goddamn painting. Only an accidental fated mate call, according to Theo, and a hefty portion of my alpha soul. The one that no one here knows I possess.

Unease stirs in my gut. They *don't* know what the painting really is... right?

Are they onto me? If they know I'm concealing my alpha vitality and pretending I'm not the heir to the most violent gang this side of the bridge, why do they even care about the painting? They should just expel me straight out.

So why do they want it destroyed so badly? I know they're weirdly religious and uptight here, but this seems a bit much, even for them.

I shake my head. Honestly, I don't have the space to think about that right now. It must be because of the dreams, but I can't find my center. I've gone from fragile to... fractured. Like I'm poised at the edge of a cliff, waiting to shatter on the rocks below.

My hands were covered in paint earlier, and I could have sworn it was blood.

They looked so much smaller, too. The hands of a child. As much as I'd like it to be, it isn't a metaphor; it's a memory. Several memories, all blending into one.

I squeeze my eyes shut until the shudders pass. This is why I keep pieces of myself locked away. I *have* to keep them locked away.

This is why I chose art, instead of the life laid out for me. The soothing sweep of paint on a canvas. The smell of the studio. It's as far from blood and death as I can think of.

Moving more carefully now, I pack up the rest of my things and leave the studio. The university is quiet at this time of day. There are no classes, so it's only students using the workspaces or professors planning their content.

Without intending to, I change direction and head toward

the library. The one the girls claimed was vandalized with blood.

The note from yesterday is eating away at me, sending shivers down my spine. I don't want to play a role in this twisted game, but it looks like I already have a role, whether I want it or not.

The killer knows me.

So, what does he want with me?

If he's already left me one note, is it possible he left this one for me as well?

I slip into the library and down the rows of shelving toward the rare book section at the back. The library is still full, crime or no crime. Students study over piles of books and glowing laptop screens. The rustle of paper is the only noise as I pad down the far end.

When I get there, the section is blocked off by police tape, but the guard they've left at the entry is fortunately distracted by two very attractive professors.

Rolling my eyes, I walk behind them without being noticed. I didn't even need to shift.

It's eerily quiet, especially in the rare books section. There's a hush over the place, like the books are protesting the vandalism.

Okay, and now I'm officially launching myself into the sun for such a wet comment.

"They're books, Jel," I mutter, ignoring how blasphemous it feels to dismiss them being harmed.

It doesn't take long to locate the scene of the crime, even though they've removed the evidence. The vandal wasn't concerned with being neat; the floor is covered in splatters of blood. Kneeling, I carefully sniff the air above the ground.

I have to bite my tongue to avoid snarling in anger.

It's human blood.

"Is this the blood of the victim, you bastard?" I murmur, trailing my fingers over the top of the dried surface. I can still feel the echo of rage and fear within it. "Why go to the effort of draining it if you're going to waste it on this?"

I stand up, turning back to face the table where it obviously happened. Movement catches my eye, and I look up, realizing I can see back into the main library through a gap in the shelves. We're separated by glass, but I can see him clear as day.

Luc.

Guilt shreds my stomach to pieces. I know I need to confess before the reporters dig too deep and out me, but I can't bring myself to do it.

How do you even have that conversation?

Hey, man, you know how you think I'm literally made for you and Fate has brought us together? I actually slaughtered your whole family.

Okay, yeah, maybe I didn't hold the knife, but oh boy I definitely could have stopped it.

Did I point the way and set my horrible family to the kill? Yes, yes I did. Unequivocally. There were several doors I could have pointed at, and I pointed at yours.

I'm so fucked.

A small noise escapes me, and even though it's impossible, Luc looks up. His eyes meet and hold mine, and we stand there, frozen. He's holding something in his hand, alongside the book he's flicking through, and now he brings that same thing to his lips in a deliberate gesture, then his collar. Then he slips it into his pocket.

What on earth?

I didn't think he was religious, but that definitely seemed like a ritualistic gesture. Just not one I've ever seen.

I step closer to the glass, inwardly searching for the line of

Fate that still connects us. Each day—each *hour*—I have to work a little harder to reject it. And it hurts worse each time.

I thought this was meant to fade. When I've heard stories of rejected mates before, I swear it's a one and done scenario.

So why is this still hurting?

As if he can hear me, Luc winces, his jaw tightening with the same kind of pain I'm feeling.

He snaps his book shut and reshelves it. Then he walks up to the glass.

Goddammit.

Lacking any other option, unless I want to encourage the asshole to follow me in here, I walk up to mirror him.

He smirks, his breath already fogging up the glass. Puffs of smoke fall from between his parted lips, swirling with the fog. It's mesmerizing.

"Someone's being naughty," he mouths.

When he speaks, I notice he takes a second too long to form the words, like he's remembering what order they go in right before he says them. He looks wild around the edges. Barely contained.

I know the feeling.

"I'm investigating." I practically whisper the words back.

He cocks his head to the side, pulling a confused face and waving his hand like he can't understand me.

Heart thudding, I step closer to the glass. There's barely an inch separating us now. He couldn't read my lips from this close if he wanted to.

My breath fogs the glass, concealing him in this strange, misty veil. Only his eyes shine through, not even shifter gold, but just his own, piercing blue.

"I'm investigating," I say in a low, quiet voice.

His answer is just as low, muffled through the glass as his eyes remain fixed to mine. "What have you found?"

My own guilt.

"Nothing yet."

He quirks an eyebrow, nodding slowly.

Then he vanishes.

I squint into the shadowy library, cursing the fog and the smoke for obscuring where he went. Is he going to jump-scare me? Because I'll stab him in an artery for that.

Movement catches my eye, and I freeze as I spot Theo standing in the shelves, watching me.

No, watching us.

He's clearly been there a while, and from the expression on his face, he doesn't like what he saw. Slight grimace, teeth bared, brow furrowed. He notices me watching and clenches his jaw, his eyes flashing golden. My alpha soul sings in delighted response.

Theo has issued a challenge, and she wants to tear him limb from limb for the insult.

I can still remember the sensation of his arm on my waist from yesterday, but that doesn't make my soul any softer on the fight. If anything, she grows more rabid.

I swallow, ignoring the pang of disappointment in my soul as I pull back from the challenge. Jealous prick of a tiger. Even after our conversation this morning, his vitality is roaring with anger from witnessing a few seconds of me talking to someone else.

But his soul doesn't realize it isn't Luc he's challenging.

I turn away and only just manage not to squeal in shock. My control is helped somewhat by the hand that presses over my mouth.

Luc grins at me and slowly lets his fingers fall away, brushing the tip of his index finger deliberately across my lips right at the very end.

"What are you doing?" I hiss at him, trying to keep even

quieter than a whisper. I ignore the flush spreading across my cheeks, and if he knows what's good for him, Luc will, too. "You'll get us caught."

When he speaks, his voice is so quiet I have to lean in to hear it. Without the glass between us, his breath brushes my face, hot and pleasantly spicy. "Then we'll have to be very... very... quiet."

The last word is more of a breath itself, caressing my lips as he leans down into my space, eyes burning.

"You're a snake," he says.

It isn't a question.

"Yes," I breathe.

"A viper," he continues, eyes narrowing.

The sharp glint of emotion in them catches me by surprise. It burns through me, and the clench of his jaw suggests he's wary. Unhappy. And yet he's leaning in close, his gaze roaming my face with that faint sense of awe he had at the party. Like I'm the treasure he's been searching for.

He's conflicted.

I have to tell him the truth. But not here.

"I don't associate with vipers," I tell him, because it's the only truth I can give him just yet. It's also the entire core of my value system, so it's definitely not a lie.

Still, when his shoulders relax and his face softens in relief, it feels like one.

I pull away, ignoring the thick twist of guilt in my stomach. It's time to focus on the task—I need answers before we're caught. I walk back to the table where the book was left. I don't think there's much more to find, but Luc doesn't suggest I'm wasting my time.

He runs his fingers over every book, using the back of his knuckles so as not to leave a print. Not that it matters, surely.

Anyone can come in here at any time. The forensic evidence would be off the charts, completely useless.

Every now and then he kneels to sniff a particular spot, same as I'm doing. Between us, you'd think we'd find a trace of the killer. Some bodily scent that reeks of malice or anticipation at the very least. But there's nothing. It's like he has no scent at all.

We finish our circuit side by side, our shoes brushing as we each straighten from our examinations—me, from the open book left on the other table, and Luc from his careful inspection of the ground. The corner of his lip curls into a slow smile.

An ache starts up in my abdomen, like an ember slowly kindling toward a flame.

It's the rut, dormant but nowhere near forgotten.

I swallow thickly, and before he can take charge, I ask the question swirling through my mind. "What was that thing you kissed, out among the shelves?"

His eyebrows lift, and he pauses for a moment before reaching into his pocket to pull out a charm.

I frown, staring at the familiar horned dragonfly, inset with bright purple amethyst. "What is this?" I breathe.

"Ssh," he whispers, propping one hand on the table behind me and leaning down until we're face to face. "They'll catch us."

Irritated, I blow a puff of air in his face, ignoring how his smile widens, and take the dragonfly from his outstretched hand.

I turn it over and over, marveling at the careful design. It's an artist's work, for sure. The sockets are far too well made for a mold.

When I look up, Luc is watching me carefully, still in the same position.

"It's a charm," he says finally. "You wear them."

"You weren't wearing it," I point out.

He huffs a laugh. "They're also good luck amulets."

"What do you need good luck for? There's only a killer on the loose."

This time, his laughter sounds surprised, like he didn't expect me to make a joke or himself to find it funny. Pretty morbid of us, I suppose, to joke at a time like this. But it still doesn't feel real.

Sinister and personal, but not real.

I almost tell him about the dragonfly I saw, but something holds me back. "Why does it bring you luck?"

The hairs on the back of my neck lift up as I ask the question, almost like there's an invisible wind ruffling through the room. Or an ice-cold touch across my skin, even though neither of us have moved.

"Because that symbol belongs to the gods."

My heart stutters, the breath catching in my throat. Sound whirrs through my ears, so chaotic and wild I almost miss what he says next.

"The dragon gods, specifically. They keep these guys as pets. It's meant to be an omen of vitality to see one. Not that that's possible, since they haven't been seen for centuries."

An omen of vitality.

Life.

Appearing against a scene of murder.

I swallow thickly. My feet are moving, backing up toward the door despite the look of concern on Luc's face.

I knew Fate was messing with us, but I didn't connect it like this. I thought the joke was on me. On my love life. But if the shifter gods are involved, instead of just Fate... that's different. It isn't Fate playing her usual games with bonds and lovers.

It's bigger.

"Jel?" Luc whispers, urgent now. "What is it?"

I can't answer him, can't alleviate his concern without revealing my secrets. My mind burns, thoughts racing, and before he can ask me for what I can't give him, I turn and run.

He calls after me, making the guard turn and shout, but I don't stop. I do what I've become so good at and shut it all out.

But the padlocks in my mind won't stay shut. Not this time.

This changes everything, doesn't it? Everything about the game I'm caught in—the rules of it, and my likelihood of survival. It's one thing to deal with a killer who's toying with me, and another thing entirely to deal with this...

Because maybe I was wrong; maybe this isn't just some sick, twisted game the killer is playing with me.

Maybe this game belongs to the gods.

10

JACE

MORNINGS IN MY HOUSE ARE A TOTAL NIGHTMARE.

My sisters careen around the breakfast table, all four of them, and scream at the top of their lungs. Our dad used to hate it, before he left us. To be honest, it doesn't bother me at all. I think it's funny. The youngest three are still trying to perfect their howls, and I haven't had the heart to tell them you can't howl when you're a human.

The oldest of them, Caitlyn—still five years younger than me—joins in by throwing the dog's toys into the fray every ten seconds. But she doesn't tell them it's a futile effort, either. She's not exactly soft-hearted, so I'm not sure what her motives are.

Possibly blackmail, for when they join her high school and threaten the cool persona she's perfected. She's smart, but it won't work. You can't blackmail people who have no dignity.

"Give it a rest, guys," I say, injecting a small amount of warning into my voice.

They ignore me. It's getting really hard to hear myself think, which is a shame, because I've been getting in some intense wallowing all morning about this fated mate situation.

If a guy can't get a free pass to wallow like a champ when destiny rejects him, when can he?

"Guys," I warn, my voice a low growl now.

The youngest, Trisha, pauses, eyes a little wide. "Are you going to bark?" she whispers.

I hold my face still, so I don't laugh. "If I have to."

Caitlyn snorts. "When are you going to give up and just roll with it?"

I flick my hair out of my eyes and lift my bowl of cereal to my mouth to drink the excess milk. "When they start listening to me."

She shoots me a pitying look over the top of her cornflakes.

I snort, shaking my head and turning away.

If only she knew just how much she should pity me. The ache of Jel's rejection still burns low in my gut, and while we can't seem to keep away from her, I don't really have much hope that things will change. She made that very clear.

Everything I've ever known about fated mates tells me it's simple: one alpha and one beta. Or one alpha and one omega.

They don't say anything about three alphas fighting over one beta. Even packs of alphas that form around an omega aren't fated. They're just... a pack. With different dynamics between each of them.

How can a pack share one person if you're all meant to be fated to her? There's no winner there—no hierarchy. It doesn't work. Alphas need a hierarchy.

And while I'm not scared of competition, fighting two alphas over a beta who's meant to be my mate just doesn't sit right with me. I know what my dad would say about it if he heard, and it's not worth repeating.

The bitter twist of anger catches me by surprise, although it probably shouldn't by now. I shovel the last of my breakfast into my mouth, focusing on the taste of soggy cornflakes instead of my own thoughts. He's right though—my dad. Trust *Jace* to be the one who ends up with a fuckup of a mate bond.

Trust me to end up with a bond that pits me against the one goddamn guy I've been in competition with since freshman year, and a punk wannabe dragon. He'd laugh himself stupid if I told him.

The prickling sense of someone watching me makes me look up, and I discover Caitlyn is still staring, her eyes narrowed this time. Her lips purse, and she pauses for a minute as if choosing her words.

Then she flicks her hair back and asks casually, "What's this I hear about you finding a mate?"

I gape at her. Freaky little mind reader. She's always had an unnerving ability to hit right at the sore spots.

The screaming stops. Suddenly, I have four sets of curious eyes turned my way. I preferred the noise.

"Nothing for you to worry about," I say pointedly.

The youngest three begin talking over each other, eagerly fighting for the nearest seat to me.

"When do we get to meet her?"

"Is she pretty?"

"What's her vita— vitall—"

I drop my head into my hands. "Vitality," I say gently.

I try to make it a stern correction, like my father would have. He was always using our mistakes as teaching moments, drilling the corrections into our heads with his seriousness and faint sense of disapproval. But it doesn't come out that way.

"What's her vitality?" Trish repeats, bouncing up and down on her toes as she leans forward to grab a banana from the fruit bowl.

"It doesn't matter," I say, and this time the memory of Jel's rejection does manage to turn my voice harsh. "We're not... compatible. We're letting the bond fade."

Or trying to.

God, it's almost hilarious, the idea that this could ever fade. Whenever I'm near her, it's like I'm a different person. My body feels lighter, and the noise in my brain—usually so deafening—drops to a low hum. Even forgetting the mate part of it, I'd follow her around the school just to feel that way again.

I sort of have, a bit. Tried to keep my distance out of respect but... our bond is like a drug. I can't stop tasting it. Is it because she's a snake, and the hypnosis of her venom has affected the bond?

Or is this just Jel and what she does to me?

The room grows a little quieter, my words ringing in the silence.

"You know you're not meant to do that, right?" Caitlyn asks suddenly, her voice low and serious. "You're not meant to let it fade."

Amusement colors my words. "Look, I don't want to say you'll get it when you're older, like a jackass, but—"

"Then don't," she snaps. "Because you're wrong. Which one of you rejected it?"

There's an intensity to her tone that tells me she isn't asking to be a pest. She knows something, or thinks she does. She's trying to help.

God, our dad hated nosy questions.

"Does it matter?" I snarl.

Two of them flinch, and I barely resist the urge to order them out. To demand silence and respect, like an alpha is meant to.

Like always, there are two voices in my head, warring with each other. Telling me which way to turn. One is my own, and that's the one I'm supposed to ignore.

But Trish looks hurt, her eyes glassy like she's close to

crying. So I reach for her, covering her small hand with mine while giving her a reassuring smile.

Though I keep trying, I can't help it. I can't help who I am.

I answer Caitlyn with a resigned sigh, "She did. But it's complicated. There are three of us drawn to her, and we don't exactly get along."

Caitlyn's expression turns serious. "Rejected mates are a tragedy," she whispers, her sisters hanging on her every word.

When she continues, she sounds like she's reciting something she read in a book. She sounds far older than fifteen.

"Fate might have the best ideas for our souls, but sometimes our bodies have lived different lives to what our souls were meant to. We've strayed too far from Fate's path already, and no longer fit with the one she planned for us."

Her words chill me. Is she saying what I think she's saying? That we can make so many wrong choices, we're no longer the people we were meant to be? I open my mouth to ask, but she keeps going, speaking more urgently.

"Jace, you *have* to talk to her, because by rejecting you, she's rejecting herself." She frowns, looking like she's trying to remember something more. Her nose wrinkles, making her look fifteen again. Then she recites: "In the moment they reject their fated mate, they can no longer deny how far off course they've gone. And if they reject their mate entirely, it means they're lost, and no one will ever find them."

I shiver, unable to help it.

Is Jel lost?

Am I meant to find her?

"Whoa."

The awed sighs from the others draw me back to the room. They're all watching me, waiting to see what I'll say. What I'll do.

I've become a living, breathing Romeo to them, tragic love story and all.

Sighing, I rise to my feet and try to look both stern and gentle. I'm sure I only manage half.

"Thank god I have a nerd for a little sister, hey." I wash my bowl and stick it in the drying rack. "I'll speak to her," I promise.

Caitlyn relaxes. The others cheer.

I escape to the sound of human howls and laughter, but it doesn't ease the chill in my bones.

How can I find Jel when I can barely find myself?

11

JEL

HALF A TUB OF ICE CREAM JUST DOESN'T SOOTHE THE SOUL LIKE IT USED to. Three scoops to go, and all I feel is nauseous.

I'm not... one hundred percent sure how I got home last night. I remember the library, and I remember Luc trying to follow me out of it. But it's all a blurred mess of my soul hammering inside me, screaming to take charge, and the awesome, terrifying sense of the gods watching my every move.

If I thought I was jumpy before, this is a whole new level of fucking embarrassing.

I stir in the morning sunlight, stretching my legs out on my couch and forcing down another scoop of cookies and cream. Momma didn't raise a quitter. And when I stop eating ice cream, I have to go to class, so. There's that.

Class means more gods and more killers, lurking in the shadows like cops at a brothel. I am officially sick of gods and killers. There's no doubt in my mind anymore that Fate is fucking with me. Us. There's a reason my painting ended up in that submission pile, calling me to the party on that night of all nights, and I officially don't want to know what it was.

Once more, my dreams from last night haunt me. Messy,

blurred faces stretch before me, paired with the aching, rasping sensation of the rut trying to break free. In my dreams, it feels possible. It feels *good*. Men kneel between my thighs. Fingers and tongues bring me pleasure while the violence within me stokes to a burning flame, promising me vengeance against the shadow that chases us.

Metal clinks against metal, and I look down to see my claws are out, rattling against the spoon. Fuck's sake.

My soul is well and truly sick of being locked up. She wants to lead us out of this danger, using her violent instincts to rip the head off the rat who sent me that Lonely Hearts notice, along with any gods that get in the way. I, personally, would rather not be a raving lunatic today.

Logic and facts. That's what's going to get me through this. Not my alpha soul.

A low, agitated hiss ruptures the silence, and I choke on my ice cream, the sound catching in my throat. I freeze, weighing both the logic and the facts and coming up with an unfortunate conclusion.

My facts are outnumbered by emotion. I need to do some damage control before I can safely leave the house.

Sighing, I get up from the couch. My legs shake with adrenaline, my heart already racing as my body senses what's about to come.

I deadlock the front door and drop the empty ice cream tub in the sink. Then, I close my eyes and let my body do what it can never, ever do around other people.

I let my soul out, just a little.

She's still tied to the painting. Both ends of the magical energy cord hook into me and the painting in turn, anchoring one to the other, so it isn't too strong. It isn't overwhelming. I can handle this.

Ease and pleasure flood me, the bond finally relaxing now

that I've given it room to breathe. Man, it's intoxicating. I've been spending so much energy holding it off, I forgot how to feel it.

If this is the only taste I get, I should enjoy it, right? Before the truth about my past and my soul comes out and everything shatters.

I press my thighs together, subconsciously seeking friction as the bond pours into every crevice of my body.

And brings my dormant rut with it.

At the first touch of that primal instinct, my eyes roll back and my head falls against the door behind me. My hands clutch at the wood, and I take a slow, measured breath in an attempt to calm the sensation.

When did the rut rise so high? It's alarming how much it's built without me noticing. I need to take a few days off and lock the doors. Clear it.

But I can't, because the rut knows we have mates now, and it won't let me take care of this by myself. No matter what I do, it will still be there. And if I try to do too much alone, without my mates... it will object.

I clench my teeth, assessing. Planning. I can hold it off a bit longer, until the bond breaks away completely. And for now, I'll just take the edge off.

The first thing I notice when I let go further is anger. It prickles my chest, scratching at me. Why are my mates not here? They should be waiting, ready. I know they're willing, so what the hell is the problem?

But thinking about my mates brings memories of them—Theo's sharp, watchful gaze; Luc's arrogant insistence that I'm the one for him; and Jace's smile. That crooked, welcoming smile that promises too much and offers too little.

As soon as the memories hit, desire wipes the anger clean. I'm back in that closet, riding Luc's fingers as they thrust back and forth inside me. Theo's breath is hot against my neck, his whispered praises encouraging me, commanding me.

This time, Jace does touch me. Luc does as he promised that night, holding his hand still as Jace swipes his tongue over my clit. Just filling me up. Reminding me that he's there. It's torture. Teasing, aching torture, because when I try to ride him again, he holds me still.

No one is allowed to hold me still.

A low hiss drops from my mouth, and when I open my eyes I can see the glint of shifter gold reflected in the fridge. I slide my hand down my front and into my shorts, teasing the edge of my pussy, running the slick wetness over my core. I wish they were here, but a distant part of me knows they can't be.

Why can't they be?

My breathing turns harsher, louder. I'm filled with equal parts frustration and pleasure as I circle my clit with increasingly rapid movements. I bite the building scream down, tasting blood on my lip as a low moan begins to sound instead.

Anger lashes with desire. I want and I *want*, but I can't have. My mates aren't here, and the rut can't understand. If the bond is still there—and it is, God, it is—then why aren't we fucking? Why aren't they in me right now? It's where they belong. It's what we all want.

I want their knot—*my* knot.

The image of it shatters me. I picture myself riding Luc, his cock filling me, his knot filling me as our sweat-slick bodies clutch at each other. Alphas don't get knotted; this is insane. This is impossible.

My body wants it so much it hurts. Pleasure surges from the deepest part of me, my toes curling as I fall back against the door, arch my back, and cry out in ecstasy.

I picture the others, too. Jealousy riding them, pushing

them as they snarl at Luc for claiming what's theirs. They fight for control, pulling me free, taking me.

I flip them, grab their throats, and take them too.

It's feral. Wild and dangerous. Back in reality, my claws shred the architrave, shaving splinters off the walls. My fangs extend at the thought of someone being in the room with me, and I know without a doubt that they'd already be bitten if they were.

The venom of a snake shifter is hypnotic. Catch the right person at the right time, and if they're not an alpha, then for a few minutes you can convince them to do anything.

Why else are the vipers so feared? Why else am I so feared?

I'm their leader, their Alpha. I might have thrown that crown back in my family's face, but the blood still ties me, and my soul won't let me forget it.

I touch myself again, grinding into my hand, riding the waves of pleasure. She isn't sated, but my soul eases, allowing the rut just enough space to back down. I feel like I can breathe for the first time in days.

My wall is destroyed.

I stare at my hands, watching with an odd detachment as the claws retract. The golden light from my eyes, reflected onto my skin, fades too.

I'm back.

"Fucking hell," I mutter, kicking a chunk of dry wall away from the door.

My attention catches on something strange. I frown, my heart thudding unpleasantly as I take a step closer to the leather object on my kitchen counter. The leather object I don't own.

My breath catches, rage erupting like a tornado inside me. The scream escapes me properly this time, and I pick up the stool from beside the counter and hurl it into the wall. The legs break off and fly away.

As quickly as it rose, my soul simmers down low again, locked in place by the painting and the magical cord that binds it. I take a deep breath, holding it, then releasing.

Then I pick up the rat mask from my counter.

It's innocent enough. Clean. No scent, courtesy of the magical herbs stuffed in the nose—that explains why I couldn't track him at the party. The only scent on the entire thing is the splash of blood right over the left cheek.

My fingers grip it tighter, the leather squeaking. Up close, it doesn't even look like a rat. It looks menacing and aggressive, like a predator. Or maybe that's just because of what it means, that it's here. Now. On my counter.

The killer was here while I was sleeping.

I still don't know his game, but he's closing in on me. He's chosen me.

I drop the mask back on the counter and turn away. A quick sweep of my apartment tells me nothing is missing, except for an extra spell kit I bought from the witch who did my painting. It only held some charcoal fog defense spells, nothing crazy. I might have misplaced them myself.

The killer came here to taunt me. That's it.

A strange sensation builds inside me. It begins slowly, curling tentative fingers around my throat. The sensation isn't fear; I'm not afraid of him. It isn't anger, either, because I can feel that just fine. I don't think it's anything to do with the rut, because the edge has burned away from that, leaving a dull ache in its place that's far easier to deal with.

Whatever it is, it's unfamiliar. So unfamiliar that it isn't until I've arrived on campus and I'm sitting down in my first lecture that I realize what it is—an urge.

I want to tell my mates about the mask.

The realization floors me. I've never gone to anyone for help like this before. Why the hell would I start now? This bond won't last. I won't let it last.

If I tell them about the mask, they'll only get more involved with me. It'll be harder to break the bond. So, no way. I'm keeping quiet.

My head turns of its own will to the front of the hall, and I sigh in resignation, knowing before I see him what's happening.

Jace stands in the doorway. My racing thoughts ease, dangerously calm and content just by his presence. I forget about the mask. Forget about everything but the sense that it will all be okay.

He makes me let down walls that should never be let down; they all do. I can't fight it any more than I can fight breathing.

He hasn't seen me yet, so I take the excuse to watch him silently, for once. I hadn't realized until now just how unusual it was that I've lost that ability. I used to be able to watch everyone; no one saw me.

Now, everywhere I look there's one of three people already there. Waiting. And even when they aren't right there, I can feel them.

It's getting harder and harder to fight this connection. This morning is proof of that, and just the memory of my fantasies and the orgasm they teased from me has me heating all over and sinking down in my chair.

Jace hovers, scanning the seats for a good spot. He's wearing a sleeveless, gray shirt, the arms cut low so that the hole comes halfway down his stomach. When he turns, his abs show through, along with the side of his pec. A hint of nipple.

He's a contradiction. There's a meanness to the set of his jaw when he isn't smiling, but when he is, he transforms. The smile is crooked and disarming, almost goofy, and it alters his

messy, sun-bleached hair from the styled mess of a fuckboy to...
just messy. Just a boy.

I like it. I like his smile a lot.

I like Theo's attentiveness, too. And Luc's determination to
go after what he wants, no matter how it burns.

My pulse thuds steadily at my wrist, a pounding, aching
beat that drags at my focus. I've always relied on logic to get me
through, squashing my instincts and hiding them away. It's
getting harder to think logically when all I can do is feel.

They make me feel.

Like an inevitability, Jace turns to me, smiles, and walks
my way.

12

JACE

CLASSES ARE MOSTLY DISTRACTED WHEN I ARRIVE, BARELY functioning. People are still talking about the murder, and everywhere you look the victim's face is plastered, along with the face of the girl who survived. It's sobering and infuriating. Even though they aren't my pack, my instincts are kicking in.

I'm not the only one.

Heads turn to me as I pass in the hallway, their eyes flashing brilliant gold as they shift just their sight. Just enough to gain a few extra senses, to determine if the new person is a threat.

By the time I've reached my lecture hall, all the hairs on the back of my neck have risen in agitation. There's a simmering pool of aggression burning in my gut, and it's all I can do to keep it in. Especially now that my soul thinks I have a mate to protect.

I pause in the doorway, trying to find that quiet, centered place I usually drop into when I'm around others. It isn't the joking, brotherly side of me that comes so naturally. Too naturally. But it isn't quite the macho leader my dad always wanted me to be, either. I found a middle ground between the two of them—silence. Usually, it's the best I'll get. Today I can't even find that.

I stick my hands in my pockets and step into the room.

A familiar head of bright red hair makes me pause just as I've decided to sit up the back.

Sitting with her would be idiotic, not only because she probably doesn't want me there, but because I'm not myself today. Or, I'm too much myself. Without the buffer of Theo, who at least brings me closer to who I'm meant to be, I'll say the wrong thing.

But already my legs are guiding me across the room to join her.

The effect of her nearness is instant. As soon as I'm within several feet of her, it's like my whole body is on a wire, tugging me forward. Heat and ease spread through me; I'm high on her presence. Even if I wanted to, I couldn't walk away.

Jel sits up straighter, the tense lines of her face relaxing as her gaze locks on mine. There's heat there, which surprises me, burning below the wariness, and it only flares brighter when my mouth quirks into a crooked smile.

But up close, I realize dark circles rim her eyes, and they're shot through with blood.

Before I can stop myself, I ask, "What's wrong, sweetheart? Has something happened?"

A complicated expression crosses her face, and she opens her mouth to speak. Then she closes it again and shakes her head. "Nothing. I'm fine."

My stomach clenches with concern, but the warning in her eyes tells me not to ask again. She doesn't want to share that with me yet.

It surprises me how much I want her to share with me. To trust me to protect her, even if it's only protection from her own secrets.

"Okay then," I murmur instead, dropping the topic for now and taking the seat beside her. Our shoulders brush, but I don't know which one of us moved into the space. "I didn't know you were in this class."

Her carefully blank expression transforms into a wry look. "So you never noticed me before Fate told you to?"

Taking her lead, I let the tension of whatever is bothering her fade away from our conversation, replacing it with a very different kind of tension.

I smile slowly at her, pulling out the charm. A faint flush rises on her cheeks. "Are you disappointed?"

"Devastated."

Warmth uncurls within me—warmth that has nothing to do with the bond. I don't think she means to, but that was almost flirtatious.

I lean into her space, propping my elbow on the armrest between us. She doesn't move back. Instead, her nose twitches, like she's breathing my scent, and her eyes flutter just a little in pleasure. Desire runs through me like a lightning bolt, and I silently command my dick to behave, or this class is about to get real fucking awkward. "It doesn't mean I don't notice you now."

Instead of rising to the bait, she narrows her eyes and hums in thought, watching me for long enough that it would be uncomfortable if it were anyone else. It's certainly a challenge, and I don't get many of them.

It's kind of hot, having a girl so unafraid of me. It doesn't happen often.

"You don't talk much, do you?" she asks finally, her eyes strangely piercing.

It's a surprisingly astute comment—moreso than she knows. "Not really, no."

"Why not?"

"Got nothing to say."

"Liar liar, pants on fire."

Startled, I laugh too loudly, disguising it as a cough when someone glares. When I glance at Jel, her eyes are crinkled with amusement, although she holds her mouth stiffly, like she's trying not to react. I get the impression she's just shown me something real. A piece of her that she wouldn't normally let out.

It makes me want to do the same. To actually speak to her, instead of letting the other person fill my stony silence.

Because she's right. I *don't* speak much, because if I do, people might hear what I'm really saying. And what I'm really saying is: I don't care. I don't care, I don't care, I don't care. Alphas are all about caring—they care about winning, about what people around them do and say, about everything.

Me? Unless I'm in the rut, I'd much rather sit down, shut up, and eat a burger.

We used to have this rooster.

Trust me, this is relevant.

We had this rooster, and I used to watch him call over the hens at meal time and proudly stand back, watching over them while they ate. He was a provider. It always struck me that I was much more that kind of alpha than the kind who'd go for you with his spurs.

A shadow falls across me, and I look up to see Theo glaring at us. Speaking of spurs. I bite down on my lip to stop the laughter; I forgot he took this class, too.

The urge to get in his face overwhelms me briefly, like it always does. He's the only thing I've ever cared about in this school, until Jel appeared; there's no one who brings out my competitive urges like this dickhead, which is probably why I keep poking at him. But even still... I have a feeling it's different. It's not what people mean when they say alphas have to win at all costs. I've always been just as happy to lose to Theo, especially when paying up on our bets tastes so good.

Theo glares at me for another second, and then shifts his attention to the person on the other side of Jel.

It's another alpha, who until now hadn't paid us any attention, and is now looking like he'd absolutely love to start a territory fight. Jel makes an exasperated sound, but Theo ignores her.

"Get up," Theo says with a scowl, staring the guy down.

The alpha squares off with him. "Make me," he says, voice pitched low.

A rumble echoes from Theo, and the sharp edge of adrenaline hits me as I realize I need to break this up. He's my... something. He's my mate's mate, and I can't let this stupidity happen.

Before I can decide what to do, the lecturer barks at them both to sit the hell down.

Theo takes a second to leave, but then he grunts and turns away. He ends up sitting halfway down the hall, his shoulders slumped in tension.

When I cast a glance at Jel, she doesn't look much better. Her hands grip the armrests, and her narrowed eyes flick tightly between the alpha next to her, and the back of Theo's head.

"Easy there," I say, touching the back of her hand gently.

It's almost like she wants to fight them. I'm as intrigued as I am confused, so much so that the ripples of my emotion catch onto the edge of our bond and reach out for her.

Jel pauses, turning to me with a puzzled expression.

"I'm fine," she says tightly, leaning back in her seat.

She sits like she's going to ignore me for the rest of the lecture, and I can't have that.

But if I talk to her too much, she'll see a part of me she

shouldn't. She's already made it clear that she sees through my silence more than anyone else ever has.

Like a true masochist, I decide to take the risk.

Shifting in my seat, I hook my elbows over the back of my seat, stretching my shoulders as much as I can in these tiny chairs. The motion brushes my forearm against her shoulder. I move to pull it back, but then she shivers—just a tight, barely there movement. Barely noticeable.

Enough to spur me on with what I've been dying to ask.

"Why did you reject the mate bond?"

Jel grows still.

The professor has begun talking, but this class is a breeze. We don't have to pay much attention. He flicks the lights off row by row for his slideshow, and we're plunged into semi darkness.

"Is now really the time?" she asks, grimacing as she pretends to focus on what he's saying.

"Depends. Are you going to hide from us forever?"

She shoots me a glare. "You can't win my heart by badgering me."

"I'm not trying to badger you," I tell her honestly.

She gives me a strange look. After a pause, she says, "I believe you."

I glance at her, still facing the front of the room, so as not to draw attention, but keeping our eyes locked together. Waiting.

Jel frowns slightly, her brow furrowing. "What *are* you trying to do, then?"

I'm not actually sure. Like always, there are two directions I could go down. Two voices I could follow.

I glance down to Theo's row, where he's sitting so stiffly he's going to pull a muscle. Just looking at him gets my back up. Makes me want to beat him at his own game, or fall to my knees trying.

I could force my way into her life, like he's obviously trying to do. Make her see me as an asset. Make her want me.

It's hard not to be pulled into his orbit, sometimes. When he wants something, he wants it with everything in him. It's magnetic.

My sister's words from this morning ring through my head, even though it isn't her voice that controls the second path. I don't know where that voice leads, I've spent so long quietening it.

"I think I'm trying to dissect you," I say finally, ignoring her sudden intake of breath. I keep my voice low, a little lazy around the edges so I sound disinterested.

"Like a frog," she says in disgust. "Real attractive."

"Not like a frog." I bite down a laugh. "Like a... thunder egg."

The word comes out before I can stop it. My jaw stiffens reflexively. It's nerd talk—the kind that would get me a lecture —but it's out now, and Jel hasn't turned away in disgust.

"A thunder egg..." she says slowly.

Something in her voice makes me turn to her. I find her watching me, but I can't read the emotion that darkens her expression.

"They're like geodes," I begin to explain, but she shakes her head.

"I know." She swallows. "They're very beautiful." Her eyes narrow. "After you smash them."

I choke back a laugh at her unintentional innuendo. "I think you could take it," I say, deadpan.

A second passes before the joke lands. The glare she shoots me is satisfying as fuck. Especially when the heat-filled smile I give her in return makes another flush of warmth rise along her collar.

The bond ripples and flares, delicious heat making me sink lower in my chair in bliss. I'd try to shove it down, but Jel melts beside me, too, a soft sigh of pleasure escaping her. Fuck, I'm in such deep shit. My dick twitches, hardening in my shorts, and it's getting harder to think around the burning need to take.

"Why do you want to dissect me?" Her voice comes out rough.

I do my best to ignore what that might mean.

I take my time before I answer, frowning into the distance as the professor flicks through slides at a snail's pace. Finally, I say, "My sister tells me that when you reject a mate, you've strayed so far from your destiny that you've lost a part of yourself. I guess I'm wondering what could have happened to you to destroy your soul like that."

Jel stiffens.

"Maybe it's a part I'm meant to lose," she says tightly.

But there's anguish in her face. Uncertainty. I'm not sure she even realizes; the scales running down her neck tell me the anguish is in her soul, not her mind.

"Maybe it isn't," I say, my voice so low she has to lean in to hear me.

I keep my face turned to the front, so it still looks like I'm paying attention, but I'm watching her. I see the warring indecision in her expression.

I know what it looks like to be split inside, torn in two completely different directions.

Maybe that's why I find it so hard to walk away from her, even though Fate has made it clear our road won't be easy.

"You don't know anything about me," she hisses, fury flashing in her eyes. "And you think you can just stampede into my life and turn it upside down? You think you have a *right* to? Like your presence is somehow going to heal me? Sorry, but your dick ain't magic."

An acidic sensation unfurls along the bond that connects

us. It reminds me of being a kid, and blaming a sibling for something you did. As an adult, I'd call it projection.

Huh. That's interesting.

"No, I don't think that." I lean in close, holding back my smile with effort. "But you've forgotten one thing."

"What's that?" she hisses, not even pretending she's listening to the lecture anymore.

"While this bond still links us, I can tell when you're lying."

I turn my head, our eyes locking at the exact moment she realizes what I'm saying, her own gaze turning wide and panicked. We're so close now, I can feel her breath hitting my mouth.

I don't think there's anything special about me—I certainly don't think I can change her life, like Fate seems to.

But Jel does.

I grit my teeth, closing my eyes and both reveling in the pleasurable heat of the bond and willing it down so I don't do anything rash. Like beg to taste her in the middle of class.

Her lips, the sharp tang between her thighs. All of her. I want it all.

I can still remember every sensation from those few minutes in the closet. Every touch, every sound. I might care less about winning than most alphas, but I'm still an alpha. The rut still burns within me, and the rut *wants*.

"I'm not your enemy, Jel," I tell her, my voice low and husky despite my attempts at control. "And I don't want to be. The others might have this pissing contest going on, trying to grind you into submission, but that's not me. I don't even think it's them, not really. I think they just don't know any other way to be."

Movement catches my eye, and I turn to see a spider crawling over the armrest beside me. I stiffen, not used to seeing wolf spiders out in the open like this. The old gods are meant to use the smallest of creatures to send their messages, which makes me wonder if this is an omen. Wolf to wolf.

I just don't know what it means.

"If it's not who they really are, then why don't they just be something different?" Jel asks suddenly, her voice a low, urgent whisper. "Why do they have to be such alpha shitheads?"

I huff a laugh, biting my lip before it can become a less dignified snort. "Well... we are alphas," I say apologetically. "But I'm safe, Jel. Cross my heart."

On cue, the rut unfurls within me, unable to take the pull of our mate so close anymore. Claws tear through the ends of my fingers—living proof that there are some pieces of us we can never fight.

Strangely, she looks like she's going to argue with me, even now. But instead she just clenches her jaw and waits, her eyes darting down to my hands.

I follow her gaze and see the claws tearing into the armrest, drops of my blood flecking the vinyl. A reluctant laugh escapes me. Case in point, babe. I lift one of those claws to her chin, watching silently as I tilt her face up to mine. The energy between us shifts. There's something new in the air. No, not new. Repressed.

I frown, unsure why I'm getting such a strong sense of suppression from her as well, when she's neither an alpha nor an omega.

"We can't change our souls," I say in a low voice, my gaze falling to her lips, watching as her tongue darts out to wet them. "That's who we are. But... the competition shit." I shrug and drop my hand. "If you want them to tone that down, why don't you ask them?

"And you think they'd stop fighting over me," she says quietly, clearly disbelieving. "They'd just let me choose, if that's what I asked for."

My mouth ticks in amusement. "Well, they wouldn't be happy about it." I cast a glance at her. "Neither would I, if you didn't choose me. But they'd still respect your wishes." I trace my thumb over my chin, idly feeling the sharp prick of the claw, thinking the idea through for probably the first time. "They'd be shitty alphas if they didn't. The pack isn't for the alpha. An alpha is *for* the pack."

She stares at me, jaw slack. I've said something that's actually gotten through to her, I just don't know what it was. Then, her expression turns shrewd. "And what if I chose you all? Would you share nicely?"

I stiffen, an unwilling shudder coursing through me at her words. The thought of sharing her, of the four of us coming together as a pack—like we almost did in those few stolen minutes in the darkness. I want it. I didn't realize, but *that's* what I want. I don't want to fight other alphas for my mate.

I want to share her with them.

Once more, that cord tugs me forward—toward a future I've never dared imagine, not while the ghost of my father's breath still burns down my neck. Jel's lips part in shock, the bond flaring with desire—mine... and hers.

The rut shudders, digging its claws into my soul. Pressure rises at the base of my spine, taunting me with everything I want and can't have. Urging me closer.

And finally, after so many years, I make the impossible choice. I follow the voice I'm meant to ignore.

"Let me kiss you," I murmur, my mouth curving into an easy smile as I tilt my head, deliberately casual. My breath stirs the curl of red hair by her lips.

"What?" she whispers, her eyes falling to my lips. "We're in class."

"No one's looking."

As soon as I say it, I realize it's a lie. Theo's looking. Jel's eyes slide sideways, to his side of the classroom. She swallows.

"Do you want us?" I ask suddenly, the words falling into the silence between us. "It can be that simple, Jel."

"You know it can't," she breathes, still looking down at Theo.

"We'll make it that simple. If you want us, then kiss me."

"No," she says, making my stomach sink in disappointment for a breath before she adds, "Kiss me."

There's something in her words that sounds like an order. It sends a shiver of delicious heat rippling through me. I barely bite back a groan, and then I'm leaning forward, capturing her mouth with mine and kissing her.

My hand snakes out, fingers sliding over her waist as I pull her into me. The seats are clunky and awkward, but our chests still slide together, her hands coming up in a rush to balance on my arms.

No one yells at us to pay attention, so I don't stop. I take it slower now, becoming greedy with it. She's melting into me like she's been wanting this for days, her appreciative hum just low enough for me to catch.

Cautiously, her hands find the hem of my shirt, her fingers exploring the skin below it. Whatever reservations she has with the bond, they aren't about this. They aren't about us, and the realization fuels the fire within me.

After a few more seconds, I ease back. "Gotta be on our best behavior here," I tease her, winking.

The look in her blue eyes takes me by surprise, leaving me with a gut-punch sensation that very few people have given me before.

"Like you'd know anything about that," she says wrily, straightening her shirt and checking to see if the professor noticed.

Theo's eyes burn into me, but I don't give him the satisfaction. He wants a competition, and that's fine, but I don't. He can work that one out for himself.

I try to tune back into the end of the lecture, so I at least know what I've missed. A few minutes pass before she speaks.

"If you were Luc," she says in an odd tone, "you'd be telling me I'll be thinking about you all day, now."

I bite down on my lip, a rush of laughter escaping me. I feel flushed and happy—unusually calm, given how much of myself I've aired in here. The bond hums, sated for now.

"How do I know what you'll be thinking about?" I murmur reasonably, adjusting in my seat so that her wrist brushes against my forearm. I pause, letting the lingering notes of her spicy scent wash over me—peppermint, and the unique smell that marks her as mine. *Mate.*

I turn so our eyes catch once more, making sure she can hear me when I add, "But I know I'll be thinking of you."

13

JEL

My front door falls shut with a soft thud, and I know instantly there's someone in my apartment. I freeze, letting my eyes adjust as my hand hovers over the light switch. Then I catch the scent and sigh with relief.

"Anthony," I say, flicking on the light and glaring at my little brother. "What are you doing here?"

"Do I need a reason?" He smiles tightly, shocking me as usual with just how grown up he looks now.

His sleeve has grown again—several intricate etchings joining the wave that was there last. I don't see any viper marks, but he knows better than to show them in front of me. They'll be on his back. Or his chest.

"No, but I'm sure you have one." I drop my keys into the bowl by the door and cross to the kitchenette, flicking on the coffee maker.

Anthony's feet scrape over the floor as he gets up. "Busted." I can hear him moving around behind me, studying my canvases. Picking things up and putting them down again. Brother shit. "Dad's asking after you again."

"Well he can just fuck off."

It's been one long-ass week, and if Dad's getting involved, it's only going to get worse. Dealing with three alpha mates is one thing; Dad is a different sort of alpha entirely. Unsure as I am about my mates, I'd take them any day.

My mind still churns with the memory of Jace's kiss. More specifically, with the memory of how much I wanted it. And when I manage to push away that memory, Luc shoves through, filling my mind with visions of the quiet, intense way he spoke to me in the library. Reminding me of the soft expression of concern on his face when I turned tail and fled—unsettled by his unwitting confession that the gods were watching.

In between those memories, Theo haunts me. I see the way he watches me, noticing things that no one else bothers to. I know it's strategic, that he's using what he learns to win this ridiculous competition. But he doesn't know that my alpha soul can read him just as he reads me.

And I see something beneath that desperate need to win.

I see a mirror, burning with the rancid reflection of everything I've failed to be. I see a conflicted heart, and since I know a thing or two about that, I can't find it in me to hate him for it.

I know these men, broken and bruised as they are, and I want them.

Anthony slides in to lean on the counter beside me and holds his hands up, eyebrows halfway up his forehead. "I'm just warning you. I've been trying to call you for days. He might come here, especially now that... well... you've heard, right?"

My hands grip tighter around the mugs I've just pulled from the cupboard. I know exactly what he's talking about, of course. It's the same thing that's been on my mind all week.

When I'm not thinking about kissing three men, that is.

"The murders," I say tightly. "They're talking about the dragons again."

"Yeah."

The instinct to protect surges. The taste of it is acrid as it hits the back of my throat. Dragons... killers... Gods... They're coming in from all sides.

I feel taunted, threatened from every angle. And not just me —my mates as well.

Why me? Why us?

I pause, tapping the counter. "Anthony, do you know what was stolen that night?"

He blinks. "From the snake pit? Not a clue. Wasn't it money?"

"Maybe... Dad said it was, and he kept going on about the insult of stealing from our vaults, but I always wondered." I shrug. "He seemed too on edge for it to just have been cash, is all."

Anthony's gaze turns sharp. Astute. "When in doubt, go back to the beginning, you think?"

My mouth curls into a reluctant smile. "Basically. Something connects that night at the dragons' nest with the party that just happened. If Dad's worked up, it's not just about money... So, what really happened?"

Anthony hums thoughtfully. "I can find out. If you want me to."

The last words are said seriously, without any air of dismissal. He doesn't want to go digging behind Dad's back, but he will.

"I think it's important," I tell him, grimacing as he nods slowly in understanding.

"Then that's that." He shrugs, nudging his shoulder into mine and leaning beside me. "Do I want to know why you're so invested, or will it make me a liability?"

I smile humorlessly. He's always been the thinker of the two of us.

"It's not that kind of problem," I tell him, shaking my head.

"You're not going to be beaten up for info. I just... I was there the other night. I recognized the same signs the reporters are crapping on about."

He sucks in a breath. "You think it's the same guy."

Anthony was too young for the attack, but his voice is filled with the same fury and thirst for vengeance that the rest of the vipers get whenever this comes up. They were duped, and it stings.

"I do. And I think he isn't finished with me." Heaving a breath, I retrieve the mask from where I stored it behind the trash can and dump it on the counter. "He left me a present, but don't ask me for details because they're need-to-know only."

I'm not telling him about the rat. Not when it might implicate him in this sick game.

No one knows about the rat. When I tried to tell my family, I got as far as saying it wasn't a dragon, and then they cut me off. They didn't want to hear.

Anthony's eyes harden, the soft face of my little brother breaking and reshaping into the face of an alpha. His jaw clenches, and he picks the mask up between two fingers to smell it. He breathes in deep, but it's as helpful as my own inspections. He shakes his head.

"Nothing left behind. This guy is arrogant, Jel. He's arrogant, and he's good." He drops the mask with a disgusted sneer. "I'll dig up your info."

Relief stirs in me, soft and unfamiliar. I nod in thanks, and it's settled. No words wasted.

The coffee maker whirrs, filling the silence. It's a comfortable silence, for all that I'm on edge and Anthony is lost in thought. It's always comfortable between us. He's the only one of my family I don't hate, and I could never hate him. No matter what he did. He's looked out for me more than anyone else in my life, and I'd do anything for him.

I'd even take over my old responsibilities, if it came to it. Fortunately, I don't have to. He was more than happy to step into my shoes when I ran away.

I fill the mugs and hand one to Anthony, who breathes in the aroma with a genuine smile. The sight softens the edges of my anger, even though it would be safer to hold onto them.

Then he pauses, sniffing the air above the mug and turning in my direction. His lip curls in distaste. "You're still on those fucking blockers."

My tentative good mood vanishes, but I'm not angry. I'm just tired.

I turn away and drop onto the couch, taking a long sip of my coffee before answering. "No, actually. I'm trying something new."

"You reek like a beta."

"Nothing wrong with betas."

"There is when it's you."

Sighing, I drain more coffee and then stand up, crossing the small space to the corner I use for my art. Anthony won't rest until he knows what I'm doing, and while his nosiness is definitely unwelcome, I allow it because he won't force anything. He won't make me stop or tell anyone what I'm doing. He'll just bark at me when we're alone, and I can handle that. Especially because he always stops when I tell him to.

He might be the upcoming patriarch alpha to the vipers, but he never forgets that he once wasn't.

"Here, look." I pull back the sheet on the painting that got me into this mess.

Anthony spits out his coffee and covers his face with his palm. "Jesus, Jel, I don't need to see that."

"Oh, grow up. It's art. Look closer—ignore the bodies."

Grumbling, Anthony lifts his hand to shield his eyes now, wincing as he squints at the painting. Then he grows still.

"Shit, Jel. What did you paint that thing with?" He lowers his hand, blinking rapidly as his eyes adjust. "It's good, don't get me wrong, but—" He breaks off, eyes widening.

"Yep," I say, staring at the painting without expression. "Snake venom. If I bleed it into the paint and get a witch to cast a tether line for me, it acts like a blocker without blocking anything. It just... holds it for me. And twists what people see when they look at the other end of the tether line—at me."

It did more than that, apparently, and now I'm suffering the consequences of three alphas that don't know when to quit.

And my own soul, that doesn't want to.

Anthony's mouth twists into a pained grimace. "It's sucking the life out of you, Jel."

"No, it's not," I snap. "It's just holding a little of my power for me. Power I don't want."

"But that's just it, Jel, you do want it."

His quiet voice stops me in my tracks. I look up to find him watching me closely. "What on earth are you talking about?"

"If you can look me in the eye right now and tell me you don't want to be an alpha anymore, I won't say another word." His jaw clenches, eyes burning. "Take your blockers, drain your power into your weird painting traps—I'll support you every step of the way."

I open my mouth, and it's like all the words catch there at once, leaving me silent. Of course I don't want to be an alpha; alphas destroy everything. They burn and pillage and do it all in the name of protection, but what are they really protecting?

Their image.

My father taught me that. He taught me everything. Aim for the throat. Leave no survivors. Protect the pit before all else.

Protect the *reputation* of the pit before all else.

That's where he lost me, the day I realized it was all for show, and there was no substance beneath it. There was no purpose for this kind of violence; only destruction in the name of destruction. He didn't care for me at all and never would. He only cared for the power I'd bring him.

A warm hiss ruptures my chest, brimming with fire. My snake rises, writhing and twisting and *wanting*. I pretend I don't know what she wants, but I do, because my father's lessons swirl through my brain even now. They're an ever-present background track to my life, which means if I ever had the power my soul craves, I'd end up exactly like the other alphas before me.

Power corrupts.

The words I need to find suddenly become clear.

"That's exactly the problem, Anthony," I say quietly. "I do want it. When someone threatens me, I want to taste their blood on my fangs. When you're in danger, I can feel the venom sliding down the back of my throat, waiting for an outlet."

And my snake, my beast... she won't stop.

My voice lowers to a hiss, and Anthony's eyes widen. I don't think he means to, but he takes a step back. I laugh, the sound broken and sibilant.

"You weren't raised at our father's knee, Anthony, but I was, and I remember every lesson he taught me. Every killer urge he trained in me, ever since he discovered I would likely present as alpha. He trained me in secret, but he *did* train me. He showed me power, and I did more than taste it. That's why I should never, ever be allowed to have it."

The things he made me do still haunt me. Will always haunt me.

I know I could tell Anthony. Of all people, he'd understand. He'd know what I meant when I told him that Dad trained me to kill by setting me on the men he'd already condemned to die; how it wasn't until later that I thought to wonder what their crimes were. Anthony would know why none of the facts change the guilt I feel.

I fall silent. It's deathly still in the room, my confession dividing the space between us in a way I don't fully understand.

"Your blood still ties you," he says abruptly. "You might have walked away from the vipers, but your blood calls you back to us."

A sharp pang stabs through my chest, making me wince and turn away. I don't know whether it's just regret, or whether there's a physical connection to back up his claim. It doesn't really matter; he's right either way.

"Then I'll move far enough away until it doesn't," I say through gritted teeth. "Are we done here?"

Anthony's face softens. He sets his mug on the counter and steps forward, arms wide. "Not yet."

My anger melts away. Laughing a little wetly, I step forward and hug my little brother. He gives the best hugs, squeezing like an anaconda, tight and warm and safe.

According to everything Dad believes in, he makes a shit alpha.

I think he's perfect.

"I'll get you those answers, Jel," he murmurs into my hair. "I'll protect you."

He's the only alpha I'd allow to. Silently, I squeeze him back.

"I'll protect you, too."

14

JEL

Now that Anthony is looking into things, I feel a little better. And after a morning spent painting landscapes filled with hundreds of the yellow roses I sketched out in the studio yesterday, my head definitely feels more centered.

Centered enough for me to realize I'm running away from my problems. It isn't only my past this nightmare is linked to; it's Luc's. I need to swallow my guilt and talk to him.

This resolve is tested almost the second I think it. Cheers, Fate. You're a love.

I come to a halt when I see Luc in front of me, arguing with the Dean. I can't hear what they're saying, and my first instinct is to fall back into the shadows and watch silently, but then I feel it—a strange tugging sensation in my chest, like the bond is trying to tell me something.

It burns. Thick like smoke. Like ash.

He needs me, and before I know it, I'm walking into the fray.

"Dean Driscoll." I nod in greeting.

Luc stiffens at my presence, but he doesn't turn me away. In fact, our bodies do that neat little bond thing where they lean into each other like magnets. And by neat, I mean ridiculous, and I want to jump off a cliff.

It's a strange reversal of the other day, in his office, and I realize abruptly that I didn't turn them away either. The awareness unsettles me. As though there was a part of me that needed them so much I let them into my world, and I didn't even realize until now.

Cliff on standby.

Dean Driscoll wrinkles his nose and gives me a cursory greeting. Then he turns back to Luc. "I must insist on those documents. If you can't provide them, we'll have to reconsider your accommodation in the Greenville apartments, at the very least."

I look at Luc properly for the first time then and realize something; he's pissed. He looks like a cornered beast. I half expect smoke to come pouring from his nostrils.

Voice very tight, he says, "The academy agreed to waive the affiliation clause in light of my situation."

Oh fuck. Several understandings hit me at once. The first being that Luc never joined another pack. When a shifter is orphaned, it's customary for another alpha to take them in, but Luc grew up alone.

Having this many shifters in close quarters, the university needs collateral in the event that territory fights break out. A pack alpha needs to vouch for Luc, and any destruction he might cause is dealt with through them, to the full extent of the law.

Which brings me to my final understanding: whatever allowance the university once had for Luc has been retracted because of me. He defended me to the Dean, called them out for foul play, and now he's suffering the consequences.

The only pack affiliation he has is himself... He's the last surviving alpha. The Alpha. And if he lives in the Greenville apartments, that means he lives on campus, in the other set of university apartments on the opposite side of campus to me. Which makes this his territory. Declaring that here, now, would be the equivalent of pissing on every lamppost from here to the university gate.

Clearing that mental image from my brain, I cough politely and wait until two furious sets of eyes turn my way.

"My brother will vouch for him."

The Dean's eyebrows shoot up, while Luc's jaw ticks with an emotion I can't read. Too bad for him, I'm his only option if he doesn't want to have a territory fight with every alpha on campus.

"Give me the paperwork," I say, holding out my hand. "I'll have it ready for you tonight."

After a long pause, Dean Driscoll makes a truly inhuman noise, mumbles something about email, and leaves.

When I shift my attention, I realize I have six feet of angry, fire-breathing shifter staring me down. Now I'm the one backed into a corner.

Suddenly, I realize what I've done. Desperate to help, to balance the debt of him standing up for me the other day, I've gone and affiliated Luc with the very monsters who destroyed his family.

Luc hooks an arm around my waist and pulls me into an alcove by the main corridor, but he still doesn't speak. Unease flickers in my chest. What does he want? Is he mad I helped him?

I was returning the favor for Christ's sake; he can't be that much of a hypocrite.

He runs his tongue over his teeth, studying me as he sticks his hands in his pockets. "Who's your brother?" he asks finally, a flicker of something edgy in his expression. "I don't affiliate with people I don't know."

"A simple thank you would suffice," I snap, deflecting.

Why the hell didn't I come up with a different solution? As soon as he hears my brother's name, he's going to leave me.

Why does that thought hurt so much? It's what I've been aiming for all along.

I wonder if Anthony would sign under our fake name, like he did for me when I applied. Then Luc might not work it out.

"You might have made things worse," he says.

It isn't an accusation; it's simply a statement of fact. A guess based on chance.

Little does he know. Boy should go to Vegas and throw it all on red.

His eyes glint, and he clenches his teeth, as if he's struggling not to say something more. Then he gives up trying.

"He's a viper, obviously," Luc grits out, and I fight down the urge to slam my head into the brick behind me and end it all.

"Yes," I answer, pretending I'm unaware of what that means for him.

He shudders, closing his eyes. The air melts between us as heat and smoke pour from his lips, his careful restraint imploding.

"Patriarch?" he asks in a voice I barely recognize.

Sweet Jesus. Is this what his reaction is to just the thought of the main viper branch? Cold dread floods my veins, and I realize my plan to stroll up to him and give him the truth on a bloodstained platter was the worst plan in the history of plans.

I need to ease into this, obviously.

"Pack." I force the word out, knowing it's the truth only by technicality. He'll be the Patriarch when our father steps down.

But he does have a pack. Two betas and an omega. He's their pack alpha.

So long as Luc doesn't ask anything more, I might escape alive.

So long as he doesn't smell the faint stench of an almost-lie.

Fortunately, Luc seems to be struggling with an internal battle. His eyes glaze over, his expression twisting into anguish. He's breathing faster now. I'm not sure he even knows where he is.

My alpha soul stirs, whining unhappily at the sight of our mate in trouble. She wants to soothe, to guard.

Equally, my mouth salivates at the thought of tearing out the throat of whoever is harming him, because the crazy bitch wants that too.

Since I'm the one harming him, and I like my throat where it is, I go for option number two. I need to distract him. Or walk him back from this ledge.

"My brother won't ask any questions you don't want to answer," I say softly, pretending he's only losing it because of that. "It'll be an affiliation in name only, just so you can escape the Dean's attention."

Instinctively, he turns his head toward me, leaning in as if compelled. His eyes still glint with violence, but there's a faint edge of humanity there, too.

I lift my hand, instinct guiding me, and stroke his cheek. A low rumble of pleasure emits from his chest, and he turns further into my hand, his eyes closing. Dark lashes frame his eyes, like soot, and a lick of flame curls between his lips when he huffs out a breath. It burns the tips of my fingers, like a candle flame, but I don't draw my hand away.

For a moment, he just breathes. My heart skitters in my chest, pulse erratic and flighty. None of this is going like I planned. As usual, base shifter instinct has taken over. Even with my soul tied up in that painting, I can't escape the call of our bond—of my own needs. My desires.

"Why would he do that?" Luc asks finally.

His voice is still too twisted up with grief. He's close to gaining control again, but I need a better distraction.

"Because you're my mate."

The words are out before I can stop them, but I'm not sure I would have anyway. It's the only answer other than the truth that he'll accept, and besides... it's the truth too, isn't it?

Luc grows still. I'm holding my breath, begging it to be enough.

He exhales slowly through his lips, a twist of smoke rising and flying away on the breeze. The atmosphere shifts from danger to intrigue, followed by a hint of desire.

What can I say? We're alphas. Violence and sex are far closer than they should be.

"Then you're accepting our bond?" he asks.

I draw in a breath, my lungs filling gratefully with air, even as a different kind of adrenaline overwhelms me. Out of one uncomfortable conversation, and straight into another...

But anything is better than the road of grief and pain he was careening down.

My alpha soul purrs in triumph. She's succeeded in soothing her mate.

"I didn't say that," I say tartly, pulling my hand away from him.

His lips curl into a slow smile as his eyes follow the movement, as if he's noticed my touch for the first time.

The alcove feels too small, even though he hasn't moved. Has he always been this tall? The shadows from the archway make his edges fade, his form blending into the stone wall, until it feels like I'm surrounded by him.

I realize it isn't just the shadows—the tattoo that creeps from below his shirt, twisting over his collarbone, writhes in black ink, the shadows playing an optical illusion with the image. It's like the darkness is consuming him.

He shifts, the leather of his jacket creaking as he watches me. "I can feel you still resisting it," he admits. His voice is normal again, but strangely hoarse, like he's been screaming. "But I don't understand why. I don't understand you at all, actually."

Great. Is there an echo in here?

"Get in line," I snap, trying to rouse myself to leave the alcove.

No matter how awkward this conversation is, though, I can't make myself leave. There's something about this moment —it feels like we're on the precipice of secrets. And for once, the secrets aren't mine.

His lips curl, unexpectedly softening his image. It's a real smile. Something I'm not sure many people see. "One of the others has already said as much?"

"More or less." Then, in answer to his silent question. "Jace."

"Jace," he repeats, his eyes roaming my face. Then his head tilts up, just a fraction, nostrils flaring like he's smelled something.

Like he's smelled Jace. On me.

Fuck.

But he doesn't acknowledge it. The corner of his mouth gives a small tick of amusement, and then he looks away. "I didn't expect to have to fight for my mate—either against her or against the competition."

A small frown furrows his brow, and he doesn't speak for a second. He reaches out to pick pieces of dead ivy from the wall, rolling the dried vine between his fingers. These ground level alfresco corridors are filled with them.

In a slower, quieter voice, as if speaking to himself, he says, "I didn't expect to have a mate at all, actually."

I blink, thrown by the sudden confession. "Why didn't you expect to have a mate?"

He shrugs. "I hear that Fate sometimes toys with the mate-less through tragedy. It's a sick game she plays on those who deserve it the least. With my past, I seemed like a good candidate."

My heart softens even as guilt spikes, thick, in my throat. "That's only an old wive's tale," I insist. "Fate doesn't play those sorts of games. Tragedy and mate bonds have nothing to do with each other, good or bad. It's just coincidence."

"Then why did we find each other the night of a murder?" he asks, eyes glinting as he looks back up at me. "Only for you to reject us all."

I suck in a breath. "Coincidence," I say, but the word comes out without conviction.

He smiles. "You really think so?"

"No."

A low chuckle escapes him. "She created that painting through you," he says thoughtfully, leaning back against the wall. "And then the painting drew you to the party... Where you met us. And the killer. Tell me there isn't something among all that."

He's right, there is. Even more than he knows, with our shared history.

But what does it mean?

Swallowing, I find myself answering his earlier question without even meaning to. There's just something about how raw this conversation is—it makes me want to be honest.

Probably because I'm knee deep in my own filthy lies, and there's nothing a sinner loves more than confession.

"I'm resisting the bond because having a mate doesn't fit with my plans," I tell him.

I try not to think about how much the bond makes me want

to throw all my plans away. How it might not match my plans, but it does reflect my dreams.

Luc doesn't say anything, but his gaze grows more intense in the silence, and I can almost feel him challenging me. Finding the holes in my logic and pulling them apart.

I rush to keep speaking. "But I'm not an idiot, either. Until the bond fades, it's going to compel you all to... protect me." I almost flutter my eyelids in distaste, but I manage to hold back in time. "With a killer on the loose, I would only make things worse if I told you all to leave me alone. And besides, mate bonds are sacred. We're bound until it fades, and I'll honor that."

He gives me a look that makes it plain he agrees.

I can smell his arousal as it mixes with the pheromones rising from both of us. It sharpens the air, twisting everything around until it's hard to breathe. My tongue shifts in my mouth, instinct guiding me to taste the scents surrounding us. To taste more than scents. I keep my mouth shut.

"So you'll let me protect you?" he asks.

The words send a shiver down my spine, even though they shouldn't. I don't want protection. I don't want anything from them.

My soul disagrees.

"I'll check in with you all," I say sternly. "And I'll let you satisfy your adrenaline spikes by confirming I'm safe. But that's it. We don't need to make this more than it is. I want the bond to fade."

Liar, liar.

"And what about Fate?"

The words are so quiet, so steady, they sound like a prophecy themselves. I breathe deeply, ignoring the richness of his scent—leather and sandalwood—or how much I just want to roll in his bedsheets, naked, until that same scent imprints itself on me.

"Fate will have to get used to being disappointed."

His lips quirk. "Someone will, that's for sure." Then he leans in, surprising me with the sharpness of the move, his breath brushing my cheek as his whispers, "You really don't recognize me, do you?"

My heart stops. I don't know what to say. I can't move, but then he keeps talking like he didn't just turn my world on its head.

"I'm in your art studio. I watched you paint the sketches for that final piece, well before the details were complete."

Slowly, distantly, I begin breathing again. He doesn't know anything yet, and I intend to keep it that way until I can work out the safest method to tell him. "Oh? How come I haven't seen you?"

The earthy scent of the old walls behind us wrap around me, giving me the impression I'm suddenly in a tomb packed in with mud and brick. The air feels colder, darker, but I'm flushed with warmth.

"You tell me," he says lightly. "You enter the room with your eyes on the floor. Set up your station. Paint, and then leave. I used to think you were shy, but..." He draws back, shaking his head. "Now I know better."

He runs a hand through his hair, elbow propped on the sandy brick, and for a moment he looks younger than normal. There's something raw about the open way he stares at me.

"I shouldn't want you, you know," he says, once more in that same quiet voice, like he doesn't mean to speak at all.

Desire floods me, sending heat racing through my core.

Almost immediately, my snake rears up in warning. A hiss vibrates at the back of my throat as I remember how close he was to the edge only seconds ago. How fractured.

My eyes flick to his hands. Are those fresh cuts on his knuckles? And we were literally *just* talking about letting the bond fade.

But then I look back up at him to find his expression searing with heat. I can't look away. Can't think beyond the need rising between us.

"No?" I ask, when the silence has stretched too long. "Then why do you?"

My voice sounds too breathless.

He's closer than before, heat rippling from his skin. A lick of flame curls between his lips, and he runs his fingers almost idly over the bricks between our heads, caressing them.

Amusement flickers in his expression, but his eyes are still too intense. "Because mate bonds are sacred."

I swallow thickly. "You trust Fate?"

"Trust isn't the right word," he says softly. "Let's call it... hope."

My breath catches. I'm left stunned by that one small confession.

How much does hope cost someone like Luc?

My stomach churns with guilt, making me sick, but he isn't finished. His eyes blaze with an inner fire as he leans in close to me, finally closing the distance between us as he reaches out to cup my jaw. His thumb brushes my lips.

"I saw those sketches, Jel, and I've seen the final painting, and they are not same. This bond is the real deal. There's a fire in that painting that won't ever fade, no matter how much you beg it to." He chuckles, voice low and self-deprecating. "No matter how much I tell myself we shouldn't exist."

"But what if we really *shouldn't* exist?" I breathe, speaking before I can stop myself.

His eyes flash. "Then we burn together."

I step closer to him, not realizing until the last second that we're touching almost from head to toe. My body presses against his, and his hands curl around my waist, fingers digging into my skin.

"You really want to burn?" I ask him, the words coming out breathless and nonsensical.

His eyes fall to my lips. "I have to." He pauses, then murmurs, "say no if you don't want it."

I look him in the eyes and I say nothing.

He spins me around, pressing me against the wall of the alcove. My palms slam against the brickwork, scraping roughly as I brace myself, but it seems like he's only teasing me.

This is just a taste.

Luc's hands spread wide over my stomach, beneath my shirt, and he kisses me hungrily on the neck. I push back into the hard ridge of his cock, gasping as one of his hands slides lower and cups me, encouraging me to thrust up into him. I do, grinding into the palm of his hand, already desperate for it. Aching.

The cord connecting us burns, writhes. I can almost see it; it's a noose around my neck, pulling my head back onto his shoulder as I pant against his cheek.

He draws his hand back from between my legs, gripping both sides of my hips so hard it hurts. We stand like that for ages, breathing raggedly, our cheeks pressed together, my ass against his cock.

We're seconds from fucking, and I can't for the life of me think why we shouldn't.

"Better not," he says with a wry chuckle. "Not here."

"You started it," I protest, but I take a step away, trying desperately to lock my feelings back up where they should be.

It's harder than I'd like it to be, and Luc looks way too fucking smug.

"Then it must be your move," he says.

15
JEL

I OPEN MY MOUTH TO SPEAK. I DON'T HAVE A CLUE WHAT I'M GOING TO say, but I'm determined to leave my mark on this garbage fire of a conversation before it ends with me pressed against a wall again.

Before I can, though, my vision is blocked by a dozen yellow roses.

"What the fuck?" I breathe. For a moment, the look of stunned confusion on Luc's face—visible only through the roses—makes it all worth it.

Then the bond flares, and I realize what's happening. The dull ache of the bond's rejection twists inside me, like it's rebelling.

Bonds aren't meant to rebel. Isn't this supposed to be my choice?

Grimacing, I rub my chest, where the pain hurts most, and lower the bouquet with one finger.

Two smug shifters appear behind it, leaning casually against the wall. Jace winks at me, making me shiver as I remember our kiss. His eyes flick between me and Luc, a knowing expression on his face.

They both know exactly what they've interrupted, and they don't care.

Theo doesn't wink. He just watches me, that same furrow on his brow as yesterday. It's like it's his thing—watching me. Not speaking to me, like Jace. Or getting in my face, like Luc seems to at every opportunity. He's way more serious and reserved than the other two, and yet...

He's the one holding the roses.

I decide to impress them with my intellect by pointing out the obvious. "You brought me roses."

Then wincing.

Theo's mouth ticks into a smile. He nods deliberately down at my hands. I follow his gaze, turning them over, and then I realize they're still covered yellow paint.

From the roses I painted last night.

"You were sketching roses in class when I walked past," he says lightly, but there's something underneath it. Something the deceptively casual tone can't hide. "And your perfume is rose."

All expression falls off my face. I blink at him, and suddenly I'm the one that's frowning. He isn't just watching me; he's seeing me.

"I—" I pause, not knowing what to say. I can't encourage him, not when I know this bond would never work. But... I'm flattered.

And the part of me that stared for hours at that painting of us all after I'd finished it wants to be flattered. If just for a few minutes.

"Thank you." I take the flowers, holding them awkwardly.

"I brought chocolates," Jace announces, holding up a heart-shaped box before the moment can get too uncomfortable.

I didn't even know they did heart shapes outside Valentine's day.

"Way better than stinking roses." He leans into the roses—which smell divine—and pulls an exaggerated face of disgust.

Laughter bubbles within me, but it's faintly hysterical and I refuse to let it out.

"We ran into each other at the store, wouldn't you know it," Jace continues lightly, his eyes sliding to Theo. "Great minds think alike."

A silent exchange passes between them, Theo's frown deepening. After the way he glared at us in class yesterday—and after he witnessed our kiss like that—I don't think I want to know what went down at the store.

"You didn't beat each other up, did you?" I ask flatly.

A sick sensation twists in my stomach at the thought. That's exactly what I don't want from them. Exactly why this won't work.

Theo's nose twitches, and he turns back to me, pausing for a moment before saying, "No more than we usually do."

His voice is oddly apologetic, and I realize—again—that he's studying me carefully enough to note my response. To know that I don't like this.

He doesn't have to do that. In fact, no other prospective mate would. This isn't how alphas display. They preen and show off and... fight.

Theo has already worked out I don't want them to fight.

"Besides," Jace interjects while I'm still trying to process this. "He's a big ol' softie underneath it all."

The smile that spreads across Jace's face is positively wolfish. I can't quite hold back the laughter this time, especially when Theo snarls and cuffs him over the back of the head in what's almost a friendly gesture.

A huff of smoke drifts between us, and I remember Luc.

With a rush of heat, my soul does, too. Tiny pricks of pain pierce beneath my nails—my golden claws, itching to come out.

The rut lingers, remembering exactly what happened the last time the three of us were in a tiny space like this alcove.

I bite down on my lip. Hard.

It doesn't stop the heat that spreads through me. The ache between my thighs.

Theo's expression turns knowing; he can smell the change in me. The corner of his lip quirks, but he says nothing.

"We were having a conversation," Luc says stiffly, jaw tight.

"Get in line," Jace says, lifting his chin. "I don't see any chocolates in your hand, Dragon Boy."

Luc's eyes flash, and smoke rises from his lips. "How about dinner? We can start with chargrilled wolf."

Jace's eyes widen. Luc is joking—I think he's joking—but there's still a razor sharp edge below the amusement. My thoughts return to their earlier assessment; something is off about him. He's fracturing.

The bond wants me to help, but I'm not sure what I'm meant to do.

Jace holds up his hands. "Alright, you can go first this time. But you've really got to up your game from now on, or—"

A scream shatters the air.

The transformation in my mates is instant, and all at once I'm visibly reminded that these are three alphas. Four, technically, although they still haven't realized that about me yet.

As one, we charge down the corridor to the music room, flinging the partially open door wide to discover a body suspended from the light. Another girl stands in the doorway with us, screaming—she must have just found the body.

For a moment, the room seems to shimmer with power. An eerie music filters through the open doorway, like wind through leaves, but I can't work out which instrument has been disturbed.

It almost sounds like humming... creepy, chilling humming.

But that can't be right. It must be the shock twisting my senses. The killer must have knocked against the harp on his way out, or sent some kind of chime jingling, even though I can't see anything.

All I can see is the body swinging from the light.

"Is she—" I begin, stepping forward, and then the body spins enough for me to see her face.

Tegan.

I retch, doubling over the nearest trashcan and vomiting up everything I've eaten in the last, oh, month at least.

Sure, I didn't like the girl, and she definitely pissed me off when she tried to get my painting, but no one would wish this kind of death on their worst enemy.

And a horrible realization is occurring to me, now that I see her like this. Tegan has red hair. Flaming red hair, just like me.

The survivor at the party had flaming red hair, just like me.

The victim... She also looked like me.

"This is going to mean a Hunt, isn't it?" Jace asks quietly, the words gagging in his mouth, like he's struggling not to vomit as well.

"A Hunt?" I ask, my voice oddly detached given that I can still taste chuck on my lips and my mind is racing with puzzle pieces I would rather just throw in the garbage and burn than slot together.

Theo glances at me. "The alphas are making plans," he murmurs. "Don't worry. We'll keep the Hunt away from you."

Oh, fuck. A *Hunt*.

True Hunts are nothing like the little pretend one at the party.

They're called when danger threatens multiple packs at once, and they're a no-holds-barred means to an end. The university has to look the other way when a Hunt is called, or they'd become collateral.

Something tells me these murders are about to get a whole lot more dangerous, without the killer even trying.

My blood chills, even as a distant part of me laughs at Theo's assurances. *Mate, if the Hunt could sense my soul, there would be nothing you could do to keep them away from me. I'd either be called to join, or you'd all be able to sense I was a matriarch alpha...*

And good luck keeping the alphas quiet on that.

I wonder what my soul would do if she wasn't bound. Would the Hunt still recognize me as a matriarch, or would it accept my abdication? Is it like Anthony says, and the blood still calls to me?

Or am I just an alpha now, and I'd have to run with them?

It doesn't matter, I guess, because my soul *is* hidden. So I can throw off the call either way.

Something catches my eye, and all thoughts of the Hunt flood from my mind.

Behind Tegan, words are written on the wall, scrawled in red: The gods will pay.

Again, that same challenge.

"Fuck," I breathe, bile rising in the back of my throat once more.

Moving almost as one, my three mates close in around me, protecting me from all sides. In any other situation, I'd shove them all away, but I know how these bonds work—what they're compelling my three boys to do, the adrenaline rising to an almost unbearable level of need.

Besides, I don't need to know; I can feel the bond flaring, too. It scrapes inside me like a living thing, begging me to protect my own, to use my alpha strength to stand between them and anyone who dares to threaten what's mine.

Like they'd let me, even if they knew I was an alpha, but luckily I've learned more than one way to protect what I need to. While they're guarding me from the front, I can protect from the shadows, using their strength as their own unsuspecting shield.

And when the killer is captured and the bond fades, I can get the hell out of this city before Fate decides she's ready for round two of my love life.

All I can think as we stand there, listening to the fading hum of music, is that Luc was just warning me about this. He said there was a reason Fate brought us together that night, and—although he didn't say it out loud—there's a reason we've come together in tragedy.

The body swings softly in the air, the music hums, and I come to the distant yet irrevocable conclusion that he's right.

I thought the first death was an anomaly. Part of some master plan, sure, but I didn't think the master plan was more murder. The murder of the dragons felt... peripheral. To what, I had no idea, but with everything the vipers stick their noses into, it wasn't a stretch to assume it was just another one of those nightmares. Just another fire at the docks, because their shipment of drugs was stolen. Just another fighting ring take-down, with casualties inevitable but not the point.

When the killer struck at the party, I was too caught up in the link to my past to think beyond that, about what it might mean. And since no one died back then—no one except the people my own family killed—murder didn't feel like it was part of the same game.

But whoever is behind this is no longer content with watching the carnage from the sidelines. The game has started over, and they're playing to win this time.

And with the secret messages he's sending me and the fact that the victims all bear a striking resemblance to my own appearance, I can't shake the feeling that the prize is me.

16

JACE

JESUS. UP UNTIL NOW I THOUGHT...

Actually, I don't know what I thought. But I didn't realize this would follow us back here. I assumed the killer was operating on some kind of singular attack. That we needed to be on guard, but unless we got in his way, it wouldn't happen again.

Shit, I even thought it might have been some kind of territory thing, like the news keeps yelling. Not that I think alphas are dangerous—any more than we need to be, at least—but it's not like it never happens. Why else do they make us sign the affiliation clause, relinquishing all territory and pack rights when on campus?

But now the killer has followed us back here, clause or no clause, and they've killed again.

And in a campus as big as Sawlefire, we were right nearby. Again.

It's starting to feel personal.

"You knew the victim?" I ask Jel quietly, holding onto her arm and leaning down so she has to look at me.

Her eyes are glazed, face slack with shock. There's still a fleck of pink paint across her left cheek, and for some reason it makes my heart twist. She shouldn't be here, seeing this. I try to shield her view, but the movement seems to snap her out of it, and she glares at me.

"Yeah, I knew her." She shakes me off, stepping back and picking at her nails.

I've noticed she does this when she's stressed. If there are paint flecks on her hands—which there are, in yellow and more baby pink like her face—she peels them off one by one.

"I'm sorry," I begin, my heart aching for her loss, but she shakes her head furiously.

"We didn't get along. In fact..." She swallows, and her next words clearly cost her. "We fought. Yesterday. She was trying to destroy my painting."

She frowns, like she's only just realized this.

My heart races, adrenaline flooding me as I realize what painting she means. I can't explain my reaction, only that that painting is *mine* just as much as it's hers, and how dare this girl try to destroy it.

"Down, wolf," Jel hisses, eyes flashing as she flicks a glance at me again. "Don't let anyone see you arcing up in here. The reporters are all over this campus. They'll be here any second."

She's right. I swallow it down, glancing back at the door and then to her again.

"Stop thinking with your—" She breaks off and starts again through gritted teeth. "Stop thinking through the bond and listen to what I'm telling you," Jel says fiercely, her voice even lower than before. "I *knew* her. We fought."

I frown, trying to pull myself away from the rising growl of fury in my throat long enough to parse what she's saying. They knew each other, okay. They weren't friends.

Oh.

Fucking hell.

I was right—this is personal. It's about Jel.

"You think it's a message." Or a setup.

Or both.

"I think I don't want to be here when the cops arrive," she says tightly. "That's what I think." She pauses, as if she isn't sure whether to say the next part or not. But then she winces and adds in a rush, "look at her hair."

It takes me a second, but then I remember the hair on the first victim, and on the survivor. My jaw clenches, my vision swimming for a moment before I get it under control.

At the sight of my expression, she gives me a wry smile. "If you're insisting on protecting me, you need to know what you're in for, right?"

A fierce need to do just that, to protect this tiny beta tears through me. My body hums in approval, the need twisting and growing until it isn't just my alpha soul leading the charge—it's wrapped the mate bond up with it.

Golden claws rip through the end of my fingertips, digging into Jel's shoulder and reminding me how close the rut is to the surface. With so many instincts warring within our fresh bond, and none of them having an outlet, my body is beginning to get confused. It thinks *mate* and *danger* and it's diving straight for the big guns.

I really, really don't need to drop into the rut right now.

"Jace..." Jel says slowly. "Please tell me that's a manicure digging into my arm, and not a very inconvenient and *insane* biological response."

A low growl rumbles from my throat. I turn my head toward her, breathing in the scent of her hair, searching for stability. She smells like acrylic paint and rose perfume. *Safe,* I remind myself. She's safe. The blood isn't hers, and anyone who smells like roses and paint in a room full of someone else's blood is *safe*.

Okay. I think I'm in control now.

"Jel?" a voice calls from the corridor, thick with shock and horror.

My instincts flare, grating at me, and I turn to see some lanky guy hovering in the doorway, dressed all in black with a snake tooth swinging over his collar. He gapes at the body, then at Jel. I think I recognize him from the party; he was talking to her before we did.

Jealousy floods me, white-hot, and with the rut riding me and the threat of a murderer still burning in my veins, it hits harder than it should. My lips pull back in a snarl, and both Theo and Luc look over sharply at the sound. In seconds they're by my side. We move between him and Jel, protecting her... and asserting our claim.

"Oh for fuck's sake," Jel snarls.

A hand pulls at my shoulder, but I brush her away.

My human side isn't in charge, not now, not while a dead girl still swings from the ceiling.

"Back away from her," Theo growls, taking another step toward the guy, who's turned hideously pale.

Jel appears in front of us, and the rage on her face breaks through my instincts. I take a step back, shaking my head and latching onto the hint of humanity that reminds me jealousy isn't cool.

"Keep that shit in control," she snarls, and I feel the other two take a step back in shock. We've all been knocked back from the edge, now. I didn't know it was even possible. How can a little beta shock me enough that the rut drops away? "Your jealousy is your own damn problem, and now is *not* the time."

She turns to the guy. "Cameron, I'm sorry."

He holds up his hands. "Forget it." The glare he turns on us singes, now we're no longer crowding him toward the exit. I'm almost impressed. "I just... are you okay?"

At the sight of concern on his face—concern for my mate—my instincts surge again, but this time I temper them with my actual personality. My humanity.

Managing a shifter soul, and specifically an alpha one is quite literally like dealing with a wild beast. My personality might be very different to my biology, but there are still situations where my soul drives the vessel.

There are some things you just can't do in front of an alpha, like approach their mate when a suppressed rut is burning.

But it's fine—I'm fine. Cameron isn't a threat.

"I'm okay," Jel says, her voice surprisingly steady. "Someone should get help."

He nods and disappears. Luc and Theo spread back out into the room, Theo guarding the entrance and Luc examining the body.

With a final glare at us, Jel moves into the corner of the room, turning her attention to the girl who found the body without a second thought.

They talk quietly for a few seconds, and then she awkwardly slings her arm over her shoulder, pulling her in to cry on her neck. With one hand, she pulls out her phone and calls someone, patting the girl's shoulder while she waits.

Ten bucks says Jel's calling the one who survived last time. Something tells me Jel is just like that. She's a caretaker, even if she hides it behind a sharp exterior, or pretends she doesn't care at all.

My instincts flare, milder than before but still overwhelmingly potent, as I remember a lesson I learned long ago: the caretakers are that way because no one took care of them.

The chocolates in my grip flex and twist, crumpling as the doorway fills again and a professor retches violently at the sight of the body. I catch Cameron's eyes over the professor's head, silently warning him.

The warning isn't to back off from Jel—the rut has eased, and I'm much more in control of myself now. I just want to let him know that someone is watching out for her. Someone has her back.

He reminds me of one of those guys who's drawn to vulnerability because it makes him feel big.

I don't like those guys. I don't trust them.

He holds my gaze and nods. Then, his attention shifts to the words written on the walls. He frowns. "The Dean's been going on about gods a lot lately," he mutters.

I don't think he means me to hear, but I catch the words anyway. Before I can ask him what he means, he leaves.

I run a hand through my hair, squeezing a little to distract from how fast my thoughts are racing. Luc turns back to us and says across the room, "The body's had blood drained, but it's no vampire. Looks like it happened after she was dead, with some kind of thin tubing. He wasn't gentle about it."

The professor doesn't even hear him. He's managed to stop heaving, and reaches for his phone to call the cops. Luc rolls his eyes and joins me and Theo. My hackles rise on instinct, but he isn't confronting me, like I'd assumed in this room of death with our instincts riding a knife's edge of violence.

It's like he's deemed me on his side. A strange sense of pride and loyalty flickers, but it fades quickly. There's still too much blood on the air to focus on anything else.

"She's been there all night," Luc says meaningfully. There's a strange pause between his words. Something is distracting him; it's like he isn't all here. I don't have time to dissect it. "And yet, we were nearby when they found her."

So he's thinking along the same lines. "Has to be coincidence, though, right? The girl who found her was timetabled here."

A cold, commanding sensation flickers in the center of my

gut, and I wince in apprehension. It's the Hunt. Word is trickling through the campus, and the alphas are coming together. I rub my sternum absently and try to hold off on following the command. We don't have long.

Luc shakes his head, grimacing. "The door was open. She was walking past."

It wasn't open when we passed it before.

Okay, that's a lot more sinister.

Luc pauses, opening his mouth and shutting it again. When he finally speaks, his voice is raspy. "Did you hear the song when we walked in?"

I frown. "Yeah, there was, like, a short melody playing. I thought it was one of the instruments."

I glance over at the drum kit and piano in the corner. They wouldn't have made the sound I heard. I should have realized.

Luc runs his tongue over his teeth, gaze turning even more distant before he shakes his head. "Doesn't matter."

Theo watches him closely, jaw clenched. But all he says is, "We shouldn't split up. Not if this is targeted."

Of course, when I look over to Jel, she's already gone. A shimmer of fabric around the corner of the doorway tells me she's taken the girl who found the body somewhere to calm down.

The knowledge does absolutely nothing to calm *me* down.

"Fuck." I kick the wall behind me. A bunch of music stands go crashing over as I stagger backward from the force. "She's never going to go for that. She doesn't want anything to do with us."

How are we meant to protect her if she won't let us? Not to mention she can slither out of the tiniest escape route.

"You might be surprised," Luc says flatly, catching one of the stands and giving me a dry look. "Before you two showed up, she was starting to agree to some basic form of protection, given how much the mate bond is screaming at us to provide."

My heart leaps, and the bond soars in triumph. It's not much, but it's something.

"Besides," Luc continues. "She doesn't get a say in this right now. Not when there's a murderer running around. One of you watch her apartment tonight. I'll do tomorrow." He stalks off before I can protest.

"Ah." Theo scratches his chin, staring distractedly ahead. "That's technically still splitting up." He frowns at the wall. "Not sure why I care," he mutters.

I don't think I was meant to hear that.

"Yeah," I say slowly, wondering whether I should insist I go alone to Jel. When I found him at the store, buying those roses, he seemed even more worked up than usual, and he's never exactly been chill.

Is he the right person to guard Jel, tonight?

But then the thought of leaving *him* alone appears in my mind, and the bond rebels, as though it isn't just Jel that Fate has connected me to. The rut rears inside me, claws tearing free from my skin.

Theo shoots me an alarmed look, stance shifting, ready to take me on. But I shake my head, closing my eyes and willing the rut back down.

I know what my soul wants, and I can give him that much because, fortunately, we both want the same thing. "Let's go together."

Theo glances at me sideways, eyes narrowed. "What, so you can show me up?" His voice is rough, and I realize too late that something has pushed him to the edge in the last few minutes.

Shame I've never been very good at ignoring his challenges.

"Don't have to try hard, do I?" I snarl, licking my lips deliberately, as if I can still taste her on them.

His gaze drops to my mouth, and his face twists in rage. For a moment, I think he's going to hit me. Properly, this time, not like all the other fights we've had over the years.

But he pulls himself back, swearing under his breath as he turns away.

"She doesn't like alphas," he mutters, giving me a dark look as he backs up to the door. "I'm not fighting you."

Huh. So he picked up on that, too.

"Well, it's what she's got," I tell him, my voice low as I begin, slowly, to follow him.

I don't realize I'm stalking him until his teeth and jaw shift and he drops his mouth in a low snarl.

I meet the challenge, my own teeth grazing my lips as I snarl at him.

He snarls louder, in aggression and warning, but his hands give him away. They twist, golden claws ripping free, and I know he wants this as much as I do.

My breath comes faster, my heart racing at the thought of the three of us together with Jel.

But Theo shakes his head, smacking his cheek to refocus, forcing the shift down.

"I'm not *fucking* fighting you," he says, and then he stalks off down the corridor.

Somehow, I don't believe him.

The whispers begin when I leave the music room. I swear, I can still hear that freaky humming, and at first I think it's that sound again. Like the killer's calling card, following me from the scene of the crime.

Then I catch the eyes of an alpha bear. The odd glint that

flickers there is far too bright for this darkened corridor, and I realize my time has run out.

The Hunt has begun.

That's just great. Right when I need to be in control of myself, so I can protect Jel above all else, an ancient binding ritual kicks in.

I try to pull back on it, resisting the call, but it's like pulling on a physical chain.

A low sense of dread spikes in my chest. If there's one thing that can control all the alphas, leading them to a very specific ritual, it's the Hunt. Everyone on campus will know where we are tonight, what we're doing.

This killer was already smart enough to use a fake Hunt as coverage for his violence. Is he smart enough to use the Hunt itself?

Correction; is he stupid enough?

Gritting my teeth, I throw my stuff in one of the gym lockers, since I'm obviously going to end up naked and covered in mud by the end of the night, and follow the whispering voice.

It seems to haunt the walls. Every alpha I pass stares at me with an eerie, silent golden light before they follow the sound, too. It leads us lower, below the renovated classrooms on the ground floor of the campus, through the basement steps near the library to the chained door at the back of the room.

The door isn't chained tonight, and the other side of the room is already full.

Growls roll through the stone walls as I step into the room. I let my soul flicker within me, let the wolf claw himself free until he's there in the basement, too. I don't need a mirror to know that my eyes flash yellow, the light of my soul glowing like all the dozens around me.

I take my place at the back, with the other wolves. A quick scan tells me that none of them are their pack's alpha yet, although two are slated to become the alphas for minor packs after graduation. That's alright. I can handle minor packs—I just can't handle being shoulder to shoulder with a pack alpha like the fucking Viper Alpha or something right now. But then, I'm pretty sure patriarch alphas aren't eligible for the Hunt.

Slowly, I let my neck relax a little, doing a final check over the rest of the room.

Theo is on the other side of the brick floor with the rest of the tigers, his hair glinting orange in the dying fluorescent light above him. He doesn't look at me, but I can somehow feel the heat from his body all the way across the room.

It's like I'm tied to him, not Jel.

Like I'm tied to all of them.

I shake the rut off, because I don't want to die down here, and continue my assessment. Apart from Theo and his cousins, there are a few panthers, several bears, the wolves, and a jackal. There are only three pack alphas across those vitalities, I think. But admittedly, my knowledge of other vitality dynamics is a bit loose.

Usually, I know enough to avoid getting into a territory fight, but that's it. I'm going to have to get my shit together and learn their faces properly. The Hunt launches when there's a campus-wide threat, and it means bringing alphas to the edge of humanity until the threat is contained, so you have to become familiar with who is in this room immediately.

No hesitations. No accidental fuckups with knowing your hierarchical position. Otherwise, in the heat of the moment, you might end up with your teeth buried in an ally's throat.

Or the other way around.

So, a couple dozen standard alphas, three pack alphas, two potential pack alphas, and no patriarch alphas at all. So they mustn't be eligible.

It's about what I'd expect for a Hunt like this.

A patriarch in here, with adrenaline riding as high as it is, would probably send the place straight into a brawl. Besides, someone needs to guard the people who aren't on the Hunt.

My thoughts shift to Luc, for some reason, and I frown when I look around again and realize he isn't here. Had he already left campus?

He should have still heard the whispers.

How did he avoid following them?

"That's everyone," a voice growls from the front of the room, and two bears take up position on either side of the door, barring further entry.

They could shut the door, but blocking an exit like that would bring our aggression to boiling point, right now.

"Who are we hunting?" a panther asks, his low voice curling through the room with a faint rumble. Like a purr, right before a strike.

"Killer from the party," the first voice continues, and I realize it's another bear.

Antonio, I think. See, sometimes I know people.

"They've struck twice now, and the second time was on campus." Antonio cracks his knuckles. "It's like he *wants* us to Hunt him."

Manic laughter breaks out through the room. Across the gathering, I catch eyes with Theo, and find he looks just as uneasy as I feel.

It's like he wants us to Hunt him.

What if he does? Like I said, if someone wanted to get all the alphas in one place, the Hunt is an easy way to do it. This guy has already taken down two alphas so far, and one beta; what if this is exactly what he wants?

While putting Jel straight in the line of danger.

I don't say anything. Dissent would be madness. But the edge of unease building within me sharpens as the meeting goes on. The alphas trade clipped words, descriptions of the scent they caught at the party or the blood that was stolen from the victims which might, in turn, lead us to the killer's stash.

"Music," Theo says suddenly, glancing to the front of the room and breaking the eye contact between us. "I heard a rumor..." He holds the bear's gaze, and my heart thuds madly as I realize he's lying. Only I can tell, connected to him in a way none of the others are, but that's exactly what he's doing. Risking his own life if they catch him out, just to protect Jel by not revealing we were all at the scene of *both* crimes. "There was music playing both times the victims were killed. Haunting music, like a little fucking—" He waves his hand in the air vaguely— "like a calling card or something. Magic."

The bear raises his eyebrow, but he doesn't laugh Theo's addition off. In fact, there's a strange note of recognition that crosses his face when Theo says that, and I mentally file the thought away to follow up later, when we won't be killed for asking the wrong questions.

I hadn't realized the strange tune had played at the party, too, but with the party itself pumping so loudly, you'd need the ears of a cat to catch it.

"Music, then," the bear says hoarsely, making me realize just how hard he's working to hold back the change.

I glance around the room nervously—they're all struggling to remain human. Vibrating with the strength of need that's swarming through them.

"Anything else?" he calls.

No one offers up any more information. No one has anything; they're all fueled by the vicious need for vengeance.

By the end of the meeting, when the aggression has reached a fevered height and the need for blood is vibrating off the walls, I'm just about ready to throw up. Both from my own adrenaline and fierce need to catch and kill, and from the absolute certainty I feel that we're playing right into the killer's hands.

It doesn't matter. Nothing stops the Hunt once it's begun. With a crescendo of baying and whooping, the alphas break apart.

It's funny. When people learn of shifters, whether they're new to the supernatural world or not, they imagine a safari. A giant zoo.

They forget we aren't animals. We're also human—and humans are a different sort of predator altogether.

Our souls are magic. Fire. No matter what our vitality—our animal soul—is, *we* are magic. And this scene before me doesn't resemble anything like a safari.

It's a fae court. Glowing eyes and souls singing with violence as a dozen shapeshifters prepare to hunt their kill.

The panthers shift first, vibrating with need and hunger, and sprint silently into the night. With a crunching of bones and a howling of magic and power, the others follow until there are only two of us left.

I stare at Theo, my fists clenched and my arms shaking with the effort it takes not to follow.

"They won't find him tonight," Theo says through gritted teeth. He paces slowly across the room, coming to a halt inches from me. "There's something wrong with this plan. It's too perfect."

"We've been drawn out," I agree, angling my body in unconscious response to his challenge. "Well..." My eyes roll back into my head with the effort of not changing, and I take a second before I can continue. Theo grips my arm, anchoring me in my body. "Fuck, I can't hold back much longer. But we need to get to Jel. We can't waste time here."

"No, I can't waste time," Theo agrees tightly. His eyes are fixed to the hand that grips me, his breathing rapid and strained. Orange and black fur ripples across his knuckles and then disappears. He swallows. "There's only one place I'm meant to be tonight."

But we have our duty here first.

Still, I can feel our other duty, too. It's like a fiery cord, dragging me away from the charging shifters currently looping the quad and to the student apartments on the edge of campus. Maybe that's why we managed to hold back from the transformation for this long; we have something that calls stronger than the Hunt.

It isn't strong enough.

As if he can sense my thoughts, Theo snarls, shoving me away from him. Abruptly, I realize he sort of can. The bond is opening to our emotions, our senses.

I know that Jel wants the bond to fade, but it hasn't. It isn't fading at all.

"There's a reason Fate brought us together now, and you know it," Theo snarls, his voice a low rumble. Fur ripples along his cheek bones, blending with his wild hair. "She isn't just some notch in your fucking bedpost." He shoves me again, and I push him back roughly.

I open my mouth to protest, since he's the one who's been acting like a goddamn frat boy on a dare, but he shakes his head and speaks over me, shoving sweat-soaked hair back from his forehead.

"She needs help now like she's never needed anyone before, and Fate saw that. Fate possessed her, painting that call through her for us all to be drawn to, and it's no coincidence that when we were, the killer struck for the first time."

"You think it's all linked," I murmur, my breath coming in fits and starts as I fight back the change for a few seconds more. "The murders, our mate bond appearing..."

For a minute, I can hear that freaky fucking music again. But then it's gone, leaving only us behind. Our skin gleams with sweat, the filthy lighting down here casting us in an eerie glow.

"I know it's linked," he insists. "Fate brought us together here, now, so that I can protect her." He throws his head back, giving in at last to the change as fur covers his face—narrow and sharp, eyes glinting. His voice is the last to change, a low rumble transforming into a growl at the last second. "And that's exactly what I'm going to do."

I suddenly realize how he's been speaking. The subtle shift to his language I barely noticed.

I, not *we*.

"You?" I snap, incredulous. "What part of her having three mates don't you understand? We're all here to protect her."

I could understand his stupid competition for heirarchy within the mates. To be chosen first. But he's acting like we're not even here anymore. Like we aren't his equals in this fight to win Jel's heart.

He's rejecting the pack, when I'm only more convinced than ever after today that we're inevitable. We need each other.

Theo doesn't answer me; he only growls, feline body pacing stealthily toward the door.

This conversation will have to wait until we're both human again.

Unless the beasts within us force it to happen sooner.

I give the shift only a second longer, fighting to remember my humanity, the other half of my soul that demands a very different set of obligations. Whatever Theo says, he's right about one thing. If we can't leave the Hunt, then we'll just have to bring the Hunt to her.

The Hunt can protect her.

That final, human thought echoes in my mind, and then I shape shift, following my mate's competition out into the night.

17

JEL

THE HOSPITAL WALLS ARE COLD AND LIFELESS, AND I FIGHT BACK THE shudder that passes through me as I walk the halls. Even with the private, hidden suites for supes—which are far warmer from all the magic and energy—hospitals suck.

I left Amelie, the Lit Major who found Tegan, getting cafeteria food to bring up while I found the room. It gives me the opportunity to sort out my thoughts.

When I spoke to Greta on the phone, I'd warned her about the second victim as gently as I could, because I know this place. I know these people. The reporters are probably already on route to hound her with questions, and no one wants to find out about the threat that way. Not when they can still feel the killer's hands in the bruises around their throat.

The fact that she's been kept under observation for several days now shows how bad the damage was, and she was the lucky one.

"One oh four, one oh five," I mutter, counting the doorways until I land at one hundred and six.

I peek around the corner, knocking softly on the doorway until Greta looks up.

Her brow furrows when she sees me, and then she relaxes into recognition. "Jel," she says with a careful smile. "I didn't recognize you, sorry."

"Don't apologize," I tell her, ignoring the awkward need to shove my hands in my pockets as I enter the room. "I think this is the first time we've actually met."

Her smile turns more real at that, and she bites her lip. "Yeah, I was surprised to find your note among my things, actually."

I shrug, definitely unable to keep my cheeks from heating now. I stare up at the ceiling, studying the ceiling tiles. "Well, it seemed like the right thing to do."

Not to mention I really hadn't thought about it. It had been subconscious. Almost instinctive.

That thought worries me a little, but I ignore it. I have to.

Every day, there are so many things I have to ignore.

"I really appreciated it," she says quickly, and when I glance back at her, she's giving me this earnest expression that makes me want to dig a pit in the middle of the hospital floor and just jump straight into it.

"Oh." I nod, probably too quickly. "Good."

She smiles. "I just meant that when I've seen you around, you seemed kind of... preoccupied."

"You can say angry."

She laughs, relaxing even more, and even though it's at my expense I can feel my own shoulders ease at seeing her let her guard down in my presence.

"Well... yeah. I just didn't expect it. But now I'm talking to you, it makes perfect sense, actually."

That surprises me. "Why?" I ask bluntly, before I can stop.

She shrugs. "You've got that decisive kind of attitude that mother hens get. You remind me of my nanny."

I splutter in shock, staring down at my grungy torn jeans

and satin button-up shirt. I've never been called a mother hen before. I gesture mutely at my clothing to indicate that obvious fact.

This time, she smirks, all her awkwardness and intimidation completely vanished after two minutes of talking to me.

"Exactly," she says cheekily. "Decisive. I know I can trust you, because you're not full of shit."

That stops me dead. Trust me. *Trust* me?!

A strange, sick feeling coils in my stomach. When I look down at my hands, I don't see them as they are now. They're much smaller, and they're covered in blood—in life.

Life I've taken.

I shake my head, keeping the distress from showing on my face. Carefully, I smirk, coming closer to perch on the end of the bed. "Do you trust me not to steal your pudding cup? Because those things are the best."

Grinning now, she picks it up and lobs it at my head. I catch it, peeling off the lid and scooping up the pudding with the spoon from her tray. "Oh, hell yeah."

"So..." Greta says, and I know immediately the mood is shifting. "Do they have any leads on who did it?"

Grimacing, I shake my head. "Speculation, but that's it." I pause, wondering whether I should ask, and then deciding I have to. "What about you? Any idea who got you?"

She rubs her neck absentmindedly, where the puncture from the syringe is still healing. "No," she says after a reluctant pause. "I didn't see him at all. Just one of those leather masks. I thought it was part of the party, at first. The alphas were messing around, starting up a fake Hunt. We all knew about it. I was expecting things to get a little feral."

Her pained wince tells me just how much she regrets it now.

I lean in closer, urgency driving me. "Any idea who was behind the mask? Were they identifiable?"

"Not really," she snorts. "It was a rat mask, but it could have been anyone. I didn't get a scent off him, and by the time I was out cold it was too late."

Damn.

Hesitant, I ask the final question—the one I don't even fully understand. "What about humming? Did you hear any humming?"

I definitely heard it in the basement, and then again today.

She frowns. "Humming? No. If he was doing that, I was passed out by then." She snorts a soft laugh. "Kind of sounds like that old academy legend, though, doesn't it?"

My breath catches. "What legend?"

She shrugs. "I can't remember it properly. Some creep walking the halls at midnight and trying to summon the gods with stolen blood, I think."

As she speaks, her words grow quieter, more serious. We share a look.

"I might check that one out," I say faintly.

"Yeah, good plan."

I let that info sink in for a minute before I remember to tell her, "There's a Hunt, by the way. They might even have caught the guy by now."

I could feel the pull as I left campus, but with my soul still bound it was easy to ignore. And it didn't pull hard... as if it still recognizes me as matriarch.

Greta stills, wincing as her eyes stare off into the distance. "Yeah, I can feel it. Even from here."

I take a closer look at her. Usually, I try to stay out of someone's vitality status, as a sign of respect. But I should have at least noticed Greta was an alpha. Maybe I'm getting rusty.

The thought bothers me for some reason. Why should I care? It's not like I'm ever going to have a pack, and certainly not anything higher than a pack, no matter what my dad wants from me. Beyond the ability to predict where trouble is most likely to come from—in the form of territory challenges and general shitty posturing—I don't need to assess other shifters.

Yet, the thought still bothers me.

Maybe Anthony was right about my painting... maybe it's doing more than just blocking what others can sense from me.

Shaking my head, I pretend I don't know what she's talking about. Like I'm just some beta or omega.

Greta frowns at my silence. I'm not surprised, after her mother hen speech, but she doesn't challenge me.

That's the trouble with spending time with people. They see through you eventually. And apparently, not after very long. Even with my painting balancing my soul and reducing my alpha scent, Greta still doesn't think I'm a beta.

"My mates are running around with them," I say quickly, distracting her with the first plausible detail I can think of as to why I'm not either brimming with eager anticipation for the Hunt or already in it. "I'm hoping they'll bring me some info soon."

Greta's eyebrows shoot up. "Mates, plural?" A gigantic, shit-eating grin spreads across her face. "I've heard of that, but I've never met anyone who had it. And they're all alphas?"

Oh, crap. "Yeah," I say weakly. "I'm not sure it'll work out. It's all very new."

I break off as I see the slightly glazed expression in her eyes. "Multiple alphas and no omega to soften them," she says breathlessly. "Can you imagine it?" Greta looks at me sharply, almost predatory. "I guess you don't have to."

The closet flashes into my mind, and a hot flush rises on my cheeks. But my mind has other ideas, apparently, because the images don't stop there.

I picture Theo's hands on my waist, his roughened growl coming low against my neck. Jace steps in front, warm and safe in a way the other two aren't—but it's only a disguise. His hands are just as rough, his lips the only softness in his bite.

And Luc.

The only safe way I can imagine being with Luc is to ride him, his hands behind his head while Jace and Theo mark their claim with teeth and claws on my back.

But that puts them all face to face.

I can see their eyes igniting with more than just passion. Hear their souls howling as beast and instinct take over. There isn't much difference between lover and prey, sometimes.

I should know. I've seen the way the men beneath me look up at a snake—the heir to the viper territory. I've seen the fear in their gasping lips as they wait for me to turn on them.

I've seen their faces when I give them exactly what they want.

"Um, excuse me, aren't you an alpha?" I splutter. "Why are you so into this?"

And why the hell does she think we're getting through a night like that without someone's throat torn out? One alpha in bed is bad enough. More than one, and it's a dance with death.

"Oh, girl," she says softly, and a touch wickedly. "You haven't seen an alpha in bed, have you?"

I splutter silently, indignant, but I bite my tongue to keep from correcting her.

"It's not all grr, grr, kneel before me." Her smile grows. "An alpha in bed is begging to kneel, if you catch my drift. We have nothing to prove to our lover, and if the doors are locked well enough, no need to protect. So all that energy, all that focus... turns to you. Two alphas?" She rolls her eyes back in her head. "We dominate packs, my friend. But there's no pack in bed—so you get it all." Then she laughs, eyes bright. "Well, *you* have a pack in your bed, and if you ever want to share the details, I'd be delighted to hear them. I can't even imagine how feral they'd be when they're not focused on caring for an omega in heat."

I barely manage not to yelp *we just met.* I think at this point it would just get me laughed at even more.

Besides... her words are doing something strange to me. They're describing a night I could never have dreamed existed.

And that's exactly what it is—a dream. My dream.

Word by word, she brings my secret fantasies to life. Everything I've ever wished for. Sex has always been too close to fighting for me, because that's what my partners have wanted. They've expected it of me, and as much as I've tried to hold it back, it ends up being exactly what I give them.

How long have I wished for something different? I know there will always be a part of me that burns too hot. Too sharp. But this imaginary person Greta is describing is the kind of lover I've hoped would one day come to me, willing to put aside who and what I am for long enough that the aggression can turn into something less dangerous. Something I could let go of.

I want to let go.

I swallow, ignoring Greta's knowing gaze and taking solace in the interruption as Amelie walks in.

"Amelie!" Greta exclaims, holding out her hands.

Amelie immediately rushes over and takes her hands, sitting sideways on the bed.

"Oh, I didn't realize you two knew each other," I say, backing up from the bed to give them room.

"Not well," Amelie admits. "I only realized you were the survivor when I saw it on the news."

Greta pulls a face. "I only realized when I woke up here. Asshole jumped me from behind, and I hadn't heard Dorothy go down."

Even though they don't know each other well, they fall into an instant rhythm I've always struggled to find with other people. It's like they were just made to connect, while I was made to attack.

Constant, neverending attack.

Aim for the throat. Leave no survivors. Protect the pit before all else.

My alpha soul whines within me, agitated and restless. I relinquish my hold on her just a little. It's safe enough here; there's no danger.

Taking a breath, I lift my hand to catch their attention. "I actually have to run. Are you going to be okay together?"

"Sure," Amelie says, giving me a genuine smile. "I appreciate the company getting over here. Thank you, Jel."

"No problem." I wave her off before she can get too into it, nodding to Greta and backing up to the door.

I leave the two of them talking earnestly, hands clasped, and wonder why there's such an ache in my heart as I go.

18

JEL

THE HOSPITAL IS STILL EERILY QUIET AS I PAD DOWN THE CORRIDORS. We're right at the end of visiting hours, when the bustling hive of activity transforms into this weird, dormant beast. The hair on the back of my neck stands up, preparing me for possible attack.

I give my reflection in a passing window a dirty look for being an idiot. No one is attacking me in a hospital. I'm heading home to a face mask, my fluffiest slippers, and a Witcher marathon, and nothing is going to stop me.

I slip my phone out of my pocket, checking to see if Anthony has replied to me yet. I'm hoping to go off grid tonight and unwind, so if he's got a bomb to drop, I'd rather he do it now. But my messages are empty, and he hasn't been online since this morning when he sent back the paperwork for Luc's affiliation clause.

At least that's done, I suppose. And under the same fake name Anthony did for me. Plus, he didn't ask questions about Luc's obscured last name.

Brothers are the best.

"Still nothing," I mutter, refreshing the chat with a frown.

I send another quick row of question marks, but his status stays red. I would have thought he'd have some answers by now, but he admittedly does leave his phone off for long stretches at a time.

I force myself to put it back in my pocket—he's probably with a girl. No one needs their older sister interrupting that.

The front doors glide open, and I step out into chaos.

"What the fuck?" I breathe, staring at the shadows flickering across the parking lot.

They move so fast it's difficult to work out what you're looking at, but the effect is eerily similar to the masked parade at the party.

Teeth, claws, talons…

Strange beasts roaming the shadowy trees that line the hospital entrance, darting between the buildings as they scope the land.

An echoing growl that nearly has me shifting on the spot in challenge.

The Hunt is here.

I glance up at the windows roughly where Greta and Amelie are staying. They're four storeys up, so I think they're safe, but still. Why the hell is the Hunt here? Is it to protect them? The previous victims?

I've never heard of a Hunt acting like this.

Four of the figures nearest me grow still. One by one, their heads swivel in my direction.

I stiffen as they change course and begin to prowl toward me. It's three panthers and a wolf. On an ordinary day, I could take them without breaking a sweat.

But I'm not meant to be an alpha.

Normally, the students in their human form don't notice that. Tonight, my scent is an anomaly that these creatures, riled to the edge of madness as their vitalities take over, can sense. I try to hide my soul again, but she's mad too. She won't go, not while the Hunt is here, at our feet.

This is why matriarchs don't join.

"Easy there," I murmur in a low voice. "I'm not a threat."

The nearest panther growls. Her jaw falls open, revealing nasty teeth and a terrifying maw.

To these shifters, I don't make sense. I don't fit the smell they're getting from me.

And that very much makes me a threat, no matter what I say.

The middle panther's eyes glow, and he lunges at me without warning, snapping the air just above my forearm as I twist out of the way inhumanly fast. I catch sight of my reflection in the window—glowing eyes, and a quick ripple of scales dancing across my face.

I'm either going to get torn to shreds, or I'm going to get my cover blown. Or both, if the rest of the Hunt clues on.

Why the hell are they here? They should be following the killer's scent. Not the victims'.

A growl rips through my throat, vicious and mean, and the wolf instantly drops to his belly.

He recognizes the beast in me, even if the others haven't properly worked it out.

"This is a pathetic excuse for a Hunt," I snarl, my eyes glinting wildly as the scales flick in and out across my hands. "You call yourselves predators?"

The panthers grow still, and two of them take a cautious step backward.

There are no matriarch alphas on the Hunt.

There's no place for us there, because the Hunt is about community. It's about the overwhelming need to band together and protect more than just one pack. It's about bonding, in the very simplest and most human way.

Patriarchs... Matriarchs... We don't bond like that.

We stand alone. Always.

My vitality rears up inside me, my soul lashing out to be free of the chains I keep putting her in, and I can no longer hold it back. Something is wrong. I can't stand to see this weak attempt at retribution, this petty stalking and patrolling.

My head tips back, my bones crunching and contracting as I prepare to shift. To lead.

A howl interrupts me.

I look up, partially shifted, my snake eyes two bright spots amid a face from your worst nightmares.

A wolf and a tiger skid to a halt between me and the others. The wolf howls again, and the tiger snarls a low, terrifying growl.

Now *these* are alphas.

My soul rumbles with delight.

Losing the last of their backbone, the other shifters flee, leaving me standing alone with my mates.

I don't know how long I stand there, panting, struggling to get my human side back in control. There's an unfamiliar feeling coursing through me. A terrible, awesome sense of something tearing and shredding itself in my throat.

Before I created the painting, I was on blockers. Before that... intense meditation and sheer iron will.

It's been a long time since I felt my soul properly. The mate bond has been calling her free for days, the rut building slow beneath the surface and egging her on with the most potent ritual an alpha can have. Add in this fierce need to protect my mates from a killer, and a dash of tonight's need to dominate these pathetic excuses for leaders... and she's free.

She doesn't want to hide away again.

Slowly, carefully, I force her back inside until the tether

from the painting takes over. It's a blanket thrown over a beast, but for now I'm safe. I'm back in control.

My two mates stare at me, confusion and desire warring in their terrible, glowing eyes. They know something is different, but they can't sense it properly through the assault of emotion coming down the bond.

I step back into the shadows, watching with resigned annoyance as they follow me. Away from the Hunt.

The Hunt isn't meant to split. But I'm not going anywhere near those other assholes. My soul can't take it. She's going to rebel.

If Jace and Theo want to follow me and risk the Hunt's division, that's on them.

"Are you sure about this?" I ask them, ignoring the way my voice rasps too low, too thick. "You have responsibilities."

Theo growls, teeth flashing in the moonlight. I glower at him, my own teeth bared in warning. Two can play at that game.

"No need to get snippy," I mutter. "I'm just saying, it's on your own damn head when the other alphas get out the wooden spoon."

Jace's mouth hangs open, tongue lolling. It's almost like laughter, and my lips twitch at the sight. Unexpected warmth surges in my chest; my soul likes this. If I stay still too long, she's going to take over again.

My eyes flash. "Alright. See if you can keep up then, losers."

I turn on my heel and run away from the hospital, giddy laughter bubbling up inside me and two shadows trailing me close behind.

We run together, our own version of the Hunt ripping through the forest that divides Sawlefire Academy from the city. But just as the Hunt is a volatile mixture of alphas from a dozen packs, ours is also disturbingly close to chaos. My soul is still fighting me, rumbling and hissing as she begs to come out.

My fingertips are stained with my own blood as the rut rears its head. Hunger and violence war within me, demanding I lead these two men into a quiet place and do what I've been craving for days. Finish what we started.

I don't want to fight my soul any longer.

Maybe it's time I stopped.

I snarl, a long, hollow sound at the back of my throat, and divert our path toward a clearing I know nearby. The echo is taken up by my mates on either side. Jace tips his head back and howls.

The wind whips my face, and a light rain starts up. The world turns into the splatter of mud and stinging cold, and somewhere in the middle of it I feel the two alphas behind me peel off onto either side. Flanking me. Guarding me.

When we arrive at the clearing, they each shift back mid-leap, and then they're on me.

I shudder as two naked men crowd me back into the trees, eyes glowing, golden metal claws unsheathed. Sweat shines across their chests, beads of it rolling over hardened muscle. They're burning up, riding the edge of the shift, the Hunt, and the rut all in one.

We never should have held off the rut for this long.

"We're in the open," Theo comments. His voice is lower than usual, with a strange echo to it, like there's more than only one of him inside. "If we're caught, we'll be locked up."

"Last thing we want, when we're meant to be catching a killer," Jace agrees, his own voice rasping.

Despite their protests, their eyes remain fixed to me. Each step I take prompts them to mirror it, their bodies half crouched in predation. Without seeming to realize it, they begin to fan out, trapping me against the large oak behind me. The only escape is the narrow channel between them, and they've laid it out like bait.

If I move, they'll pounce. On a night like this, where they've just chased the scent of a killer across the city, it's a fifty fifty shot whether they'll remember they want to fuck me, not kill me.

My soul preens, chest swelling with delight and anticipation. We can take them.

My eyes glow, the eerie yellow light bouncing off their faces. I keep my claws hidden behind my back; the trump card they aren't expecting.

"I don't intend to get caught, boys," I murmur, surprised at the strange echo to my own voice. It feels new. I don't remember other ruts happening like this, although I suppose I've blocked them out. "Now, are you going to stalk me all night or are you going to fuck me?"

Theo growls, his claws tensing, knuckles rippling like Wolverine.

But it's Jace who pounces.

He spins me, his strong arms curling around my neck as he pulls me flush against his body. The hardened ridge of him presses against my ass, and his breath hits my cheek, warm and faintly thick with adrenaline. My hands come up to clutch his forearms, golden claws digging into his flesh.

He doesn't notice.

"That felt too easy," he murmurs, licking a long, slow line up my neck. "You wouldn't be letting me win, would you, little beta?" His voice drops lower. "Because I don't need your help."

I turn my nose into his jaw to breathe in the rich scent of his arousal, preening at the feel of his fingers clenching into my arms. His shifter scent overwhelms me.

"I don't let alphas win," I hiss, fluttering my eyes closed in a deliberate challenge.

I let alphas think they've won, and then I rip out their throats.

Any second now, he'll see the claws. He'll know what I am. I flex them a little harder into his forearm, relishing the scent of blood as they break his flesh. Waiting.

I ignore the human part of me that's screaming to stop. To keep hiding.

A soft sound comes from in front of me, like something dropping to the ground. I blink my eyes open, confused, and find Theo kneeling before me. My mouth drops open, a quiet gasp emerging as he looks up at me. There's a fierce glint in his eyes, a promise.

He lifts his hands to my jeans and pops open the button, pulling the zipper roughly open before sliding them halfway down my thighs.

I tilt my hips, lifting up into him as he breathes a hot, deliberate breath over my core.

As Jace resumes his steady attention over my neck, my soul arches within me, fierce with ecstasy. I don't know where to focus, what to feel. He's fixated on the scent glands below my jaw, and it's tantalizing because I know he wants to bite me. Mark me.

Alphas don't get marked. The thought should enrage me, but instead it fills me with the most taboo sense of longing.

I wonder if part of him can tell the scent is wrong. Artificial.

Then Theo swipes his tongue over my pussy, and I can't think at all; only feel.

My legs part, restricted by the jeans but wide enough to let him slide two fingers between my thighs, teasing me by rubbing slickness over and over without going inside. His tongue beats faster, flicking over my clit as I arch my hips and thrust into him.

This is only the beginning. The rut hasn't properly come out to play, but it's here, it's building, and I don't intend to lock it away again.

"Can I mark you?" Jace asks against me, lips sliding, hot and wet, over my skin, just as Theo thrusts two fingers roughly inside and begins to fuck me.

I cry out, head tipping back as a wave of pleasure rises, so close to the edge, and finally, unwillingly, bearing my throat to Jace. He snarls in hunger, teeth shifting, sharp points digging into my flesh. I know I should stop. Alphas don't get marked, but I *want*. I want it more than anything—

Pain.

Pain floods me, turning my cries into harsh, jagged screams. Jace falls away, clutching his head, as Theo staggers backward, landing on his elbows. The rut. It's objecting, punishing us, demanding we—

Luc. It's because Luc is missing.

Our first rut can't happen without Luc.

I let out a scream of frustration, pulling my jeans up over my hips and staggering away. The rut doesn't want anyone marked until we're all here.

Theo rolls onto his knees and drives his hands into the ground, ripping up earth and sodden grass, snarling in anger.

The air shifts as the rut, still lingering, burns with a different sort of fire. We can't stay like this. We can't be near each other like this, not if the rut has lost one of its only two outlets.

Passion or violence. There's only one left, and it's already been stoked too far.

I think of Theo's eyes on me throughout the day. Watching me, claiming me, even as Jace kissed me senseless. Even as Luc cornered me and covered me in the scent of his dragon smoke.

These boys are seconds from a territory fight, and now that my head is a fraction clearer, I know I can't risk them discovering I'm an alpha. Not here. Not when they're already squaring off.

Theo's agitation burns, rising rapidly as he climbs to his feet. With a shudder, he shifts, feline body disappearing into the shadows—the terrifying figure of a predator winding through the trees.

Jace shifts and lunges for Theo's throat, sending the two into a rolling dive into the mud. My fangs rip through my gums, venom coating my tongue, and I hiss in rage and agitation.

Turning, I sprint out from the trees, toward the main street that leads to the apartment lanes. The sound of fighting still carries from the trees, and any ordinary humans walking past here would be right to think something hellish and demonic is happening. Fortunately, there shouldn't be any in this area. Not so close to the university.

As their mate, I should intervene. Or at least be on hand to heal the wounds.

But I can't stay, not when I am what I am.

I make it into my apartment building, hair plastered to my face and mud coating my legs. Kevin, from down the hall, gives me a shocked look, and I just salute him and keep walking until I reach my door.

It's only when I'm inside with the door locked behind me that I let myself fall to my knees, mud-streaked hands clutching at the floorboards. For long moments, I fight the blackness threatening to consume my vision, dragging me into unconsciousness, and just breathe. It takes me a long time before I'm back from the edge enough to feel human.

I'm not human. Somewhere in the last few years, I'd forgotten that. I'd forgotten what it means.

But now I've remembered.

I drag myself over to the window, staring out at the distant trees and the rain lashing the canopy. I hope they don't destroy each other tonight. I hope what happened tonight doesn't destroy me.

Deep in the darkest parts of me, my soul rumbles in ecstasy. That small taste of freedom has fueled her.

As I collapse into sweet oblivion, my final conscious thought is that I'm no longer sure she can be contained at all.

19
THEO

THE EARTH BEATS BENEATH OUR FEET, LEAVES AND MUD SCATTERING, coating us. The rain pours down in a deluge. Somewhere in the city, the Hunt is prowling, guarding the shadows from this sneaking, haunting killer that somehow keeps escaping from under our noses. But out here, the killer is forgotten.

It's just the two of us, and this has been a long time coming.

The wolf stalks me through the trees, his glowing fae eyes the only sign of him among the growing darkness.

I slink among the foliage and wait. He can't hide forever.

He lunges. I meet him on two legs, clawing viciously through the streaking rain as he tries to sink his teeth into my shoulder. The Hunt still floods me, calling to me. It tells me he's the enemy, and I believe it.

Everything is the enemy tonight.

The sharp tang of my mate on my lips only fuels me, guiding me forward into a confrontation I should have forced days ago.

The wolf pulls away and retreats. But there's something connecting me to him—a pulsing, anchoring cord. I can feel him through it, how he thinks, how he feels.

I follow it.

The cord between us sizzles with fire, and the rut burns like an answer within me. I've been stoking its flame far too close to the edge, playing with it like it's a game. The rut is no game. Tonight was a reminder of that. The rut has rules, and we've ignored every one.

It's kill or be killed. Pleasure, devotion, and violence barely held together by the thread of ritual. If you're mated, the first rut after the bond is together.

No matter how many mates there are.

After tonight, there should be one less.

Something barrels into me from the side, teeth lunging for my neck. I duck at the last second, spinning around and lashing through the darkness.

My claws rip through his flesh, sending a spray of blood across my face. It's getting harder to remember the side of me that's human. Getting harder to remember why I only want to defeat this wolf, not kill him.

Someone howls in the distance, then another and another. The Hunt isn't far. I wonder if they've caught their prey, like I have.

But then the earth spins, the star-flecked storm clouds suddenly above me and a too sharp sensation burying into my neck.

The wolf flips me, the earth pounding into my back and sending sprays of mud up around me. His jaws latch around my throat and something in me just—stops.

Submits.

I grow still.

His breath hits my skin, landing right on my scent glands, teeth pressed to mark me. Alphas don't get marked, and the rut refuses to let him bite me without our mate present, the pain already rising once more like barbed wire through my chest.

I should use the break to my advantage, flipping him and slashing his chest open, but I can't. My own soul holds me captive, paralyzed with the sudden knowledge of my willing submission.

For a second, I wanted him to mark me.

Jace's hot breath reaches my skin through the fur, and against the ice-cold of the building storm, it burns. I've lost. It's a different kind of loss, this time. It doesn't feel like the others. Like the temporary wins we've traded in every other competition we have.

I've lost to Jace.

A whining rumble burns in my throat, and I shift back—suddenly more vulnerable than I've ever been beneath his wolf's teeth.

After a beat, he follows, shifting back into a man before slowly easing his teeth free from my neck.

He braces over me, naked, sharp eyes glinting as the eerie shine to them slowly fades. His long hair falls over his face, sticking to it in streaks. Blood still oozes from his shoulder, where I swiped him, but he doesn't seem to notice.

"Yield," he tells me.

My jaw clenches, teeth gritting together so hard it feels like they're splintering. "I can't," I spit out, even though I already have.

Do I lose Jel now, too? Has my moment of weakness cost me everything?

Will she be in danger because I failed to protect her?

I imagine how we look from the outside, how I look. Pinned to the ground by the smaller competition. Defeated. The imaginary reflection haunts me.

Jace frowns, his brow creasing in both confusion and a vicious anger I rarely see in him. "Then you're an idiot," he snarls. "We both want the same thing, so why do you keep fighting over it?"

I stare up at him incredulously. "Because we both want the same thing."

Has the Hunt messed with his brain?

He snarls and moves as though to bite my throat again. A jolt of heat runs through me, my muscles tensing as I prepare to flip us, to get him under me instead, in a very different way. But he doesn't bite. He just shakes me by the shoulders and glares.

"We want the same thing *together*. We can work *together*."

My fingertips burn as claws rip through, and this time I do flip us. I pin him beneath me, golden claws digging into his throat. The arrogant prick doesn't even flinch; he grins, that lazy, crooked smile I know so well. He knows I lost, and I can't take it back. For a second, I nearly tear through his jugular for the insult of his calmness. For making me lose.

I feel him stirring beneath me, the hard length of him pressing into my thigh.

"Tell me again how these souls can have her together," I mutter, my voice tinged with hysteria. With shock.

Centuries of ritualistic need burn through me, aching and begging for release.

This is the side of being an alpha we don't share beyond our packs. Most of the time, it's power and strength. Heightened senses gifted by the gods, so we can protect our people from harm—including from within, from weak, twisted leaders who would run them into the dirt. But it comes at a cost.

These souls might be ours, but they aren't us. I am not my alpha soul, and he isn't me. And the constant battle between them, the fight... there are times when it's harder for the human in me to win.

Jace doesn't move immediately. Just watches me, eyes half

lidded and predatory. Then I feel him twist—somehow he gets his thighs around me, flips us again, and—

"Because you're going to learn to share," he says, gripping me by the throat, his own claws out now and a fierce light burning in his eyes. He leans down, gets in close and whispers, "Because you want to."

I want to.

My instinct is to argue, but when I have no argument to reach for, I realize the truth of it. I blink up at him, my clenched hands falling away from his arms, releasing his skin with droplets of blood.

He's right.

For years, I've fought to win at all costs. But who really wanted to win?

I don't think it was me. I just didn't want to lose, to be destroyed beneath so many feet and jeering hands. Beneath the schoolyard bullies who hurt me.

This, right now, beneath the sharp heat of Jace's hands... it doesn't feel like losing.

I hold his gaze, and then I let go. Of everything. I sink back into the mud and earth, and let the coolness soak me through. The strangest sensation meets my wrists—it feels like cold metal falling away. Like chains snapping.

An unreadable expression crosses his face, and before I can react, Jace kisses me. My body surges toward him, my hips thrusting as he grinds down into the hard length between my thighs. It's messy and quick, urgent, his mouth almost a weapon as he devours me.

With one last, aching slide of our hips together—a tease more than a promise—he pulls away to look at me properly.

Bright green beetles scurry by my face. Tiger beetles. The gods are watching, but I was already well beyond denying that. I thought I'd been given a test—one where I had to prove I was the strongest, most worthy protector for my mate.

What if this bond was never a test, but a gift? It wouldn't just be the gift of a mate. It's more than that... It's an answer to a fear I've carried for a very long time—a fear that makes me fight to win even when I don't want to.

It's the gift of a pack. A pack so strong it doesn't need me to prove myself at all.

We can protect her together.

Above me, Jace relaxes, the lazy grin creeping back onto his face. The glow to his eyes fades, and he drops back onto the ground beside me. Mud cakes his stomach, already drying in the ridges of his abs, his cock. Rain-damp hair covers his face. He's filthy.

We both are.

"Fucking hell," I mutter.

I hold my hand up above me and study how the golden claws glitter in the moonlight. I'm no longer shifted, but the claws remain, ready to come out, shift or not. They're nothing to do with my vitality. This is just the rut—waiting. It's a ticking time bomb edging me closer and closer to ecstatic destruction.

Jace laughs, the sound high and strange, as he looks at my hands. "We can't hold onto this much longer." He runs a hand through his hair, fingers sliding in the mud. "I've never had a reaction like this to a beta. I thought only omegas brought out a rut like this."

I shrug. My body still stings, but I'm enjoying the sensation. The heavy weight of release. "Must be a mate thing."

"Speaking of mates..." He glances at me. "We're meant to check in for the Hunt, but..."

"We left Jel."

The night returns to me in fits and starts. I remember the

sharp taste of Jel on my tongue. The sounds she made. The sight of Jace holding her still for me, his muscles straining as she writhed against my mouth.

I remember the tiger in me rumbling with desire, unbridled lust consuming us as we chased the rut we'd been promised—only to come slamming up against a brick wall.

I don't know what happened after that, but she must have run. Our territory fight must have scared her, and she wisely escaped home.

"We have to check on her," I say, pulling myself upright. "The Hunt can wait—we already knew they weren't going to find anything tonight."

It's after midnight, so its call no longer controls us.

Jace nods, decided. "Yeah, I doubt anything happened." He follows me upright. "You left your phone in the change rooms before the Hunt, too, I'm assuming?"

I grunt in affirmation, hoping I'm not the only one who also has a spare set of clothes as well. The thought of putting him in my clothes right now... It makes me shudder. Not with disgust, but with something else entirely.

Possession. Want.

He claps me on the shoulder, and I go ahead and shudder anyway. The look he gives me turns knowing, but he says nothing. Only lets his touch linger a little softer before he pulls away.

"We didn't make a bet," I grit out, irritated by the gesture for some reason. "You don't need to touch me like that."

"You don't need to make a bet to have me take care of you."

Shocked, I turn to him. He looks different—sharper, somehow. And yet less aggressive than before.

There's a confidence to him I never noticed. It relaxes me. Makes me feel like I don't have to fight for this one—my pack has got it.

"You finally won," I say casually. "Maybe you'll be our pack alpha, in the end. Make your family proud."

The words don't even sting. It's like something inside me has just washed away.

Jace looks over at me, eyes bright and startled. After a beat, he laughs—a low, genuine sound, rich with affection. "My old man would never be impressed by me," he says proudly. "The only way I can defeat another alpha is to seduce him into sharing his toys."

Startled, I laugh. He winks at me, undaunted by his own confession or the strange new ground we find ourselves on. I pat him on the shoulder, too, letting it linger a moment before I pull away.

We shift and race each other back to campus.

20

JEL

I MUST FALL ASLEEP ON THE FLOOR, BECAUSE WHEN I WAKE UP IT'S TO
the cold press of floorboards sticking to my cheek, and warm
sunlight streaming through the window.

Too warm.

Warm and... snuggly.

Blinking my eyes open, I stiffen when two familiar scents
hit me, seconds before my body registers the warmth of an
arm thrown over my waist and another looped beneath my
neck. Theo and Jace are here. Covered in mud, their hair still
plastered in damp streaks to their face, but breathing as
steadily and heavily as if they were in a five star honeymoon
suite.

"Er..." I poke Theo in the cheek, my voice foggy with sleep.

Am I dreaming?

His breath catches and then breaks in a long, low sigh as he
stretches. His shirt rides up, revealing mud-soaked skin, hardened with muscle.

I distantly notice an unusual stirring of warmth in my chest
as he blinks sleepy eyes open to watch me. The warmth grows
when Jace stretches behind me, using the arm around my waist

to pull me on top of him as he does, my back pressed to his front.

"Good morning, darling."

"It is, isn't it?" I murmur, a touch dazed, not really thinking the words through as my body reflexively uncurls into a delicious stretch.

My wrists brush Jace's hair, and he plants a kiss on my neck.

Theo laughs, the sound coming out in a surprised rush. His head appears above mine, blocking out the ceiling, and his expression seems... softer. Even his hair has lost its gelled perfection and simply hangs, scruffy and soft, above my face.

He waits a beat, assessing my reaction as he plants a hand on either side of my body—both our bodies. Whatever he sees on my face must equate to permission, because he brushes a kiss over my lips, holding for a moment as my breath catches in shock, and then withdraws.

They didn't kill each other last night, and something has changed.

The realization kicks through my chest with a sharp jolt, waking me up properly and bringing my brain from sleepy enjoyment of my two mates to *what the fuck is happening?*

"Don't tense up," Jace whispers in my ear. "Go with it. It can be this simple."

But he lets me go as I slide down between his legs, sitting up and looking at the two of them in confusion.

"Simple?" I repeat, shaking my head. "I don't think we could ever be that, but..."

But maybe we could *be*. Maybe we already are.

It isn't just them; something has shifted in me as well.

My soul unfurls within me, a pleased hiss on her tongue, and I realize abruptly what it is that has changed. She's here, with me. Not completely unlocked, but the cord binding her and changing my scent is fraying. I could snap it, if I wanted to.

I swallow thickly, watching the way the sunlight highlights my mates' shoulders, the wisps of their still-drying hair. There's hope in their eyes, in the way they hold themselves. Hope and interest.

I've always known I'm covered in a thousand fractures and breaks. And especially now, I'm poised at the edge of a cliff, ready to smash on the rocks below. I thought I had to fight the fall. To hold myself together with superglue, but maybe I don't.

Maybe shattering from the fall is a good thing. I can take it, and when my mates rescue me from the rocks, they won't find a fractured, broken mess. They'll find a geode instead.

I run a hand through my hair. "We should talk," I begin, but Theo's phone buzzes, interrupting me.

He grimaces down at it as it keeps buzzing, several messages arriving in a row.

"Someone is missing from the Hunt," Theo says after he's flicked through them. "Just a sec. They think we're missing too."

He taps the phone and holds it to his ear. I can hear low murmuring from the other end, someone lashing out.

"No," Theo speaks over them. "Didn't run. We had pack priorities."

His eyes flick to me, and he holds my gaze, his own fierce. My stomach flips, and I fight down the excited stirring of my soul. Pack. This is our pack.

"That's what I said," he snaps, a rumble of anger in his voice. "Would you abandon your own pack like this? The Hunt comes first, but the Hunt was over when we left. Our mate was in danger."

The voice continues, louder, and then abruptly cuts off.

Theo drops the phone, running a hand through his filthy hair and grinning. "Yep. Got a fucking earful."

"Where's the other guy?" Jace asks.

Theo shrugs. "Don't know yet. Probably the same thing as us. It was Will Adelaide; do you know him? He's a wolf."

Jace pulls a face. "Distantly. He's not one of ours."

Theo opens his mouth to speak and then stops abruptly. A harsh expression crosses his face. Then Jace's. Their nostrils flare, irises glowing a bright yellow as they climb to their feet.

They cross the room to my kitchen counter. There's only one thing they could be tracking.

I could hide it. I could kick them out and enforce the distance between us again.

Instead, I sit there, calming the racing of my heart and watching as they pull the rat mask from behind the trash can. Interestingly, now that I'm paying attention, I see how my own instincts flare, too. At the sight of that thing, I want to kill. I want to maim.

I want—no, *need*—to protect my mates from the threat that fucking mask represents.

Theo explodes. "This is the victim's blood," he snarls, holding the mask out between us. "What the fuck, Jel? Why is this here? Is this the killer's?"

"He's targeting her," Jace says so quietly, so softly, you could mistake it as gentle.

When I look in his eyes, I feel a shiver of fear that very few people can elicit in me. He might have a laid back personality, but you'd be an idiot to think Jace isn't an alpha.

I've been running from the inevitable. I might not like dealing with alphas, but I am. I'm dealing with three of them—and a fourth, more unpredictable than the rest for how her soul has been stashed away and repressed.

And maybe... maybe I should have been looking at the truth of that, instead of running. These men are alphas, but their personalities don't match the alpha men I've known all my life. Not even close. Sure, their instincts rise when poked, but when it comes down to choice, they choose differently. They choose kindness and respect—even deference when they want to. When it's right.

Maybe I should be learning how to work with these instincts, instead of shoving them away. I need to see the man as a whole, alpha instincts and opposing personality together as one. Maybe that way, I won't end up with strange killers targeting me in my bedroom while I sleep, putting myself and my mates in danger.

"So I know the killer," I say. "Sort of. The killer knows me, anyway."

Their eyes go gratifyingly wide. Before they can speak, I hold up my hand.

"But I'm not telling you this without Luc. He needs to be here."

We need to find him.

Anthony was right. This isn't me. By blocking the worst of my violent soul away, I've blocked off a piece of me that I never want to lose. And it's costing all of us, transforming our bond from something that should be a gift from Fate into a twisted mess of lies and injustice.

Lies and injustice; the opposite of everything an alpha *should* be, even if I've never met one who actually upheld those values.

Maybe it's time I became that alpha instead of waiting for them.

Luc isn't going to take the news well, but with Theo and Jace there, we might be able to walk the explosion down to a cooking fire instead of a wild fire. For the first time, I'm thinking the presence of alphas might help rather than make things worse.

I startle when a hand touches my face, so lost in my thoughts I didn't realize Theo had stepped in closer. He brushes my cheek, cupping my chin and tilting it upward as he studies my face.

"Are you safe?" he asks quietly.

"No," I answer.

None of us are safe. And Anthony still hasn't fucking gotten back to me with info on what this killer's game might really be, so who knows what his next step will be?

Theo shudders, his nostrils flaring as the grip of his fingers very subtly increases. But after only a second, he relaxes them again. He drops his hand to my shoulder. "We have to protect you, you know that. It's in our nature."

I war with my own nature for a good thirty seconds as I struggle to respond to that one. Instinct tells me to flip him onto the ground, straddle him, and hold him down until he realizes who and what he's facing.

But I can't. Not until Luc is here and it's all out in the open, for better or worse.

"We'll talk about it later," I grit out. "For now—we have somewhere to be. Once we find Luc, I'll explain everything."

When we find Luc, we'll see if our pack can withstand the truth of who and what I am.

21

JEL

THEY CLEARLY WANT TO ARGUE, BUT THEY DON'T. WITH HARDLY ANY complaints, we quickly eat, get ready, and head onto campus.

Fortunately, I'm so close to the university that we're there in a few minutes. Less fortunately, the campus is mayhem after the second killing.

Theo and Jace close in on either side of me. At some point, Jace has pulled a lollipop out of his pocket, and he sucks on it obnoxiously. When he sees me looking, he winks.

The wind ruffles our hair, and I feel strangely out of step with the whole world. I breathe in the scents of a dozen shifters, searching through them for my missing mate. He's been here, but it's too faint to track. It's easier to follow the pull of the bond; it leads me further into the quad.

Reporters haunt the front steps of the admin building, and the faculty staff have set up a number of blockades preventing them from entering further into the campus. It hasn't stopped them. Whispers from passing students carry on the wind, mingling with attempted interviews by the press; it sounds like the academy legend theory has taken off. The only trouble is, no one seems to know what it is.

I hear the vague summary Greta told me three times over by the time we've crossed the quad, and it hasn't solved anything. Someone walking the halls, trying to summon the old gods with stolen blood. Supremely unhelpful. Why does he want the gods? How much blood does he need?

Why did he fucking kidnap me?

"We need to find this academy legend," I mutter over my shoulder. "Our killer is clearly inspired, and no one seems to remember the source properly."

"I'll get my sisters onto it," Jace offers, pulling out his phone and tapping out a message. His mouth curves with fondness as he types, only half paying attention to the rest of us. "If anyone can dig up the nerd dirt from history, it's Caitlyn."

The sensation of someone watching me makes me turn. I glance behind me and catch the Dean's eye over the top of two badly disguised reporters badgering a student. Even from here, I can tell they have a camera hidden in their jacket.

At first, it looks like he's furious to see me. The unexpected intensity in his eyes floors me for a moment. It's like he's glaring, but that isn't quite the right emotion... It isn't anger. It's something just as strong, but a different flavor.

Before I can work out what it is, his attention returns to the reporters and he approaches them.

Maybe he was just angry at the reporters.

I shake it off.

"You should check in with the Hunt while we're here, too," I add in a low voice. "They'll be wondering where the third guy is, if he's still missing. They'll want your help."

Jace shrugs. "Let them wonder. We're staying together." He shakes his hair out of his face and swivels the lollipop to the other side of his mouth.

Theo nods. "After that fucking mask, I'm not letting you out of my sight."

"You are aware that I might want to be out of your sight, sometimes?" I ask him, one eyebrow raised. He stares at me flatly, and I sigh. "Right. Still not having that conversation yet."

Soon.

My shifter soul feels warm and content within me. She isn't worried about the impending conversation. She wants these men to know us. To fear us.

Subtly, I tighten my hold on her leash. Okay, so I can't put her away again. I've got that memo loud and clear. But I can still hold her while I make the decisions, and since I'm not a fan of pissing off three alphas just for funsies, I intend to do exactly that.

We follow the pull of the bond. It leads us past the music room, still cordoned off and reeking of blood and death. The hair on the back of my neck rises, and it doesn't settle as the bond pulls us through the halls and down toward the basement entrance.

The smell of death hasn't faded.

"Can you still smell blood, too?" I ask.

"Yes," Theo grits out, glancing over his shoulder as if silently measuring the distance between the music room and here.

We take the steps to the basement slowly. It's normal for students to come this way; the basements are the quickest route to the excess sports storage, and they connect to the back entrance for the underground library collection and several old bathrooms long since retired from modern plumbing and now used exclusively for hookups.

But today, the blue-stone passageway is eerily quiet.

No students pass us, and the bond pulls us deeper. Our footsteps echo, and the sound of our breathing is hauntingly loud. Golden light shimmers, growing stronger as our eyes each shift to our better senses.

The light glints off the walls, catching on something wet.

Jace grows still, his lollipop poised in front of his mouth. With a shadowed expression, he reaches out and brushes his fingers through the wetness.

Blood.

He sniffs it, eyes glinting. "Tegan," he says quietly.

Not a new victim then.

Is he taunting us? Trying to scare us? My heart thuds in my chest, but it isn't fear that's coursing through me.

"Do you hear music?" Theo asks quietly.

I frown, slowing down. It's distant, but now he mentions it —those same three notes, over and over. One high, one mid range, and one a deep baritone.

My eyes meet Theo's, and the rage there reflects my own soul back to me. "It's him."

My fangs shift, extending from their sheaths and pressing into my lips. Jace drops his candy and flexes his hands, claws breaking free as he wordlessly takes point. Theo slides behind me, his presence a comforting, solid assurance that my back is covered.

Something flutters in my line of sight, and I rest my hand on Jace's shoulder, silently halting him as I turn to the shadowed alcove I hadn't noticed until now.

It's full of dragonflies. Bright purple dragonflies with horns perch on the walls, wings hovering up and down in slow beats.

Bringers of vitality. Stuck to walls of blood.

"Do you get the feeling we've pissed off the gods?" I mutter.

"What on earth makes you say that?" Jace asks.

Something in his voice makes me turn. A wolf spider crawls over his open hand, and he watches its path with a sick sort of fascination. "These guys are messengers," he says faintly. "From the gods, if that part wasn't clear."

"So what's the message?"

"Don't ask me; I'm not the dragon," he says with a laugh. "I can't speak to the gods."

As if realizing what he's just said, he looks up at us, brow furrowed.

He's right. Luc can speak to the gods, in a way. Has he been speaking to them this whole time?

What have they been saying?

I glance at Theo and jerk my thumb at the spider. "You still committed to your '*a kiss pays the messenger*' routine?"

His lip twitches, but after a hesitant look at Jace, who now appears to have ascended to a new realm, reaches out to cup the spider in his palm and drop it on the ground.

"Guess we know which one of the pack gets spider removal duty," I say, keeping my voice deliberately light.

They each shoot me expressions filled with heat, and we turn back to the tunnel. I focus on the shadowy distance, searching for a sign of the killer. The music still hums, but it's distorted and distant. Like a vintage record player three rooms over.

"Where's Luc?" Theo asks, his voice pitched low and quiet.

Jace holds his hair out of his face and sniffs the air, head tilted back. "Halfway down the passage. Alive."

We move silently, predators tracking a scent. The bond ripples, tugging on my chest and flaring, bringing us subconsciously closer to one another. Our pack is almost complete.

One of the doors down the far end of the corridor makes the hair on the back of my neck stand up, for some reason. I squint through the shadows at it, marking it, trying to discern a scent. But there's nothing. No scent to make out, no sign of anything out of the ordinary.

And my mate isn't behind it, so it's not a priority. I mentally flag it as something to check out and turn back to the front.

Jace pushes the door open to one of the bathrooms, and we come to a halt.

Luc rests inside, his head clutched in his hands. Panic, shock, and confusion flood me, assaulting my hold on logic and control. What's happened? Is he hurt?

He lifts his head and stares at us, his eyes unseeing as the door slams, echoing, behind us.

I realize the song is coming from him. He's humming it.

Fuck. I've been so caught up in my own mess, I didn't understand what it was doing to him—how close he's been to the edge this whole time.

The distant gaze. The look in his eyes right before we found Tegan. The way he disappears when the rest of us can't help but be drawn together. I should have realized.

My instincts flare, gripping me in a choke-hold as under-standing hits me: I haven't protected my mate. I've failed him.

"Luc," I say softly.

The expression in his eyes shifts slowly to recognition. "Jel," he says. He turns to the others, one by one. "Theo and Jace. You're here."

His voice is jagged, filled with harsh edges. My eyes fall lower, to the blood on his knuckles.

The sinks are broken, and the flooding trickle of water suggests it was recent.

"We've come to get you," Jace says, his crooked grin in place as he slowly crosses the room, hands held out to show he's harmless. "I knew dragons were a bit subterranean, but I can't say I share your taste in lairs, man."

A dragonfly zips in front of Jace's face, and he pauses, narrowing his eyes.

"Been having any conversations down here?" he murmurs, flicking a glance at me and Theo. "Anything you want to share with the... pack?"

The word ripples through us, pulling us closer, but Luc doesn't respond to it. He simply huffs a broken laugh and turns to Jace.

"Conversations with the gods, you mean?"

"That would be a good place to start."

Theo's mouth tightens in grim amusement, and he moves a little closer to me, ready to step in front. Pins and needles prickle at my fingertips; I clench my fists, searching for calm among the rising apprehension.

Luc runs a hand through his hair, gripping it tightly.

"They're taunting me with that fucking song," he says, teeth clenched. "Fate won't quit with me, and I can't take it. I don't want to be this violent shit of a kid anymore. I just want peace —I want to go home."

He's rambling, every word edged with rage. How long has he been falling into this darkness?

Like a cloud passing across the sky, the room shimmers. Impossible, cavernous depths reflect from the dusty mirrors above the sink that Luc clearly smashed with his bare hands; and within those depths rests a throne of twilight.

A woman sits on that throne, and as we lock eyes, she greases me off with the biggest glare I've ever had the pleasure to receive.

The image vanishes and the bathroom returns.

I startle, hand flying out to steady myself on the wall. Did I imagine it? It was over so quickly, and it's so dark down here.

But Luc's eyes widen in fear; he saw her too, although I think the others missed it. Then, too quickly, his expression darkens with something else. Anger. Pain.

He rises to his feet, fists clenched and broken porcelain at his feet.

Theo takes a step backward, covering me.

"Scared a few students on my way down here," Luc says, a feral grin creeping onto his face. "They'll be saying I'm the killer next."

He begins to laugh, the sound echoing off the tiles.

Whatever the gods are trying to do with him here, Luc is spinning into violence, his soul riding him in desperation. We need to pull him back, but you can't ignore souls when they've reached this point. They aren't human. They're a whirlwind of unmet needs, a golden coin spinning on its edge. All you can do is choose which side lands face up.

Violence or passion.

Luc said we'd burn together, but he's imploding on his own down here. And I never noticed.

I swallow, steeling myself as my own soul rises, the too-long-ignored rut simmering inside me, pushing me to end this and save him. But Jace gets there first.

He steps into Luc's space, forcing those cold, blue eyes to move, slowly, to him.

"You've got a choice here," Jace says in a low, rough voice. "You've always got a choice. So what will it be?"

"Back off, wolf," he mutters, the sound coming out too throaty. "I'm leaving, or someone gets hurt. That's my choice."

"No you're not," Jace says, stepping in closer until he's barely three inches from Luc. "You leave now, and you'll end up with more than slashed knuckles. Not to mention the vicious comedown from all that energy you're burning." His voice lowers. "I've seen you at that fucked up little gym with the broken equipment. I know what you're doing in here."

"Who the fuck do you think you are?" Luc snarls, but Jace doesn't back down.

What is he doing? He can't really think it's a good idea to provoke Luc into a fight. Not here, not now.

Jace lifts a hand, guiding it to Luc's chest. I expect him to jab Luc violently, starting a fight. But he doesn't.

He rests his palm over Luc's sternum.

Luc's expression flickers in shock. "What are you doing?"

It doesn't come out like a challenge, this time. The words are rough, broken.

"Ssh," Jace tells him, and, shocked, he falls quiet.

His lips curl into a faint smile, like he's pleased with Luc. A shiver of desire races through me.

"What do you need?" Jace asks.

"Nothing," Luc spits out, the answer choking in his throat.

"Try again," Jace says calmly.

A long pause passes between them. Then Luc's gaze flicks to me, so heated my knees go weak.

"I'm losing it," he says quietly, still staring at me. "I don't think I can walk back from the edge on my own." He takes a deep, shuddering breath, before saying, "I need her."

"No," Jace corrects him. "You need us."

Then he kisses Luc.

Luc doesn't move for several seconds, staring with wide eyes at the face suddenly so close to his. Then desire takes over.

He grabs Jace by the collar, pulling him in closer and kissing him fiercely.

Jace's mouth curves into that same crooked grin he always has when things are going his way. It makes my heart flutter, my eyes widening in surprise as he slides his hand from Luc's chest up to his throat, gripping him as he kisses back with a quiet, fierce determination.

Theo reaches for me, pulling me out of the way as they go staggering into my space. His hand doesn't leave my waist, even when I'm no longer in danger of being sent flying.

As Jace and Luc fumble at each other, their movements becoming more urgent, almost desperate, Theo's fingers curl over my hips. It's like a reflex, as though he doesn't mean to, but the second we both notice, it becomes deliberate.

Heat surges through me. I lean into him, unable to take my eyes off Luc and Jace, but equally unable to resist Theo's hands. His comfort.

A wooden bench goes screeching across the tiled floor as Jace and Luc grapple. For a few seconds, it's almost like they're fighting. Luc shoves Jace backward, glaring at him for a beat before clashing their mouths together again, lips swollen and bitten red. And Jace doesn't take the shoves; he pushes Luc away, crowding him against the wall, his leather jacket hanging off one shoulder and his white shirt skewed beneath Jace's fist.

But we can feel it—what this really is. The bond tingles with it, with the rightness of what's happening. It feels like waking up this morning, with the sunlight streaming down and three warm bodies curled together.

Jace's fingers close around Luc's throat, savagely gentle. It's a claiming. A promise of protection and pack.

Luc stiffens, shudders, and then melts. His hips drive up into Jace's thigh, the two of them grinding and thrusting as the action shifts into something different. It's no longer a fight, and yet the edge of it is sharp and unyielding. Luc's leather jacket creaks beneath Jace's hands, echoing beneath the wet sound of their mouths colliding.

As quickly as it began, Luc surfaces, his eyes bright with desire and confusion. He's back from the edge. It's only by an inch, but it's enough.

"Tell me," Jace tells him, hand still caressing his throat in both a threat and a promise. Their mouths brush together as he speaks. "Tell me what's breaking you."

"No," Luc snarls.

He shoves Jace's chest, but when he moves back, Luc chases

those inches in another kiss. His mouth is possessive, desperate, his expression broken open in need.

Jace slides his hand to the back of Luc's neck, holding him close, their foreheads pressed together. "Tell me," he repeats. "I can't help you if you won't tell me."

This time, when Luc shoves them apart, they stay that way.

"Because I'm a dragon, you idiot," Luc snarls, his voice broken in pain. "Haven't you worked it out? I'm the only one left. The killer took them all from me, and now he's back."

My heart clenches at the grief in his voice, at the shock rippling through the bond from the others. It's no surprise they hadn't worked it out. It was ten years ago, long before they would have paid attention to things like that. And it isn't like we've been glued to the news these last few days. Whispers are everywhere on campus, but whispers are a far cry from the details of Luc's past.

Jace stares at him, body stiff with shock.

The faint drip of water from the broken taps is incessant, grinding into my brain as it echoes on the grime-coated tiles. I can't focus. Can't think. This place is too hidden, too far underground.

How long has Luc been down here?

"This city should burn," Luc whispers. Then he scrubs a hand across his face. "No, they shouldn't. I don't mean that. I just—" He falls quiet, his eyes still covered.

Jace's expression softens. And then he draws him into a hug.

Luc's face twists, broken, and he wrestles with Jace, trying to break free. But Jace doesn't let go, and after only a few seconds—far sooner than I expect—Luc sags in defeat.

No, not defeat. Surrender. His arms come up around Jace's neck, and he turns his head into his cheek, gripping him like a lifeline.

I wait for the bond to break apart, but it doesn't. Even now, when it should be severing my connection and casting me aside, it only draws us closer, and that knowledge shatters something inside me.

I have to tell him the truth. Now.

I open my mouth.

Someone knocks on the door. The sound is so ordinary, so incongruous to this broken, forgotten bathroom, it sends a sick feeling of dread through me.

I turn to see a plain white envelope slide beneath the door, moving as if in slow motion. It's like a memory, a vision of a time in my past that I never witnessed. A note sliding beneath a door, sending my family to the slaughter.

It's happening again.

My heart stops, an almost divine recognition seeping through me as I realize what's in that envelope before it's physically possible for me to know. Maybe the knowledge isn't divine at all. Maybe it's just my shifter senses finally working with me —the whiff of blood coming from the paper, as if someone with dirty hands delivered this message, and the acrid stench of a Polaroid print hidden within the envelope. Both would be enough to raise my suspicions.

Or maybe this was the gods' message all along. A warning —reuniting us at the killer's fingertips and then stopping me moments before I could confess to my sins.

Luc and Jace break apart, frowning. They don't know what's happening. But Theo takes one look at my face, rips the door open, and races into the corridor. But he needn't bother. He won't find anyone.

They didn't last time either, when the kidnapper delivered the false photograph to the vipers, framing the dragons as my captors.

I pick up the envelope, addressed to me, and open it.

I stare at the word written on the back of the photograph

inside, my senses locked down so the noise of the world feels like it's coming from a distance. *Shoe factory.*

The only shoe factory I know was abandoned years ago, down near the dock. With my heart beating in fast, painful thuds, I turn the photo over.

22

JEL

THEO RETURNS, EYES BLAZING AS LUC AND JACE STAND ON ALERT ON either side of him. "No one there. Jel, what is it?"

Of course he didn't find anyone. My parents didn't either; only the note saying I'd been taken to the dragon's nest. The note, and a single photograph with the dragon symbol swinging from a man's neck and my tiny, terrified body in his arms. Just like this one. Only it isn't me, this time.

"Anthony," I whisper.

My brother sits on a wooden chair, his head slumped forward, his body bound with ropes. Beside him, a blurry figure tightens the ropes. He'd be indistinguishable to most people, but I know that snake tooth necklace.

Cameron.

"Who is that?" Theo snarls. "Is that your brother? Who's tying him up?" The snarl turns to a growl, orange and black fur rippling over his hands. "I know that stupid necklace. I'll fucking kill him," he says in a low voice.

"No." My tone pulls him up short.

He stares at me, eyes glinting with anger. "It's what needs

to be done, Jel," he says carefully, frustration creeping in. "Don't worry—we'll take care of it for you."

Despite everything, I nearly laugh out loud. These idiots still don't know what I am. They have no idea who they're dealing with. And it's all my fault.

"I said no." An edge of power creeps into my voice, and Theo frowns. Before he can work it out, I move on. "This has happened to me before, and the kidnapper was framed. It's a setup."

More than that, it's a message. The photo is exactly the same as my own, using an incriminating piece of clothing and everything. If I tell the boys that, we'll all be on the same page.

In my mind, the dragonfly wings glisten in golden shifter light. I look over my shoulder, drawn to the mirror where that woman appeared.

A flash of dark, terrifying eyes stare out at me from the glass. It shocks me enough to break through the dissociation, making me shudder.

Not yet. The gods are saying *not yet*.

Anger tightens my chest. These bastard gods are screwing with me right when I need to run free.

But I'm in this mess because I argued with Fate, so maybe it's time I listened. Either Luc needs to remain ignorant of our shared past in order to do something else first, or when I do tell him, it's going to kick off an explosion that will prevent us from saving Anthony... Whatever the reason, I'm going to trust in Fate for once. Even if it pisses me off.

I look back at the photograph. At Anthony. The dissociation burns away until all that's left is fire. My vision turns red, the sheen of the photograph glinting gold as my eyes shift.

I know the killer is gone, but I don't care.

I start to run.

The distant sound of feet hitting pavement behind me tells

me my pack is following, and I don't bother waiting for anything else. There's a trail I can follow. Barely there, but distinct. It smells like... arrogance. A smug, territorial challenge that the killer can't hide with the spells he's used to mask his body's scent.

He's no longer taunting me from a distance; he's playing with me. Toying with me.

We tear across campus, retracing our path from this morning almost to the letter.

The scent ends at my apartment. He came here after we left.

The mask on the counter is gone.

That's a message, too.

I lean against the wall, breathing in harsh, ragged breaths. My mates enter seconds behind me, lingering only because they checked the exits. Guarded the doors. They're good alphas. They know how to protect, how to care.

"He's not here." Jace leans his arms against the wall, head hanging between them and his hair falling limp over his face. "And we're wasting time. Your brother's in trouble."

Luc doesn't speak, but the jagged edges of his breakdown haven't completely left him, even if he does seem more whole than before. He watches me, face stiff, his body held rigid with tension.

"Where does Cameron live?" Theo asks, barely panting. His face is a mask of rage. "Jace is right. We're wasting time."

I flick the photograph with my fingers. "This is too neat," I tell them, dropping my head back against the wall and staring at the ceiling. I can't even look at the photo anymore, so when Luc slips it quietly from my fingers to study, I let him. "He's my art TA—of course I recognize that necklace. But anyone could be wearing it."

Slowly, reluctantly, Theo backs down. Then the atmosphere shifts. "He *is* the one from the party, isn't he?" he asks.

I sense danger brewing, but I nod. Theo's lip curls, and Jace steps up beside him, eyes flashing. He brushes damp hair away from his forehead and glances between us.

"Maybe it's worth questioning him anyway," Jace suggests, the words a low rumble.

"Couldn't hurt," Luc agrees.

"You don't think that's exactly what the photographer planned?" I snap. What part of *it's too neat* don't you understand?"

"We'll be gentle," Luc purrs, smoke rising from his nostrils. His eyes glint dangerously. "At first."

"Just got to check out his story," Jace agrees.

I can't believe this. It's happening in front of my goddamn eyes.

"I don't give a shit about neat," Theo snarls. "Someone has to pay."

Below the edge of righteous anger, I hear it—the jealousy.

Theo will go in, guns blazing, and he'll take it out on Cameron, even if he isn't the kidnapper. He'll say he was reckless, to get set up like that. He'll say Cameron's carelessness endangered me.

He'll use me just like my family did. Using our bond, their love, as justification for revenge.

I won't let it happen again.

"Whatever you're thinking, it ends now," I tell them, injecting a decent amount of command into my voice, but not quite enough for it to be a bark.

But I will if I have to.

Theo rumbles a low growl, deep in his chest. He glances sideways at me, immediately trying to conceal the tick of irritation in his jaw, but it's too late. He doesn't want me taking charge. He thinks this should be left for the alphas.

He's right, it should.

I'm the alpha.

"Jel," Luc says sharply. "This is what we do—leave it to us."

"No," I growl, my voice sharper now. "This is what *I* do. You have no part in this. If anyone is rescuing my brother, it's me. And if you beg me really nicely, you can tag along."

They gape at me, mixtures of incredulity and annoyance on their faces.

I open my mouth, the first bark I've given in years building on my tongue, but when I go to release it—

Nothing happens.

My soul, it's still blocked. The frayed cord holds her strong, and my command isn't coming out right. *Fuck.*

"Lock her in the bathroom," Theo says to Jace, interrupting my moment of shock.

He hasn't even noticed anything odd happening. None of them have. Theo turns to me as Jace spins me around and whirls me into the bathroom before I can protest. It's the closet all over again.

There's a note of apology in Theo's voice, but it's hardened. He's made up his mind, like any good alpha would.

Like I had, but I hadn't factored in the repercussions of my earlier decisions. The ones Anthony kept warning me about. Now I really, truly regret tying my soul to that painting. My alpha decisions don't mean shit if I don't have the soul to back them up.

I settle for giving Theo a death glare.

His jaw clenches, and he turns away as the door closes in my face. "You'll thank me later, when we return with your brother."

The door slams, and my chest heaves with rage as I stare at the unmoving wood. I can't believe they've done this to me again.

I know exactly why they have.

But I'm not letting them get away with it, not this time. This isn't a random party with a stampede of raging alphas outside the room and a fake beta in need of protecting. This is my brother.

If time wasn't so important, I'd kick this door down, rip that painting in two, and tear shreds off all three of them. But that's wasted seconds—plus minutes when they inevitably continue to argue with me. Anthony may not have minutes.

Shitty alphas go for the kill without considering strategy. They let their decisions be ruled by their emotions—their rage and ego. I'm not a shitty alpha.

And I can't tell them the truth, or Fate will grease me off again. Turns out it's a lot harder to follow Fate's instructions than I thought, and I can't help but feel it's a little malicious payback on her part for not listening in the first place.

So, looks like I'm in this on my own, as always.

I turn to the window, narrowing my eyes as my mind jumps through calculations. The only problem is, I'm five floors up. But I'm also a snake, for fuck's sake. I can climb buildings—something these idiots have forgotten. I can make that distance.

I dig through the cabinet above the sink, grabbing a knife I keep at the back just in case, along with a pack of aspirin and a couple of the more heavy duty painkillers. I don't know what condition I'm going to find my brother in, and that just makes the fury burn harder.

Colder.

I begin to strip, working quickly while I can still hear them making plans. Throwing my shirt down on the floor, I drop the knife and the painkillers into it, then throw my jeans and shoes in, too. Then I bundle the whole thing up, tie a knot, and throw it out the window.

There's a pause in the conversation outside as the water-damaged sash slides up, but I don't wait to see if they work out what I've done. I shift, scales rippling over my body, my tongue flicking out to taste the emotion on the wind, wafting from the room next door.

Determination. Strength. Power. All good alpha qualities.

Well, they would be if they weren't using them against me, like utter twats.

I slither over the edge of the window and down the wall, dropping lightly to my—naked—feet and dressing as quickly as I can.

I'm over the fence and into the distance before I even hear a shout.

23
JEL

I'M WELL AWARE THAT THIS IS A TRAP, BUT I'M SICK OF OTHER PEOPLE springing traps meant for me.

The photo is far too neat, too incriminating. It's exactly like the 'evidence' that sent my family charging at the dragons.

The fact that they're trying to use it on *me*, after they've already used me as bait in the same trick, fills me with an anger I can't explain. This is personal in a way I don't fully understand yet, but I know it is. It always comes back to me.

The vipers were sent to retrieve *me*. The new victims were chosen as a message to *me*. And of course, the Lonely Hearts warning, saying they know what secret my guilty heart protects —that I could have stopped the murders and didn't, because my alpha soul craved blood.

Finish that off with a taunting little photograph of the alleged killer with my brother in danger, hand delivered to my doorstep, and I'm officially over this fucking riddle.

This killer is playing a twisted game. One that started ten years ago, and somehow throughout it, I've been both the bait, the idiot falling for the bait, and... I suspect... the prize.

I don't know what the fuck he's doing, but it's time for it to end.

How dare they touch my brother?

I race through the streets, and as I do, I work on mentally unraveling the tether that links me to my painting. I can't destroy it from here, but there are two ends to the connection. I can destroy this end; it will just take longer.

Already, though, I can feel it falling away, burning up as I call my soul free. As I call her home.

"You've been waiting for this, haven't you," I murmur as I skid around a filthy dumpster and down another laneway. "You hussy."

The fierce rumble from my chest is completely out of my control. It nearly makes me laugh. She's happy to be home, and it turns out I'm happy to have her.

I run faster, each step more freeing than the last as senses return to me that I haven't felt for years. I'd forgotten them. I'd forgotten just how good it felt to be powerful. The windows I pass shimmer with an eerie light as my eyes glow, my shifter soul rearing up in delighted madness. I don't rein her in.

As I pass through viper territory, I pause for a moment. It shames me to admit, but I consider calling in backup. Who knows if I can take this asshole alone? But with my family at my back, there's no question. Everyone knows what a viper can do.

I keep running, leaving them behind me.

I swore I would never crawl back to them. They could throw whatever they liked at me. They could beat me, blackmail me, and try every trick in the book to control me—I wasn't going back.

For a while there, they did. Until they realized I was serious. I can't go back on my word now. And besides, there are still too many unknowns when it comes to who has my brother and what they're planning to do to him. My family aren't known for their ability to strategize in the face of complexity. You call on them when you want violence. Pain.

I don't know if they even have my brother. The photo could have been faked. And I seriously doubt Cameron is the killer. It's too neat.

My family wouldn't care; they'd kill him anyway. And with him, any chance of getting to the bottom of this latest twisted play.

I duck through the side lane that runs behind the shopping district—a filthy little alley that no one ever goes into unless they're dealing or worse. It's empty, thankfully, but right at the end something catches my attention.

A camera, poised at the top of the alley and angled to look down it.

Who the fuck wasted money on a camera here? The cops don't care what goes on in this part of the city. It'd cost them too much paperwork to care. Besides, I've been through here recently and there was nothing.

Someone's territory is expanding.

I skid to a halt, wasting precious seconds on a very bad feeling. And that's when I see it—the tiny viper logo branded onto the camera.

The vipers are watching this alley. Which means someone, right now, is watching me tear down here like the hounds of Hell are chasing me. And I've just stopped and given them a full view of my face, just in case they missed it. Fuck.

No time to worry about that now. I vault the chain fence at the back of the alley and keep running.

Anthony hasn't answered his phone in days. The more I let that thought simmer in my mind, the more frantic my fear becomes.

As I realize that, my father's voice enters my head.

"Alphas are never ruled by fear, Angelica," he tells me, his face shadowed as he stands in the open doorway to my training room. "If you attack in fear, you've already lost."

Somehow, his words sink through like nothing else, and I begin to shift my emotions, locking them away one by one until I've become someone else.

Someone I haven't been in a very long time.

My hands look too small; a child's hands, covered in blood. I ignore them.

When that first delicious hit of repressed rage and righteousness hits me, I think for a second that I can do this. I can hold the vengeance I need to hold without losing myself.

But then she comes, and like always, I forget the rest.

I don't know what it's like for other alphas, weaker alphas, but it's always been like this for me. This magic comes from somewhere outside of us, an ancient instinct that calls up all the power of those first shapeshifters, all the energy they harnessed and transformed into a complex caste system to defend their own, and it lets that energy rule. Our bodies become vessels for those first shifters and the power they gave us.

Bit by bit, I feel that power overtake me, replacing emotion with ice-cold, animal instinct.

The broken window beside me flickers, and I swivel on a breath, prepared to attack the intruder before they can move— but then the movement takes shape. It's no intruder; it's me.

My eyes glow with an inner light, bright white with hints of green. We stare at each other, my soul and I, mesmerized by the sight. I don't look human.

I'm not human.

Glistening scales flicker over my hands, rippling free from my skin and then fading as I fight back the change. They catch the light from my eyes, iridescent beneath the early morning cloud-cover.

I remember the first time my father made me kill. He taught me how to go for the throat of the quivering man knelt before me. He trained my senses to sharpen until all I could taste and feel was blood and movement. Blood, to know when the kill was done, and motion, so I could stop him escaping.

The man begged; I took his life. I didn't feel a thing until the human in me returned, and then... I felt too much.

I shudder as the memory washes through me, changing me. It doesn't feel like a costume or a mask, and that's so wrong because it should. It should be a role I'm playing, not who I am. But as I let that old, familiar power surge through me, it doesn't feel like a mask at all. It feels like I'm shedding my skin.

Scale by scale, it flakes away until all that's left is the truest, rawest form of me.

I slow my steps as I approach the factory. Despite the lack of fear driving me, I have absolutely no plan. But I'm guessing they're expecting a snake instead of a woman. Which means the pipes aren't safe, and neither is the subfloor.

Grimacing at the thought of unexpected flooding or gas, I slide off my shoes and approach the side of the building. There's only one entrance this way: a window ten feet up the brick wall.

Looks like I'm up for round two of impromptu rock climbing.

They're expecting a snake slithering in the low entrances, the tiny gaps. But what they don't know is I have a lot of human skills, too. Bracing myself, I leap at the wall.

Okay, so maybe this isn't *entirely* a human skill. But I can't ignore the possibility they've set up sense traps to incapacitate me as soon as I shift, so we're doing this human style. I wouldn't have made five floors in this form, but I can do ten feet.

I anchor my hands and toes in the grooves of the brickwork,

edging carefully up. Three points of contact at all times, and thank God I'm flexible.

A hysterical giggle threatens to escape as I realize anyone watching this probably thinks they're looking at a goddamn alien. We're talking full X-Files shit.

Reaching the window, I crack it open and hoist myself over. Finally, perched at an advantage, I survey the factory.

Fury nearly breaks through my strategic mask when I see him. A low, hissing rumble starts in my throat, my fingers gripping the broken window so hard they slice open on the shards. The scent of my own blood wafts upward, and I force my breathing to slow so I can plan my next move carefully.

Anthony slumps in a chair in the center, bound by rope and, at least in appearance, abandoned.

There's no movement, no other sign of life. Only a strange whirring sound, like an old tape player that's reached the end of its loop.

The sound stutters, pops, and then a voice emerges. It's difficult to pay attention to it when my blood still runs cold, the power guiding me through a slim, uncompromising funnel of violence and vengeance. But slowly, I force myself to take in the words.

"Don't you want to make them pay?" The recorded voice asks in a creepy, singsong tone. "Blood for blood, that's how it goes."

I grit my teeth, my arms straining from the effort of holding myself here. "Fucker wants to cosplay Jigsaw, does he?" I mutter, losing a little of the cold edge to the pure frustration this asshole brings out in me. "I get it. You're pissed off at the gods. I mean, who isn't?"

The distorted, unrecognizable voice continues, looping round and round as I perch in the corner of the window. But even when I scrape some plaster free, shuffling around noisily, nothing moves. For a second, I think I see that fucking leather rat mask that's been haunting me, but when I glare into the shadows, there's nothing there except for an oddly rat-shaped bit of graffiti. Creepy, but inanimate.

The cold strategy fades a little more, overcome with heat and anger. But that's fine; there's no one here to kill, anyway.

When I'm certain there's no one around, I drop lightly into the room and walk carefully over to Anthony. I'll wake him up, and then we'll take on this fuckhead together. No one has a chance against two Viper Alphas.

I'm almost smiling at the thought when I realize something is wrong. My body is moving strangely, like I've been drugged, but I haven't eaten anything except my own breakfast.

A sharp pain erupts in my skull, and the world shimmers white around the edges.

Dropping into instinct, I spin and attack.

24
LUC

JACE SNARLS, SLAMMING THE DOOR ON THE EMPTY BATHROOM. "SHE'S gone."

Sound rumbles in the back of his throat as he begins prowling, followed closely by Theo. The edges of my vision flicker as the dragon in me fights to come out. But the last thing I need is to shift, as much as I might want to.

"Does she even have a weapon?" I snarl.

My voice is still rough around the edges. I can't remember how long I was down in the darkness of the basements, listening to that song haunt me. The world out here seems too bright, and I keep having to concentrate just to get words out properly.

Between the looming rut and my own painful memories, it's getting really fucking difficult to focus. But it's been marginally better since they found me... The break feels dormant, instead of imminent.

Jace's touch somehow eased the pain, and I'm beyond asking why.

"Her fangs?" Jace suggests. "That'll give her some hypnosis, if he isn't an alpha."

"It's not enough," Theo counters.

He's right. It's not enough. My soul flares, begging to take control and save our mate. But I fight him down, closing my eyes until I can see with nothing more than human sight.

I'll need him soon, I'm sure. But not yet. For now, I need a little longer with clear thought, and my vitality doesn't allow for much human clarity—not that I have so much of that these days, either.

More than the other vitalities, dragons are... well. Power. My soul belongs to the kind of magic that hasn't existed within this world for centuries. And when the shift occurs, it takes with it the sight I'm used to, in favor of magic. Literally.

I can't afford that loss just yet, not until Jel is safe.

Fear rises in my chest, followed quickly by anger. Doesn't she know we're here for her? Locking her in that bathroom was to keep her safe, and now she's endangered both herself and her brother by splitting our attention.

Why does she keep running from us? From our guidance? I know she's no omega, but I've never met a beta less willing to submit.

We're a pack, and we should be together.

I snort, two plumes of smoke rising to obscure my vision. I think that's the first time I've uttered the word, even to myself.

"What's the fastest way to this shoe factory?" I ask, my voice catching on the fire in my throat. The bookshelf in front of me singes.

Theo throws a glass of water on it and eyes me warily. "Well, *technically*..."

Ah. He has a point.

But I've never let anyone... ride me... before.

Theo and Jace watch me, twin gazes of apprehension on their faces, and it would almost be hilarious if we weren't running out of time.

"Meet me on the roof," I tell them, then I fling open Jel's window, kick my legs over, and drop as the world turns to fire.

The ground rushes to meet me, bronze edged and burning as my sight changes to encompass all that a dragon sees. I stretch my talons, my jaw shattering and reforming as the shift begins, and I claw my way into the sky seconds before impact.

Even with danger looming, I suddenly feel alive again.

I've had no chance to shift, to *exist*, since term began. If I did, the children in that college would finally know what they were dealing with and I'd be knocking back territory fights every fucking day. It wasn't worth it.

But fuck I missed this.

The wind sweeps over me, through claws and scales, and all at once I catch the scent of her. But before I can go chasing, I need to pick up the other half of our pack.

I land with a crunch on the roof, concrete tearing to rubble beneath me. The two of them are already there, eyes wide, hearts racing so loud it sets my teeth on edge. Their forms shimmer with blackened flames, embers twisting and coiling with smoke.

Most shifters look like this through a dragon's sight—their energy is a black hole. An ouroboros of power, both burning and ice-cold all in one as our shifter souls dance through a body that isn't theirs. Shifters are an impossible flame, resting in one of two states, and the ebony fire reflects this.

For a moment, I think I see shimmering threads of light pulling me to the fire within these men, like the threads between me and Jel.

That can't be right. She's my fated mate; not them.

Unless... they all are. We're all fated.

What was it Jace said to me before? I don't need her; I need them. All of them.

Slowly, the action entirely unfamiliar, I bend my forelegs

and kneel before them. The shock ripples through them like a physical barrier, marking their resistance. I don't blame them; my sharpened sight means I can see my own reflection in their irises.

The gritty, depthless black of my scales ripple across my body, their angle distorted in the convex reflection. It doesn't matter. The real life effect is just as bold, because my scales glimmer with the steam that rises from my skin.

There is too much water in this atmosphere compared to the realm my ancient soul came from, and the air surrounding me transforms into a humid mess. It keeps me warm, and the smoke that curls from my nostrils as I face the two hesitating shifters only adds to the fantasy of my appearance.

I don't belong here. The very air rejects me, and a wrong word will have my vitality burning the building down to its foundations.

Without my dragon clan, I don't belong anywhere at all.

"Get. On. Board." I grit out, my voice rumbling through teeth that are more suited to feast than to speak.

It seems to break the spell. Jace huffs a nervous laugh, but his eyes shift on instinct, their glow matching my own.

The two of them share a look, hesitant for only a second before Jace climbs onto my back. Theo follows, letting his apparent rival climb up first in an unusual reversal of their competitive role.

More things to ponder.

Later.

The city falls away beneath us, and it's lucky Jel lives in the university apartments or I'd have a lot of explaining to do, because it's a long time before we're behind the clouds. The warehouse appears in seconds; at most, we could only be a minute behind Jel. We may even be ahead of her, if we can just—

Then I see it. The smoke.

Flame lashes from my lips, and I dive from the sky earlier than I should. But who gives a shit if the Council have to deal with some damage control; the goddamn warehouse is on fire.

As we plummet, I feel the hands on my back turn to claws, digging an inch into my scales, and I love it. I love knowing they can hurt me, because it means they're strong enough to protect me, too. To protect all of us.

The lingering torment from earlier fades even further, because now, I'm finally fighting something.

Now I can win.

We smash through the glass front, the whole building rocking from the damage as half the building crashes down. This place is too small for me. I transform immediately, just as a tiger and wolf launch themselves at two shadowy figures in the center of the warehouse.

The fire is spreading.

"Theo," I yell, coughing as the smoke sinks into my lungs. That's strange. Smoke doesn't usually affect me. "Check the back!"

"On it," the growl returns, and a flash of orange and black disappears into the fire.

The wolf is prowling, circling something that's still just a shadow to my eyes. I shift my sight and immediately wince as a sharp pain knocks me backward. Odd thing number two. I don't like this.

I slip my hand into my back pocket and draw out my knife. It's usually the last thing I attack with, but something has me on edge.

The sight works, though, because I can see what Jace is circling now. It's nothing. A shifting, rippling form of smoke that seems weirdly sentient. The other form, the one I assumed was Jel lying prone on the ground, doesn't move at all. It's a body, but it isn't Jel's. I think it's her brother, knocked over and still tied to the chair he was photographed in.

I freeze, my senses reaching out as the thing mirrors Jace's movements, down to every lunge and parry.

"It's a diversion," I murmur, spinning around.

I should have known. As if anything could knock Jel out so quickly when she was running into a known trap.

That's when I catch sight of her, on the other side of the burning building, smoke billowing all around.

There's a man before her, leaning in the doorway that leads to the back offices. I can't see his face, but the rage spiking in my gut tells me exactly who he is.

I slip sideways into the shadows, using the steel pillars as refuge while I edge closer. As I come near, the figure steps back into the corridor and Jel follows.

"No!" I snarl, running to catch them.

Wait, there's... Something isn't right. I prop myself against the doorway as I reach it, fingers gripping tightly into the metal frame. My body feels wrong. My instincts are screaming from every direction, but I can't sort through them to make a decision. I can't see properly.

This smoke has something in it.

He's drugged us.

The warehouse sways before me, distorted like the haze in a steam room, and I'm beginning to feel like Alice staring into Wonderland. I think we've found the source of the fire, but even that doesn't look right. There's no fuel. This building is metal; it should be scorched and broken, but not lit up like a bonfire.

And the smoke doesn't look right.

Red fog rolls through at my feet, and on the other side of it, I see the killer properly.

He stands in the doorway of another room, eyes fixed to Jel

as she struggles to reach him. There's something eerily off about him, like the smoke, but I can't place it. Something besides the creepy leather rat mask, anyway.

Then it hits me.

He's in the thick of the smoke. That shit is billowing around him, all over his eyes, curling through the breathing holes in his mask. He's surrounded by it, but he isn't affected like we are.

My brain is tweaking just enough that his composure wigs me out. It's like he isn't human, like he's some kind of Freddie Krueger freak crossing realms but remaining untouchable.

Snarling, I double my efforts, clawing my way forward one support beam at a time. My skin ripples, the dragon in me desperate to fight this threat where I can't, but I can't let it free. I don't know what this drug will do to that half of me, and instinct tells me it won't be good.

Instinct tells me he *wants* us to shift.

I turn my head, wincing at the pain, to look back through the open doorway into the warehouse.

Theo and Jace have completely collapsed. Whatever this drug is, it hits harder in our other forms.

An unexpected fury rises within me, even as my body weakens further. Who is this asshole? What is he doing to us, and how is he doing it?

"Stop running from me, you weakass little shit!" Jel demands, staggering upright from a nasty coughing fit.

The smoke writhes at her feet, lunging like a living thing, searching for her. A surge of pride sweeps through me when I watch her fight. She's clearly as drugged as we are, stumbling more with each step and wavering back and forth like a hypnotized snake, but she lashes with a violent hiss every time that smoke moves against her.

She stands tall despite how the drug pulls her down.

Blood drips from her forehead, and her nails bite so hard into her palms they're cut raw, but she doesn't back down. She fights like an alpha.

I can't help the soft chuckle at the thought—my solitary beta mate, lunging at a serial killer like she has a whole pack to defend. I kind of like it.

But right now, she's too isolated to win. Whatever he's doing to us with the smoke, however he's doing it, it's coming from all sides. I swallow thickly, holding my breath and lunging forward until we're shoulder to shoulder. I pause for a beat before twisting to guard her from behind.

"You know, the final girls are meant to be more desperate," I mutter to her, holding down the sharp edge of relief that over-whelms me as soon as my back presses against hers and my body registers her as safe. "That's how they win. Through their overwhelming virtue and their terrified, innocent use of envi-ronmental weaponry." I laugh, the sound ending in a choke. I jerk my head toward the slim, elegant dagger in her hands, still coughing. "You brought that from home."

"That's why I'll never be a final girl," she snarls, brandishing the knife with familiarity. There's an odd note to her rage. It's familiar in a way I can't quite pinpoint, but the answer feels so close.

Once more, I'm hit by how unbetalike her fighting style is.

Jel casts a glance at me sideways. "I'm just the collateral damage. I'm the angry bitch that gets taken down first, and the audience won't admit it but they kind of cheer a bit because she got what was coming to her."

Her eyes flash, and my soul sings in recognition that soon solidifies into an unexpected truth.

I freeze, every nerve and instinct sharpening in agitation as I finally see the woman next to me for what she really is. Holy fuck. The low growl rips from my throat before I can stop it, but thankfully she just thinks I'm mad at the killer.

This has nothing to do with the killer. This is all her, and everything she's been hiding from us.

Not a beta. Not a beta at all. And while logic dictates I should only react like this to an omega, once more Jel has turned everything I ever expected on its head.

I'm more turned on than I've ever been in my life.

My mind whirrs with predictions, with *questions,* but I can't argue or demand answers because with a shriek of rage, she launches herself at the red-tinged haze.

And falls right through.

There's nothing there. He's gone.

The building above us screams in protest, and another beam begins to fall.

"We have to go!" I yell, grabbing her shoulder and pulling her backward. "Jace and Theo are unconscious, and the building's coming down!"

As I grab her, she's halfway through an instinctive shift, rage twisting her features into a forked tongue, shining scales, and bright, lidless eyes. But when she hears my words, she freezes.

"Mates," she hisses, the 's' catching even as she returns to human form, her flaming red hair billowing around her face among the smoke. "Anthony!"

Then she runs.

I don't think about what I've just seen; I don't have time to. I just run through the smoke and heat until I reach Jace and Theo, grabbing an arm each and dragging them to the entrance. Jel has already grabbed her brother, dragging him free from the building and collapsing, her energy gone, still too close to danger. I'll have to move her as well.

I don't have time to think, not if I want to get my pack to safety.

But I do notice one thing as the building comes down, as the flames lick over the final remnants of the structure and collapse it inward into fire and ash. There's yet one more thing linking us to this killer—something I didn't notice until now.

This fire is dragon flame.

25
JEL

I WAKE TO THE LOW MURMUR OF A FAMILIAR VOICE, AND THE ACRID stench of smoke. Slowly, my memories of the nightmare in the warehouse come flooding back.

"Easy," Luc says, and I know it's him without even opening my eyes.

The familiar energy between us surges, and I'm too wrecked to even summon up the guilt that should follow.

I shouldn't feel this way with him, but I do, and I'm sick of fighting it.

"Fucker crept up on me," I groan, clutching my head and trying to sit up. "Got a jump start and then he—" I shudder. "Where's Anthony? Is he safe?"

Strong hands hold me down. "Don't move. You're both safe."

The sound of sirens whirr in the background, too close for comfort.

"We have to go," I protest.

Go. Why do we have to go? The urge overwhelms me, but I'm also nauseous as fuck and my thoughts are all messed up. Warehouse. Fire. Asshole.

Where am I again?

I shake my head, cutting off the scream that wants to erupt as the memories slot back into place, this time staying there. That's right—we have to go because the fire wasn't Rat Face's goal. It was the bait.

"Something was really off about that setup. I don't trust it."

My brain is still working at half speed, but I can remember enough about the warehouse to know it didn't add up. God, did he drug me? He must have drugged me. But there was this energy to him, like a triumphant anticipation.

It turned his scent all wrong.

A killer standing over the intended victim should have smelled like victory, especially with how much of an advantage that drug gave him. The scent I got behind his creepy rat mask wasn't victory, it was like... A mad scientist. Like I was his experiment, and he was watching it all unfold.

And even though I was drugged and at his mercy, he didn't touch me. He wouldn't fight me—stepping back into the smoke each time I got close. When I tried to talk to him, to goad him into answering me, he just laughed and said nothing. If he had me right where he wanted me, why didn't he do anything?

Unless he was waiting for something else.

The question is, what the fuck was he waiting for?

It doesn't matter. I don't care what he wants with me, so long as Anthony is safe. And I'm sure I remember dragging him from the smoke before the fire really set in.

"Anthony," I mumble, the words tasting like bile.

"Your brother is fine," Luc says, an odd note to his voice that I can't understand right now.

Huh. My eyes are still closed.

Groggy and unnerved, I blink my eyes open, squinting through some kind of gunky muck that seems to be the aftereffects of that fucking smoke. With all the grace of a fainting goat, I begin to make sense of the shapes surrounding me.

"So," I say neutrally. "We are now in a boathouse. Anyone want to explain that one?"

Jace grins. "Felt like a swim after all that fire. Don't you?"

Despite everything, I laugh. It hurts.

"Urgh, fuck." I clutch my head and sit up. "Where's Anthony?"

"I'm right here, twerp."

My entire body relaxes at the sound of his voice, even though it's raw with smoke inhalation and far quieter than it should be.

"Who are you calling twerp, dingus? I'm three years older than you." When I look around properly, I see him crouched in the corner, elbows hooked over his knees as he leans back against the wooden wall.

There's a look in his eye I can't decipher. Then his gaze flicks to Luc and back to me, and suddenly I know. He's recognized Luc, and he wants answers.

I didn't give him Luc's background when I got him to sign the affiliation clause, and bless him, he never asked. Something tells me my little brother won't be so quick on the favors next time.

Dread sinks in my stomach, and I shake my head minutely, holding his gaze. His lips press tighter together, a furrow deepening in his brow, but he doesn't say anything.

After a moment, Anthony clears his throat and mutters, "Thanks for picking me up, I guess."

I snort. I can't help it. "Picking you up?"

Finally, he grins. The lopsided, easy grin I know so well. "I totally had it covered."

There's blood in his teeth, and I get a sudden vision of what kind of scene must have gone down for the killer to get Anthony alone. He's the middleweight state champion. He eats guys like Rat Face for breakfast in a fair fight.

Like the smoke, like the drugs, this would not have been a fair fight.

"We could see that," Theo says in a low voice. There's amusement there though, so I'm not too worried.

It's the other two I'm concerned about.

Jace keeps glancing at Luc like he's waiting for some bomb to drop, and Luc... For all that he can't take his hands off me, checking me, making sure I'm okay, he also looks like he might want to murder me.

Tit for tat, I suppose.

"Whoa, that's a bit grim," I mutter, closing my eyes and wincing.

"What is?" Luc asks.

"Nothing."

Tentatively, I steady myself against the wall and climb to my feet. All three of my mates protest the entire way, but they don't stop me.

Maybe they're learning.

"Why do you want to get out of here before the cops arrive?" Anthony asks, too sharp as always. "You thought he was setting you up?"

"I don't know," I hiss, frustrated. "Nothing about it adds up. Why light a fire and let us escape? Why refuse to fight me or talk to me, but stick around to watch like some creepy mime?"

Luc clears his throat, interrupting us. "The fire was set with dragon flame."

Silence drops through the boathouse. How many dragons do we know in the Caldburg City area, apart from Luc? Zero. And with the news running recaps on the terrible murders ten years ago every time they release an update, there won't be a person in the area who doesn't know that.

He wasn't setting me up; he was framing Luc.

Theo lets out a slow whistle. "Bottled fire or fresh, do you think?"

Luc snorts. "There are no dragons left here to give him fresh flame."

There's an uncomfortable silence at his bluntness. Anthony tries to catch my eye, but I refuse to let him.

"Alright, first things first," I say.

My voice comes out sharper than I intend it to, and Theo and Jace fall to attention immediately—followed, just as quickly, by confusion. They're following an alpha, and they don't know why.

She's back. My soul is back.

Interestingly, Luc doesn't look confused. The odd gleam in his eye brightens, even as he shifts his stance subtly enough to indicate deference.

Fuck. What does he know?

Shaking my head, I continue. "We need to figure out what the trap was for, because it was bigger than burning me alive or framing you for arson. He was waiting for something with that smoke, and he was smug as hell about it. Everything was going exactly as he'd planned until you arrived." I pause, frowning. "No... even then, he was smug. We all played exactly into his hands—he was definitely framing you. So what was he trying to do with that?"

When I glance at Anthony, he's shaking his head, a wry smile on his face as he watches the four of us.

"I didn't see who grabbed me, and it was done away from cameras," he says, scrubbing his hand roughly over his hair. He looks exhausted. "I got a few good knocks in through the fog. He did something to the air... some witch spell. It was like fighting in charcoal."

My stomach twists, and I feel violently, painfully sick all of a sudden. My missing spell. That's how the killer got him.

Anthony grins. "But I think I knocked out a tooth. Would've had him on the ground if the fog wasn't drugged." He sighs, dropping his head back against the wall and running a hand over his neck. My heart sinks as I see a familiar, painful wound. "And yes, he took my blood."

"Shit," Jace hisses. "And you didn't recognize anything about him?"

"Nope. Only thing I can remember is that snake tooth necklace around his stupid neck." Anthony's words turn sibilant with anger.

I don't blame him. Cameron's necklace always bothered me too. But that's twice now that the necklace has been highlighted to us. And once through an apparently impenetrable fog, where he could see nothing else.

"What are the odds that your memory is too hazy for a face, but you saw the identifying necklace they just so happened to include in the photograph that sent me to you?" I shake my head. "It's too neat. Feels like a frame job."

Anthony nods. "Was thinking that myself. This guy's too good to leave a necklace on. But then, sometimes people are stupid..." He shrugs. "Do you want to take that risk? I think we shake the guy anyway."

Theo and Jace rumble in immediate agreement. Anger flashes through me, fiery hot with just a sliver of ice. "No."

They stop, once more with that stunned confusion. I grin, my alpha soul purring at the sight of their submission. She's barely been out an hour, and already she's taking over the place.

"Jel," Theo says in a voice like he's about to argue with me.

A low hiss starts at the back of my throat, and I cover it with an exasperated sigh. "There's no point rushing into anything just yet. Let's work out why he was framing Luc first—that's more important."

His voice pitches lower, rough around the edges and a little incredulous. "You're going against your brother. He's patriarch alpha, isn't he? I can smell it. Why the hell are you contradicting your alpha?"

He isn't speaking from some sense of puritan hierarchy, although that would be valid; he thinks Anthony will kill me if I keep challenging him. I can smell the shock and fear coming off him—it almost overrides his confusion. If Anthony were to go for my throat, Theo would defend me, as my mate. But I can see from his face now that he isn't happy about it. He's protective, but he's not an idiot.

Anthony clears his throat, ignoring the confused look Jace gives the two of us.

"He's got a point," Jace says slowly. "Unless the bond has messed your allegiances up..."

I can't help it—I laugh. "No, honey," I snarl, "I'm not deferring to you instead of him."

Behind me, Anthony snorts with laughter that he quickly tries to hide.

"I told you this would end in tears, Jel," he says, twisted amusement in his voice. "I just hadn't realized how spectacularly you'd fucked things up." He starts laughing, the sound faintly delirious. "How did you bond to three alphas and they don't even know?"

"What would end in tears?" Jace asks, his eyes glittering an eerie gold as his shifter soul begins to get edgy. "What don't we know?"

"You should listen to Anthony," Theo insists. "We'll take care of it. I'll make sure Cameron isn't roughed up—if he doesn't need to be."

Visions of the blood dripping onto the front step of the dragon's nest shatter my mind, and something inside me flips. The words drop without my intention.

"I said no." There's no mistaking the order in them.

It's the first bark I've given in years, low and undeniable.

My jaw firms, and my eyes slide away from the shock and confusion on Theo and Jace's faces, moving toward Luc. It's his reaction that matters the most, because it's one step from realizing what I am to realizing *who* I am.

This isn't how I wanted it to come out, but it's how it did, and I'm done hiding.

I freeze, my eyes locking with Luc's. He watches me calmly, his eyes piercing. Almost triumphant.

He already knew.

"Well I think that's my cue," Anthony says lightly. "I'll see what I can dig up about who took me. Let you know what I find. Our network might know a thing or two." He leans in, murmuring in my ear. "Don't know how much they're caught up on, but when they're in the loop... It was venom. Venom was stolen from the vault, and a number of experimental alchemies created from the venom." He glances at me meaningfully. "Drugs."

My eyes widen, thoughts racing as I try to put the pieces together. It's still too messy.

Anthony leans back, ruffling my hair as he goes, a simple brother to sister gesture, but he deliberately alters it. His body twists, angled away from me in deference, and I know exactly what he's doing.

He's reminding them I'm the Alpha.

He's forcing this confrontation to happen.

"Asshole," I hiss, ignoring the ratcheting tension from the room behind me.

"Suck it up," he murmurs. "It's who you are."

It is. And more than that, it's who I'm becoming.

Then he lifts a hand and leaves us alone.

26

JEL

THEO IS THE ONE TO BREAK THE SILENCE. HIS VOICE COMES OUT rough, his breathing audible like he's been running a mile.

"When were you going to tell us?"

Forcing the casual expression onto my face, I turn around and shrug. "Does it matter? I thought we agreed to let the bond fade."

"You know damn well that's changed."

I do. I do know it's changed.

I think I'm the last to say it out loud, but we all knew it.

Sighing, I let my defenses drop. The bond between us reels in triumph, lunging at my senses and flooding our connection with everything I'm feeling.

Almost imperceptibly, Theo relaxes as he feels the complexity of my emotions. He wanted to know I wasn't stonewalling him. Well, this is the best I can do, buddy boy. Can't really handle soft words right now. You want soft words, you get a beta.

You should get a beta anyway.

Jace frowns, stepping forward as if compelled. "You still want this. But..."

"It's four alphas," I snap, still too rattled to deal with this maturely. "What even *is* this?"

"Fate."

The answer comes from the place I least expect it.

I turn to Luc and see the fire burning in his eyes. He's all in, even knowing my secret.

One of my secrets.

If I thought there was any chance we could walk away from each other, maybe I would try to keep the walls I've had for ten long years. I might let him think of me as the girl that got away, instead of the girl that ripped his heart to shreds in the cruelest twist of Fate imaginable—bound to the source of his tragic pain.

But we're past that. We're not walking away, and I think deep down I've known that for a long time. Just as I've known the rest.

I have to tell him the truth right now, no matter if it breaks him.

Do I tell him here? Or take him outside alone?

He'll burn the fucking boathouse down.

"I need to talk to you," I say, holding his gaze. "Before this goes on any longer."

"Before what does?" he asks, lips curled into the faintest of smiles.

Light glints from waist height, and I glance down without thinking. Claws. Golden claws.

He isn't even trying to sheathe them.

Fuck.

"Walk it back, *mate*," I tell him softly, my voice barely more than a breath. Theo and Jace stiffen in automatic response to my tone. "You don't have all the facts."

"I have enough."

His voice burns. He's riding the edge of too much instinct.

Too many days of trying to protect his mate from a killer. Twisted games playing out in the background behind us. Lust burning, rising, like smoke from a dragon's breath.

He's just pulled me from the fire, and he doesn't intend to let me walk away this time.

"Theo. Jace."

I call them both into line with me, the action instinctive. It shocks me when they fall in without question. We face off against Luc, smoke now pooling from his nostrils in the dingy light of the boathouse.

His stance eases, just a little.

Maybe I can save this.

"We're going to my apartment," I tell him, command him.

He shakes his head slowly, lips still twisted into that tiny smile. "That's not how this works, darling."

"Oh?" I can't keep the snarl from my voice. Theo and Jace echo it from either side of me, but I can't tell who it's at. They no longer feel at my side, but they're not at Luc's side either. "Then tell me how this works. *Cupcake.*"

He barks a laugh, blue eyes glinting as he tips his head back. They aren't glinting with the light; it's his shift. His vitality tearing forward.

Luc straightens, his eyes sliding from one of us to the other, one by one. I don't know what he sees with his dragon sight, but it brings a change over him—slower, more laconic. Smug.

"We'll have to fight for heirarchy," he says simply. "I never realized that was the missing piece. But it is." He snarls, long and low. "The fight."

My heart races, my soul singing for blood. Especially now. Especially here, because this is a different fight altogether. Sure, it will end with teeth on a throat, but the throat will be willingly bared.

And a different fight altogether comes after that.

He's right, though. The fight is the missing piece. We're all trapped in cages of our own making, desperate for a fight we can't have because the opponent can't be fought. Me, with my hidden soul. Luc, with a killer who haunts him and won't show his face. Theo, with the invisible demons he pretends aren't chasing him. And Jace, who from the beginning has only ever been fighting himself.

We're primed for the fight, and Fate bound us together with the one pack who could take it all. Take it and release it, so we can finally reach what comes after.

I swallow thickly, trying to tamp down my desire. This isn't going right; I can hardly think straight. It's no time for a fight, but tell that to his vitality. Tell it to mine.

We waited too long to address this.

I waited too long.

"Luc," I warn him.

"Angelica," he hisses back, prowling closer, body angled ready to attack.

Fuck it. I guess we're doing this here.

"You think I have no family. That my ties to the vipers are so diluted they may as well not be there. You're wrong."

Luc grows very, very still. I close my eyes, my fists clenching as my vitality tries to fight its way out of the surrender I owe him. I don't let it. I force myself to open them, to look him in the face when I tell him the truth.

"My family are *the* vipers, and they haven't forgotten me," I say, the words falling into silence.

Jace chokes out some kind of shocked noise, broken off immediately by what sounds like an elbow to the ribs. Theo has picked up on the mood, even if he doesn't know why.

"Which vipers are *the* vipers?" Luc asks so quietly I barely hear him.

"Marcus."

The patriarch alpha. The one who ordered the attack. My father.

The boathouse is eerily quiet, dust motes swirling sluggishly in the air between us. My heart races a hundred miles an hour, and I'm so close to the edge. To lashing out. I can't imagine how Luc feels, and I can only hope the building is still standing when this is over.

His face is unreadable. I keep going.

"That night my father took out your nest, it was a setup. I was the bait, and something in my family's vault was the prize. They stole it, and now he's back for more. This is bigger than we know, Luc. The killer is the same one who kidnapped me—the one who framed your family and set the vipers on them in retaliation."

I swallow, straightening my shoulders and preparing myself for the final blow. The confession that will ignite his attack.

"And you should know... when I realized it wasn't a dragon with me, I didn't tell them, even when I suspected something was wrong. I had suspicions no one else could have, and I didn't share them. I pointed to your door, because I wanted the vipers and the dragons to fight." The words almost choke me, but I force them out. "My alpha soul woke that night, and she wanted vengeance. *I* wanted vengeance." My mouth twists in shame. "I wanted someone to bleed."

As if on instinct, Luc's own hands clench at my words, the golden claws painfully bright in the dim lighting. They don't draw back. Smoke drips from his open mouth, and his eyes glow so bright I fear we might be on the edge of something none of us can return from.

"Your family," he says slowly, his words edging into a high-pitched hiss I've never heard before. "You. You're an actual viper." He stops. Shakes his head. Laughs. "You're *the* viper. The alpha heir. You're the one we hear rumors about—who gave up her inheritance. Her crown." He spits the word like poison.

In a manner of speaking, but I don't argue semantics.

"Yes."

I've never seen Jace so silent. Theo, too, though his expression is harder to read. He won't take his eyes off me, but it isn't his vitality watching me. It's just him. As though he's seeing me for the first time.

After what feels like an age, Luc speaks again. The fire is gone from his voice this time, but it's somehow worse.

"So," he says bluntly. "It all comes back to you."

I open my mouth, but what can I say? It does. For ten years, I've carried this weight, and I'll never be free of it if I don't end it now.

"It does."

"I need..." He breaks off, and for a moment, I see the pain behind it all. The agony. "I'll be back," he growls, then he twists, folding in upon himself with an anguished snarl, his body writhing as it stretches and contorts into a flash of scales and terrifying mass.

He bursts through the roof of the boathouse, timber and metal sheets collapsing around us.

That's building number two gone down. No wonder he rarely makes a full shift. Ten bucks says he makes it a hat trick before the week is out.

I cover my head with my arms, slices of torn roofing cutting bloody shreds through my skin.

Then he's gone, leaving me hollow, torn, and alone.

27

JEL

After several slow, sluggish minutes, I come to the odd realization that someone is talking to me. I'm not alone, like I'd assumed.

"Maybe he'll calm down by the time he's back?" Jace offers, but his face is tight, the words falling flat and lifeless. I appreciate the effort all the same.

"No," I say, my words impossibly steady. "He'll be back to pick up where he left off. You don't calm down from something like this on your own, and he definitely doesn't."

No one contradicts me. We know our mate.

The boathouse feels oppressive without him in it. Even broken to pieces, it's dingy and small—far too similar to the hideouts my father would choose. I can't stand it.

I can't breathe.

"Jel?" Someone is speaking, but I can't work out who the voice belongs to.

My hands clench so tightly the nails bite into my skin. This isn't the end of our argument, and stopping it in the middle is just making it worse. My soul flickers in agitation, wild and burning with aggression. She needs to attack. She needs to defend.

"Ssh," that same someone says from in front of me, their hands held out to either side. "Put it away for now, Jel. It's not gone—it's just locked away. Wait until he comes back."

Until he comes back.

This man is right. I can't ride this anger alone, and my vitality won't let me pass it off. I have to lock it away until it can safely come free.

I have to find another way to unleash this energy.

The man grins. Theo. Theo grins. "There she is," he says in delight. His eyes flash with amusement and something deeper, something heated. "Now. We've got some catching up to do. So let's get you home where we can talk... in private."

The Uber ride home is full of tension. Theo refuses to take his hand off my thigh, and Jace seems to think he has permission to tease my hair. The thing is, he does. And he knows it.

Something has cracked in the bond tonight. The sensation is no longer marked by a push and pull; instead, I'm falling, closer and closer to the three men I've tried to shove aside.

At least they're falling, too.

Jace's fingers trail through a curl by my cheek. He lifts it and leans in, blowing soft, warm air against my skin and laughing as I shiver.

"You know, we've been thinking," he says in a tone so casual it's clearly fake. "You don't have to choose any of us at all."

It sounds like he's saying I can walk away from this bond. I'm not an idiot. I know what he's saying, and the thought makes my heart pound and a flush of heat rise along my chest.

"I think we've all figured that one out," I say dryly. "We're well past the pissing contest at this point."

I can't say I understand what this next stage means, but I do know we're in it. We're well and truly over the finish line—this is bat country.

He blows in my ear again, and I turn reflexively, my lips almost brushing against his, we're so close together. He pauses, eyes heavy lidded as he gazes down at me. "You're not following me," he says. "You don't have to choose."

My brow furrows, even as my eyes fall to his lips. It takes me a second to chase the words back to any sort of meaning. "I know I can have you all if I want," I whisper, the hairs on the back of my neck rising as Theo leans in to kiss me. "The problem is, having you all would be a total disaster."

"Why's that?" Theo asks against my skin, ending the words on a soft, deliberate bite. A claiming bite, even though it doesn't break the skin.

I should beat the shit out of him for that alone. Instead, I melt back into him, ignoring the scandalized expression of the driver as he adjusts the mirror so he can no longer see us.

Prude, choosing naivety over safety. What if we get rear-ended?

"But see, that's the thing," Jace murmurs, his lips somehow finding their way to my collar. He pulls back to keep speaking. "We *thought* it would be a disaster, when it was one beta and three alphas. How the hell would we keep it reined in for that? There's no hierarchy there to submit to, only the challenge. We're alphas, Jel, we thrive on competition, and our instincts..." He pauses just to breathe, his eyes flashing gold. "Well, you know all about our instincts."

"Which is why this is going to work." Theo slides a hand over my stomach. It's still chaste, above my waistband, but it burns with the promise of so much more. "Because we're on equal ground, now. It's no longer three alphas working out how to share one beta. It's all of us. *You* don't have to choose."

Oh. I hear the distinction this time—the subtle emphasis on

a word I wasn't expecting. I hadn't realized it, but that was exactly how I saw it. They were all fated to me, and I had to balance all that aggression without any of us rising to the killing edge.

But the slow adjustments in our bond tell a different story, don't they? One the boys didn't notice until now, because they were so convinced I was the prize to be shared among them.

But the truth of it is, we're all fated. Together.

We're a pack.

I bite down on my lip, just managing to restrain the sound. Laughing, the two of them pull back, but their hands remain on me. It's a casual touch that means more than I want to admit.

"I know you don't like alphas," Theo says under his breath, voice pitched low in my ear. He almost sounds apologetic. "And I'm beginning to understand what might have made you this way. What they did to you."

Not just what they did; what I've done. I don't correct him.

"But we're going to show you there's more to our souls than violent chaos."

I shiver, my lips parting as a sudden burst of desire hits me.

Jace grins. "And even the violence doesn't have to be chaotic. We can follow rules, Jel." He makes the word 'rules' sound dirty. "This is our pack. We get to decide what that means."

Theo hums in agreement. "I respect you, so I'll let you fight your battles and I won't step in until you ask." His voice darkens. "But I *am* an alpha, Jel. If anyone hurts you, I will skin them alive. And I know you'll let me, because you respect me too."

"See?" Jace murmurs, voice thick with amusement. "Rules."

The promise sends a sick sense of joy running through me. My soul is in heaven, screaming in delight. We've found them. We've found the men to guard our back while we defend ourselves from danger.

While we defend our pack.

The second my soul broke free, truly free, she's been tearing my insides apart, screaming at me to stand between my mates and the danger that's coming. She's so loud, I can barely think.

I'd forgotten what the instincts felt like.

But just because it's hard to think like a human around them, it doesn't mean I can't. And it doesn't mean they won't. Theo has been watching me ever since he met me, not just to win my favor, but to understand me. He understands what I need, and it's time for me to understand what he needs, too.

"Rules," I tell him, resting my palm on his. "And respect."

He takes it and turns my hand over, kissing the center as he holds my gaze.

I open my mouth, hesitating for only a second. "What do you need?"

"You," Theo answers instantly. Jace brushes my hair from my neck and kisses me.

"To protect you," Jace adds. "To protect us."

Then we're agreed.

I let myself feel the intoxicating pull of the bond. There's an energy growing between us. It's been growing since the party, and it's finally been given space to appear.

As if on cue, I feel a prick of pain beneath where my hand rests on my thigh. Looking down, I see the golden metal of my claws digging into my skin. It almost makes me laugh, especially when Theo's hand flexes and his own appears. He doesn't even notice.

I glance at him, and then at Jace, both of them watching me with hungry eyes. Giving them a pointed look, I return my attention to our hands, where our claws reveal the truth of what's building. It's more than sexual tension. Our instincts are riding high, desperate to bring an end to this dance. The rut can last for days, and for days we've held it in chains.

Freedom is coming before this night is out. I can feel it.

"It's alright," Theo says, his voice almost unrecognizable. "Without Luc, we won't do anything."

He's right. One of us is missing, and going into the rut without him isn't possible. Even if it was, it wouldn't satisfy anything, and we'd be even more likely to emerge in a bloodbath.

I sheathe my claws, but I can still feel them just below the surface. I don't think they'll fully retreat now until they get what they want. What my soul has been craving since I painted that goddamn mating call.

But for now, we'll wait. There are so many other ways we can have fun in the dark.

And this time, when Luc realizes he can't outrun me or our fate, *I'll* be the one who's waiting for him. This time, we burn together.

28

LUC

THEY SAY VIOLENCE ALWAYS LEAVES A MARK, BUT THE PLACE WHERE MY family died has nothing. No reminder. No scar. There isn't even a drop of blood to tell the story of what happened here.

If you tore open my brain, I think all you'd find is evidence of that night. The blood, the screams. Fire, but not enough. Until today, fire has always been a comfort for me—it meant safety, and even if it didn't win the fight, it was the closest chance at victory.

Today, it nearly took my mate from me.

But my mate's family took everything from me first. Her blood calls to mine, woven with Fate, but should I reject her like she first rejected me?

Do I trust the fire or the blood?

What if I can't trust either?

Frowning, I walk onto the empty lot that marks my family's home. It's mine, technically, but I've never come back until now. Three years ago, I paid contractors to knock down the burnt husk, raking the earth over until there was nothing left. It's an abandoned meadow these days, and I'm wondering if I did the wrong thing.

If everything is linked, there might have been a clue. But if that's the case, it's lost now.

I don't even know why I'm here. I should be with Jel, challenging her to the fight that roars in my blood. She lied to me. Or deceived me at least, even if she didn't lie.

Ever since she told me, my vitality has rippled beneath my skin. He wants to come out. He wants to tear someone limb from limb, now that our family's killer is finally so close.

Except she's also my mate, and my soul craves a different sort of aggression there entirely.

Being around her now would be explosive in the worst way.

The quiet sound of someone clearing their throat distracts me. I look up to find an elderly man dressed in overalls watching me. It's the gardener, here for the monthly decimation of my meadow, it seems.

I narrow my eyes. I swear I've seen him on campus recently. Does he have a contract for the grounds as well?

"Two of you in a month," he says grimly, and my breath stills. "Seems a bad omen if you ask me."

"Who was the first?"

The man shrugs. "Some other fire breather. Dug up the place before I told him to get lost. Last Wednesday, or thereabouts."

Impossible. There are no others, not here.

Which means it's someone who *isn't* from here.

"Did they dig up anything in particular?"

The gardener is already fitting headphones to his ears, kicking his ride-on into action. "Nothing that I saw," he yells over the noise.

But what was there to find?

A slippery thought slides into my mind. The flaw in my grief-fueled logic. This isn't just about Jel; it's about me, too.

It doesn't just come back to her. It comes back to us.

Skulking at the tree-line, I watch the man make his slow, methodical lines across the property. Back and forth. Curls of smoke drip from my nostrils, surrounding me inch by inch in a cloud of smoke. The man looks over every few seconds, when he makes a turn, and the sneer on his face tells me just what he thinks of fire-breathers.

Looks like I'll need a new gardener after this. Sure, there isn't much he can do to a meadow to harm me, but I'm starting to rethink the value of this place after what he's told me today.

I take a deep breath, and then another, preparing myself. Then I slip into my dragon sight.

The world burns. My friendly gardener's shifter soul reveals itself in a swirl of blackened smoke. After a while, you learn how to read the images—well enough, at least. I'm looking at a mouse, I think.

No surprises there.

I let my sight roam further, but there's nothing here. No magic left; the land has been razed. The energy that once made it a home burned to the ground long ago.

My home is gone.

I reach for my pendant, silently begging the gods once more for answers they refuse to give me. But this time, as soon as I touch the metal, pain rips through my stomach. I double over, clutching my abdomen, and the world twists sideways.

I'm staring up at the sky, but it's twisted and dark—night time.

There are too many stars.

Dozens upon dozens of stars whirl through the sky, rippling as though I'm on a playground and some nasty kid is spinning me too fast.

"I'm gonna fucking be sick," I mutter, clutching at the grass beneath me.

It isn't grass.

My meadow is gone, and I'm left with dirt and bones.

Don't tell me the gods have finally decided to answer.

The sound of children's laughter breaks through my thoughts. I don't want to look. I know what's waiting for me just out of sight, as much as I try to resist seeing. But this won't end until I witness what the gods have chosen to tell me.

I turn, mouth twisted in a pained sneer as I haul myself to my feet over broken bones and charred earth.

"No," I hiss, staring in horror at the resurrected house before me.

I trail into silence, barely remembering what I was thinking. All I can see is how similar this house is to my memory of it— and how many pieces I had forgotten completely.

The pots by the door, filled with snapdragons in a joke my aunt liked to play. The box of chalk I hid beneath the step. The scent of baking bread and other concoctions from my collection of uncles hovering in the kitchen, who liked to tinker with new recipes every week. I remember all of that.

I don't remember the bars on the basement windows, or the piss-stained fence from the neighborhood dogs, who couldn't understand why they hated our house so much or why they could never mark it properly. I don't remember the stink of fear, or the charred edges to the windows from how many fights ended in flame.

My earliest transformations were in that basement. It isn't unusual for the more dangerous shifters. Especially wolves, who can stray too close to the moonlight in those early days, and become a different sort of beast entirely.

But I still remember the cold. And I remember what I could hear through the vents. Whispers upstairs, when they thought I was too deep in the agonizing, uncontrolled shift to hear them.

They spoke about stealing something back. I never heard

what, or from where, but my mind shoves Jel's words at me
once again.

Something in my family's vault was the prize.

Without meaning to, I growl, long and low. The laughter
from inside the house pauses, as if they can hear me. It's impossible, but a longing opens up within me that makes me believe
it anyway.

I step forward.

That same pain reappears, sharper this time, and a cold
hand snatches my wrist.

A silky, feminine voice murmurs soft words from behind me
as the world spins again. "Don't you know how to listen, boy?"

The coldness sharpens into chains, locking tight around my
arms and ankles and yanking me down. I cough up dirt and
grass as I fall once more through the earth. There are no stars at
all this time, not even strange ones. The ground consumes me,
burying me so deep below the surface I don't think even fossils
could find me.

"Likely not," the voice says, as if she can hear my thoughts.

I spin, my eyes glowing, illuminating the darkened chamber
as I find a woman sitting upon an earthen throne. Her black
gown ripples over crossed legs, moving as if alive. I decide not
to look too closely at it.

Not that I could, since looking at her dress would mean
looking away from her eyes.

Her eyes terrify me.

Is this some kind of dragon goddess? Am I looking at the
source of our ancient magic?

She laughs, proving—unfortunately—that she can read my
thoughts. "I'm not your dragon god, no," she says, her eyes
narrowing in thought as she regards me. "Is this how you
thought they would look?" She shakes her head. "Forget that, I

don't have time to hear your thoughts. You have fifteen seconds to tell me why you can't complete this simple task."

"What task?" I stammer, pulling ineffectively at the chains still tugging me toward the ground. I wonder if they'll keep going, if she isn't happy with my answer. Maybe they'll just drag me to the center of the fucking earth. "I don't even know what I'm doing anymore."

"Fifteen."

"Fuck's sake, you don't mess around do you?"

She smiles, as if I've said something particularly funny. "Fourteen."

Task. What task?

That academy legend Jel mentioned said something about the gods...

"You want us to stop this killer?" I ask slowly.

She rolls her eyes. "Thirteen."

Okay, not good enough, I take it. "Well, what am I meant to do?" I snap. "Fate's fucking with me, and I don't know who to trust anymore. I don't know what I'm *doing* anymore."

Her eyes flash. "I have sent you so many clues and *still* you assume I'm playing tricks?" She takes a deep breath. "Twelve."

She—oh. Oh, fuck.

Fate raises one eyebrow. "Eleven."

"Alright, alright," I try to hold up my hands in placation, but the chains won't let me. They pull me an inch further into the muck at my feet. "You're not fucking with me."

"Ten," she says through gritted teeth.

If this isn't a game... If I'm speaking to Fate right now, then the task she's talking about is our mate bond. She thinks I'm screwing up the bond.

"This bond is already screwed up," I snarl. "Her family killed mine. How the hell is she my fated mate?"

"Nine—you know I really thought you were smarter than this." She narrows her eyes. "Think about what you asked for."

What I asked for? When have I asked Fate for anything? I never wanted a mate, I only ever wanted—

Unless...

She isn't talking about what I asked for in a mate. She's talking about what I asked the gods for every day since my family died. A new life.

"This isn't a new life," I tell her flatly.

"You're in single digits, I may point out. Eight."

I grunt, closing my eyes, forcing my irritated brain into overdrive. It's impossible. All my agony has been stirred up at the front of my mind for days now. Set off by the reappearance of that killer. I can't think past it, can't see past the swirling mess.

All I wanted was a new life, and this isn't it. I wanted peace. I wanted—

Oh.

"I didn't ask for a new life. I asked for a new home."

Home is never a place. It's always people.

She pauses, lips parted to announce another number. Very slowly, her mouth curls, eyes shining brightly. "Very good, Luc."

This is the home Fate picked for me? These three?

As if in answer, my soul rears up. The golden claws that never quite sheathed since Jel revealed herself to us break free, tearing through skin so violently that droplets of my own blood decorate them.

He has no issue with a mate like this, a pack like this. Violence, sex—it's all heat and fire to him.

I start to laugh.

We're hours at most from a rut, and we left it way, way too long. Any chance we had of this working has probably been lost; each of us is now bordering on unhinged.

I think I've completely tipped over.

"Don't be so pessimistic," Fate says. She leans back in her chair, smiling to herself. I think the wall writhes behind her, and I refuse to look close enough to be certain. "Unleash the beast, Luc. Give your soul what it wants."

"My soul doesn't know what it wants," I snarl, bloodlust surging in me. Do I want to fuck Jel or do I want to kill her?

There's far too thin a line between violence and passion when it comes to the rut, and with four alphas, and one whose hands are soaked in my family's blood...

I just don't know which path my soul will choose. The fire or the blood.

"Sometimes," Fate murmurs, smiling, "the future is not yet written. And you just have to accept that." She picks a piece of dirt from under her nail and sighs, almost with relief. "It's been interesting meeting you, but your fifteen seconds are up."

Then she shoves me, her boot connecting painfully with my sternum as her smile fades. Her parting words echo after me, long after her face has vanished.

"My gifts are not set in stone. The future is not written, but that doesn't mean you don't know what you want."

I fall and I fall and I fall.

Until I'm back on the surface.

I wait for the feeling she's awoken in me to fade, but it doesn't. It builds.

My hands clench into the earth beneath me, claws puncturing the dry, cracked ground with more than an edge of violence. With my soul clawing free like this, I can taste the old blood on the wind. Their deaths here were not gentle. They were not earned.

There are too many secrets here.

As if from a distance, I hear the sound of the mower stop. I have to leave. I can't speak to this man or I'll tear him apart.

I need to get to Jel.

I need her.

I need to tear her apart for what she did to us.

No.

"You gonna be alright there, son?" the gardener calls out, still walking toward me.

"Stop moving," I grit out.

He sees my face for the first time and freezes. His expression grows slack, his skin suddenly pasty white.

I've no idea what I look like, but I can feel the scales rippling over my cheeks, and the world is still covered in burnished gold, so my eyes must be glowing.

My claws won't retract.

There's a hunger in me I can't feed. Not here. Not with this man.

"Stay back!" he calls, voice quavering as he stumbles backward. "Don't come any closer."

I can't help it—I laugh. As if this idiot would have any control over whether or not I leave him alone. For a moment, I consider showing him that sorry truth.

But then I catch the scent of something glorious. Something rich and bright. It makes my soul sing and the dragon in me keen with delight.

It's gold, pure gold.

There are three of them.

Not just my pack—my mates. All of them.

Lifting my head to the wind, I breathe in the scent. North.

Shifting without a thought to who sees me, I take to the sky, following the threads of my destiny to the fate I've been rejecting.

It's time to go home.

29

JEL

My apartment is eerily quiet when we arrive, like the whole building is waiting for us. It wouldn't surprise me if there was something supernatural in the air, given Fate and her meddling fingers.

She's wanted this for days, now.

If I'm honest, so have I.

But first, I want to unwind. I feel like I could sleep for a hundred years, after today. My body is burning with so much energy and adrenaline, I think the slightest touch might make me explode, and not in a good way.

"What were you tapping about on your phone on the way up here?" I ask Theo as I drop my phone and keys on the counter. "You looked way too smug. I thought tonight was about calming down."

"Go and get changed," Theo orders me gently, ignoring my question and still looking way too damn smug. "Something comfortable. Give me about fifteen minutes."

Anticipation shivers down my spine. What is he planning?

The only space to get changed without an audience is the tiny little bathroom off the side of my apartment. It's more like an overly large toilet than a bathroom, but it's not like that matters. What am I going to do with all that extra space anyway? Take a bath?

Baths are for rich people. People who can afford the luxury of pampering themselves—or who are loved enough to have someone do it for them. I'm not that kind of girl. Just like final girls are the good girls who never give their family shit or know the exact vein to rupture for a quick death.

At least I'll make this psycho pay before I go down. I'm promising him that much.

Sighing, I grab my thin cotton pajama set and escape into my overly large toilet to change. Theo's right. I need to take the night off and get comfortable, whatever that means.

I peel off my shirt and jeans, taking my time, slipping into the delicious softness of my hot pink loveheart pajamas. It clashes horribly with my hair—bright red curls sproinging free of their bun—and I kind of love that. I lean closer to the mirror, smoothing a few curls down and then letting the rest do their wild, frizzy thing. I practice smiling in the mirror, searching for a sign of the girl I know is hidden deep down beneath the bull-shit. Beneath the anger.

The smile looks predatory, so I stop. I guess I'm too angry to find her just yet.

It's probably for the best. I've got a killer to hunt. And before that, I need to fill my mates in on everything I've lied to them about so far.

I straighten my shoulders, push open the door, and—

Stop.

Theo leans back against my kitchen counter, arms folded and a smug twitch of one eyebrow as he regards me. Despite the arrogance, there's an air of hesitation about him—something that ripples down the bond with soft little tweaks. Jace perches beside him, elbows propped on his knees, a hopeful grin on his face.

In the center of my living room is a giant, claw-foot bath tub. It's filled three quarters of the way with steaming water, and I can smell the luxurious oils from here—lavender and something sweeter. Maybe rose.

"What are you—" The words die in my throat with an embarrassing choke.

Theo glances down at my novelty slippers, eyebrows lifting. "Never thought I'd find chicken feet sexy," he deadpans.

The hesitation in the bond spikes, acrid, but when a tear escapes my eye it vanishes. Theo crosses the room and lifts my chin with one finger.

"You need to relax," he says softly. "And I had a friend who owed me a favor. We return the tub next week. Until then, it's yours. And I give a damn good massage."

"This isn't how it's meant to go," I choke out. I don't explain myself any more than that, but he gets it.

I mean this, all of it. The fact that they're still here after what they learned today. The easy smiles on their faces. Alphas can prepare baths for their omegas, doting on them during the heat or at other times when their protective urges ride high. Or, an omega might wash their alpha as a mark of submission—a prelude to what comes next, in the bedroom.

What Theo is offering doesn't make sense. Alphas don't do this for other alphas. If my father could see us right now, he'd challenge Theo and fight until he was bleeding out on my carpet.

All of this is wrong.

The tub.

The gesture.

The casual submission of alpha to alpha.

The bond that pulls all three of us closer—and stretches

somewhere in the distance, to the fourth one of us who should never have been allowed to bond with me at all.

"We're all in new territory," Theo agrees. "So we're working it out as we go." He shrugs, backing away slowly, drawing me along with my hand clasped in his. When we reach the bath, he trails our fingers through the water. It's pure bliss. "I've never seen anything that said we can't take it in turns."

"Turns," I repeat vaguely, half bewitched by the steaming water in front of me. "Like... You're the beta today, and I am tomorrow?"

Theo chuckles. It's a low, dark sound that snaps me out of my musing. My head whips up, and his sharp gaze holds me captive. "I'm not a beta, Jel," he promises, his rich voice sending shivers down my spine. "And neither are you. What I mean is... tonight, you need us. And when we need you, I know you'll be there, too."

The words sink in somewhere deep inside me, to a place I've never accessed. Warmth spreads through my body, making my toes curl and laughter bubble up in my chest.

He's right. It could be this simple. Alphas go where we're needed—we protect. And now, I need protection. Not from the enemy; I can hold my own there just fine. No, I need protection from the darkness that haunts me. From the quiet urges that tell me to bleed something dry. It doesn't matter what, so long as there's blood. Something, anything.

Even me.

Slowly, deliberately, I unbutton the front of my pajamas. Their eyes follow my movement, soft with affection at first.

The affection shatters as soon as the fabric slides free.

With hungry eyes, they watch me strip and slide into the water. And then, like a signal's been flipped, they pounce.

Jace prowls to the front of the tub, reaching in to draw my foot free—never once taking his eyes from mine.

But it's a dangerous game, a distraction that Theo takes advantage of, moving behind me to sweep my hair from my shoulders and slowly dig his thumbs into the hard, tense muscle.

They're moving on instinct. The competition they've fought for so long vanishes as a new game emerges: one where they hunt together.

For the first time in my life, I think I might like being prey. Especially because I've been promised the same in return.

Maybe all these complicated alpha rituals are bullshit, and it just comes down to us. Our styles. Our choices. Maybe it's all bullshit.

I let my eyes fall closed, deliberately taunting my mates as if they aren't worth my wariness. A low growl comes in response, and my own hiss sounds far too much like pleasure.

"Where's that massage you promised me?" I ask, still with my eyes closed.

My voice comes out steady. Somehow, I'm still holding it together, even though the effort of that control is starting to feel like razorblades slicing through me.

The air between us burns, thick with desire. When Jace's fingers gently wrap around the arch of my foot, squeezing softly, his touch is like fire.

But then Theo's hands soften, the massage no longer digging into the painful knots of my shoulders but instead just... resting there.

Something in me shatters.

It's like back at the boathouse; my breathing turns ragged and strange. I can barely drag it in, and each exhale becomes harder and harder to push free, like there's nothing there. Theo's hands press against my collarbone. At least I can remember who he is this time, but it doesn't help me because I can't bear this feeling. What is it? What the hell is going on?

"Ssh, Jel. You can fall apart here."

I squeeze my eyes tightly shut, so I can't feel the tears slip free, but soft thumbs wipe them away. I shouldn't be like this. I've never wanted my alpha soul, but goddammit I don't want this either. I'm not meant to *be* this.

It's unnatural.

Someone's hands are on my thigh, and I force my eyes open so I can at least see who it is. Jace watches me, his eyes bright with emotion.

"I'm not meant to fall apart." I choke the words out through gritted teeth, tears blurring my eyesight. "I'm the Viper's Alpha."

Something flickers in his expression, but he doesn't argue. He just says, "I know, sweetheart."

"No, you don't," I spit out, the words becoming a hiss. "Or, you didn't until like five seconds ago, and now we're just ignoring it? My family killed Luc's! Why am I sitting here having a fucking bubble bath?"

I can't even name the number of lives I've taken at my father's direction. But their faces haunt me, and if I remember who I am then I have to remember them, too. If I fall apart, those memories are what I'm falling into.

Jace lifts his eyes to Theo's above my head, and they share a look. Then, before I can stop him, Theo plants a hand on the top of my head and dunks me below the water.

He only pushes for a second, but it's enough to send me sprawled beneath the soapy bubbles, water hacking through my throat. I rise coughing and spluttering, rage turning my vision red.

"What the fuck do you think you're doing?" I hiss, swiveling in the bathtub until I can glare at Theo properly.

The fierce light glancing off his jaw tells me my eyes are glowing.

And the answering glow, coupled with the darkening pupils and the parted lips tell me something else.

Seeing me like this turns him on.

Heat pulses between my thighs. It's sharp, aching, and full of need. I need him so badly. My claws rip free, digging into the metal of the tub, screeching.

Theo stops me with one hand in the air. He actually stops me. Something in my soul recognizes him, and the moment of confusion lets me walk back from the edge, just a little.

"You *were* falling apart," Theo says slowly, deliberately. "And then you were angry."

Jace leans over my shoulder, dangerously close to my teeth, and clearly loving it judging by his scent. "And now you're horny."

"Fuck you."

"Only if you're a good girl."

My mouth falls open in shock. Even when people think I'm a beta, they don't dare talk to me like this. Who does he think he is?

My mate grins at me, sun-bleached brown hair falling over his forehead in a sudsy, sweaty sweep. He tosses it back with one hand. "Jel, falling apart isn't forever. And you've got a bit further to go before you can release it all. You don't have to do it all at once."

"Release," I repeat, ignoring the flash of heat in his eyes, and the soft grunt from Theo. It's damn distracting.

"I've been thinking," Jace murmurs, lips brushing my shoulder. "When exactly *is* an alpha meant to let go?"

"Never."

"Mmm," Jace answers. His tongue swipes up my ear, making me shudder. "We can't show weakness to betas or omegas. And even with our mate, there's a limit. They need to know we can still protect them." He lifts a finger to my chin and turns my head until I'm facing him. "Doesn't that seem fucking stupid to you?"

All of a sudden, it does.

My father thinks it's a sign of strength to remain stoic in the face of anything. My mother always admired his fierceness, his aggression.

But this is between me and my mates. My family has no place here.

Holding eye contact without blinking, I nod and very slowly begin to sink back in the tub. I'm facing the other way this time, and when Theo's hands reach for my foot, I place it, dripping, on the edge.

"So, what do I do?" I ask flatly. "I'm not going to sit here and cry for an hour."

Theo shrugs. "You could though."

"Well I'm not."

Jace brushes my hair free and places another kiss on my shoulder. "Just... let go."

I close my eyes, sinking back into his touch as his kisses turn hungrier. More dangerous—teeth scraping over skin.

Theo lifts my foot to his mouth and licks over the arch. I suck in a breath—I've never screwed anyone with a foot fetish before, and I'm coming to the horrifying realization that the person with the fetish might just be me—and fall deeper into the water.

He sucks my toe into his mouth, pulling free ever so slowly.

"Theo," I say warningly.

"Let go," he interrupts me.

I'm sick of fighting. The thought hits me like a truck, and I somehow find the strength to do exactly what he's telling me to do. Tears leak at the corner of my eyes, even as Theo's mouth travels higher up my calf, wet kisses mingling with soap and lavender oil. I must taste overwhelming.

I want to taste him, too.

The strange relief of crying mixes with the heavy weight of my relaxed muscles, and, as if they're a doorway to another world, desire breaks through. Suddenly, I'm so fucking horny I can't think. My chest still aches with overwhelming emotion—fear, rage, guilt—but I want these two more than I can imagine.

Someone chuckles.

A hand slides into the water, pauses for a moment at my stomach, and then slips between my thighs.

"Yes, please," I whisper, my head falling back against the metal of the tub as Theo's fingers slide over my clit.

Pleasure consumes me, my body so sensitized from their dual touch that my nerve endings are already crying out for more. It's ecstasy. His touch is everything I've waited for, and I know we've done this before, but it was nothing like this.

Their touch before was a tease. A game.

Playtime is over.

My claws grind into the rim of the bath, and I hope Theo's friend isn't aesthetically motivated because I think I might be handing this tub back a little worse for wear.

The rumbling growl from one of my mates answers my unspoken question; they're as gone as I am.

The fingers sliding between my slick folds take on a sharper edge. I feel Theo's claws raking, feather-light, across my skin. My eyes flutter open, and I watch through heavy lids as he strokes me.

His own face is shadowed, pupils blown wide as he watches me. My clit aches with pleasure, my hips gliding upward to rub against him without my conscious thought.

"My rut is coming," I tell them in a voice that sounds nothing like my own.

"Let it," Theo answers.

He's barely recognizable, too.

The hands that caress my shoulders slide up to my neck, Jace's claws pricking my skin as he tips my head back and kisses me.

"Why hold back?" he says against my mouth, kissing me again before I can answer. "Luc will be here soon."

His other hand drops below my breast, sharp with those golden claws, and I know we're coming up to the point of no return.

"Because we're three alphas, and alphas kill each other in the rut, especially when one is missing," I point out, my words oddly languid given the subject. A warm hiss starts up in my chest, almost like a purr.

I've never felt that before.

"You think you can take me?" Jace asks with a smile.

Theo slips two fingers inside me and I gasp, falling back against Jace's chest.

At some point in the last twenty minutes, he's removed his shirt. I turn my head so my cheek slides against his sweat-slick skin. He's so hot to the touch.

Theo moves them deeper, his fingers angled so his claws are mostly retracted. There's only the barest hint of anything sharp, a reminder but nothing more.

"I know I could take you, Wolf Boy," I hiss, and he bites me.

His teeth sink into my shoulder, a snarl tearing free from his throat. I bite down a scream, while the rich scent of blood wafts in the air. He's barely broken the surface, but it's enough to mark me. To claim me.

Alphas don't get claimed; we claim.

"You'll pay for that," I moan as Theo twists his fingers over that perfect spot, his thumb sliding over my clit as he adjusts the angle.

"Not before you come for us," Theo points out, grinning. "Which means first point goes to us."

"Your scoreboard means nothing if I tear your throat out."

He growls in response, his eyes flashing golden. At that same moment, his fingers stroke me in just the right way, and my head falls back again. I cry out, my moans swallowed as Jace kisses me, my own blood on his lips and my orgasm tearing through me until my whole body shudders from it.

"Good girl," Theo tells me before it's even over, so unbearably smug as he delivers the line like the insult it is.

"I'll have you on your knees," I promise him, but I can barely get the words out through the desperate need raging through me.

I've never had a rut like this. I've never known it could *be* like this.

I need to regain some sense of control. We can't start what we can't finish, and without Luc... Someone will die.

Even with him, someone might die, but I like our odds better. If Fate is so determined for this to play through, she must have a plan. There are easier ways to kill me if that was all she wanted.

"Breathe," I say out loud, and I'm not sure if I'm telling them or myself.

It isn't enough. I can't back down from this edge—I can feel the rut taking over me.

God, I don't think I can hold it any longer. Why is my soul fighting me on this? We shouldn't be able to go through with a mate's first rut when all of the mates aren't present.

Oh.

A slow grin curls onto my face, mirrored in the feral smiles of my two men. Luc is near. He's coming back to us.

To fuck or to fight, I'm not sure, and my alpha soul doesn't care.

Either way, she gets what she wants.

She's finally getting what she wants.

30
LUC

THE THREADS OF MY SANITY ARE BARELY HOLDING ON WHEN I ARRIVE AT her apartment. It's dark, the light of the moon guiding me as I force my way through her building entrance and up the stairs.

I'll fix the hinges tomorrow.

For now... my pulse races, my breath forced into a slow exhale that does nothing to soothe me. I'm beyond soothing.

Fate told me that just because the future is unwritten, it doesn't mean I don't know what I want. I thought she was trying to encourage me. To tell me that there is never any certainty when it comes to the rut. When another alpha interferes with a mate, it's a fight to the death. It always has been. And there are four of us.

I thought Fate was telling me that my desires will override the risk, and I need to trust that I want to protect Jel more than I want to attack.

Now, I'm not so sure she was saying that at all.

I know what I want. I want to consummate the bond between my pack, my mates. I want the rut to finally burn the edges off everything that has been building between us. To take the fire of our impossible connection and bind what can never be tamed.

I also want to destroy the person who killed my family. The human side of me knows that wasn't Jel. Of course it wasn't her.

The rest of my soul doesn't care.

She was there, she witnessed the destruction. She pointed the way.

And our souls demand blood for blood.

It's the crux of our shifter nature: ritual upon ritual, upholding the fae magic that possesses us. The ritual of the rut was already a problem, but now we're also dealing with vengeance.

The future is unwritten.

I prowl the darkened corridor outside her apartment. Somehow, I can almost feel the terrifying presence of Fate at my back, although after actually meeting her, I would have thought she'd have better things to do.

Before I can change my mind—or acknowledge the faint sound of feminine laughter that definitely comes from the end of the corridor—I knock on the door.

Movement sounds from behind the wood, and I stiffen as my senses come alive. I smell... lavender... rose. Bathtub oils.

Theo. Jace.

A snarl drops from my lips, and two of the doors behind me audibly snib their deadlocks.

"Come out, Jel," I murmur, listening to the hitch of her breath from the other side of the door. "We need to talk."

"Talking is the last thing we'll do," she replies, and the sheer heat in her words stokes the embers within me to a roaring flame.

I breathe in again, overpowered by the rich scent of clean

skin. She's naked behind the door—maybe a towel. I think I smell linen.

"Then we need to fuck," I snarl, the words pitched low. "Whatever we do, we need this. Can't you feel it?"

She laughs, the sound edged with violence. "Just making sure you were ready for it."

The door opens, and I take a breath just to drink it all in.

They're all here. My mates. My pack. The light is dim, illuminating little more than a sphere of orange around the bedside lamp. I barely notice it, my eyes drawn, instead, to the giant metal tub in the center of the room.

I assess it approvingly. I believe two people could fit in that with ease, so long as they were willing to share a lap.

Heat curls through me, and Jel's eyes fall to the growing ridge at the front of my jeans.

My claws scrape into the architrave, scouring the wood, as I pull my weight inside the door. "I hope you didn't pay a big deposit on this place," I murmur, watching the pounding skin above her heart as she glances at my clenched fist.

She doesn't speak for a moment, her pupils darkening as she wets her lips. Finally, she lifts her gaze back to me. "You talk a big game," she says in a voice so casual I want to rip that towel off her and force her to her knees, just so she'll admit what this is. What we're playing with. "But you're late."

I grin, take another step inside the apartment, and slam the door.

The sound echoes through the tiny space, rattling the windows.

As if prompted by the sound, Jel shifts only her face, becoming something fae and strange as the scales ripple over her cheeks and her eyes light up like the moon.

This is the rut, but it's a rut unlike any I've experienced before. There are no words exchanged, no healing brews drunk to ensure the alpha doesn't accidentally harm the omega in a moment of aggression. There is no exchange of ritual at all, because this ritual is far beyond any we've been prepared for.

I'm so close to the edge now, I can barely remember my own name.

"This is our last chance to speak, human to human," I tell her—tell them all. "What our souls have started... it ends tonight, one way or another." Fight or fuck. Destroy or... consummate. "And even Fate doesn't know how it will go."

Their only answer is a low growl, picked up one by one until it echoes from every corner of the room.

I smile. Good.

Then Jace attacks, lunging between me and the mate he's chosen, for now, to defend. He nearly gets my throat. Fire ignites within me, instincts I've long kept hidden tearing free.

I thought I'd never have to return to being that boy again, but Fate had other ideas. One more time before it all comes crashing down, it seems.

Ducking into a low roll, I come up behind Theo and wrap my claws around his neck.

"Move and I rip it out," I tell them in a voice I hardly recognize.

Theo stiffens beneath me, and I can smell the uncertainty in the air. It drips, thick and odorous, into the room. They don't know whether I'll do it.

It's insulting.

I dig one claw into his skin, smoke curling from my nostrils as a bead of blood drops free. Theo winces, and I dig in a second claw, then a third.

Jace takes a wary step backward.

Jel doesn't move.

Snarling, I shift just a couple of teeth, my jaw. Bones pop and reform in agony with this partial shift—the forms too large for my human body. My reflection in the glass is monstrous, and I tip my head, adjusting to the pain, ready to bite—

She strikes.

The speed and strength behind it floor me, sending me crashing into the kitchen counter and over, onto the tiles behind it. She's already disappeared by the time I land.

I barely know her name. All I know is she took something from me, and these two men are defending her.

I'm in enemy territory, although the scents are strange.

My scent is here.

I shake my head, clearing it as I rise to my feet slowly. I shift my bones back but twist my hands into proper claws. The air still tastes strange. There are too many unexpected scents.

My mate.

But instinct tells me to kill.

She watches me. I dig my claws into my own palms to try to remember her name. If I can remember her name, I can keep something with me in this rut. I can turn the edge of violence into something better.

Skin on skin, bodies writhing. My mate screaming my name.

All our names.

She lunges again, but something is off. I see a weakness; she's too slow on her left side. Her non-dominant hand.

An alpha shouldn't show weakness.

A low, grinding rasp drops from my throat. I step to the side; she mirrors me.

Her breathing isn't right. It's no longer the steady, focused breathing of a predator. She's drawing breath in ragged pants. Sharp and shallow, like she's wounded. Instead of using the opening to my advantage, I'm annoyed.

No; I'm furious.

"You're still holding back," the tall one with the spiked hair snarls at her, and it sounds deranged. Unhinged.

His scent is confused—he's no longer on her side completely.

Our souls can sense something is wrong, and we don't wait around to assess potential threats at the last minute. We eliminate them.

Her scent is a threat.

She flicks a glance to the side of the room. Assesses. Changes her mind.

"The painting," she grits out, pointing to the canvas-covered painting off to the side of the room. It's closest to me. She would have to step into my strike zone to reach it. "One end of the magic is still tethered. Slice the cord—but don't destroy it."

The painting.

Desire burns like fire through me, and just for a moment this fight shifts into what it's meant to be. I remember us. Jel's scent consumes me, arouses me, and the overwhelming addition of two strong male scents only sends me higher.

I flick my hair out of my face and take a step toward the painting.

I want to destroy it. Even knowing it's of us, and the thing that drew us together, I want to destroy it because it's destroying a piece of my mate. With my sight open, I can finally understand how she's using this painting.

The venom alters her scent. It's hypnotic, like snake venom has the tendency to be, controlling how people think and what they see. So with a little magic to connect her to the venom in the paint, her alpha soul becomes linked to the canvas. It rests away from her, creating distance, while the link then alters what people see when she's standing in front of them.

Anyone who looks at her smells a watered down version of her. A beta. Someone less than who she is meant to be.

But she put too much of her soul into it. She's destroyed the end of the cord inside her, but she's left a piece of her inside the painting, and it's crying out, vibrating with need.

What her soul needs is us.

This painting is crying out to us, even as it locks away the most core part of her being. Binding her. Containing her.

With deliberate, careful intent, I hold onto the last shreds of my humanity and do only as she asks. With my shifted sight, I can see the layers to this world that humans can't. There—magic. An anchor of power connecting her to the god-imbued treasure she created.

I reach out a single claw to the air between the painting and Jel, and slice through the cord binding my mate from me, freeing the last of her soul and sending it home.

It combusts, blackened smoke bursting from the air, and the room is suddenly filled with the scent of alpha. My alpha.

Mate, prey, and enemy all in one.

My humanity shatters.

"We have a score to settle," I tell her, shifting my sight back as I face her. I want to see her in this world, without magic to distract me.

Someone howls, and the part of my mind that remembers names and faces doesn't bother to emerge. I don't need it; I have instinct to guide me.

My mates are here, and this dance ends now.

A figure darts in my path, furred and low-slunk to the ground. Wolf. His chestnut fur shines in the light of the moon, and my soul tugs me forward to him.

A flash of orange distracts me.

Then I'm flying, my shoulder bursting with agony as glass rains down around us.

Cold wind hits my head. My face. I'm hanging half out of the window, broken glass still falling down as Jel's scaled, fanged face hovers above me.

She pins me easily, an unexpected strength filling her. When I duck to break free, she follows, whiplash fast, and pins me again.

How many times have I imagined fighting a viper? In my nightmares, I've taken them down over and over. I've ripped their fangs from their mouths, torn them in two, and even when they shifted back to human they were no match for me.

This viper fights like nothing I've seen.

She fights like she doesn't have to think about killing; she's done it too many times.

How many times *has* she killed? My mind shoves a name at me—Marcus. Father. Patriarch.

Under his reign, it has to be too many. Far too many.

"You're all the same," she hisses at me, eyes wild as she grips my throat and holds me in the rain. "You'll kill anything that isn't yours." Her voice chokes with fury—and something deeper. "And you'll kill that too."

She's right. I will.

There's nothing left. I can't sense anything except pain. Longing. She took my family from me, and there's a price for that, no matter who she is.

I'm going to kill her.

My arm is pinned beneath me, but I can just free my other. I close my fingers around a shard of glass, gripping until it slices me and blood drips free.

But then Jel vanishes, her shriek of rage cut off as enormous teeth sink into my shoulder and throw me into the room, like a cat playing with a mouse.

The tiger stalks closer, flanked by a wolf. My eyes dart

between them, assessing. If I'm not mistaken, the tiger defers to the wolf.

Confusion sweeps through me, muddling my instincts. No one defers to anyone in the rut.

I growl, opening my mouth to breathe a little warning fire. The tiger pauses, ears tilting toward the wolf.

A spark of shock flickers in me. I wasn't wrong, the tiger isn't operating alone.

But it isn't deference. Not quite.

They're working together.

"How the fuck are you doing that?" I grit out.

The tiger only snarls, a low, gritty rumble between his teeth.

They stare me down, circling step by step to widen their net around me. The animal in me—all of me, by this point—lashes out, frantic, hunting for a way to take them both down. But the human side of my mind has returned, clawing its way from wherever it goes dormant during the rut.

Analyzing. Questioning.

Their movement is unnatural; it suggests a way to move beyond the rut while still being in it.

The impossibility of it breaks the final barrier to the human in me. My sight shifts once more, this time while I'm looking at my mates.

The blackened flame that marks our shifter souls burns, stretching toward the sky as the rut calls our vitalities to their peak, and I *see* them.

Our souls.

And their chains.

The tiger's soul is taller than I imagined, dwarfing the wolf beside it. But they both fill the room, ridiculously high, easily three times the size of the true animal. From their wrists swing broken chains, like dark shadows.

The chains around Jel's wrists and mine are locked tight.

I shift my sight back. "You're completely in the rut," I murmur, backing up to the wall. "But you aren't lost to it. How?"

Already, I can feel my own will to remain present fading once again. I'm losing the very thing I'm accusing them of keeping.

The wolf throws his head back and howls. Unfettered. Free.

At ease with his own desires.

In an instant, the answer hits me. My humanity isn't meant to temper the beast, just as the beast isn't meant to control the human.

It's meant to be a partnership.

How long ago did we lock the gods' gifts in chains for fear of what they would do? Petty little men, we couldn't handle the power we'd been given, and so we twisted it. Ruined it.

We kept our beasts in cages and expected them to play nicely when we let them out.

A slow, menacing sound alerts me seconds before I go flying. I land among the glass, a hoarse shout of rage escaping me as I twist for position. On the other side of the room, I see the wolf go down, and then the tiger, knocked flying by a force so fast and strong they never stood a chance. They don't get up.

The rut ensnares me again, but it's different this time.

I don't disappear within it, and together, my beast and I face our mate. I realize with a distant sort of certainty what's about to happen if I can't convince her to stop.

She's going to kill me.

And rather than hurt her instead, I'm going to let her do it.

Rain hits my face, tearing through the broken window and soaking me. I should be cold, chilled to the bone, but the water rises off me as steam. Smoke from my nostrils curls through it, obscuring our faces as my skull grinds back into the broken glass beneath me.

Violence and passion live in equal measure within our souls, but the key to surviving their turmoil was missing until now. Until I discovered those chains and saw them for what they were.

The key is in the shift.

Knowing when to give and when to take. Otherwise, you're nothing more than the worst of humanity. No better than the vipers who took my family from me on the flimsiest of excuses —pride, anger, and ego. Justifying their violence in the name of love.

That isn't love. That's an excuse to do whatever the hell you want.

Love is fluid—a constantly changing mess of needs and desires and intent. It's a call and an answer. The chaos of finding a home in a place you would never have looked. And right here, in this moment, love isn't violence; it's surrender.

I fall back, body sinking into the thick rug, my eyes fixed to her face. If she's going to kill me, I want to see it happen. I want to see all that energy lit up like a lighthouse, guiding me home, as she finally stops hiding her soul from the world.

"Jel," I murmur, wetting my lips, trying to make her see me, not whatever it is she's really fighting. Whatever she's turned me into—just like I'd turned her into the source for all my pain. The only viper I could fight. "Look at me."

She looks, and there's a flicker of something there. But there's too much of the rest. Her chains are too strong—too tied to her humanity and misguided attempts to temper one with the other.

Her fangs extend.

A drop of venom slides into my open mouth, and a dazed sort of fog descends over me immediately. It reminds me of the fire in the warehouse, although this feels different. More raw. More enticing, like I've fallen into a cage, but the bait was so intoxicating I'd do it again willingly for just one more taste. It doesn't hypnotize me, because I'm an alpha, but it does soften me for the few seconds she needs.

Our eyes lock together, shifter gold on blue, and I wait patiently for death.

Two shapes barrel into her, knocking her from me, holding her down. The venom in my bloodstream fades, and I leap to my feet, head spinning. She rages, cries. When she shifts, she nearly breaks free, her fangs lunging for me again and again. But then the tiger rumbles, a low almost inaudible sound.

He shifts back, naked, vulnerable.

The wolf shifts, too.

Theo and Jace hold her, backs pressed against the windows, chests heaving. She lunges for them, fangs dripping, but pauses at the last second.

She sees them. Sees them for all that they are—all that they're choosing in this moment.

They wait, staring her down, throats far too exposed.

Her eyes flicker, and it isn't just her soul I'm seeing there. It's all of her, as well. It's her humanity, rearing up and standing side by side with the shapeshifter that lives inside her.

For a moment, they're equal.

She shifts back.

Naked, she falls against their legs and exhales.

"Shit," Jel breathes.

I drop my head back down and close my eyes.

"Jel, I forgive you," I say, speaking into the darkness.

I feel her stiffen, even from the other side of the room. I keep going, knowing this needs to be said, or we'll just end up back here one day.

I open my eyes. "Think about it. Do you really think the vipers let a ten-year-old girl lead them? Stop. Picture it."

She does. A frown creases her forehead, and she chews on

her lip. I can almost see the scene playing out in front of her—a child, barely stepped into her shifter caste, and more than thirty grown shifters. Alphas among them.

She might have been told she had power over them, but she had nothing. They killed because they wanted to.

"But I wanted it," she protests. "I wanted them all to hurt each other. Vipers and dragons alike. I was just so angry." Her voice trails off, almost broken.

I almost smile, looking around at her trashed apartment. "I bet you did. Seconds ago, we all wanted that in here, too. Jel, this is the price and responsibility of having an alpha soul. We want these things in certain situations. We crave them."

I think of our chains, our beasts. How we've gone about this wrong for centuries, fighting the instincts of creatures that should be our partners. Our pack.

We blame the beasts when it goes wrong, but Marcus Vario isn't a monster because of his shifter vitalities or his caste. He's a monster because that's who he is.

And his daughter has spent years running from him; I'm not about to join the chase.

I reach for her, resting my palm on her thigh when she pulls away. "We crave these things, but it doesn't mean we take them. Instinctively, we know when one side of the coin is needed and when it isn't. Your guilt tells the truth of who you are, not your anger.

"You aren't the kind of alpha who says the end justifies the means. Look at how you wouldn't let us shake Cameron over for that trap at the warehouse. You value justice and loyalty, and you put your values first. Always.

"Ten-year-olds don't understand violence, not like adults do. They were the adults, Jel, not you. Don't forget the guilt—it makes you who you are. But stop carrying the shame they're never going to feel."

Her eyes grow wide, her lips parting as she stares at me. I feel something shift in my chest; a cord strengthening. Solidifying.

Our bond is whole.

"I saw our souls tonight," she says hesitantly. "They were standing together. Side by side."

My mouth breaks into a smile. "That's how they should be."

The room spins, wind howling through the broken glass. We'll have the cops knocking tomorrow, I'm sure. But this apartment block is full of shifters. They know this is a rut, and so no one will interfere.

We have tonight at least. Which is a blessing, because the rut isn't over.

And now, without my worst aspects driving me, without my fear chaining and distressing the beast that shares my soul, I can truly enjoy it.

I clench my hands, golden claws driving into the carpet. A hum of heat flickers within me, guiding me. It was easy to ignore the hard heat between my thighs before. It's harder now, especially with Jace and Theo on display.

Their bodies burn hot, their skin covered in a thin sheen of sweat.

I turn back to Jel, and find her already waiting.

31
JEL

THE HEAT IN LUC'S EYES SENDS A SHIVER RACING THROUGH ME. There's an ache between my legs I'm only just noticing, but it isn't new. I can still feel the ghost of Theo's fingers inside me. Even through the fighting, I could feel him, feel them—the phantom touch spurring me higher and honing my instincts into sharper violence.

Violence that almost went too far.

I want to be hand in hand with my beast, like Luc says we should be. I want to believe the rut isn't dangerous, and we know how to flip the coin to the side of the fire that's needed. But I don't know how I can trust that when the price of failure is so high.

I reach behind me and pull the thin cover off the bed, draping it over myself. I'm too exposed like this, with the rut's fire turning into the kind of desire I can't escape.

I'm scared to touch Luc, after what I nearly did. And he knows it. I can feel it.

I can feel everything from my mates. The swimming, disconnected, painful ache of the half-rejected bond has gone.

In its place is... so much. Just so much. Emotion, need; whispers of thought. I don't know what to do with it all.

Luc's expression softens, even though the heat remains. Then, unexpectedly, he turns to Jace. A slow smile creeps onto his face as he takes in Jace's body. Sweat-soaked skin. Cocky grin as he leans back on one elbow, completely naked. A silent conversation passes between them, and then Jace turns to me.

"Should we show her what she's missing out on?" Jace asks.

His voice doesn't sound quite right. It's too full, too echoing. Kind of deeper.

I blink, startled as it hits me. It's deeper because there are two of them. Jace's voice, and... his soul's.

Both here.

I've always known the rut as a ritual where the beast has to be tamed at all costs. Where we have to hide away, locked in a single room, with every effort put toward damage control.

This is something completely different. Nothing is tame here, and it certainly isn't locked away.

It doesn't need to be.

Luc peels off his shirt with one hand and throws it at me. It's damp with sweat and blood, completely ruined. Holding his gaze, I bring it to my nose and inhale, eyelids fluttering unwillingly closed at the rich scents, before I throw it behind me.

When I open them again, his gaze is hungry, and Jace and Theo have already moved in closer, crowding him back toward the bathtub that somehow survived our foreplay.

The water must be ice-cold by now, but Luc turns and breathes a thin stream of fire into the water, and the steam soon returns.

"Come here," Luc says to me, his eyes blazing with heat and power all in one.

His soul is almost visible, the dancing shadow of a dragon

flickering in and out of sight. I blink, but it's still there; has his own shifter ability affected me through the bond?

I flick my gaze to Theo, to Jace—their souls rise, too. Unbound.

We never cast the ritual circles for the rut.

Oops.

"No, I don't think so," I say gently, but I let the sheet fall a little lower, the curve of my breasts rising above it.

Three sets of hungry eyes fall to my nipples, and Jace gives a moan at the back of his throat.

Luc's smile widens, as though I've said exactly what he wanted me to.

"Then suffer alone," he says lightly, and he drops into the bath.

His sigh of bliss is the most obnoxious sound I've ever heard.

It's ruined in about three seconds when Jace drops into the other end, sending water splashing over the side. Luc's eyes snap open, a snarl of agitation ripping free, but Jace shuts him up by grabbing the back of his neck and pulling him forward into a brutal kiss.

Luc's shoulders stiffen, his claws flexing, and then... he softens.

A low growl rumbles from his chest as he slides an arm down Jace's back, below the water, and pulls him closer. Their mouths slow, the kiss deepening and turning into something lazy. It's like they can't get close enough to each other, Luc's body surging up to meet Jace's, their hands clenching, pulling.

I thought alphas wouldn't be able to handle the jealousy of sharing, but it isn't like that at all. Not for them, and not for me. These are my men, and I'm theirs. There's no jealousy here; there doesn't need to be, because I want them to be happy. I want them to have pleasure.

I want to provide, to protect. To care.

And watching them like this, servicing the beasts within them through the ritual of the rut, every kiss and touch meeting a need our human bodies can barely contain... it's everything I've been missing. My mates. My pack.

Luc tilts his head, sliding his free hand to Jace's jaw so he can angle the kiss deeper. Harder. One of them moans, and the other echoes the sound in a harsh, desperate plea.

I can feel that kiss, right down to my toes. Heat burns through me, the rut rising and flaring. Something shatters, something that feels like cool metal around my wrists, and all that's left is *want*.

I want them.

And there's no reason I can't have them.

Theo gives me a wink and pulls up a barstool beside the bath. He drops his feet in one end of the water, eyes fluttering closed in pleasure.

Jace glances over his shoulder and then climbs higher, giving Theo more room to stretch his feet forward. To widen his legs so the jutting, hard ridge of his cock is clear.

Jace makes Luc's lap look like a throne.

Water flicks up the sides, but it's such a big tub that even with Theo's feet in one end, there's still room for mine. If I don't mind slipping in beside their rutting.

Jace's hand is below the surface now, and from the way he's moving—a slow, lazy slide of his hips while Luc groans and thrusts up beneath him—I'm guessing he's got both of them in hand.

It isn't a display for me. They aren't putting on a show they think is hot, or trying to please me in any way.

Shit, I think they've forgotten me.

My mates are lost in each other, bringing each other pleasure, caring for one another with the single minded devotion of an alpha.

And just the thought of that brings so much heat and pleasure to me that before I can help myself I'm whining like an omega and rising to my feet.

The sheet falls away.

Three heads turn my way, eyes glowing. Theo reaches out a hand, and I take it, my claws grazing his skin without breaking it.

He lifts one foot from the water and guides me between his legs, so I'm leaning back into him. Then he props his foot back on the bath, caging me. Trapping me.

"You wouldn't be trying to tame me there, would you, alpha?" I ask him, leaning my head back onto his shoulder as he drops his mouth to my neck.

The shock of hearing a second voice below mine sends the heat in me soaring, screaming for release. She's here; she's with me.

"I wouldn't dream of it, mate," Theo murmurs against my skin. "But if you want, you can ride me on the bed while these two finish."

I moan as the image thrusts its way into my mind, but before I can suggest a thing, Luc and Jace growl in protest.

I glance down to see they're at opposite ends, arms propped on the sides, watching us.

"No one leaves this bath," Luc orders, smoke curling from his lips.

Theo grins, a slow, triumphant grin that makes his eyes glint in the light. "Stay put, then," he tells Luc.

Then Theo kisses me, one hand beneath my chin. He holds me in place, tongue entwined with mine in a slowly deepening, breathless dance. It's just like in the forest, but this time, it's

Jace who climbs out of the bath, dripping wet, and kneels before me.

His hands grasp my hips, and he licks a long, aching swipe across my core. My ass falls against Theo, and I spread my legs and moan into Theo's mouth as the tongue between my thighs flicks faster.

Theo pulls back, a wicked grin on his face. Still gripping my chin, he turns my head a little toward the front, so I'm facing Luc. "We've done this before, you know," he says, tone full of lazy arrogance. "Did she tell you?"

He knows damn well there's been no time. We haven't stopped since the forest.

Luc's eyes flash, heat and jealousy riding for position. I can't look away, can't take refuge in the wall or the floor. He flicks his hair out of his eyes, dripping black strands revealing that sharp, piercing blue, and frowns. "When was this?"

My only answer is a whimper as Jace slides two fingers into me, making my eyes roll back.

"Last night," Theo says, smugness oozing from his voice. "You missed out."

"You'll have to make it up to me," Luc snarls.

Jace's tongue moves faster, flicking over and over me. I begin to pant, the pleasure rising, chasing so close to the edge. I close my eyes, but Theo gives my chin a little shake.

"Watch him as you come," he orders me.

My eyes snap open. I'm furious that he's given me an order like that, but then I see the smug triumph on Luc's face and I realize this is their game—they're teasing me.

Two can play at that game.

I hold his gaze as my orgasm tears through me. My mouth drops open, breaths coming in high-pitched, rough pants, and I let every careful ounce of control I've kept over myself and my reactions over the past years shatter.

Luc's eyes darken, his brow furrowing in a desperate expression. Water splashes over the side of the tub as his knee jerks up reflexively, and Theo's grip on my jaw tightens to the point of painful.

His cock twitches against my ass, and he grinds it into me, pushing me against Jace's mouth. "You did so well, babe," he murmurs into my ear as Jace rises to his feet.

I smile, but it isn't the pleased, affectionate smile he no doubt wants from me. Luc startles, eyes blazing as the corner of his mouth ticks in amusement.

"Did I?" I purr, my voice pure warning.

Theo doesn't notice. He answers with a low rumble, nuzzling over my neck. His teeth bare against my throat, and I wait until the moment before he bites me to pull away.

A snarl of frustration rips from him, but I grip his chin just like he held mine and hold him still. Shock spreads across his face, followed quickly by desire. His usually spiked hair falls across his forehead, the gel completely gone now through sweat, water, and the rut. It softens his appearance, and I get the abrupt sense that he wants to kneel for us.

It isn't just a sense. It's the bond, telling me.

"Sit on the couch," I tell him, my lips so close to his that my breath brushes his mouth. He tries to lean in, but I don't let him, my fingers clamped tight around his jaw.

I did so well, did I?

Let's see if he can do the same.

"You, too," I tell Jace, my mouth twitching at the undisguised interest in his entire demeanor.

Now that he's relaxing into himself around us, the himbo energy I caught a glimpse of at the beginning is only getting stronger. The contrast between the sure, steady way he leads and his own blatant desire to share and be shared fascinates me.

They all fascinate me.

They sit together on the couch, relaxed and regal despite the fact they don't have a stitch of clothing between them.

"You," I say, turning to Luc. He reclines in the bath, perfectly at ease, but his eyes give him away. They burn like fire. "On the bed."

He holds my gaze for a second longer, and then he gets up. Steam rises from him, his body warmer than it should be with the dragon inside riding so close to the surface. He crosses the room and lies on the bed, arms crossed behind his head, droplets of water rolling off him.

I take a moment just to admire. The full moon shadows his muscles, creating dips and lines over the ridges of his arms. The unexpected softness of his stomach when he lies back. I can see the muscle tensing when he stretches and shifts his legs, but on the surface he's relaxed. Surrendered to this moment, like we all have in our own ways.

I want to paint him.

Instead, I straddle his hips, sink down onto his cock, and ride him. Just like I imagined.

His gaze caresses my breasts, my thighs, his attention fixing for a long time on the point where we come together. I slow down, teasing him, watching the way his brow lifts with desire and need.

Soft noises come from the couch, accompanied by rough breathing and the wet sound of mouths mixing with skin. I look over my shoulder to find Theo and Jace kissing, their hands on each other and their mouths hungrily taking, exploring.

But their eyes don't leave the bed, greed filling their expressions as I begin to move faster.

"Eyes on me, sweetheart," Luc murmurs, his voice low and thick with the shadow beneath it. The beast within.

My snake hisses, rising, as I turn back to kiss him. His claws drive into my skin, sharp points of blood spilling over my hips as he tries to guide me, pistoning up while he slams me back down. Our souls flare, crying out, reaching for each other.

The bed dips as Theo and Jace join us, caressing our bodies with lips and tongue and teeth as we rise to the edge and fall over together.

Pressure builds at my core, between my thighs, shocking me until I realize what's happening.

His knot fills me, and it's almost too much when my own swells, too. I'm used to holding men in place for several minutes after sex, although I refuse to let my soul knot them often. But holding men down was a different sensation to this... The beta men beneath me loved it, writhing as the viper alpha forced them into submission.

Now, it feels like I'm the one who's held down. Out of control. Unable to move.

Luc's eyes widen, and he begins to laugh—a soft incredulous laugh that makes him seem strangely, abruptly vulnerable. Then his eyes darken, and his smile turns wicked.

"You're stuck," he says with amusement. "At our mercy."

To prove it, he thrusts slowly up into me. I gasp, my eyes rolling back into my head as my soul hisses with ecstasy. I lift with him, my body rising, but between my thighs, nothing moves. Not even an inch.

It's fucking hot.

Sibilant noises drop from my mouth, and Luc's breath hitches in desire. "Behind," he orders. "And right there."

I blink my eyes open, dazed with pleasure, wondering what on earth he's talking about.

And then Theo touches me. My oversensitive clit pulses, shocking me, almost hurting me.

Luc smiles. Sweat rolls from his neck, over his collarbone, shimmering against the red flush on his chest. "If you want us to stop, you have to bark."

Desire surges white-hot within me as I leap to play the game he's started. Hands touch my clit, sliding over and over, bringing me to the edge as I cry for them to stop.

They don't stop, and I don't bark.

Luc's knot grips me, holds me, my muscles clenching and fluttering as Theo makes me come again. Then again.

The room spins, moonlight dazzling me as my head tips back and I stare up into the stars. Someone pulls me back against them, the velvety head of their cock nudging between my ass as their teeth close over my throat.

They don't enter; they just tease me, sliding back and forth. I smell Theo at my neck, feel him through the bond as his teeth break my skin and he marks me.

The hand between my thighs disappears, and Jace's tongue licks over me. There's a mouth at my breast; the person behind me isn't there anymore. I can't move away, can't think. There's nothing but pleasure surrounding me. I arch my back, pushing my breasts into his mouth as Jace replaces his tongue once more with his finger. He circles my clit, slick and fast, and it's too much. It's too much.

I come again, and this time Luc's knot pulses within me, his head tipped back as he comes with another cry.

I whimper as the knot swells larger, overstimulated and desperate with desire, the rut guiding me, pushing me to take and take.

And be taken.

The hands ease, turning softer as my hips rock. A mouth licks the wound at my neck, healing it—Jace. In return, I sink my teeth into his throat.

He laughs as I claim him, the scent of blood filling the air.

Finally, finally, our knots begin to ease. The pressure disappears, and I miss it. I want to be filled again; want to hold again. Be held.

How could I ever have thought I would be with anyone but an alpha? Three alphas?

Languid, I ease backward, slipping free of Luc and falling back into the arms that hold me.

"My turn," Theo whispers, before he guides me to the window.

As we leave the bed, he snatches up the sheet and shoves it to my front, possessive. "No one else sees you like this, tonight," he growls.

I can't help laughing. My legs nearly buckle from exhaustion, but I hold the sheet to my breasts and lean one hand against the window. Our reflection stares back at us, golden eyes shining in the moonlight, the wind howling through shattered glass at our feet.

He plants his hands on my hips and takes me.

I press my forehead against the glass, lips parting in need. "Alright," I gasp, "but if you get something of me, I want something of you."

"It's yours," he growls, his relentless pace never slowing as he thrusts into me. "Take it."

I laugh, breathless. "Luc," I call without looking. "Take a photo for me."

Theo shudders, his fingers driving harder into my hips, but he doesn't stop.

Jace laughs wickedly, and I can hear the two of them fumbling for someone's phone on the bed. I don't care whose.

"You can't vet these shots, big boy," Jace calls as Luc snaps a photo. Then another. "Think you can handle that? We've got thirst traps of you now that you're never gonna even see."

Theo snarls in answer, his pace quickening, his eyes never leaving my face in the reflection.

Jace appears beside him, and they take turns. Every time I'm seconds away from coming, they'll trade places, the other leaning against the window to watch. Soon, all I can do is close my eyes and brace myself, my body aching with overwhelming pleasure as they drive into me over and over.

With a howl, Theo comes, thighs trembling as he slams into me. His arms bracket me, muscles thick and tight. When he slides free, Jace enters immediately, his cock slick with Theo's spend as he thrusts, faster and faster, and finally comes.

An exhausted wolf whistle from the bed has me turning, looking over my shoulder to see Luc reclined with one arm behind his head, grinning. A bolt of heat runs through me, but it's different now. Softer. More human.

The rut is letting go.

I smile at him, leaning my head back against Jace as he places slow kisses to my neck. I let the sheet fall. Theo grunts, picking it up and shoving it to my chest. "Jel," he says warningly.

"Theo," I reply, mimicking his tone.

His eyes soften, and he leans in, kissing me softly. He drops the sheet. I slide my hand between his thighs, cupping him gently, making him shiver. He grins against my mouth and pulls away.

"We should sleep," he says, reluctant, but his voice betrays him—we're all wrecked.

Theo leads the way back to the bed, with Jace and I following. But my legs are weak from exhaustion, and at the last second I stumble, sending Jace forward, too. We catch onto the closest furniture.

Our combined body weight proves that, transcendental orgasm or not, the laws of physics still apply.

The tub flips, water sloshing over the edge, filling the apartment.

"Oh, fuck!" I hiss.

The boys break into motion, slipping and laughing as they leap from the bed, grabbing mops and brooms and towels. It's infectious. I start to laugh, long, choking peals of laughter that feel like they'll never stop.

"God, it's everywhere." I catch the broom Luc throws at me and join them, sweeping the water out the broken window.

It sloshes down the walls, joining the rain. But, Christ, there's so much of it.

It's falling through the cracks in the floorboards.

I hear shouts from below. See lights flicking on in the apartment downstairs.

"Bolt the door," Luc orders, laughing so hard he's doubled over. I think it was meant to be a bark, but it didn't come out that way.

Jace rushes to obey, slipping on the floor, and throws the chain over the door just before a loud knocking starts up.

"Do you have a leak?" A hysterical voice calls through. "The storm's flooding the building! Check your electronics!"

"We're on it," Jace yells back, voice as low a rumble as he can manage.

The voice disappears.

"Oh Hell," I mutter, clutching my face. "This is fucked."

Theo slings an arm over my shoulder and leads me to the bed. "It's tomorrow's problem," he says fiercely, planting a kiss on my cheek.

Before I can protest, the other two have joined us, Luc beside me and Jace curled up at his back.

"But—" I begin.

"Sleep," Jace commands.

My soul hisses, sated and sleepy. And most of all, warm. Warm, like she'll never be cold again.

I yawn. "Okay," I whisper.

To the dulcet sounds of the apartment occupants yelling, the storm raging, and the wind whistling through the cracks in the window, I fall asleep.

3²
JEL

I WAKE SLOWLY, STRETCHING WITH A LUXURIOUS SIGH IN THE MIDDLE of the bed. My right side is warm; two bodies are curled up there, breathing heavily. Content.

My left side is cold. As I stir, blinking awake and coming into proper awareness, I notice there are voices.

After a split second of urgent adrenaline, I recognize the voice as the tinny, affected tone of a TV reporter doing an interview.

I sit up, squinting across the room. Theo sits at my kitchen counter, a grim look on his face as he stares down at his phone. At first, I assume it must be because of the water damage, but when I look around, the apartment is... kind of okay. He's set up a fan on the floorboards, and patched my window with a blank canvas and duct tape, and everything else is kind of fine. Damp, but fine.

Which means the problem is something else. My heart thuds.

Quietly, I get out of bed and pad across the room to him. He welcomes me with an arm around my hips, pulling me into him. "It's not good," he warns in a low voice, still not looking away from the screen.

"Lay it on me," I mutter.

The reporter stares menacingly into the camera, and I realize with a jolt that she's out the front of the academy.

"For how long will Sawlefire Academy protect the very people who should be brought to justice?" she demands. "And can we expect this level of bribery and corruption to be evident in every facet of the school's operation? We're joined now by Ms Caddel, head of the community group M.A.A.V. who are calling for an overhaul of the school board until this serial killer is caught."

My brow furrows, my sleep-addled brain struggling to follow what she's saying no matter how much adrenaline my body pumps into it.

"What is she talking about? Is the killer a student?" I whisper, but then the guest says a name that freezes me in my tracks.

"Angelica Vario, daughter and heir to the notorious Marcus Vario, patriarch alpha of the Caldburg City Vipers, should never have been allowed to attend Sawlefire Academy. Not while she still stands to inherit the line of succession, and certainly not while Luc D'Amour was in attendance.

"The alpha clause is meant to protect students by bringing any territorial disputes or vendettas to light, where the school can appropriately weigh the risks of those alphas being allowed on campus and install a more appropriate hierarchy. It has clearly failed us here because there is no record of either Angelica Vario or Luc D'Amour ever signing one."

"Those liars!" I hiss. "They've warped the truth. Luc signed one late, and I have one under a fake name."

"Is that really better?" Theo asks dryly.

"Yes!"

The guest keeps speaking. "And I dare anyone to look at the targets of these murders—all women, all redheaded—the locations of these murders, and the brutal method of killing, and tell me we aren't talking about a retaliation of some description. Putting these two alphas together in one place was going to make one or both of them crack, and they have. They have!"

"But we can't be sure yet that they're involved in the murders," the reporter interjects in a supremely unconvincing tone. Thanks a million. "Surely this is a very unusual method for two patriarch alphas to enact vengeance on each other. There have been no territorial displays between the two, no indication at the crime scenes of any alpha bloodletting."

"We can't be sure *yet*," the guest replies, pursing her lips. "And I have it on good authority that there is some new evidence coming to light just this morning that will change the way we view these crimes." She leans back, smug. "So, we shall wait and see, Margaret."

"He tipped them off," I breathe, horror making my words sharper than I mean them to be. "The killer tipped them off about Luc. About me. This was his plan at the warehouse—if they hear about the fire being dragon flame..."

It must be the new evidence.

Luc and Jace stir, sitting up together. They've obviously been listening for a while. My bedsheets pool around their waists, and the morning sun no longer looks comforting. It highlights the tension in their jaws, the washed-out paleness to Jace's cheeks.

Luc's eyes are murderous, dark shadow transforming his expression from the face of my mate to someone dangerous. Jace rests a hand on his shoulder, squeezing gently over the flame tattoo that covers Luc's skin there.

His face is equally shadowed, equally dangerous.

"The killer is splitting us up. Weakening us. How long do I have?" Luc asks.

"Why now, though?" Jace mutters. "He could have tipped off the press at any point."

It hits me that this is really happening. Our past has been aired in the worst way, at the worst time, right when there's evidence to plant Luc at the warehouse.

The screen changes. They're interviewing a man I don't recognize.

"He's dangerous," he says in a terrified voice, ears pricking back and forth like an animal's. Brown fur pokes out the tops, and the ears round a little. Like a mouse.

Or a rat.

Luc turns sharply, narrowing his eyes at the screen. "That's my fucking gardener," he snarls. "He saw me last night. That's why it's happening now—they've got a witness."

"Your gardener," I repeat slowly, thinking of those twitching ears.

I shake my head. It's no time to speculate now. It might not have been the killer who tipped off the cops, but there's no doubt in my mind that he's going to pounce on the opportunity and add his carefully prepared framejob to the cloud of shit raining on us. He was probably just waiting for the right moment.

"You have to get out of here, Luc," Theo says roughly. "Do you have somewhere to go?"

"There's a cabin in the mountains." Luc stands, pulling his black Henley over his torso. "I'll let you know where it is when it's safe, then we can regroup. Jel, you should come now."

"It might make things worse," I tell him, thinking it through carefully. "They think this is some kind of retaliation against what my family did to you... But it doesn't make sense. Until the warehouse, no vipers have been hurt. Do they have any grounds to hold you?"

Luc shrugs, checking his pockets for his phone and wallet, scanning the room—presumably to make sure he leaves no trace. "You heard her—victims are all redheaded women. Maybe they think I'm taunting you. Or I've just cracked and I'm killing anyone who looks like you. Doesn't matter, we can't fall into his game. He's too many steps ahead, and we still don't know what his goal is."

Frowning, I hold up a hand. "Hang on. What did the reporter just say? About the Hunt?"

Theo turns up the volume and taps the live play back a few minutes. We all stop dead as the signs of carnage flash onto the screen.

"What the fuck happened?" I breathe, my eyes wide as I take it in.

Blood lines the walls, mixing with the left-over fur and hair of what I can only assume was a half shifted wolf. It's difficult to make sense of it with the photos only showing the aftermath, but it looks like he'd been taken out somewhere in the academy's basements, below the library.

It's the missing wolf from the Hunt. And when the camera pans back, shoved away by an angry Dean, I realize I know that door. It's the one that caught my attention, right before the photo of Anthony arrived.

Again, the killer is taunting us, playing right under our nose.

"Tuesday's Academy Hunt ended in tragedy, when a young alpha wolf was brutally murdered on campus grounds. The Hunt is an ancient tradition, steeped in the academy's roots as a Guardian Place for the Gods.

"In ancient times, academy alphas would regularly set aside their minor disputes and engage in a campus-wide patrol ordained by the gods. Predators were taken down and laid on the altar of various deities, ensuring the academy's good fortune and the safety of its students."

"On the altar," Jace breathes, leaning forward and pointing at the screen as it replays the chaotic footage of the scene before. "He's made an altar in the corner there. That's not murder. That's a sacrifice. Look at the blood."

Shit, he's right.

Symbols have been scrawled in the blood, but the camera won't focus on them long enough to identify. Maybe they don't want us to.

"But it seems the long-held tradition has fallen to the wayside in place of sadism and depravity. One of the Hunt's participants was struck down in a brutal attack, leaving police to speculate whether the outdated practice should be banned."

The camera cuts to a policeman. "There's no evidence this is the same murderer, and every suggestion the Hunt participants were stirred to madness chasing this criminal, before they eventually lost control completely. Look at the altar. Look at the sacrifice. The Hunt is unruly," he says flatly. "It's the worst of a shifter's instincts all stirred up and thrown in one big gladiator ring. Maybe it served a protective purpose once, but I can't imagine one now. It's not how I'd protect my pack, and the Hunt on Tuesday night failed to protect anyone." His eyes glow just as the camera cuts away.

"They're saying the Hunt took down one of their own." My voice sounds strange to my own ears.

"The Hunt didn't do this," Luc says firmly. "That shifter was already missing. This is the killer again, diluting his tracks. That wasn't a Sawlefire ritual altar. I didn't recognize any of those symbols, did you?"

We shake our heads.

Luc's jaw sets into an even grimmer expression than before.

"This is calculated. There's no evidence of instinct gone wild, of predation. Not animal predation, anyway. This is human. This is sadistic."

"It's him," I agree. "But why aren't they connecting those dots?! They really just think the Hunt went feral?"

"It's what the killer wants them to think," Theo says, speaking for the first time in a while. There's a coldness to his voice, his words. It makes me think of the look I see in his eyes sometimes, and I wonder what this is reminding him of. "But he doesn't strike me as the type to waste time losing focus on the wrong thing. Even when he framed Luc, he was also baiting you, Jel. Targeting you. He's efficient. This is his game, and he's playing to win. Which means sacrificing the alpha was important. This ties in."

"How?" Jace mutters, tapping the video backward to stare at the crime scene. "It's nothing like the other murders. They'd have mentioned if blood was taken from the victim again, and the scene is completely different. There's no message—not one we can read, anyway. He isn't trying to scare us or bait us. Just those symbols." He winces. "Unless he wants to wig us out thinking of the gods."

"Or unless he's really talking to the gods," Luc says quietly.

We fall silent.

"No blood was taken," I say, forcing my brain to move slowly as it puts the pieces together, even though my soul wants to leap from the window, track this asshole's scent, and attack the first sign of danger she sees. "And this is a sacrifice to the gods. What if the previous murders weren't his main goal? What if this is what he was planning all along, but to make the sacrifice, he needed that blood first? The other victims weren't the goal, they were..."

"His shopping list," Theo finishes with a snarl.

Jace's eyes suddenly glow, his head whipping up and

casting his face in eerie light. "You said in the warehouse you felt like his guinea pig. What if last night wasn't just about setting Luc up? What if he was testing something on you, as well? Two birds, one stone."

"The drug." Luc stops trying to edge out the door completely, his need to escape overcome with this sudden revelation. "The drug in the smoke. He's been searching for enough blood to make this hypnotic drug. Or maybe not enough blood, maybe the *right* blood. That's why he tried for two victims that first night."

"This is a lot of maybes," Theo growls, but his brow is furrowed in thought. It makes sense. Too much sense.

The answer comes to me, sickening in its certainty. I turn to my painting, thinking of the hypnotic power of the venom in it, especially when it was mixed with more magic. With the right power, it could control my alpha soul and keep her hidden. It could control how people saw me.

I remember the warehouse and my body losing control of itself, sluggish, in the smoke. Hypnotic.

"He needed blood and venom."

Anthony said it was venom that was stolen that night. What else is as hypnotic as snake venom? And when you add blood magic to the mix...

He already had the venom, but Luc is right, he would need the right blood. He would need alpha blood, at the very least. Likely snake alpha blood.

Viper alpha blood.

Theo frowns, reading my urgency and terror, but not knowing the source. I open my mouth, searching for the words, but they choke in my throat. My mind conjures a vision of Anthony, strapped to that chair, and the tiny puncture wound in his neck.

I wondered why he hadn't taken more, or killed him. But he

didn't need to. It was just enough blood to test a sample. The drug would work, but it wouldn't be strong enough. It wouldn't be the final form of the drug, because Anthony isn't truly the alpha.

I am.

"This has been about me all along," I mutter, my voice catching, rising. "Luc isn't taunting me, like the news thinks, but the killer certainly is. He knows what I did to my soul—what I did to myself. It was ruining his plans, and so he had to make me stop."

He knows I've been blocking my soul.

He's been luring it out.

Fists clenched, I pull away from Theo's warmth, backing up until my feet hit the wall. The killer probably worked it out that night in the alley, when he got a proper read on my scent. When he realized I wasn't just dulling it around other people for safety; I still smelled like a beta when I was alone, because I was properly blocking it.

He set up this net to get me on edge, to rile my instincts until my soul burst free. It took him ten years to work out how to use the venom, and he's sick of waiting.

"We need to get the details of that legend," I say. "The sacrifice, the symbols, the hypnotic magic... The legend is about a ritual. Humming that creepy fucking song—it probably isn't a song, it's a chant. But that legend has gotten mixed up so many times over the years, no one knows what the ritual was trying to do. We need to know."

Jace reaches for me, but I shrug him away.

"There's no time. He's been running rings around us for days; we're doing exactly what he wants us to. We have to—"

A knock sounds on the door, loud and insistent.

We turn as one to Luc, whose face drains of color.

"Run," I tell him. "*Run.*"

33

JEL

THE DOOR BURSTS OPEN, KICKED DOWN BY THE ASSHOLE COPS ON THE other side, and Luc sprints for the window.

"Freeze!" the first cop yells, aiming his gun at Luc.

Scales ripple over his skin, fire burning from his throat and scorching the windows. He's partially shifted, the window cracked enough that his torso is out of it, but the cops are too quick.

They fire a net at him, and as the silver-coated thread comes into contact with his skin, he howls in pain.

He can't shift like this, not with that material on him. Those bastards.

Luc falls out the window, writhing in the net, and it's only his half shifted wings that save him, slowing his fall just enough that it doesn't kill him on impact. Instead, he just hits the earth below my window with a sickening thud, rolling from the hedge onto the garden bed and roaring as he tries to break free.

"You could have fucking killed him!" I yell, the words sibilant and hoarse.

Three of the cops stutter, confused by the power in my

voice. But their leader barks an order, and they race out, down the stairs to handcuff Luc where he's fallen.

"I'll kill them," I hiss, already turning for the door, but Jace and Theo stop me.

"Don't give them a reason to take you, too," Theo snaps.

Jace doesn't say anything. He just holds me, surprisingly strong. I nod reluctantly, my chest heaving with ragged breath, as I step back toward the window.

They've finished apprehending him, now. But they're leaving the net on, so he can't break free in the car. It must hurt, but he shows no sign of the pain. His expression is stiff and blank as he casts one look behind him, up to us in the window. His gaze seems to say *don't do anything stupid*. But I can't make any promises.

Already, my snake writhes in fury, planning a dozen ways she can take down the people holding my mate captive.

The human side of me knows it will only make things worse. Fortunately, it's the human side in all of us that wins tonight. For now.

The last thing we see is Luc's forehead, pressed to the window of the cop car in furious defeat as he drives away.

***

The killer is nowhere in sight, and yet it feels like he's surrounding us. The air has thickened with his presence in the time since Luc was taken. It's too dark in my apartment; the storm outside seeps in through the broken windows and damp floor.

"I'm dying here," Theo rasps, clutching his head. "I need something to fight."

He pauses his relentless pacing to lean against the wall with one hand, eyes closed. The metaphorical tiger in the cage is real, here.

"This is torture," Jace agrees, and even his voice is too low, too close to the edge.

They're right; we can't stay here. My snake is losing it, and I don't know how long before she takes over.

But where do we go?

Theo's checked with his family lawyers to see if they can do anything, but his parents won't touch it. Jace has hounded his sisters continuously, to see if they've found anything on the legend and the ritual. He only stopped when Caitlyn threatened to turn off her phone.

Luc's gone, the killer is winning, and we're out of ideas.

"What have we missed?" I ask absently, staring up at my ceiling with my head tipped back on my kitchen counter. "There has to be something we've overlooked. Some piece of information he's left behind."

"What about the sacrifice?" Theo suggests suddenly. "The wolf. If it's different to the other murders, there might be something there."

Hope flickers in my chest. "It could give us a scent—something to follow or fight," I agree carefully. "It'll stop me marching down there and fighting the police, at least."

"Wait," Jace says, holding up his hand. "Doesn't your family own the police? Why didn't we already think of that?"

My blood freezes. "You can't be serious."

"Am I wrong?"

"No, you're not fucking wrong." I clutch at my hair, tugging the strands until my scalp burns. "No way. I can't do that to him. He'd rather die than owe my family anything."

"Then maybe he will," Jace says harshly. "The alternative is to leave him alone in there—right where the killer wants him. Who knows what he's planned?"

I swear, loudly and at length. Theo and Jace wait it out, twin expressions of amusement on their faces, despite the seriousness of the situation.

Eventually, I stop swearing. I have no choice.

"Only Anthony, though," I say, holding up my hand before they can object. "He'll be enough, especially since he signed that affiliation clause for Luc, and trust me... you don't want the rest."

They stay silent while I call my brother. Jace loops an arm around my waist, pulling me into his lap on the stool as I explain the situation to Anthony. He'd already clued into half of it, his voice grim as he tells me the snake pit is in an uproar.

"We're running bribes in every direction," he says in a low voice. I can hear yelling in the background. "The Mayor is trying to get into the pit. Stick his nose in. The reporters have stirred the shit up too far."

I frown. "Dad hasn't bought him off already?"

Strong, gentle hands run through my hair. My chest rumbles with a hiss of pleasure.

"Not yet. Give it a day. I think we might be up for a new election if he keeps this up." Anthony's voice is dry with black humor, and I wrinkle my nose at the thought. "Anyway, that's not why you called. So. You really want me to do this?" he asks.

There's something in his voice I don't fully recognize. He's hesitant, when Anthony is never hesitant. Not with me.

I guess the last thing he did for me got him kidnapped, so fair's fair.

"What else am I going to do?" I ask honestly. "The killer has been one step ahead of us this whole time, and as far as we know, he's got Luc right where he wants him."

There's silence down the line, and I can imagine Anthony doing his slow little nod, thinking it over. Weighing the decision.

"You're right," he finally agrees. "Dad won't like it, though. I'm warning you. There'll be consequences."

I laugh without humor. "I think it's a little too late for that warning, but thanks."

He huffs a quiet, humorless laugh of his own. "I'll be down at the station as soon as this is sorted. Two hours should do it. Meet you there?"

That'll give me time to figure out how to let Luc know that the affiliation clause he didn't want to sign with my brother is about to save his life. Maybe I'll even think of a way to tell him without losing a limb.

"See you then."

"And in the meantime," Theo says roughly as I hang up, "we can study that sacrifice."

Chills run down my spine, even as my soul stands to attention. It's time we quit hiding in the shadows. This killer has led us around for too long.

"After me," I say, my voice hissing quietly.

It doesn't take long to cross the campus, and with one mean looking bodyguard hovering over me, and one slightly less mean and admittedly distracted bodyguard covering the rear, no one bothers us. I get a lot of nasty looks though, and when I cautiously sniff the air, I smell fear.

News spreads quickly.

As we enter the admin block, Jace looks up from where he's been tapping away on his phone, his gaze triumphant. "She's found the source."

"The source for what?" Theo asks.

"The academy legend. There are like twenty different editions of the school gazette that reference different academy legends, but this one's the oldest, and it talks about a book of rituals stored in the basement stacks." He waves his phone in my face. "Told you she was a mini genius."

I raise my eyebrow. "Exploiting your sisters already, for shame."

He lowers the phone. "Hey, we're not the nerd team sitting behind and reading slayer handbooks in the library. We're the front line. We need to prioritize different things."

"Was that a Buffy reference?"

He laughs under his breath. "When have we had time to look this up, Jel? I wouldn't even know where to start."

"Okay, but you know Buffy did the research too, right?"

He points a finger at me dramatically before holding the phone up again. "But did she enjoy it? No. Because she was made for different things."

The tiny text is almost illegible, but Caitlyn is right. The article is only a snippet, barely going into detail, but the humming, the blood... It's all there.

I grab the phone and read a section out loud. "Annabelle Lansley, who has dedicated her thesis to the topic, has determined after thorough research that the current iteration of events are likely pranks from the witches at Dremen Academy. However, the ritual itself, and its history, is soberingly real and should not be taken lightly. Let the student body's response be a warning of the dangers of mass hysteria."

I curl my lip. "Condescending prick. But you mean your sister looked up her thesis and it's in the basement stacks collection?"

"Why is it down there?" Theo frowns.

With a snort, Jace takes his phone back. "Caitlyn thinks they just didn't want anyone to stumble on it, but they couldn't wipe it completely or it would make people curious."

"So..." I say slowly. "Quick detour for the thesis, then on to the sacrifice?"

My heart races, mind churning as I plan through our next steps. Maybe we're finally starting to get somewhere.

"You need a reference to see the stacks," Theo says, trailing off.

Crap.

Well, am I an art student, or not?

I swing into an empty lecture hall and scan the tables for a forgotten notebook. Bingo. Three minutes later, and I've added a pen. Quickly, I draft out a note in my best forged handwriting and sign it from the Dean out of spite.

He's never liked me. He can help me out this one time.

"Okay, let's do this." I tell them, my voice low in case anyone is listening. "But first I need to pee."

Theo growls. "Can't it wait?"

"No." I smile sweetly and duck into the nearest bathroom.

I fold the note and move to slip it into my pockets, only to meet air.

Crap. No pockets in this bloody skirt.

Maybe I should have paused for a second before asserting my dominance when it comes to bathroom matters.

With a sigh, I arrange the note carefully above the sink, where it won't fall or get splashed, and then hurry into a cubicle.

I'm nearly finished when the door swings open and two girls walk in, talking loudly. I can practically feel the tension from the other side of the door as it slams shut, and I can only hope Theo and Jace don't decide to barge in here.

Then I freeze, realizing what's about to happen seconds before it does.

"What's this?" There's a rustle of paper.

They're picking up my note. Reading it.

My eyes flicker and glow, scales rippling over my bare skin. I don't need any setbacks right now. We're on a tight schedule.

One of the girls snorts. "Some journalism major is obviously hunting for a scoop on that legend, then. God. Why can't people shut up about that? It's everywhere."

I pause, my skirt halfway up my ass and my lace underwear hanging out as I try not to breathe and miss anything. The murderous urge to get my note back fades as logic takes over—they might know something.

The second girl grunts in annoyance. "If I see that viper chick, I'm going to nab her. Maybe if we give *her* to the gods, they'll all piss off and stop bothering us."

Then again, maybe not.

There's a rustle of clothing and a huff of laughter. "There were spiders all over my fucking desk this morning. So gross."

"So gross." They fall silent. Then: "That dragon boy is cute though."

This time, my blood boils. I lose several seconds of conversation as my soul screams for vengeance.

One of them smacks the other, and they both laugh.

"You're insane, Mads."

"What? He's not the killer."

"He might be. They locked him up this morning."

"No! Really?"

"God, you loser. Did you really miss that?"

"I had track!"

"Whatever." More silence. "I don't think he is, either. I think it's her. She's finishing the job for her dad, and then she'll become a god and win back the vipers after they kicked her out."

My heart begins to thud wildly in my chest. What the hell is she talking about? I'm not even mad she's accusing me, or that she's messed up the truth of how I left the vipers.

It's the casual way she said I'll become a god that's caught my attention.

Why would she think that?

Fortunately, the other girl doesn't get it either. "What are you talking about?"

"That's what the legend's about, Mads. Make some sacrifices and you get to become a god or some shit. I don't know. I've heard like five thousand versions this morning because *no one will shut up about it.*"

Everything stops. My heart, my blood—it all just ceases to pulse. She can't be serious. This is so far beyond reasonable that it's cycled right back around to plausible.

Because why else are the gods so invested?

"Oh shit," I breathe, steadying myself against the wall as it all sinks in. I finally pull up my skirt and button it.

Fate's interference would all make sense like this, wouldn't it? If these sacrifices are some kind of ritual that lets the killer become a god, and our pack can somehow change the course of this game... then wouldn't that be a love story worth toying with?

It all fits: the gods watching everything we do; Fate's insane decision to bring our pack together on the night of the murders; the fact that I'm bonded to Luc at all, when it sounds like that night ten years ago was the start of it all.

The killer tried to use my family as a slaughter machine to get the sacrifices he needed, but for some reason it didn't work, and now he's trying again.

Does the school know about the legend? Is that why they've tried to cover it up, by hiding all reference to it in the basement? I've always wondered why our school was so weirdly religious.

And why the Dean has always seemed to hate me so much. He probably thinks the vipers tried to become gods ten years ago, just like this girl obviously does.

The bathroom is silent, so I flush the toilet and throw open the door, only to find the girls still putting on their lipstick.

Great.

I've successfully avoided everyone all morning, only to be caught with my pants down. Almost.

I go to move past them, reaching for the sink on the other side and completely ignoring them, but it seems fear has made the two betas find their bite. They stare me down, the girl on the left twitching nervously but nonetheless committed to greasing me off.

It's going to take a lot more than that, that's all I can say. This isn't high school.

"So. Becoming gods, you say," I say conversationally when it becomes clear they're not going to let up. I turn and lean my hip on the sink, picking up my note with deliberate slowness and crossing my arms to regard them. "That's gonna suck. Doesn't anyone know what hubris is anymore?"

"You know all about it, don't you?" the nearest girl says in a hushed voice. She's the one who's been sharing the legend. It's always nice to put a face to a voice. "You let the killer in the door."

I pretend to raise my eyebrows in shock. "Now, now, momma always told me not to answer the door to strangers."

She gives a fake, shrill laugh. "People are dead because of your family! The dragons were murdered, and now you're finishing the job. We all know you're behind it. You can't hide forever."

The silent girl finds her voice suddenly. "You've got a lot of nerve showing your face here."

"Yeah," the first girl agrees, and her words end on a snarl. Her eyes glow, fur sprouting over the back of her hands as claws tear free. "Too much nerve."

I know I'm on a tight schedule, but come *on*.

"I've got more than nerve, you piece of shit," I snarl, letting my eyes glow with fire.

The silent girl squeaks, cowering at once, but the other girl lunges with a roar, shifting into a giant, white wolf mid-leap.

The part of me I like to keep buried uncurls with delight. I can't hold her back; my soul breaks free.

I was a fool to think I could hold her like this. She's never hiding away again, and I don't even care. I'm almost relieved. This is the fight I've been waiting for ever since I came to Sawlefire. At last, the truth is out about my past.

And they've all reacted exactly like I knew they would.

My soul takes over.

After ten years of being trapped and smothered, she doesn't hold back. Fangs rip free from my gums, a partial shift that transforms my mirrored face into a scaled demon. I dodge the wolf, grab her by the throat, and slam her into the mirror.

Glass shatters, deadly rain pouring over us the wolf twists free. Her friend whimpers, snarls, and shifts.

Two wolves crouch before me.

I could kill them with two strikes.

The door slams open and I smell my mates behind me, flanking me. They'll protect me. I crouch lower, preparing to lunge.

One of the wolves trembles violently, and I smile. A quick bite at her throat, and my venom will do the rest. Toxic and potent. She'll lay down at my feet and beg me for the privilege.

A low growl echoes from behind me, bouncing off the tiles. I stiffen, assessing the danger in a split second. I can only sense my mates, which means—

They've turned on me.

I tip my head back and begin the shift in full, ready to strike, but a hand snatches me around the neck and pulls me backward, into a hard chest and a scent that does more to soothe me than any words could.

"Not here," Jace whispers into my ear, while a giant tiger appears before us and blocks the wolves from attacking.

They drop lower, ears flattening. The tiger rumbles.

"You don't want this."

My soul hisses, dramatic and hurting and furious. But if anyone knows what I want, it's my mate. She listens to him, letting the scales disappear one by one as I lean back into Jace's touch.

With his free hand, Jace picks up my clothing and the dropped note. And then we begin to back out of the bathroom, using Theo as a shield.

The lights flicker.

My fangs extend, dripping with venom, as the scents in the room change. Not quite another person, but... something.

The lights go out.

Someone screams, and I feel warmth brush against my arm. But it's the wrong kind of warmth. There's something disgusting about it, repulsive.

Fingers claw their way to my neck, gripping tightly, choking my air until there's nothing left. He begins to drag me away from the others. This bathroom is the nearest to the stadium, so it's massive, and it connects to three small supply closets. If he gets me in there alone...

I lash out, beginning the shift, tasting him with my forked tongue. I'm going to hurt him. I'm going to tear his throat out for this—for all of it. But pain erupts in my neck before I can complete the change and I stutter, losing focus.

My howl comes out in a spluttering whimper, my blood flow seriously cut off, and all I can do is punch through the darkness. The killer slams backward, the hiss of a shower turning on covering the chaos of growls and frightened lunges we've left behind.

I land two good uppercuts into a solid form, even with my

oxygen depleted, but it isn't enough. The killer drops me, and when I lunge for him, my arms only find air.

A voice whispers nearby, "Welcome back."

The screams grow louder, and Jace snarls behind me as he shifts into a dangerous mass of fur and teeth.

There's a scuffle, and the sharp scent of blood.

The lights slam on, too bright for my shifted eyes. Words scrawl on the mirror.

Your blood is mine, viper. I'll see you at the end.

34
JEL

For a moment, we all freeze, nostrils flaring, souls screaming for vengeance. For pack safety among the danger. I'm on my knees; I fell at some point when the killer attacked me. My fangs are still out, scales covering my naked body in patches.

But there's no scent.

There's no scent to track, just like at the party, just like every other crime scene.

I bring my hand to my neck, where the pain is. It comes away sticky with blood.

He got it.

He got my blood.

Was it enough? Why didn't he kill me like the others?

What does *I'll see you at the end* mean?

"Jel," Jace says, his voice cracked and broken as he shifts back and snatches his clothing from the floor. "They're going to blame you. Your pheromones are all over this bathroom; it stinks of your rage. We have to go."

My eyes lock with the nearest wolf's. Her tongue lolls out of her head, and her eyes are wide with that panicked animal look that tells me we've no way of knowing what she's taking in.

Maybe she sensed him for that brief second, like I did. Maybe she can work out that, since the message is targeting me, I didn't write it.

Maybe she's too lost in panic, and she'll go straight to the cops with my name on her lips as soon as she shifts back.

Jace tugs me backward and I follow, stumbling into action.

We get out of there as fast as we can, the two wolves already sprinting past us toward the campus gates. It isn't fast enough.

Everywhere I look, I see signs of him. Blood smeared on the wall. Rats etched in juvenile graffiti on the walls.

The announcement system crackles into life, and a faint, eerie tune spills over—snatches of that tuneless song, the chant, drift over the announcement system before disappearing so quickly it's as though my mind made it up. It didn't though.

Has he been following us all morning? Caging us in, waiting for the perfect moment to strike?

We're lucky he didn't murder those girls.

Jace keeps his hand clenched firmly around my arm as we run. My snake rears up several times, hissing at him in protest, but he doesn't even flinch. He knows I won't strike; this is just heat with nowhere to go.

More and more, I feel like we've nowhere to go. He can track us without us sensing him. He got in and out of that bathroom without a trace. Everywhere he points, the reporters and the police follow. There's only so long he'll keep this up before he stops pointing anywhere that isn't us.

He has Luc. Or, at least, he has him where he wants him if the killer isn't physically with him. But then, maybe he's both, because who says he's not a cop?

Doubt creeps into my thoughts. Who is this guy, and if he was smart enough to dupe the vipers and the dragons in one, can we really defeat him on our own?

Theo keeps his tiger form, circling us whenever we slow,

guarding the rear.

When we finally feel far enough away, we duck into an empty classroom and fall to the floor, chests heaving.

Slowly, breath by breath, we steady. The rise and fall of Theo's chest, still in his tiger shift, is more calming than I want to admit. Coupled with the loop of Jace's arm around my waist, I come down from the high of violence quicker than usual.

It feels different, this return to humanity. Like it isn't a return at all. Our beasts are still with us, and they refuse to leave after an encounter like that. But I feel grounded within my own skin. Like the alpha within me and the face I wear outside aren't so far apart after all.

"Maybe we should all go to that cabin," Jace suggests. "We're no good if two of us are locked up, and I don't like your chances after that, Jel. Sorry."

With a rough shake of his head, Theo transforms back. Naked, burning skin presses into my body from behind, heating me in more ways than one.

"We're no good anywhere," he says in disgust, voice rumbling low in my ear. "He's taunting us."

Jace holds out his clothing and then grimaces. "Er. Looks like I only grabbed your phone and jeans. Sorry."

Theo snatches the jeans and gives a low grunt of distaste. "I'm going commando too, by the look."

Jace's grimace turns into a leer. "Shirtless and commando beneath those jeans. Looks like the campus is in for a treat."

The sound becomes a growl, and Theo lunges for him, grabbing him around the neck and trying to flip him. Jace laughs, the sound rough in the back of his throat, and hooks his arms around Theo's waist, heaving him over and onto his back.

I shake my head and walk away. I suppose it's better they get some of that fury out. We need our senses on high alert.

The killer is here, and even though he got what he came for,

I can't help sensing him everywhere. In every shadow. Every flicker of movement.

As if proving my point, the faint hum of that song strikes up from the speakers outside the classroom. It's hauntingly sweet, sad and low with only a few notes to sell it. But boy do they. It doesn't stop playing, and a sick sensation of dread hits me as I realize this might be the beginning of the end.

He's drawing out the Hunt. Riling them up.

The sounds of my mates' scuffle behind me pause, but I ignore them, making my way down to the locked cupboards at the front of the room. Lost property is meant to be stored in admin, but it has to make it there from the classrooms and lecture halls first. And most people are too lazy.

After three tries, I pull the door hard enough to break the lock. We're in luck. Someone's left a gym bag behind, and the shirt inside looks only a little too short for Theo.

My nostrils twitch, a familiar warm scent filling them as a presence settles by my shoulders. When I turn around, Theo is standing right behind me.

I hold out the bag and open my mouth to speak, but he stops me, resting his hand on my shoulder and taking the bag before dropping it on the ground.

"Jel," he murmurs, his hand lifting to my cheek. "Pause."

I huff a laugh, incredulous. "We're on borrowed time here, in case you hadn't noticed. "What the hell do you want me to pause for? You want someone else to die?"

The thought of Luc being taken haunts me. He can't shift in prison, not even a little. He can only fight as a human, and this killer has begun to feel anything but human. The gods feel closer than ever, and I'm no longer sure they're on our side.

"I want you to rest." Theo's brow furrows, that familiar seriousness overtaking him. "If only for a few minutes. You're short on blood, you're afraid, and you're losing sight of the plan."

My jaw drops. "How dare you! You're making me sound like a frazzled omega or something—"

But he cuts me off again, thumb swiping over my lip. "And so am I."

I'm so shocked at the confession that when he kisses me I don't pull away. After a second of stunned silence, my body softens, melting into him, and my hands come to rest on his chest.

I can feel his heartbeat fluttering beneath his skin. He's burning up, hot with fire. But that fire burns on only two sides of a coin for us, and I don't want to give in to one when I so desperately need the other. Violence. Passion. I can't have both at once, or my soul might forget what's important.

I need to keep my edge.

"We need to fight," I protest against his lips, my eyes falling closed as he kisses me again, sucking my bottom lip into his mouth. "We don't have time for this. I'll get caught up in it and forget."

"You won't forget," Theo assures me, his lips trailing to my neck. "You know when to fight. You've always known when to fight. But I don't think you know when to rest."

My heart stutters, all of a sudden beating louder. I feel like I'm on the precipice of something. "What do you mean?"

A hand comes to rest on my hips, and my entire body shivers. Jace's breath hits my skin, his other hand gently moving my hair free so he can kiss the curve where my shoulder meets my neck. "He means he's a big ol' softie who's only just learned that losing and letting go can make you a better fighter." He kisses higher, below my ear. "And he's desperate to pass on the lesson."

A low hiss of pleasure escapes me. "That makes no sense. I can't afford to lose."

"Not to the murderer," Jace agrees.

Then, so quickly I don't see it coming, he takes me by the hips and pulls me back between his legs, where he leans at the desk behind him. His hand fists in my hair, gripping tightly, pulling me backward.

"Five seconds, Theo," he growls. "Take her."

Take me?!

My lips part in shock, heat pulsing between my thighs, as Theo steps forward and kisses me again.

It's different this time. Memories of the rut burn through me, flooding me, overwhelming me. His hands brace down on the table, either side of Jace's thighs, caging me there while Jace holds me in place, counting down from five under his breath.

And Theo takes me. He devours my mouth, his tongue curling lazily as he deepens the kiss. Biting me. Claiming me. He pulls away only to latch down on my neck, his teeth breaking the surface of my skin over where the rat-faced son of a bitch took my blood.

The scent of blood hits my nostrils again, but it's not a violation this time. It's a willing offer. A ritual between my mate and I. Passion offered and claimed.

Like a burst of light, I feel my soul come alive once more. The terror of the fight in the bathroom fades, while the adrenaline that shakes through my limbs bursts into an almost eerie sense of calm. Of power.

A truth hits me rapidly, one that I hadn't allowed myself to feel, because it felt like giving up. Like losing.

It might be necessary for the safety of our packs, of our community, to hunt this killer down, but violence is fucking exhausting.

Passion is the rest. It's the other side of the fire; the rekindling of the flame. And like our shifter souls breaking free of their chains, the answer to our dual lives doesn't lie in control.

It lies in balance. In knowing when to flip the coin and let the fire burn on the other side.

The rut burns in me, nothing like at its peak, but a low simmer all the same, and suddenly I *get it*. What Luc was trying to explain.

The rut isn't a loss of control. It isn't a dangerous side effect to be controlled through ritual. It's restoration. It's rest.

It's passion restoring the means to protect.

Theo pulls away, a smug grin on his face. "Better now?"

"Much," I growl, shoving him backward and stepping free.

My body burns. I'm ready to take on a dozen of these bastards, head to head.

But first, we have a library to infiltrate.

Theo tugs on the shirt from the gym bag, raising an eyebrow when it comes only halfway down his abs.

"You look very eighties," Jace says approvingly, eyeing the slight midriff. "Rock it." He moves past us, giving me a kiss on the cheek as he heads over to the window.

Theo growls, wrinkling his nose at the smell. But we need to be clothed if we want to get out of here, so he has to suck it up.

"Don't suppose it's worth sticking to the original plan?" Jace asks, peering out the window.

The library is opposite, the warm midday sun shining on dozens of students gathered around the front with their lunches.

"I don't think we should draw attention to ourselves by handing over the note," I agree. "But I want that thesis." Frowning, I settle on the only other option. "I'll sneak in again. You guys split up and check out the part of the basement where the wolf was killed. I won't be far. It's just down the hall."

"We're not splitting up," Theo says flatly, and it's Jace that growls this time.

My heart flutters, annoyance warring with a lighter feeling, something closer to joy. "Fine." I roll my eyes. "I guess that's when everyone dies anyway. We never want to split up."

"Now you're thinking like a final girl." Theo grins. "So what's more important—thesis or crime scene? We might only have the chance to do one, so we should pick which is first."

I hum in thought. "If the thesis has information on this ritual, it should explain what those symbols are more than just looking at them would."

"Yeah," Jace interjects, pointing at the library. "I don't fancy staring down ancient Babylonian and just waiting for a burst of inspiration if the answers are just down the hall."

Decided, we inch the window open and check the scene. It's busy, and the low hum of frantic activity tells me the word is spreading about the bathroom and the blood.

In fact, it's more than just a rumble. The Hunt is prowling.

"Look," I point to the edge of the quad, where three panthers roam in a tight circle. "It isn't dark, though. What are they doing?"

Frowning, Theo closes his eyes. Almost immediately, he winces and snaps them back open. "Yeah, I can feel it," he rasps. "It's calling."

Jace rubs his chest absently. "We can fight it until dark, since they're starting early. After that... I'm not sure."

I purse my lips and nod. It's as good as we can get. Now, we need to get that thesis and escape from here before the Dean finds us.

Or more specifically, finds me.

Those girls will have told someone by now. My time is running out.

We slip out the window one by one and keep to the shadows, cutting across the quad as casually as we can while concealing our faces.

We aren't exactly the inconspicuous types. With my hair,

Theo's bulk, and Jace's striking face, we draw attention on a good day.

This is not a good day.

Heads swivel in our direction, fingers pointing. Whispers fall behind palms.

In the shadows, more alphas rise. They're already shifted.

One or two are close to the rut, golden claws driving into the cobblestone. I swallow thickly. More than anything, I do not want to come across another alpha in the rut. We're meant to hide away when it happens. It's *illegal* to do anything else.

But the law has abandoned us, if it was ever with us at all. I should have known better than to ever trust it. I should have tracked this piece of shit down before these murders ever began.

"New plan," I whisper, quickening my pace. "Forget staying hidden. Just get in there, get the thesis, and get out."

The doors fall with a heavy thud behind us, and several low growls start up the second we enter the library.

I mark three alphas by the exits, and two more covering the middle.

The Hunt isn't resting at all, anymore. After the death of one of their own, they've made this a twenty-four hour affair.

It makes me wonder how many hours we even have left before this dumpster fire erupts. A low rumble sweeps through the library, picked up and echoed by alpha after alpha. Their faces lift, eyes flickering with fae light. Theo snarls, his warning drowning out their own. I let my own eyes light with challenge. Let my fangs sink through my gums and rest, just visible, on my lower lip.

The librarian glances at us and holds very still, her ears twitching.

Ignoring subtlety, ignoring distraction, we walk past their deadly challenge, and open the door to the basement.

35
JEL

We only have minutes before that mob attack, so I'm praying they keep shit organized down here.

Theo tails me, guarding me as I run through the cobwebbed, shadowed shelves. Fortunately, the librarians here rock. It's creepy as hell down here, but it's organized. I thought we'd find a bunch of crumbling cardboard boxes at best, but it's as neatly laid out as the rooms above.

Spiders scurry alongside us as we slow down to check the numbers on the shelves. I see a few brightly colored green beetles as well, crawling oddly in the shadows. I don't miss the way Theo glares at them. Their splotchy-patterned back, almost like tiger stripes, tells me all I need to know—nosy, unhelpful gods—and so I ignore it.

"We're looking for 398.2, according to Caitlyn," I whisper to them, not sure why I feel the need to be quiet. "Which direction are the numbers going in?"

"We're going the wrong way," Jace whispers back.

A loud slam echoes into the hallway—a door being thrown violently open. I swallow thickly, and the shelving around us illuminates in a soft, golden light as our souls rear up.

"Three of them," Theo says sharply, nostrils flaring. "Bears. From the study tables."

I remember them immediately. Tall, hulking men with mean looking faces. Will they take us to the Dean, or just attempt to kill us where we stand? Both are bad, but I think out of the two, the Dean is worse. The Dean means the cops, which means we can't get Luc out.

And that means we're all right where the killer wants us.

"Lovely," I mutter, and I start to run again. "At least this place is a bit of a maze. Maybe we can lose them in it."

I skid to a halt, my heart racing as I stare at the figure at the other end of the stacks, almost completely hidden among the shadows. He stares back. Expressionless. Face concealed behind the leather mask of a rat.

He's everywhere. How is he everywhere?! And *why*, if he's already got what he needed from me?

Is this the end he promised me?

My body lights up with fire, with renewed energy from those stolen moments together with my mates in that empty classroom. My fists clench, and I'm filled with the terrible need to take this asshole down. In movies, this would be the final sacrifice, where the best friend launches a stupid, heartfelt but futile distraction so the final girl can get away.

If it saves just one more victim, it's worth it.

I snarl, low and quiet in the back of my throat, shifting my fangs so they slice free.

Startled, not yet sure what I'm fighting, Theo and Jace move into offensive stances beside me. Low growls emanate from both of them.

"What is it?" Jace snaps. "Where?"

"That way!" a voice near the entrance grunts, drawn to the sound.

I whip my head in their direction, eyes narrowed, gauging the distance. When I turn back to the front, the rat is gone.

Did I imagine him?

"No," I hiss, furious. "He's gone! He was right there, I swear."

I blink, squeezing my eyes tight and opening them again, but the shadows are still empty.

He's messing with my mind.

"No time," Theo growls, guarding our back. "Get the thesis and run."

We stumble down the aisle, nerves on edge, searching for a sign of the missing rat. There's nothing there, nothing but the eerie sense of being watched. Of being prey.

I find the shelf, find the call number, and snatch the book from the shelf.

"Got it."

We turn back to the doorway just as three bears close in.

"How are you feeling right now on a scale of alpha to Goldilocks?" Jace mutters. "Because I'm feeling very blond and curly looking at these three."

He's not wrong. These guys are huge. Menacing. The idea of them chasing us down and winning is not a stretch. Once shifted, they could probably just sit on us until the Dean got here, and we wouldn't be able to do a thing.

I hiss out a long, slow breath. "I don't want to hurt them," I mutter. "Not unless we have to."

Theo glances at me. "You know what that means, then, yeah?"

I frown. "No?"

"We're going to have to hurt books instead."

Then, before I can stop him, he grabs onto the bay in front of us, heaves, and sends it crashing down between the bears and us.

"What!" I yelp, but there's no time to stop. We sprint for the exit, stopping to pull over more bays every few seconds.

Snarls of rage and confusion follow us. Alphas don't run from a challenge. Not unless they're weaker.

And yet, we're winning.

I hear the bears stumble and slow, books flying in their path, metal shelving units crashing to the cement floor in loud, echoing smashes.

When we reach the door, we pull a half-sized unit through with us, slam the door, and barricade it. Checking to make sure I still have the thesis tucked in my waistband, I nod to the others, shake off the adrenaline, and sprint once more.

We race back to the stairs, but Theo pauses, grabbing us both by the arm outside the room with the crime scene tape.

"Two seconds," he urges, pulling us with him. "Guard me."

I stumble, covering my nose as Jace retches and nearly chucks in the doorway. God, it reeks of death in here. It's even worse than the other scenes, because this is death and magic.

Not the good kind.

I take a cautious step inside, scanning the room for any clues while Theo sweeps quickly around it, checking the corners methodically.

Jace stares at the blood-covered walls and shakes his head, his jaw clenched in a grim, tight line. "This doesn't look like a scare tactic," he mutters. "This is real."

Theo grunts affirmation, and then pauses just inside the doorway to kneel down. Grimacing, he looks up at us. "Skin," he says, nodding to a fleck of something so small I can't even see it. "And marrow."

I can't see it, but I can smell it.

"Skin and marrow," I repeat, wrinkling my nose. "Why?"

"He hacked a bone." Theo rises. "But the news didn't mention that."

"Let's go," I hiss, shivering and looking over my shoulder. "They're already slamming the door. They'll be out in seconds, and that rat could be anywhere."

My hand comes up of its own will, covering the wound on my neck. Theo's expression darkens.

"Yeah. Let's go."

We clatter up the stairs, back into the library, and slow to a walk, trying to make it look like we aren't being chased by three pissed off alphas. I don't think it works. Several heads turn our way, eyes narrowed. Assessing.

I am so done with this shit.

I shove past my mates, past the alphas whose eyes remain fixed on us, glowing eerily, and sideways to the emergency exit.

Everyone in this room wants me dead. That counts as an emergency.

Then, finally, I tumble into clean, open air, followed immediately by Jace and Theo. We made it out.

A hand lands on my shoulder. My fangs are out, eyes glowing before I can stop them.

"If you bite me, Angelica," Dean Driscoll's voice comes very close to my ear. "I will see you put away where even your all-powerful family can't find you."

I spin around, backing up until my feet hit something warm —Jace. His arm closes around my waist, pulling me into him.

"You lied to me," the Dean says after studying the three of us for a moment. "You said you had no viper affiliation, despite your heritage."

"I rejected them."

His answering smile is almost pitying. "Their claim on you still holds. It isn't that easy to abdicate from a lineage that can trace their ancestry back to the gods."

My mouth falls open. "Back to the what now?"

He grunts, an annoyed sound, and adjusts his glasses. "Don't go getting ideas. No, you are not a god, Angelica. The bloodline is far too watered down. But why else do you think you were able to create that connection with your painting? Do you think just anyone can call out to the gods like that, if they aren't dragons?"

The painting.

This is why the university wanted my painting.

My body buzzes with adrenaline, my brow furrowing at the Dean's nervy, intense energy. My eyes fall, landing on the hand that reaches for me, almost placatingly.

The fingers are stained with blood.

My head whips back up, our eyes meeting—my own wide with horror and rage, while the Dean's are confused.

I step back further still until my mates flank me on either side. "Is that why you want my painting? Because it's interfering with your sick ritual?"

My heart races, the alpha soul within me fighting to overcome my logic and humanity entirely. I want to let her, but I can't. Not until I know for sure.

I can't lose my humanity yet.

I sniff the air, trying to guess if he's the one I sensed in the bathroom. He smells how he always does—nothing like that strange, cool absence of the killer. But the blood.

The Dean frowns, but then his eyes flash gold as he looks down and realizes what I'm saying. "Don't be ridiculous. This is from the walls." He wipes his hands over his trousers, but when he looks up at me his eyes are too dead. Too cold. "But I will need you to come with me, urgently, and don't even think of running this time."

If he's the killer or not, it doesn't matter. I don't trust him.

"Fat fucking chance," Theo snaps, stepping between us. His

face twists in rage and pain as his rising shift enables the Hunt to strengthen its call to him. "Run, Jel."

I don't ask questions; I run. Theo can handle himself, and if the Dean really is the killer, then we're not safe until we know how to prevent his ultimate goal.

I race across the quad, dodging students and professors, my lungs burning as I head toward my apartment. Something tells me I need to get that painting. This all comes back to the painting. I don't know how, yet, but it does.

Jace runs beside me, barely breaking a sweat, and the low rumble of fury behind us tells us Theo has abandoned his eighties digs and is charging too.

A flash of wolf blurs on my right.

The Dean.

Snarling, Jace leaps toward him, shifting mid flight to take him down just as he lunges for me. They roll, jaws snapping, blood red against the sharp whiteness of their teeth. I can't tell who's winning, and I can't afford to. I keep running.

A flicker of purple shines above me, distracting me. I look up to find that dragonfly hovering above us. The gods are watching.

They'll be watching until this ends.

Vipers and dragons and gods. Somewhere in that mess lies our answer.

I look back down, my apartment building so close I can read the signs on the gate, but my moment of distraction cost me. A wolf collides with my side, taking me down in one strike, rolling us together with his jaws clamped tightly around my neck.

By the time I'm upright, the Dean has shifted back, his wiry forearm hooked tight around my throat. Mud splatters up from the ground as the storm clouds above us open up.

He's naked, of course, because this is just my day.

"Think you're fast enough?" he snarls at Theo, every inch of his usually posh exterior vanished.

With a crunch of bone and sinew, Theo and Jace shift back. Three naked men stare each other down while I fight to calm the snake inside me.

"What the fuck do you want?" I choke out, digging my fingers into his forearm.

The golden claws of an alpha are always there, though it costs more to pull them free without the rut. I'll pay the price if it means I can stick them in the Dean's throat.

"You have to destroy the painting," he grits out. "It's how the killer will complete the ritual. He just needed a method of control and a conduit, and you've given him both because you're a stubborn little brat who wouldn't listen."

His arm tightens around my throat. I snarl, lashing out furiously, claws digging in deeper until blood runs in rivulets over my fingers.

Theo and Jace edge closer, eyes wild. They're way too close to the edge, with both the Hunt and their own instincts to protect their mate pulling at them.

"Who the hell are you, that you know all this?!"

"Think how this school was founded, Angelica. Guardians. We *guard*." He sighs, lowering his voice to hiss in my ear. "Time's running out, and this killer is arrogant. He's been trailing you in the shadows for days. He's going to step out of the darkness soon, but if you keep running around as stupidly as you are now, you'll miss the reveal. He'll be hiding in plain sight and laughing at you all the way down to Hell."

"Fine," I hiss. "If I promise to destroy the painting, will you let me go?"

"I'll even light the match for you," he says snidely, reminding me how little I like this guy. Still, he is helping us.

"Then—"

I don't get the words out. A gunshot echoes over the field, my body heaving from the force. I look down, expecting blood, but there's nothing, nothing in front of me, just—

The arm around my throat goes slack.

My alpha soul takes over, getting me to my feet and away from the dead body of the Dean.

36
THEO

"Jel," Cameron pants, lowering the gun. "Are you alright? Did he hurt you?"

That little shit of a TA appears out of nowhere, coming from the direction of the apartments. The scent of gunpowder fills the air.

He looks like a theater kid playing at an action hero. Everything from his black turtleneck to his Italian leather shoes is wrong. And yet, the gun is smoking, and there's a body pooling with blood on the ground. Cameron flicks his black hair out of his face and looks around at us, harried. The stench of his confusion grows stronger the longer we go without saying anything.

I flick my eyes down to his collar; his necklace is missing. That's a begrudging point in his favor; the killer stole his necklace for the photo after all.

Jel just stares at him, her jaw slack. Even I'm struggling a bit to process the fact that her TA just shot the fucking Dean.

We don't have time for this. Her brother is due at the station any minute; we need to get Luc back and get out of here. I'm sick of running around like this asshole is the predator and we're the prey.

"Are you insane?" Jel hisses, staring from the body to Cameron and back. "He was—what did you—"

Cameron frowns, the arm holding the gun lowering just enough for me to stop bristling instinctively. At least he isn't aiming it at my mate anymore.

"It's the Hunt," Cameron says. He still reeks of confusion, but his voice is deliberately calm as if we've all missed something obvious. "They've gone mad. Two tigers just tried to take down a freshman omega." The furrow in his brow deepens. "I did see what I thought I saw, didn't I? The Dean was about to bite Jel?"

I clench my fists, knuckles popping as a low growl catches in my throat.

Jesus. This guy isn't even an alpha, and he's obviously so hot on Jel he's trying to protect her. What kind of shifter carries a gun?

He just killed the first person who seemed to know what's going on.

Grinding my teeth together, I feel them elongating, filling a mouth that's growing rapidly wider than it should be. I want to bite this asshole, but I know Jel won't like it if I do.

Then again...

Jel's hands twitch reflexively, and the shimmer to her eyes is taking on a fierce quality that suggests she's struggling to hold back a complete shift as well. Would she bite Cameron?

Maybe I should just sit back and watch.

But we really, *really* don't have time.

Sighing, I step in between them. "It doesn't matter. Look... Cameron—is that your name?"

His eyes flash with anger. I give a warning growl, my teeth extending as my eyes shimmer with a bright yellow glow.

Cameron startles, so terrified that for a moment he almost looks repulsed.

"Yes," he snaps, finding something resembling a spine. "It's Cameron."

"Cameron, I'm not sticking around to sort this shit out, and neither is Jel. We can't afford the cops right now, so you're fine on your own, right?"

Cameron stares at me, expressionless. There's a scent of incredulity coming off him, mixed with shock and something more complex. But he doesn't show any of it on his face. Maybe that's how he's survived the chaos long enough to get a gun. There are already sirens in the distance. Campus security yells somewhere out of sight.

Will the Hunt even let the police on campus? Shadows flit across the edges of the field. It's getting harder to hold back from joining them. From losing control completely.

Jel steps forward. "He's right," she says firmly. Her eyes still glow, but she seems to at least have her fangs under control now. Her speech comes without any sign of a lisp. "Cameron, there are security cameras pointing right at us, so they'll know you had good cause to shoot out of self defense. But we're leaving now."

His expression flickers, the mask breaking. I'd almost say he's wary beneath it. "I thought you alphas were meant to be about protecting those who need it, not your own interests," he says, staring me deliberately in the eyes as he says the last words.

I hold his gaze, keeping my face still so I don't frown. What is this guy doing? Why is he taunting us?

Unfortunately, with Jel's background, it was exactly the right thing to say to throw her off balance. She snarls and steps forward. "I *am* protecting people," she snaps. "I'm protecting my pack, and far more than that if I'm lucky. And right now, you're *in my way.*"

He smirks. For an asshole who just screwed up our only lead, he's far too triumphant for me to play nice with right now. I bristle, hair sprouting along the ridge of my neck, my hackles rising. I step forward.

"People like Luc? Locked up in a cell?" Cameron shifts onto one leg, the other propped, like he's ready to run. "Everyone says he's behind the murders. Looks like you've been protecting the wrong people, and he's right where he should be."

Jel growls.

He puts his hands up, backing away but still with that irritating smile. "I'm just saying. You don't know everything about him and his family. Apple and tree, you know?"

That's it.

"I give you three seconds," I tell the guy. "Fair warning, and all that, since my mate takes issue with unnecessary bloodletting. Seems a decent enough compromise to me."

Cameron's eyes widen in shock and outrage. "I just saved your life," he protests.

"Two," Jace says, a low growl in his voice.

I hadn't even realized he'd moved around to guard the back, but there he is. Silently in position.

"No, you just made things stupidly complicated," I correct Cameron. "Are you going to stick around until we hit one, or do you have a survival instinct?"

Cameron darts a look at Jel, but whatever he sees there isn't what he wants. His face hardens, and he runs.

We don't waste time after he's gone. With a quick glance at the Dean, and an unexpected twinge of guilt and regret at the sight of his unmoving chest and vacant eyes, we move.

Everyone knows the victim is only dead if you can see the body, but the Dean's is right there. No mistaking it.

Running up the stairs to Jel's apartment, we trade plans in quick, decisive commands.

"We'll destroy the painting, and take the thesis with us to read when Luc is safe," Jel says.

"Better idea," Jace argues, "we give the thesis to my sister, and she can summarize by the time we're out of the station."

Jel glances at him admiringly. "Your sister really is great, isn't she?"

"You know it."

We reach the doorway of her apartment and freeze.

Someone's been here.

The door is busted off its hinges, the tiny space tossed over as the thief hunted for something. As one, we turn to the cloth-covered canvas on the easel.

It's gone.

"Well," Jel says, voice tight. "We were too late."

She doesn't say anything for several minutes, just staring at the easel, her chest heaving. Jace and I check the place over, but there's no sign of who it was. No cameras we can check.

When she speaks, it startles me.

"He's closing in, and I can't even see him," she says quietly. "He's in the shadows. He's in my goddamn *mind*." She runs a hand over her neck absently, expression twisted in pain.

Something catches her eye out the window. She steps forward, frowning, and traces a shape on the glass with her finger.

Jace and I fall in beside her, squinting.

When I realize what it is, my blood boils, while Jel's breath escapes her in a rush. It's only visible in the heating; a child's finger drawing on the window pane, visible as the hot air from the room hits the cold, rain-splattered window.

It's a rat.

"I'm going to find you, asshole," she hisses, her breath

fogging up the glass and obscuring the image. "And I'm going to fucking kill you."

She swipes her hand through the image, destroying it, and turns away, leaving her ransacked apartment behind her.

We take an Uber to Jace's house and drop the thesis off with four girls who seem to have the energy of a thousand. Then we ride on, to the station. Unlike the hospital, it's completely supe. Completely shifter, actually. So at least we don't have to hide our vitalities.

But that doesn't mean it's safe.

"You should wait out here," Jace says, nodding toward a shadowed bench on the other side of the road. "You've no idea what's been reported by now, and just because they didn't take you this morning doesn't mean they won't take you now."

Jel bristles, jaw dropping. "They can try!" she snaps. "I thought the whole crux of this plan was the vipers have power here. If Anthony can bail Luc out, he can stop them from taking me."

"Yeah, but we don't know if he can yet," Jace points out reasonably, lip twitching.

But before the argument can go on, a roar sounds from up the stairs, through the open doors. We freeze, staring at one another, and then we run inside.

The place is in an uproar. Anthony stands in the center, arms folded, a cool expression on his face, but the white of his clenched knuckles tells me he's close to losing it. I'm not surprised. Just stepping into the energy in this room has me close to the edge. Already, I can feel my instincts rising, feeding off the static charge of the numerous challenges rolling through this station.

We've got to be seconds away from someone breaking, and I don't like our odds.

When Anthony sees Jel, he turns and drawls, "Can someone

please tell your pigheaded idiot of a mate that I'm trying to help him?"

A rabid snarl draws my attention, and I turn to see Luc at the other end of the station, behind the bars of an overnight cell. "Get him out of here," he huffs.

The silver cuffs around his wrist sizzle, and where smoke would normally be curling from his nostrils, there is only red-rimmed, raw skin. He can't shift. He can't defend himself.

I grip the edge of the counter, the wood splintering as I fight not to bust through and get him out myself.

"Luc, he's got your bail," Jel snaps, ignoring the police officers who've appeared in front of us, trying to simultaneously usher us out and calm us down. "And he can prove you signed the affiliation clause."

Jace takes up position by the door, arms folded. It's my usual role.

I clap my hand over my face, dragging it slowly down, pulling at my skin. He's going to get us all locked up.

"I don't care if he's got my bail. I don't owe vipers *anything*." The last word is practically inhuman.

"I'm going to need you to leave," the nearest cop says, reaching for her gun. "Or we'll be forced to—"

"So if I take the money from him and pay it, then what will you do!?" Jel yells, eyes flashing with fury, ignoring the cop like someone who's never been profiled before. I rest a hand on her shoulder, trying to calm her. "I get that you have to draw a line, but this is fucking stupid."

"Ma'am," the cop insists, drawing her gun. My stomach drops.

But then a new voice appears, and everything just... stops.

"A fine display of police authority, we have here," the man says, voice rich with sarcasm. "And resources, too."

Anthony stiffens, and Jel's face turns pale. No need to ask

who's just entered. I don't want to turn, don't want to see him, and yet I can't stop myself. I turn around.

Marcus Vario, head of the vipers, stands in the doorway to the police station.

"Mr Vario," the policewoman stammers, dropping the hand that rests on her gun. "We weren't expecting—"

"Release him," Marcus says, ignoring her and flicking his hand at Luc's cell.

A policeman hurries to unlock the door. Behind it, Luc stands rigid, his face pale with anger. His lips have turned white, they're pressed so hard together. I don't think he knows what to say. What to do.

I can't imagine what this is like for him.

The man who murdered his family. Standing right in front of him. Engineering his freedom, as though they're old friends.

"See?" Marcus purrs, mouth curved into an awful smile. "Ms Caddel has grossly exaggerated her little story in exchange for fifteen minutes of fame. The boy recognizes me and accepts my gesture of goodwill. It's water under the bridge. Uncuff him."

I half expect Luc to shift right then. To tumble down brick and mortar and dragon flame on this unsuspecting station, for just the chance at revenge. It's sheer arrogance that Marcus allows him the chance. Arrogance, and power.

But he doesn't. He stays still. He doesn't say a word.

He also doesn't leave the cell.

Jace stares between them, eyes wide. And Jel doesn't move at all.

With a little sigh, as if everyone in this room has disappointed him, Marcus crooks a finger at Anthony. "We're going."

Then he claps his hand on Jel's shoulder, and without a word, steers her from the room as well.

Suddenly unfrozen, Luc startles, stumbling free from the

cell. Jace's mouth opens too, an indignant sound escaping. Marcus turns, but he isn't looking at them. He's looking at me.

I know men like this. They start off as tiny bullies on the playground, tormenting the little kid who's too young to shift. Taunting him. Hurting him.

And then they grow. And they get power. He could have us killed with a snap of his fingers.

But what will he do to Jel?

I take a step forward, but Jel glances at me, pleading with me. And because I respect her knowledge, her authority when it comes to her family, I watch them continue down the stairs and into the waiting car outside.

As the car drives off, she slumps against the car window, as if she's suddenly unconscious, and it abruptly hits me what's just happened.

I fall to my knees outside the station, and my two mates drop beside me, equally destroyed.

37
JEL

WHEN I COME TO, THE FAINT BUZZ OF WHAT SOUNDS LIKE ELECTRICITY sends the hair along the back of my neck prickling upward. My fingers twitch, nails digging into a cold concrete floor.

When I can finally squeeze my eyes open, I discover the source of the buzzing. It's nothing too bad—just a bunch of server cabinets badly contained. It's enough to tell me I'm not in some kind of torture room, like I'd thought.

But this might well be worse.

I'm in my parents' basement.

I grit my teeth and stand up, methodically checking the exits. I used to get locked in here occasionally for training rituals, and there used to be a broken lock on the third window—if that tiny rectangle of muddy light can be called a window. I could fit through as a kid, and definitely as a snake.

But when I climb up on the pile of rotting cupboards, they've fixed the lock, and the window holds firm.

Sending out a mental apology to whichever viper kid suffered the cost of my frequent escapes, I jump back down and face the only exit. Light peeks through the dusty windows and the bottom of the stairs, so there's plenty of daylight still.

Plenty of activity, too, judging by the movement I can hear above me.

If Dad could just throw the killer down here with me, I could fight the bastard and at least put this temporary imprisonment to good use. It would be just like old times, too. Except instead of it being some hired goon who pissed off my dad, it would be someone who pissed off me.

I feel like I'm owed that, after the scars I earned down here.

But the door remains closed, and there's fuck all I can use in this forgotten place to get out. It's used too often as a prison. The vipers aren't going to make stupid mistakes.

Although, they don't seem to have taken my phone off me. I pull it out of my pocket and flip through idly. Still have reception. But I guess since everyone saw me get taken, it doesn't exactly achieve much if they know I'm in the basement. Anyone with a brain could guess I'm in the basement. It's always the fucking basement.

I fire off a message to my mates anyway, but there's no response. Which, honestly, is more worrying than my own situation. If my dad got me back in his clutches, he can get them too.

I know his style. He'll take me publicly, because it's his right, and the others will disappear silently as a threat to anyone who questions his right.

A message pops up, and I almost drop my phone. But it isn't from the guys.

It's from Greta.

I flick it open. She hasn't contacted me since the news went public that I'm the viper heir.

Hey snake, thought you might want to see this.

A link pops up straight after. I can't read the tone of her text, but it doesn't sound like the girls in the bathroom. Maybe she won't turn on me immediately.

But then, Greta is an alpha. She's not going to drop to the passive aggressive lows of those girls. She's just going to go for my throat. Guess I won't know until I open the link.

Subconsciously rubbing my throat in protection, I click the link. A news article pops up, and a video starts playing immediately.

My dad's familiar, arrogant drawl sounds tinny down here, on my shitty phone speakers in his shitty basement.

"If you want something done right around here, you have to do it yourself," he says, signature grin in place—right below his dead eyes. There's never been any emotion in them, and even looking at them now, they send a shiver through me.

Not because I'm afraid of him. But because I'm afraid of the part of me that looked up to this man. That listened to him and did anything to earn his praise.

"Mr Vario, does this mean you know who the killer is? Are the vipers involved with the murders? Does the city have to fear gang violence going forward?"

I raise my eyebrows. What a ballsy reporter. Wonder if she'll disappear.

Marcus's grin widens, his eyes turning somehow flatter and more dead than before. Snake-like. "It means my daughter is returning to her rightful place at the head of our tender community," he murmurs, his gaze caressing the reporter in a terrifying promise. "Her talents were wasted in Sawlefire Academy, and since the proper authorities have failed to reduce this threat, it's time we stepped in."

The reporters try to hound him for more, somehow forgetting he's a viper—or not caring in the face of a new scoop. But he turns easily away and carves a path through to his bike.

I close the video, not needing to see any more.

The vipers and their fucking reputations. They've turned this into a PR stunt—they've turned *me* into a PR stunt. In one smooth move, he's going to claim me back for succession and earn the city's favor. He's going to make me bring them the killer's head on a pike—something I was already going to do, but of course, now it will be in his name.

I can't believe I ever thought he cared about me.

He's lying, I tell Greta, not sure why I care what she thinks.

My dad would call it a weakness.

No shit, she sends back immediately. *Someone filmed you being taken from the station. Any fool could see you were pissed.*

Pissed is too soft a word. I was murderous, but I couldn't do anything or he'd have taken my mates then, too. At least now, they have a chance of escape.

Are the guys okay?

If someone filmed me, maybe she saw where they went, too. I just hope they weren't foolish enough to follow me. They should be reading that thesis now and getting some real answers.

The bouncing dots appear several times, kicking my unease straight up into fear, before she finally says, *They're not with you?*

My blood runs cold.

Greta isn't an idiot who creates facts from assumptions. The only reason she would ask that is if my dad took them, too.

When I don't reply, she sends: *I've got your back, babe. Hang tight.*

I snort. Sure. I'll believe it when I see it.

The door at the top of the stairs slams open, and heavy footsteps enter the basement. He walks slowly, without hurrying for anyone. And in the same show of power, I don't get up from my seat on the floor. I just tilt my head back against the concrete walls, my wrists resting on my propped knees, and wait.

"Angelica," Dad says, running his dead eyes over me. "I'd hoped we could talk about this sensibly."

"Then you shouldn't have started with a kidnapping. Sensible people tend to go for coffee dates, instead, just FYI."

He grins, the eerie sight sending shivers down my spine. After twenty years, I finally know what it reminds me of. His smile reminds me of a snake yawning, stretching its jaw right before it swallows its prey whole.

Dad folds his arms and leans back against the railing. "And clever alphas don't make their presence known on an enemy's surveillance system. Would you like to explain that one?"

For a second, I don't know what he's talking about. Then it clicks. I barely fight back a groan. That fucking camera in the alley, on the way to the warehouse.

I knew I shouldn't have looked at it.

That's why they started paying attention—because they realized I was. Which meant it was something worth watching.

"If I'm such a shitty alpha, why do you want me back so bad?"

This time, his smile doesn't make me shiver. It's a straight up knife through the heart. I don't know what's coming, but I know it's bad.

"There are many ways for an alpha to fulfill their duty," he says idly, his gaze falling to the muddy windows, as if he's turned pensive. It's all an act. It's always an act. "Some lead, because it's what the community needs from them."

A false expression of sadness crosses his face. "But you, Angelica. The community needs something very different from you."

He crosses the room in two quick strides. I realize what he's doing at the last minute and leap to my feet. I duck his first swing, but his second grazes me and knocks my hits off to the side.

The needle stabs me in the neck, and the drug courses through my veins.

I wish I could say it was the cold that made me too sluggish to beat him. Or that I was still stiff from being thrown down into a basement. Something frustrating and pathetic, to be sure, but human and understandable.

But it wasn't.

It was the same thing it always was. The fact that he's my dad, and for just a second, a second that cost me any chance at winning, I didn't see it coming.

"What have you—" I slam my hand over my neck, trying to will the drug out of my system, but I can already feel it working on me.

"A little sedative," he says casually, stepping back. "With a mighty kick. Only works on alphas." Finally, his smile morphs into what it truly is—a sneer. "If that's what you can be called."

A drug. A drug that only works on alphas.

Even my sluggish brain puts the pieces together rapidly. He's using the same venom-blood combo on me that the killer has been using. Except his drug is the real deal, full strength, because it's mixed with the proper Alpha bloodline. His blood or mine. The only two that work.

Was that why the killer could stand in the smoke without succumbing? Maybe the mask wasn't the filter at all; maybe this asshole isn't even an alpha.

I shake my head, clearing it from thoughts that can't help me now.

Dad has already turned away.

He begins up the stairs again, footsteps never faltering even as he continues speaking to me. "Sometimes, the most important role a leader can fulfill is to differentiate between the time for fighting and the time for sacrifice. A ritual like this, my girl, already so far along, will not be resolved by fists nor fury. This upstart of a killer has done one good thing with his measly life.

This ritual will bring us straight back to the gods—to their favor."

He pauses, a rare moment of emotion breaking through. It's triumph. Sick, twisted, arrogant triumph.

"What began that night we took out the dragon threat will end now," he says softly, almost to himself. "This city will no longer be under the delusion that they can trick us. Steal from us. Defeat us."

He glances at me, as if seeing me for the first time. "No one touches a viper and lives."

My blood runs cold. This is still about that night, for him. It's still about the insult of that rat stealing from him and tricking the vipers to do his bidding. It eats away at him.

It's made him lose whatever sanity he once had.

And this ritual will bring him more than vengeance. If the girls in the bathroom were even half right, it will bring him the kind of power he's always craved. The power he believes he deserves—the power that the killer has challenged him for.

Through the groggy influence of the drug, all I can think is *he can't be allowed to get it.*

Not this kind of power.

Not the gods'.

He's nearly at the door now.

"Of course, we won't be using the Hunt sacrifices he's prepared. I don't know what petty game he's playing there, but it's just a waste of good alphas if you ask me."

No. Please no. "You're not sacrificing them," I beg, too far gone by the drug to care how I sound.

"Your mates?" He sneers. "No, Angel." My stomach turns at the pet name. A reminder from when I believed we were a family. "We'll be sacrificing you."

38

JACE

It's Luc that gets us out of there, even though he has the most reason to fall apart.

"Move," he snaps, voice low as he glances around the streets. "We have to go."

I blink at him, my mind working in half time. I don't want to move. I want to collapse, like Theo has. Even if I know I can't do that safely, not yet.

"Move," Luc hisses again, grabbing Theo by the arm and pulling him upright. "There's no time. I know she should be with us, but she isn't, and at least she's safe from the killer."

Theo grunts, disbelief etched into his face as he slowly rises to his feet. "Yeah, because she's deep in the snake pit."

"She's gotten out before, she'll do it again," Luc says quietly, shoving him forward again and pulling out his phone to grab an Uber. "This piece of shit killer is our biggest threat—he's Jel's biggest threat. Don't lose sight of that now." His voice becomes a snarl, low in the back of his throat, and his eyes glint gold. "It's time to eliminate the threat."

In a few minutes, we're speeding down the back lanes toward my house. The tree-lined streets pass in a blur, slowly fading out into grass-lined, and then eventually just concrete. The fences get messier and wirier the further we go, too, until we finally reach a wire fence with no grass at all.

The Uber driver sneers as we open the doors. I don't care; I'm used to it. But Luc opens his app and deliberately cancels the tip, blue eyes flashing with anger as they meet the Uber driver's in the rear view mirror.

A surge of warmth curls in my gut, and I squeeze his shoulder as he gets out.

"So, we're here to get the info, locate the ritual, and take the bastard out, right?" I ask as we hurry up the path.

We're here to hunt him. My soul knows it, my mates know it, I know it.

"He's going down," Luc answers, a puff of smoke obscuring his face for a moment.

The door swings open before I can get out my key. I wince. It looks like my sister has been waiting for me, and she's pissed.

Caitlyn raises an eyebrow, like the little shit-stirrer she is, and doesn't move from the doorway. "I'm not your gopher."

Theo covers a startled laugh with a cough. Badly.

"Never said you were," I say lightly, my brain whirring as I try to get out of the storm I know is coming.

"You can read, I assume?" she continues, both eyebrows lifted now. "So I'm not sure why you wanted me to read some dusty old thesis for you. Unless, of course, you're taking advantage of your sister's generosity." She narrows her eyes. "Which would be really mean."

I lean both arms against the doorway, blocking the others from view for a moment. "Please, Caitlyn. This is urgent. I'll do anything you want if you can just tell me what that ritual means."

Her expression softens, a flicker of surprise crossing her face. "Alright," she says slowly. "But you owe me." Pursing her lips together, she adds quietly enough that the others can't hear, "I want you to stop trying to replace Dad."

My heart twists. "Done," I tell her softly. "That old bastard can piss off and stay gone this time."

Her grin lights up her face, and she steps back from the door. The wind chimes stuck to the front of it jingle. "Then come on in. I've got a messed up tale of deicide for you."

"Deicide?" Theo mutters as he follows me down the hallway.

He looks too big for my house. His shoulders hunch over in the narrow hallway, and he looks around at the framed photos on the wall with an almost hunted expression. Luc is completely silent, and seems even more distant than usual.

"God-killing."

Luc and Theo glance at one another, jaws tight, and keep walking.

When we reach the kitchen table, Caitlyn sits down with a flourish, swiping her empty bowl of cereal to the side and moving a familiar bound stack of papers.

"Okay, so the legend is about a wish," she announces.

Theo chokes, eyes wide. "A wish?" he growls. "What kind of fu—" He glances at me. "Messed up wish do you get from this kind of ritual?"

"Anything," Caitlyn answers primly. "You can ask the gods for anything. But... the legend comes from what the first person asked for." For the first time, she looks a little queasy. "He asked them to die."

Silence meets her announcement. There's a chill in the air that has no source, like it's coming from my bones themselves. After a moment, Luc clears his throat.

"So, what, he tells them to keel over and they just do?"

"How else would you kill a god?" Caitlyn asks him, her tone the peak of logic and practicality.

It's gratifying to see the look on Luc's face as he's forced to deal with the whirlwind of strange intellect that is my sister. It's the same look I get, and it's nice not to feel like the only one.

"I guess so," he murmurs, frowning down at the table as he leans forward. "Do you have an account of that first time? The one that started the legend?"

"Sure do. This page here." She points and begins to read. "The rat roamed the halls of Sawlefire Academy, humming a chant that would summon the old gods. Just three notes: one low, that called to Fate, who lives beneath the earth; one middle, of the human realm, where shifters reside; and one high, to reach the heavens.

"Of course, the Hunt was summoned to take down the arrogant omega who thought he could speak to the gods. But, using powerful blood magic, he found a way to control and annihilate the Hunt that stalked him. In turn, he sacrificed three hunters: one to open the gate, one to call the gods down through it, and finally—on the ritual altar itself—the third hunter, whose blood spilled upon a conduit and allowed the gods to speak. With a queen by his side, to represent the rat's selflessness and his right to rule, he could finally ask for his wish."

Caitlyn clears her throat and lets her voice take on a spooky tone. If I weren't so creeped out already, I'd tell her to stop. It's not the time for humor. But I can't find the heart to tell her it's real. It's happening. "But he had no right. The queen had been tricked, because the rat's wish was simple: for the gods themselves to lay down their lives and die."

The room stays very, very quiet. Luc's face has turned pale, and Theo is gripping the edge of the table so tightly I think it might be all that's keeping him up.

"So our rat heard the legend and decided to pay homage," Luc says finally.

Caitlyn's eyes widen, and I squeeze her shoulder in silent

support. I didn't want to tell her, but maybe it's better she knows.

"Yeah," Theo grunts. "Beginning ten years ago, when he went after the viper's drug and set them on your family."

Luc clenches his jaw, staring down at the table in thought. "He knew he couldn't take down alphas on the Hunt on his own... So he stole the drug that night, when the vipers were occupied. Blood magic, like in the legend. But he didn't realize the dragons didn't have the blood he needed to mix with the drug. He drained them all, and it wasn't enough, so the ritual never began."

"Why did he think the dragon blood would work at all?" I ask, frowning. "The vipers had the drug and the venom."

"Maybe he just thought any powerful shifter blood would do?" Luc suggests. "He couldn't kill the vipers without the drug, so he arranged for them to kill the next best choice and then came in after, like the little scavenger he is."

Caitlyn scoffs. It's a small noise, but we all turn to stare at her. "Or," she says slowly. "The dragons sold whatever this drug is to the vipers."

Silence. Then: "I heard them," Luc breathes. "From the basement—they spoke about stealing something back. Stealing it *back*." He looks up at us, eyes bright. "You're right, it was their drug. They must have created it, but it needed snake venom to work. So they worked with the vipers, or tried to pay them off, or something, and it went wrong. The vipers took it."

"No wonder they were so quick to take you all out," Theo says in a low, quiet voice. "You were a liability."

"I think you still are."

The fear in Caitlyn's voice has my instincts rising in a second. My eyes flash, teeth shifting and ripping free from their gums as I turn to the kitchen window. A familiar black car has pulled up outside.

I last saw it transporting Jel away from me.

A tall, stern-faced man steps out. Marcus Vario.

"Ten bucks says Jel doesn't know he's here, and she isn't going to be told," Theo says gruffly, straightening up with a glare.

"No one's taking that bet," Luc snarls. Fire erupts from his lips, making Caitlyn startle.

I stand between her and the door. "Caitlyn, get your sisters and hide in the basement."

"But—"

"Now!"

She goes, collecting my sisters from the back room and ushering them downstairs in almost complete silence. I'd be impressed, but she always impresses me.

"Meet him on the porch," I murmur to the others. "I don't want him smelling how near the girls are."

We shut the front door behind us just as Marcus comes to stand on the front step.

He smiles. It's a slow, mean smile that doesn't reach his eyes. He fixes his attention on each of us, one by one, lingering the longest on Luc.

"I had you followed," he says lightly, after he's finished whatever assessment he's been conducting. "Hope you don't mind."

I bite my tongue and wait. I'm not falling for his games. He's on my territory, so he knows exactly what he's doing by challenging me like this. Just as I know he'll win if I take the bait.

After a tense silence, Marcus drops the smile. "I'll get to the point," he offers, turning to Luc. "Are you currently in contact with Michael D'Amour?"

His tone makes him sound bored, but the golden light of his eyes tells a different story.

Luc frowns. "My uncle? He's dead." His mouth twists as he spits out, "You should know that."

His fists clench by his side, and the bond rattles with the effort he's putting in to hold himself back. To keep from murdering this man where he stands.

Marcus gives a small laugh. "Why would we kill our supplier? Use your head. Even when he was addled and missing his precious formula, he might still have been valuable to us, if he hadn't tucked his tail between his legs and run away." He clicks his tongue thoughtfully. "No, it was only the others who had to go. Michael is very much alive, and apparently determined to be a pain in my ass."

His supplier...

Oh. Oh shit.

Luc's eyes widen at the same time my brain connects the pieces, slotting them horribly into place. Luc's uncle betrayed them, selling the drug to the vipers. In return, they spared him.

Not even out of loyalty, but out of a chilling sense of practicality.

"Addled?" Luc asks, his face pale. "What do you mean? What did you do to him? He was never addled."

Marcus just stares at him, his face unreadable. Finally, he gives a sigh, as if we're inconveniencing him. "When he couldn't keep his mouth shut about our little deal, we had to contain the issue somehow. A witch's spell to destroy his memories, and a simple commandeering of the formula was enough to render him harmless."

There's a slight emphasis on the word *him* that sends shivers down my spine. Especially when paired with that flat, bored tone, like the massacre of Luc's family was nothing more than a convenient excuse to run damage control.

"Now, are you sure you aren't in contact with him? Word

has it he's been digging up the lawn at the old dragon house, and I for one would love to know what was buried there."

Luc doesn't move, doesn't breathe. He's straining so hard from holding back his soul that he's shaking. Finally, he says, "He worked for you. He made you that drug."

Marcus grins and leans forward. "How does that make you feel? Want some revenge? Or maybe you want to use him like we did and get back at us instead?"

Luc's control shatters.

A snarl is the only warning before he shifts. The porch cracks beneath the weight of his limbs, bones crunching as they double in size. Triple. It isn't a full shift, only enough to distort his legs and jaw, his jeans tearing to reveal shining, obsidian scales rippling over muscled thighs. His teeth snap, monstrous below frightening yellow eyes.

I stumble backward, dragging Theo with me, fur rippling over our hands and arms as we prepare to fight to the death. Our death.

Marcus's two henchmen lunge for the guns at their waists, but Marcus stops them with a hand in the air, disturbingly calm.

Worryingly calm.

My heart races, an ominous, wordless prediction rising in my veins. I turn back to Luc.

"Stop," I bark.

Only Theo listens, freezing by my side.

"I don't need a sidekick to kill you," Luc snarls in a broken growl, right before he lunges.

I don't see it happen; I only see how impossibly fast Marcus moves—the surge of electricity from the taser that buys him seconds as Luc slumps forward. Seconds shouldn't matter, not in a fight against a dragon, but then the syringe slides free from Luc's neck, and it all falls into place.

Luc drops to the ground.

Marcus's smile widens. Without looking at his henchman, he says to them, "Dear me, we certainly can't leave him now. Not when he's so obviously deranged with fantasies of revenge, and..." His voice lowers to something slow and deliberate. Triumphant. "Not now that he knows all our secrets."

My blood chills. He told us deliberately, so he'd have a reason to take us in. It's doubly chilling, because he never needed a reason. It's not like he has to justify his actions to anyone. Telling us about Michael D'Amour is a power play, to show us that Marcus doesn't see us as a threat.

The second reason it sends shivers down my spine is because we know what he did to the last people who knew about this.

The two guns pointed at Luc's prone body tell me exactly what will happen if we fight. I can't risk it. Especially not with my sisters so close by.

My focus is to get Marcus off this property, away from my family, and while keeping my pack alive. My father would have died before giving in without a fight, but then, he never really thought about anything but his own pride, did he? He never thought about what alpha protection might truly mean, in the moment.

It's a price we have the privilege to pay, not an entitlement we're owed.

Our flame burns with more than just violence—two sides of a single coin that only represents one thing. Family. Pack. Protect what you love; love what you protect.

A violent man will never win this fight. So, I flip the coin and let it burn.

I hold up my hands, sacrificing my pride and my freedom for the people I love.

After a beat, Theo does the same, the low rumble in his

chest fading.

Movement across the street catches my eye, and I turn to see a vaguely familiar face watching us in shock. I blink, realizing who it is—the almost-victim we saved at the party. Greta, or something. Well, at least someone apart from my sisters will know where we've gone.

"What do you even think Michael is doing?" I ask Marcus as he herds us toward the car.

Is Michael D'Amour back now because he knows something about how the drug works? Maybe he can help us outwit the killer, if we can escape Marcus's clutches long enough to find him in time. It can't be a coincidence that he's waited ten years and only shows up now.

Marcus waves a hand, not bothering to turn around. "Seeking revenge on me, perhaps. Perhaps revenge on the rat that stole his precious drug. Who knows who he blames for his own mistakes? We can't afford time for amateur hour at this stage of the game, so Michael and any of his resources, like yourselves, have to be eliminated. It's nothing personal."

Nothing personal.

I watch as they shove my mate over our laps, handling him roughly before surrounding us and pointing their guns at our heads. I think of Jel, betrayed by her family, and Luc, who just discovered a fresh betrayal himself.

I imagine my sisters huddled in the basement, smelling the aggression that will linger long after we're gone.

Maybe it's not personal for him, but it is for me.

The fire in me simmers, burning hot with everything I would do and sacrifice for the ones I love. I'll let those embers burn a little while longer, because I know something Marcus, in his violence and arrogance, doesn't. The coin will turn once more before this is over.

And when it does, he'll be the one to pay the price.

39
JEL

THE ROOM BEGINS TO SPIN. IF THIS HIGHER POTENCY OF DRUG WORKS at the same speed as the one the killer gave me in the warehouse, I've got about ten minutes before I'm completely out. But there's no guarantee. Could be faster. Probably is, since Anthony's blood was just the test case. This is Dad's drug; it'll be his blood.

Besides, it's straight in my veins for fuck's sake, and in the warehouse I was trying not to inhale. Taking shallow breaths.

My breathing turns shallow now, but it's not by choice.

As soon as I pass out, it's over for me. I've no idea how much the vipers know about this ritual, but if their network has grown as much as I think it's grown, judging by that expensive camera in a random alley, I can't assume they're not ready to sacrifice me as soon as I drop.

I have to get out of here.

Using the last of my strength, I pick up a heavy paint tin and hurl it at the window. It shatters into a dozen pieces, but the tin bounces off bars behind it.

Bars I could handle; it's the mesh between them that poses a dilemma.

With the basement swimming, blurring my vision until I'm seeing at least two of everything, I crawl over to the wall and attempt to navigate the bookshelf.

The furniture I climbed in seconds before now proves an impossible mountain. I take it one shelf at a time, calling on the reserves of my soul to bring forth claws, which I drive into the wood.

The world wobbles dangerously, but I make it up one shelf. Then another.

This time the bookshelf wobbles—for real. I cling to the shelves, aware of how ridiculous I must look. I'm barely two feet off the ground, grappling for dear life as I fight not to flatten myself with a bookshelf.

My phone vibrates, too long for a message. Someone is calling me, and there's only one person who does that.

Gritting my teeth, I mutter "Anthony," to myself.

The name somehow anchors me. Steadies me. I've got one person on my side in this godforsaken place, and if I can just get out of this fucking room, he can do the rest. He can alpha the shit out of me if he just saves my life.

"Anthony," I say again, jaw clenched as I use the shining light of my idiotic little brother as a beacon.

Inch by inch I claw my way up the wall, golden claws driving into the brick, sending mortar dust sprinkling down below me.

My phone continues to buzz, its urgency serving as the kind of boot camp mantra those asshole personal trainers wish they could be.

"Anthony, you little shit, you better be ready for a mutiny," I hiss, my words turning sibilant. "Because it's time our dad got what's coming to him."

Yellow light flickers on the dirty white-washed walls as my

eyes glow, my body seeking to pull strength from anywhere it can.

I don't let the shift take me yet. I don't know what the drug will do to my snake body, if it will work faster or slower. With my luck, I'll drop to the ground like a fucking slug. It's not worth it.

Besides, I can't bite my way through mesh.

I reach the top, and urgency spikes through me as my adrenaline gives one final kick. I don't have long. The drug is winning, and there's only so long sheer spite and the dream of patricide can fuel me.

I tear at the mesh, digging my claws through the tiny holes and pulling until my fingers bleed.

A golden claw rips from my flesh and falls to the ground. I barely even feel it. The mesh is giving way. Bit by bit, it's tearing at the edges. Just enough for something small and thin to fit through.

Who says size is everything, hey?

With the last of my brain cells, I take my phone and shove it through the hole. I'll have to go without clothing for a while, but at least I can call an Uber.

The tang of blood fills my lips as I grin, staring at the hole I've made. Golden light flickers off metal, my fangs elongating as I bite into the mesh, ensuring I don't fall when I've come so far, and begin the shift. My body lengthens and twists, writhing up onto the ledge.

My brain bounces around like a juggler on steroids. This drug is definitely worse while shifted. Way, way worse.

Through foggy vision, I force my body through the hole and out into the grass. I can collapse out here. Anthony will find me. I just need to get to Anthony.

My phone stops ringing abruptly, and a panicked shout

makes me look up. Distinctive red hair catches my attention—
Anthony is waiting just within the fenceline. He must have
known I'd be down there.

But he isn't looking at the basement.

He's looking at the two vipers in front of him. Their forms
are partially shifted, gigantic snake bodies writhing on top of
meaty, tattooed legs like some kind of fucked up hydra.

Anthony begins to shift, eyes like flame, and I want to
scream *no, it's a trap*, but the words won't come out. I can only
hiss, panicked and broken.

Who are these men? Have they turned on my father? Trying
to steal his heir for some reason?

I start to shift back, panicked, but my body is halfway
through the hole still, and my soul and body together scream
out in agony. My soul takes over, forcing us back into snake
form, blood oozing from a dozen new wounds.

I spin around to watch, praying he's made it free.

So far, he's ducked all their attacks. The two freaky hydras
are bleeding from several long gashes. One of them has shifted
entirely, a gigantic anaconda-like snake twisting across the
hilly mountain of our land.

Anthony can beat this. He's fought hundreds of men in our
father's training rings. They don't stand a chance.

But something is stopping him from shifting. Why won't he
shift? Ripples of scales cover him and retreat, over and over. It's
like he's consumed the blockers they give us during our first
shifts, to help us feel the beast before it takes over. But why the
hell would he have taken them?

The first man shifts back, scales still covering his body as he
pulls out a gun. My heart leaps into my mouth, but I needn't
worry. Anthony sees it.

He ducks the bullet and comes up spinning. Even if he can't

shift, he can fight, and pride swells my chest. Pride for my little brother.

My vision blurs, made foggy by the drug pouring through my system, and I begin to wiggle a little clearer from the hole. I'm nearly free. We're nearly out of here.

A shadow crosses my sight.

I think it's the drugs at first—the whole world is swooning —but then a familiar form steadies among the chaos.

A rat. Not a real one—a leather one.

A man in a leather rat mask.

No. *No!*

The two vipers fighting my brother have disappeared. Where did they go? My vision swims, sending double, triple of the scene in front of me across my sight. I can't make sense of it. Anthony is panting, doubling over, shaking as the shift he's trying to make still won't come.

Someone has drugged him, too. They've used the shift blockers on him.

The killer has planned this.

I open my mouth to scream, but only a violent, frantic hiss comes out. I try to shift again, but the mesh and the bars rip through my skin, and my soul won't let me die like this, halfway through a basement window. She doesn't let me shift.

Anthony doesn't see it coming, his attention is fixed inward, on his uncooperative body. He misses the shadow behind him.

An arm scoops around his neck, holds him tight.

A knife slices into his stomach.

Blood, there's so much blood.

I watch my brother go down, his body sliding ignobly over the top of the hill, out of sight.

The rat turns to me, two horrible leather masks swimming in my vision, aligning again and again to the face of the man who just killed my brother. He stares right at me. Then he disappears.

He's gone.

They're both gone.

My brother is gone.

40

JEL

I DON'T KNOW HOW I GET OUT OF THERE. INSTINCT TAKES OVER, MY soul quitting her constant battle with me and simply kicking me out completely. I let her.

No one sees me. I should go over the hill, see if there's a chance to save him. I only saw the body fall; I didn't see him die. But my soul doesn't let us stay to witness, not at the expense of our safety. She gets us out of there, out of the broken window, over to the copse of trees by the main house. Somehow, she even brings my phone, although there's no point, because there's no Anthony anymore to call me on it.

Anthony's gone.

I didn't protect him. I promised I would protect him, and I *didn't*.

I couldn't.

It doesn't matter why; I failed him.

I shift back and lean against the trees behind me. I can't be seen from most angles, but a naked girl in someone's backyard eventually attracts attention. Especially when she's covered in bloody cuts from wire mesh.

I have to get this drug out of my system. Shifting has only sped up the process. I can barely think, barely breathe.

If they find me like this, I'm done for.

It's my own fucking blood—or my father's blood. The details don't matter, because it's still mine. How can it hurt me like this? Mixed with venom, sure, but I'm a *snake*. None of this makes sense. I don't understand how this wonder drug even affects me. But I guess that's why I'm not in the drug peddling business.

I blink up at the sky, confused at how blue it is between the trees, and why I'm staring at it, before realizing that my head has rolled back. I try to force it up again, but it won't move.

The dry mouth has stopped, and I'm at the drooling stage. Feels like I'm going to drown in my own spit, which is as fun as it sounds.

My arm shoots out in front of me, gripping the air in a fist. I frown, staring at my fingers as they turn back and forth, searching. What the fuck? I am totally not doing that.

My other arm flings out, twisting around. It clasps my other hand, and okay, now I'm officially freaking out. It's like something else is controlling me.

Like—

Oh, God. They are. This is how they're planning to get my sacrifice. They'll make me walk there on my own two feet, and smile the whole way down.

Sick dread floods me. The idea of being controlled by the vipers, walking straight to my own death, is a fate worse than anything I've imagined. I walked away from them years ago, and now they're making me just... walk back.

I can't take this. I have to get this drug out of my system, but without an antidote, I don't know how.

My eyes flutter closed, but even as I fall back against the

tree, close to passing out, my body lurches and rises to my feet. They can control me even when I'm passed out.

Adrenaline surges, giving me one last ditch effort to fight this thing off. I force my brain to work. The key to this drug has to be the snake venom—it's paralyzing and hypnotizing.

Mind you, it shouldn't be on *me*. They must have found some way to disguise it from my system, so my body doesn't recognize it and doesn't realize it has the antibodies to fight snake venom off.

My eyes snap open.

My body doesn't recognize it. But it can't be foolproof. They can't disguise snake venom from a snake permanently, can they? It's like a mask. I have to rip the mask off.

My mouth contorts into a pained grimace, my jaw unhinging as fangs tear from my gums. Maybe I can kick my system into action if I remind it what it's meant to do. If I force it to look for danger.

Or, maybe I'll just paralyze myself because they've blocked my antibodies somehow instead of tricking them, and I'll be the first dickhead snake in history to die from their own venom.

I'll take those odds.

I lift my forearm to my mouth, wrenching it from the invisible grasp that's trying to lead me from my hiding place, and drive my fangs into my flesh.

Agony rips through me. A scream catches in my throat, garbled as I try to hold it back. The tang of venom hits my tongue, and I bite deeper, harder, tearing into my flesh.

I pull my mouth free and slump back against the tree. Is it enough? Or is this about to become the stupidest death in the history of deaths?

Something tugs at my arm, pulling it forward. Weakly, I pull it back.

It takes a second, but it goes.

My arm does what I tell it to.

Hope rises in me, my heart fluttering with the first positive sensation I've felt since I crawled out of that basement.

I step backward, into the trees, further down the dip in the valley that runs toward the back fenceline. An invisible force tries to tug me forward, toward the house, but I overpower it easier now.

Exhaustion floods my body as it grows heavier, weary with the effort of fighting off this drug—the unexpected surge of venom my body had to deal with. But it's heavy with my own weight, my own exhaustion.

They aren't controlling me anymore.

My poor, tired body is working in overdrive, and I'm going to feel this like a bitch tomorrow, but I suddenly feel so lit up with energy I could take on the entire pit and win.

I slow my steps, focusing on making them steadier, sturdier. I've reached a secluded area that feels safe enough to pause, so I take a breath to regroup. Just for a moment. I'm about three meters from the fence, but it will be guarded, and I need to make a plan before I navigate that.

I fall to my knees, skin hitting the cold earth and reminding me I have no clothes.

Something digs into my palm, cold and almost painful as my fingers grip tighter around it. I frown, trying to make sense of what it is when I'm otherwise completely naked.

Oh.

Of course, it's my phone. I turn it over and stare dully at the screen. Several notifications flash up at me, but only one truly grabs my attention. I remember my phone ringing as I was climbing free, before it abruptly cut off and... everything else happened.

Anthony left me a voicemail.

Driven by some kind of masochistic urge I can't explain, I hit play and hold the phone up to my ear.

"Jel," he says urgently, his voice low like he's trying not to be found. Just that word nearly makes me burst into tears, but I'm strangely numb. Detached. I listen without a single expression on my face. "I know where he's keeping you, but he won't let me anywhere near. He doesn't trust me."

I can't listen to this.

I don't hang up.

His voice lowers further still. "Listen to me, Jel. You know what Dad's like—he's going to try to convince you you're nothing. He's done it your whole life, and you've never been able to see it. All that alpha shit you hate—he did that to you deliberately. So that even when you took his place, it would still be him. Always him. He didn't want you to be an alpha; he wanted you to be his little alpha vessel."

There's a rustle of fabric, like he's checking the coast is clear, or ducking further into the shadows.

"He's tried to erase you, Jel. Brainwash you. Make it so there's nothing left, and look, I get why you ran. Fighting that shit off is hard. I get why you just... blocked it. Why you turned to your paintings. It was the only way you could keep a piece of yourself alive.

"But he's got you now, Jel, and I refuse to let him win. How much longer are you going to let people tell you what you are? What that *means*? You're an alpha, Jel. And that word doesn't just belong to Dad. It belongs to you." His tone turns fierce, and something in me stirs. Lifts. "It's time for you to get your shit together and step into who you're meant to be. It's not what Dad told you you are. It's not what any of those university shitheads told you you are. But it *is* an alpha, and you're going to get yourself the fuck out of that fucking basement and meet me by the back gate. Okay, Jel? Now! Get up!"

I get up.

My brain buzzes with a thousand thoughts, all clamoring and crashing into each other. Anthony's right. He's always right.

I walk, strangely calm, toward the back gate. There's a shed nearby, where Dad would sometimes take people to shoot them. He won't have shot my mates yet—not until they can witness his plans for me, and probably serve as more sacrifices as needed—but he won't have let them run free. They're a liability.

Sure enough, when I get to the barbed fence that runs along the back of our wooded property, there are two guards posted at the door.

My eyes flick to the side window. It's boarded up, but there's a gap about the size of a mouse.

Dad always tried to make me compensate for my smaller shifter size. He said it was an embarrassment.

The corner of my lip ticks into the faintest of smiles. My heart still thuds wildly, grief driving my chest into agony. But for now, I shut it off.

I throw my head back, bones shuddering as the shift takes over, and fall to the ground. I'm inside the shed in seconds, with no sign of the drug in my system anymore.

On the floor, my mates are bound to one another. Luc is passed out, but Theo sees me coming and grins through blood-covered lips. When he speaks, there's no sign of sedation or paralysis—they haven't been drugged yet.

And they won't be.

"Hi there, little snake," he rumbles.

Jace's head jerks up, his brown eyes falling on me. They soften as his hands clench, mouth twisting in triumph. "We wondered when you'd show up."

41
THEO

SHE SHIFTS BACK, HER BONES CRUNCHING INTO POSITION, SNAKE EYES shimmering as they turn first shifter-golden and then their usual deep blue. Lying on the filthy ground, covered in blood and trembling from the after effects of whatever she's gone through to get here, she should look vulnerable. Broken.

She doesn't.

A fierce energy hums through her, steadying her shaking limbs and filling her gaze with a terrifying fury. I wouldn't want to get in her way.

It's time to put someone else there, instead.

She rises first to her hands, then back up onto her knees. With rough, jerky movements, she undoes the ties holding us together and leans back to give us space to stand.

"Don't suppose you've got an extra tshirt lying around," she asks, voice raspy. "I seem to have misplaced mine."

Jace tears off his shirt and tugs it over her. It's cut off at the sleeves, but it's long. It works as a dress for now.

I move to Luc, untying the last of his bonds and tapping him gently awake. He's been in and out of consciousness since we arrived.

He blinks up at me, blue eyes only half alert. He's struggling, trying to shake it off, and fortunately it looks like we're nearing the end of the potency.

It's been about eight hours by my count, so if we weren't nearing the end, I'd be hella fucking worried.

"You good?" I ask him in a low voice. "How are those urges coming along?"

We worked out early on that the drug does two things. Paralysis and hypnosis—both properties of an ordinary shifter snake bite, but somehow kicked into intense overdrive with this drug. A normal bite would induce mild effects for five minutes or so, and it has little to no effect on an alpha.

This has effects I've never seen before. Complete bodily control, no eye contact necessary.

When we worked that out, we figured it was better if he stayed unconscious.

Luc's eyes focus on my face, his expression a little sharper than before, and he nods carefully. He lifts his arm as I watch, studying it, and shakes his head. "No other urges to move. Just my own."

Good.

I leave him to reorient himself and cross to the door. We can't have long before the final ritual starts. The final sacrifice.

The night we've all been waiting for.

The killer is planning a big scene, and I can't imagine what he'll do if we don't show.

There are still two guards outside, but they're distant enough they won't hear small noises.

Jel joins me. "My dad wants in on this ritual, too. He's going to skip over whatever sacrifices the killer has planned, and just use me instead."

A sick sensation, like bile, stings the back of my throat. Her dad is planning to sacrifice her. "Jel." I reach for her, but she holds up a hand, silently asking for space.

That's when I feel it.

A riptide of grief, sucking me in even as she holds it back.

"What—" I ask, my voice twisting in pain. But it's not my pain. It's hers. I just don't know why.

She meets my gaze, eyes shining with tears. "He killed Anthony."

"Your dad?!" Jace starts forward, eyes wide.

Jel shakes her head. "The killer. He was here. Taunting me, like usual."

"Oh, sweetheart."

I step forward, not crowding her, just letting her feel the warmth of my presence, my silent offering of strength as I run my hands over her shoulders. Up and down.

It doesn't feel real. But why wouldn't it be? He's killed before; there's no reason he wouldn't take her brother.

She shivers beneath my touch, but she doesn't lean in. "Not now," she breathes, just quiet enough for me to hear. "I can't fall apart now."

"And you won't," I tell her, standing back.

Jel clears her throat, shuts her eyes, and then begins to pace, her hands clenching into fists at her sides. "How long do we have?"

Jace steps in front of her as she spins back around and hooks his arm around her waist, stopping her. He pulls her in tight and murmurs in her ear. Where I would get a shove for daring to interfere, he gets away with it, but the thought doesn't come with the sting of jealousy, like it might have once.

I'm glad she can accept what he offers her, just like she took what I offered her, too—those hushed moments of acknowledgement. And Luc, with his ability to poke and prod until the fire beneath the surface roars free and cleanses the toxicity it was concealing; she takes that too.

We're all in this pack thing, together. We each offer something different. I wouldn't have it any other way.

When Jace pulls back from her ear, he answers her earlier question loud enough for us all to hear. "Long enough to catch him and make him pay."

She freezes, turning to look up at him. Her eyes were flickering before, but now they begin to glow, the pupils narrowing to two slits.

His mouth ticks, a hint of a smile, and he grips her by the chin to kiss her. A low moan falls from one of them, but it's over too quickly as he pushes her gently away.

"Make him pay," she echoes, still with those fierce, fae eyes.

"I can walk," Luc confirms, steadying himself against the wall. "We need to move now, though. Before they come back."

"Where is the ritual? Did your sister find out anything?"

"Not the location," I answer as Jace shakes his head.

We share a look over the top of her head. The same sense of resignation and disquiet slips down the bond from each of us, and I know he feels the same thing I've felt for the last hour.

"We don't need to," I tell her. "He's using the Hunt as his supreme sacrifice, and it's been calling us since the sun went down."

She stares at me, expression unreadable. After a moment, she nods.

"So we follow the call."

The Hunt guides us home. Jace and I transform in the shed, then wait for Jel's signal to leap on each of the guards and tear out their throats. They go down in a gurgle of shock and rage.

No time to reflect. They would have done it to us.

We leap the back fence and cut through the forest. It winds around the side of the city, where the mountains meet the first spindly buildings. The Hunt thrums in my veins, commanding me.

Jace lopes beside me, eyes alight with power and energy. Somewhere behind us, Jel and Luc run as humans. I don't worry whether they can keep up; my only focus is on reaching the source of the violent power coursing through my bloodstream.

Shadows follow us, flitting in and out of the trees. At first I think it's the rest of the Hunt, closing in. Then, I realize the ritual has begun.

These are gods.

Snarling, twisted faces rage at us from the darkness, their eternal life disrupted as an earthly force commands them to join us.

They lunge at us, claws swiping over our skin, but it's only a warning. They aren't here yet.

We run on.

A dark-haired woman leans against a tree, her eyes fixed on Luc as he passes, but with a sardonic lift of her eyebrow, she disappears.

Another shadow appears through the gloom, running stride for stride beside Jel. I spare a glance to see which god has joined us, and snarl in rage.

A leather rat mask shines through the gloom, the silver moonlight reflecting eerily off its curves.

I roar, but Jel has already noticed, ducking and spinning to face him just as haunting electronic laughter fills the forest.

Like a shadow, he's gone, leaving only the lingering notes of his song in his wake.

"Keep running," Jel snarls, her voice drowning out the song. "I'm going to kill him with my bare hands."

I realize where we're going minutes before we arrive. Back to where it all began, of course. Because Fate likes poetry.

"I'll check the perimeter," Luc says, peeling away to roam the outside of the house.

I transform back as we enter the party, not that anyone seems likely to notice if we're shifted or not, or even that we're naked. There's something incredibly off about the way everyone is moving.

The bass pounds through my body, making my head pulse and my vision dance. At first, I think they must have drugged me at the snake pit after all. Then I realize the drug is here.

It's everywhere.

In the ventilation system, in the filtration system leading to the pool—the steam rising from the pool. It's in the fog machines drifting by our feet.

One by one, drunken dancers stumble and sway, their limbs dead but their bodies kept maniacally upright by some distant puppeteer. Every third body or so moves the same way. I cover my nose and shift my sight to make sure, unable to use scent to confirm. But my soul knows as soon as I look. It's all the alphas.

This drug only affects alphas.

That's what the killer's game has been about from the start, I realize. Alphas. He's targeting and sacrificing alphas to the gods.

The only remaining question is why.

A rippling tremor races through me, making me shudder. Convulse.

"We have to get out of here," I warn the others, my body shivering as it attempts to fight off the drug that's trying to seep in every pore. "It's everywhere. He's got the place filled with it."

"It's too late," Jel says in a cold voice, her expression fixed in a scowl of rage. "Look at the doors."

I turn. They're locked, and the windows are boarded over.

Neon lights bounce off the fog, the dancers writhing and screaming in joy. None of them realize what's happening, what's about to happen.

The Hunt is still calling.

"With this drug, he's going to control the Hunt. We don't have long," I warn her, my eyes catching Jace's. "We're about to become a liability. You're the only one who can throw off the drug."

Terror fills me at the thought of what he'll make us do. How he'll use us.

If Fate is on our side, Luc won't be inside yet. He'll have avoided the drug, and since he isn't part of the Hunt, he might still be able to help Jel.

Cameron appears in front of us, like a twisted dream. But he's only here to talk, his body swaying slightly as he leans one arm against the wall and focuses on us. His drunken gaze narrows in confusion as he skims over my fighting stance, the clench of my jaw. Of course the drug isn't affecting him; he's a beta at most. Possibly even an omega.

"I pulled the security footage." He lifts his voice above the music, smiling at Jel. "They let me go. Self defense."

He keeps smiling at her with that fixed, unnerving stare of someone who can't see straight. When she doesn't answer, his jaw tics in anger.

"I thought you'd care," he says, leaning in closer.

"Tell me again tomorrow," Jel snaps. "I'll care then. I've got bigger issues tonight."

Cameron's eyes glow, his lips pulling back like he's about to snarl.

I growl at him, a low warning threat, and he pauses. His eyes flick over, and then he backs away, lifting his arms in defense. "I'm going," he says with an aggressive grin, and then he stumbles into the shadows.

"Jel," Jace rumbles, his eyes flickering, jaw clenching as sharp canines appear in his gums. "I can't—it's happening."

A ripple like a roar runs through the crowd, picked up one by one until the entire room echoes with it. There's no way we can hold it back now, and if the Hunt is rising then that means we're at the end of the ritual.

The killer will be hunting, too, and Jel is on her own.

Jel's eyes widen and then glint with determination, with fierceness. I have a moment where my heart fills with sheer admiration for this woman in front of me.

Then the Hunt and the drug take over, and everything else is lost.

42

JEL

I SEE THE MOMENT MY MATES' AWARENESS FADES. THIS ISN'T LIKE AN ordinary Hunt, where their souls might take over but at least their human awareness is still present enough to have some input. These alphas are drugged and controlled.

I need to get out of here.

While the alphas are still shifting, bodies contorting among the mass of scared partygoers who've just realized something isn't right, I make for the stairs. I'm sick to death of basements; it's time to fight from above.

Cameron's house is huge, and it takes me almost the full shift to reach the base of the stairs. Already, I'm surrounded by several large panthers, their eyes glinting through the drugged fog.

But they turn away from me. The killer hasn't set them to hunt me down yet, and I don't know what that means.

He told me he'd see me at the end. Well, this is the end, so where the hell is he?

I clatter up the stairs, body pumping with adrenaline.

Screams follow me, but I don't turn around. I hope the pounding snap of wood splintering means that someone has made it outside. That they've escaped before the Hunt is unleashed.

When I reach the landing, the sounds from the party become oddly distant. Distorted. I can feel the bass thudding in my chest, but the screams and snarls themselves are almost too warped to notice. It's like the TV is on behind some far away closed door.

And then they fade completely. I don't know what that means, but it sends shivers through my body. I'm so full of adrenaline now, my limbs are shaking.

I slow down, ducking into the first room I find—someone's bedroom—and scanning for signs of life. There's nothing. Not a rustle, not a moving shadow.

Where has the killer gone?

And where have the gods gone?

I walk over to the window and try to open it. Even though the drug doesn't affect me the same, I'm feeling a little woozy with all this vaporized venom in the air. But the window is stuck, and it won't lift up.

I smooth my hand through the condensation on the glass and peer down. There's no sign of Luc anywhere. Maybe he's had the good sense to do some recon before joining us.

Or maybe the killer was waiting at the perimeter, when Luc went to check.

Swallowing down my fear, I turn away from the window.

And come face to face with the killer.

I freeze, my blood filling with adrenaline and rage. He stands in the doorway, rat mask fixed in place, standing as still as some kind of freaky statue. There's a long knife in his hand, and it occurs to me in a series of quick calculations that I haven't had a chance to assess his skills yet. He's taken down or killed five alphas so far, and that was before he got his stolen drugs to work.

I'm not facing off with him in a tiny bedroom on his turf.

He tilts his head to the side, assessing me, waiting for something. I let him have that second, preparing my body for the attack without pulling back to telegraph the move, and then I lunge, slamming the door just as he lurches forward. He hits it hard, splintering the wood. A glint of metal appears through the gap, twisting and writhing as the wood snaps further. He stabs again, and again.

I wait a beat, holding until he withdraws for another attack, and then I push the door into him again. Harder, this time. A vindictive smile twists onto my face when I hear him grunt. His strength is impressive. Likely potion-induced. When he drives his knife into the wood again, it grazes my cheek, leaving a slice of blood.

My hand comes away red when I wipe it. So, he has good instincts, too. He might not be an alpha, but he can scent my positioning behind the door. And he keeps his cool.

I shift my tongue, flicking it out and pulling the scents and chemicals back into my mouth, tracing them over the glands there. There's still no identifying scent rising off him, but this close I can detect a hint of emotion. So, while he might not be operating out of rage, it's definitely there, lingering in the background. Along with an odd note of disgust—repulsion.

I can use this.

"You didn't have to go to so much effort, you know," I call out through the door. My voice echoes with a second, lower tone as my soul rises in anticipation. We flick our tongue out in delight, tasting his mounting rage. "If you wanted my attention, baby, all you had to do was ask."

There it is—that disgust. It flickers, uncontrollable, making me smile. It's his weakness. Especially because disgust and fear go hand in hand.

He pulls back, wild with fury, and I swing the door wide.

I meet him with a slash of golden claws across his chest. He stumbles back, giving me space to lunge again. To shift my teeth and sink them into the meaty flesh of his bicep.

He tastes foul, but it does the trick. He stutters and falls back a step, a low snarl of rage dropping from behind his mask as his body stiffens in anticipation. Snake venom is a beautiful thing, sometimes.

Do I kill him first, and then unmask him? Or do I want him to know my face in death?

Decisions, decisions.

I shift my eyes, watching the golden glow illuminate the dips and lines of his rat mask. I should have five minutes of partial control over him, if he isn't an alpha. Five minutes of playtime.

The glow shimmers, hypnotic, and I hiss, "You want to lay down tribute for the gods? Dance for them, little killer." My tone shifts and dips, deeper now, two of us together. "Dance for me."

He straightens, limbs unnaturally stiff, and begins to sway. Charmed. Hypnotized.

The shadows in the corridor writhe, eyes and faces appearing and then fading. The movement shudders and blooms, spreading wider, further, and I realize the walls are covered in bugs. Thousands of bright green beetles, of furry spiders. And dragonflies, poised with their wings gently swaying, ready to take flight.

Whatever my ancestry and latent painting abilities may be, I can't speak God. But I'm pretty confident I have their blessing to end this.

My shifted form isn't strong enough to strangle him, so I'll have to do this at least partially as a human. But I know now that my human self and my shifter soul were never as far apart as I once thought. They're side by side, and it's together that we'll take this bastard down.

But then the killer twists unnaturally, limbs flailing outward, and shatters the control. I grunt in annoyance, pulling back. In the space of a breath, he lunges for me, leaving me barely enough time to twist out of the way. The knife drives into the wall, sticking to the drywall and buying me seconds.

I use those seconds to run, assessing what I've just seen. I was right about the potions. The question now becomes, how many more does he have up his sleeve? In a fair fight, he would already be dead. But this asshole has never had the balls to play fair.

I need Luc.

A bathroom appears to my left. I grab the architrave and use the momentum to spin inside, slamming and locking the door behind me.

The window opens easily, and I'm out there and on the roof before the killer even appears.

My heart races, and I force my breathing to slow. Searching for calm. For my center.

My soul guides me there, and it isn't cold at all, like my dad always trained me to believe. It's a warm, churning sea of *knowing*. Of calm, passion, and logic all mixed into one.

I back away from the ridge, wondering why the killer hasn't appeared yet.

"Afraid of heights, there, buddy?" I call out.

There's no answer.

There's no sign of Luc, either. Frowning, I crouch into a solid stance, walking forward one silent step at a time. I let my eyes unfocus, roaming the surrounding land in quick, methodical sweeps. There's no movement. If the Hunt swarmed outside, like I thought, they're eerily still. Only the muted sounds of thudding bass break the stillness of the night.

Chills dance across my shoulders. Where is everyone? Where is the killer?

Movement catches my eye, making my heart leap, but it isn't Luc. A figure stands by the pool, illuminated in the blue light from the lanterns, and waits for me.

How the fuck did he get there when he was just upstairs?

Frowning, I check the surrounding land for a trap, but there's nothing there. With one last final taste of the air—thick with growing malice and something tangier, stronger, which I think might be the ritual itself—I leap off the roof.

The grass is soft and springy as I duck into a roll and come to stand ten feet before the killer, with only the pool between us. Neither of us move.

He wants me to follow him into the dingy poolhouse, where he can get me alone. Does he think I'm a fucking idiot?

"I don't think so, baby," I call out, waving to my relative safety behind the fence. "Why don't you come out here and we can talk nicely."

The killer tilts his head to the side, mocking me, pretending to consider. Then, very slowly, he shakes it. No.

Well, can I blame him?

"Then we have a stalemate," I call back. "I'm not coming into your little room of death, and you're not coming out where you might, you know, suffer the consequences of your actions." I give an exaggerated shrug. "So. Where does that leave us?"

"Jel?"

My heart sinks as a familiar voice emerges from the side of the building. He must have avoided the Hunt by going down the side of the house, but oh God, not now, you idiot.

"Stay back!" I yell, but it's too late.

Cameron steps into the shadow of the poolhouse, and the killer lunges. If rat masks could smirk, this fucker would be giving me a thousand watt grin right now.

Cameron stares at me, eyes wide with fear as he tries and fails to save himself. It's over in seconds.

With one arm hooked around Cameron's throat, the other holding a knife to his neck, the killer takes a step back into the poolhouse.

"Follow or I slit his throat," the man in the mask calls.

I blink, startled to hear the voice. Even more startled to realize I don't recognize it. I thought after he'd toyed with me so personally, I would know the bastard behind this, but maybe not.

Cameron's eyes silently plead with me, and I know deep down I've completely run out of options.

"You really are a fuckstain on humanity, you know that, right?" I call back, but I'm following. I know a hostage when I see one.

I had an excellent plan, a brilliant plan, to not fall for any of his tricks. But unfortunately, this isn't a trick. It's the one thing that would get me in there—the one thing I stand for. Protection. Loyalty.

But if that asshole thinks he's getting between me and the door once I'm in there, he's got another think coming.

I start cataloging exits, planning how I can incapacitate the stupid rat as soon as he's within striking distance and get Cameron to freedom before the killer brings down whatever ritual knife he's been saving for me.

There's a tangle of pool equipment at the back of the room. If I can maneuver him into that I can gain a second in focus. It should be enough to disengage.

I take another step, then another, pausing in the shadow of the doorway. I'm not taking another step until he shows a weakness.

If he just needed me in the poolhouse, that means he has some way of trapping me there. I don't intend to give him the chance to pull it off.

But then I see it. I don't know how I see it, with his opaque little eyes, but something glints behind the holes in his mask. I smell malice, and sense the triumph in his gaze.

The hand holding the knife shifts, and I realize what he's doing. How far he'll take this, because of course he will. This hostage isn't his shield, it's the bait, and what good is hostage bait to an alpha if the hostage is ultimately safe?

"Jel!" Cameron whimpers, the sound garbled, the room moving as if in slow motion. I try to reach him. I try to stop the knife.

I'm too late.

It slits across Cameron's throat in a horrifying spurt of blood. He crumples to the ground.

"You—" I begin, but instinct kicks in and I duck to the side just as the killer throws the knife at me and lunges to the side.

It skims past my ear, slicing the top almost in two before it thuds into the wall. I clutch at the bleeding stub on reflex, my hands slick with blood, but I barely notice it. My brain races to get ahead. I'm inside the poolhouse now. He's got me where he wants me; I can't let him lock me in. I have to get him talking again. A villain that monologs is a villain that fucks up.

Ego, man; it'll get you every time.

"What the fuck is wrong with you?!"

The killer doesn't move. Doesn't speak.

Did he only have one knife?!

But then he lifts his fingers to his mask and begins to peel it back, inch by inch.

I keep my face still, but inside I'm screaming *what the fuck?* Is this how he plans to trick me into whatever trap he's made this poolhouse into?

Because damn, that's a good one, I am a curious bastard after all.

But it's not good enough.

I back up toward the door, step by step, never taking my eyes from the killer.

The mask comes off just as I reach the final two feet of the room. If he can somehow stop me from leaving with two feet of ground when there's three meters separating us, he can have this one.

I stay to see the mask come off.

Tussled black hair falls free above cold, blue eyes. My brow furrows, my heart racing in confusion and apprehension. I don't know this man. I've never seen him before in my life. Why did he reveal himself like this, like it meant something?

What's so important about being in the poolhouse?

I freeze, hands braced, my legs poised to leap backward, toward the door. But I can't move until I spot the trap. Where's the trap?

Wait.

Where's the body?

The door shuts behind me with a soft click.

I spin around, rage and fear clouding my mind when I see the smiling face standing in front of the door.

"Corn syrup," Cameron says, wiping his fingers through the blood at his neck, and grins.

Corn syrup.

Did... Did this motherfucker just *Scream* me? Five hundred slasher films, Jel, and you didn't see this one coming.

Then the reality of what's just happened hits me. Two of them. There were two of them.

Scenes play out in record speed in my mind. The mirror writing, written while the killer's arms were around my neck. Two victims at the party, so soon after one another. The killer appearing at the poolhouse when he'd just been upstairs.

Cameron leaving my apartment building right before we discovered the painting had been stolen.

Killing the Dean, who was the first person to help us.

My adrenaline surges, my whole body feeling like it's vibrating from the strength and shock of this betrayal. I should kill him now. I should take him out. I've only got a split second before they do whatever it is they've been planning from the start.

I've only got a second to do what's most important.

"Why?" I ask, my voice full of rage.

He cocks an eyebrow. "Isn't it obvious?" he asks. "I'm sick of you fucking alpha brutes running everything. It's time for a change. No more alphas. No more gods who only favor the strong." He smiles. "Just me."

Well. There's no accounting for taste.

Something the Dean said just before he died rushes back into my mind.

This killer is arrogant. He's going to step out of the darkness soon, but if you keep running around as stupidly as you are now, you'll miss the reveal. He'll be hiding in plain sight and laughing at you all the way down to Hell.

The necklace in the photo with Anthony; it was Cameron after all. The Dean was right. It wasn't a mistake; it was deliberate. Arrogant.

I start to laugh, a low, hysterical laugh that sounds almost deranged.

A projectile hits me from the other side of the room and everything goes black.

43
JEL

"Wake up, darling," Luc's voice murmurs into my ear. "They've gone to prepare a lovely coffin for you, if you don't fight back now."

"Don't want a coffin."

"Of course you don't." He nuzzles my neck, voice still soft. Gentle. Coaxing. "But you were stupid, and stupidity ends in a coffin."

The fight with the killer comes back to me. The poolhouse. Cameron.

Fuckers, the lot of them.

"No, I was protective, and I lost," I groan back, clutching my head. "There's a difference. Can't win 'em all."

They used my best assets against me.

Oddly, I don't regret it. Like Luc said, these values make me who I am. They mean I'm not my father.

"So they're preparing a coffin, are they?" I mutter, trying to prise open my eyes with my fingers.

"They are indeed."

"Who even are they?" I still can't believe the killer was half unknown. That's so unsatisfying.

"That sniveling rat-faced piece of shit, Cameron, and my uncle."

My eyes snap open. "That blue-eyed guy was your uncle?"

Luc nods, expression grim. "He got one over on me, made me think he was here to protect me for just long enough that I turned my back."

I grin. "So, you were stupid, too."

He grins back. "Maybe." His expression turns sober. "We had a nice little family reunion. He told me everything. They've been working together for years. Cameron was the vipers' test subject... for the drug and for other things... mostly venom, I believe." He gives a humorless laugh. "He was their lab rat."

The snake tooth makes a twisted sort of sense, now. I almost understand why he was mad at us all.

But then I remember Tegan, Dorothy, and Greta. I remember the wolf from the Hunt who died, and my brother. Cameron took his revenge out on innocent people, and he's dangerous. Twisted.

I have to protect my own, and all the others he wants to hurt as well.

"I'm guessing your uncle was the man in the first photograph, then, ten years ago," I murmur, clutching my head. "The red herring that got my family running to your doorstep."

Luc's eyes flash. "Yes. I gather my family weren't pleased when he let slip he was working with the vipers, and they kicked him out. Then, of course, Marcus destroyed his mind and stole the drug. So, Michael betrayed us all for the sake of revenge on everyone who'd ever wronged him.

"The drug was originally designed to work with his own blood, but whatever Marcus had done to him ruined that. He'd assumed it would still work with dragon blood though, so when Cameron and Michael planned their revenge on the vipers, they figured this was the best plan to take down everyone at once. In their hands, the drug would be the right kind of blood magic to appeal to the gods. They'd have power they'd never dreamed of before."

"Doesn't anyone know what hubris is anymore?" I groan.

Luc chuckles and kisses my head, continuing to fill in the blanks in a low, steady voice while he rubs soothing circles over my back. "But Marcus had modified the drug, and it didn't work with dragon blood at all anymore. So their plan failed. Michael buried the venom and the drug on my property and fled, while Cameron stuck around to work out what kind of blood it needed. He eventually discovered it was the viper alpha line, but he couldn't take down Marcus or Anthony on his own, so he gave up. But then he found out about you..."

"Because of my painting," I realize suddenly, my eyes snapping open. That fucking painting. "So he called up a little double-crosser's reunion, am I right? Cameron needed your uncle to get the drug back from where he'd hidden it, and to help him mess with us until my soul came out again."

Luc nods grimly.

The poolhouse comes slowly into focus, and I get to my feet. Luc stands back, giving me space, but as soon as I'm steady, he's there again. Fingers trail the skin below my shirt, tracing up my thigh. His breath is hot on my neck.

I can feel the hard ridge of him against me as I press between his thighs.

It doesn't mean anything alarming, like I once would have thought. The rut is long gone; we aren't going to get sidetracked tonight. It simply means this is who we are, violence and passion as two sides of the same coin. Always. Where one flares, the other is close behind.

With my soul by my side, as a partner instead of an enemy, that duality no longer worries me. I know when to shift from one to the other. I know where violence is needed, and when it's toxic.

I know how to serve my pack.

We protect. We guard. And we take what life gives us with two hands and never look back.

I lift my hands to Luc's shirt, one on either side of his collar, and grip the fabric. I pull him down to me, kissing him fiercely. Brutally.

His mouth curves into a smile against mine, smoke curling from between his lips. He's shotgunning me with dragon breath.

I lean back and blow, the smoke obscuring his smug face.

"I don't suppose they left me in here because they were done with me," I say dryly.

His expression turns grim. "Look out the window."

I look.

It's happening over the pool, I suppose for the water element. Or maybe a cheeky bit of cultish drowning. Who knows?

The lights are on, flickering eerily through the drifting smoke. But that isn't the freakiest bit. No, the freaky part is the Hunt.

Crouching monsters surround the water, still as gargoyles. Panthers sit beside wolves, some of which have collected the smaller alphas around their necks. Stoats, smaller cats...

It's a strange, fae collection of creatures acting against their instincts. Still and silent, their eyes glow through the fog, and their attention never lifts from the man in the rat mask standing at the head, laying out candles and...

Oh yuck.

Trophies. That must be the sacrifice part. Sacrificed in ritual, and then presented to the gods.

The flash of skin and marrow from the basement haunts me

temporarily, before I shove it aside and go back to paying attention.

The Hunt watches their predator like old friends, when they should cut him down where he stands.

"This is fucked up," I murmur. "What's the plan?"

The door is partially hidden from the ritual, but breaking through it will draw attention I'd rather not have. I run my hand along the windows, searching for a break, but it's pretty clear that they've done something to them to deter our escape. There's a slimy substance coating the outer sill, and while I might be immune to one drug now, there are a dozen more they could give me. I don't want that shit on my skin.

"Getting out quietly is going to be difficult. And the second we go out there, the entire Hunt tears us to shreds," Luc points out, staring grimly at the slimy stuff as I point it out to him. "I don't want to kill anyone who's under his control, so we can't even fight back."

I wince. He has a point. Just then, my eyes land on two shifters standing silently on either side of the rat. A tiger and a wolf.

"He's going to sacrifice them first," I whisper. "What does this ritual require? How long do we have?"

Luc gives me a quick run down, but when he reaches the end, his words trail off as he stares at something in the distance.

"The gods are already here," he whispers.

I follow his gaze. Shadowy creatures rest just out of sight, in the courtyard behind the pool. In the shadows of the house and garden. Horned men, women with long, twisting claws and bright eyes. Gods of indeterminate gender, clothed in fabric that looks like stars. They all shimmer a little at the edges, like they aren't fully here. But I don't think that will last.

I can see why they're so pissed about this ritual. No more gods, Cameron said.

Which, I suppose, would make him the god in their absence. The rise of the god killer.

Not on my watch.

A low humming buzzes from the trees, from the two killers in their deceptive sweaters and jeans. It's a chant. Speakers buzz as the chant echoes over and over; ancient rituals in a modern age.

As we watch, one of the fae figures lifts a horn to their lip and blows.

The sound is eerily familiar. The same three notes, except they don't cycle this time. The second note joins the first, followed by the third, until they blend and sing an eerie chord into the night.

I frown, my mind whirring. "Why does the ritual grant a wish?" I mutter, staring at that strange horn. "Why the fuck would it grant a wish? This isn't elementary school. And how can you just kill all the gods in one go like that... Talk about a loophole. It's so *easy*."

Luc makes an incredulous sound behind me.

I wave my hand, shushing him. "Yeah yeah, all the murder, I know. That's not easy, but if you want the gods to pay, why would you balk at a few sacrifices?"

The answer hits me. I turn to Luc, eyes wide. "It doesn't grant you a wish; it gives you control of the Hunt."

The *real* Hunt. As in, the gods' Hunt, that our little baby Hunt is based on.

The horn blows again, sending shivers down my spine. That sound doesn't belong on earth. It transforms the night into something else—something belonging to the Underworld. To the gods.

Luc's eyes widen. "He didn't ask the gods to die; he sent the Hunt after them."

We fall into silence, watching out the window.

"They're all here," I whisper. "Waiting. We can't have long."

My eyes fall on the painting that sits behind him. My fucking painting. The conduit to the gods, which he must have stolen just before he shot the Dean.

It all makes sense now—why he wanted it in the show. Why he was so insistent I include it.

Luc's jaw tightens. "So, now come the last of the three sacrifices, and then you. The queen. You'll be the main event, Jel. The queen by his side while he sacrifices three hunters in exchange for the horn."

And then kills me too, for funsies, no doubt.

"Are you the third hunter, with Jace and Theo?" I whisper. "Or does he just want you to watch?"

Luc shakes his head. "He's already done two, remember? He only needs one more."

My heart stutters, fear and confusion warring until I connect what Luc has already realized.

The wolf in the Academy basement.

And Anthony.

A broken sob catches in my throat, and it's only Luc's cool hand on my waist that holds me steady as I realize my brother's tribute is beside one of those candles. It doesn't take me long to locate it. One of the tributes is a broken, bloody finger, still half shifted into a clawed beast.

The other is a tooth.

A simple, gleaming snake's tooth. Bile rises in my throat.

Ritual slaughter, ritual bloodletting, and a token offered as tribute. Those were the two sacrifices that opened the connection to the gods, calling them down here so they could witness the end.

There's only one more hunter to kill tonight, which means he isn't taking both Jace and Theo like I thought... he's only taking one of them.

Sick dread fills me, choking me. I gag, doubling over to retch silently at my feet. The idea that he's only taking one of my mates from me is somehow worse.

How could I ever be without one of them? I need them all. They're my pack.

He's not getting a single one from me.

"So how do we reach him without the Hunt turning on us?" I growl. "Do you have a gun?"

"Better," Luc says in a low voice. "We have you."

"Huh?"

I turn to him, and his eyes flash golden—not with power, but with heat, desire. "It's your blood in the drug, Jel. Your family's venom. There has to be a way you can take over control."

Shit, maybe he's right.

It's our drug, after all. It's connected to us. To me.

Movement outside the window catches my attention, and I turn, horror catching in my throat—but it isn't the ritual.

The movement is something else. Shadows pour in from the garden, between the silent gods and through the Hunt.

Snakes.

Hundreds of snakes.

"The vipers have come," I breathe.

Rage and anguish consume me, but I force the emotions down. They don't matter. It doesn't matter who takes this psycho out, even if I want it to be me.

It just matters that we protect. That we restore safety.

I grit my teeth and tell myself it doesn't matter if my dad gets the killing blow.

Maybe one day I'll even believe it.

But then the snakes come to a stop. Several of them shift back into towering men, skin glistening between the fog and steam under the moonlight. My cousins and uncles.

I wait for them to strike down the killer; then I can take out Dad before he sacrifices me.

"Jel," Luc says warningly. "What is—"

They shake hands, and my stomach drops out from beneath me.

My father steps through the fog, holding out a small glass vial. More of the drug, I assume. So they can dope me up with too much for me to fight.

My heart races, eyes darting back and forth between them, searching for the lie. Searching for the truth.

It's there, in the glint of Dad's eye. In the tight twist of hatred on Cameron's face as he peels off his mask and casts it aside.

They'll betray each other. There's no doubt in my mind this is no solid alliance. But they still formed it. For the sake of their reputation, of their name—of *greed*—they've shaken the blood-stained hands of my brother's killer.

That's when it hits me.

There's no way this little rat made it through an entire pit of vipers without help. There's no way he got out of there alive without them letting him free.

"Anthony," I whisper.

They sold him out. They let that murderous bastard onto our land, drugged my brother, and let the killer take him. Anthony said Dad no longer trusted him, but it was more than that. It was payback for helping Luc at the station. For helping me.

"If Cameron was their lab rat, then your father knows him," Luc says softly, urgently.

I stiffen. He's right.

More pieces fall into place, toppling like dominoes.

As soon as my father's network discovered that the killer was a rat shifter, he would have been able to put the pieces together. He's probably known since Anthony started investigating the rat mask, after the warehouse.

Anthony said he'd see what he could dig up on the killer, then. He even said he'd use our father's network. Why didn't I realize? Why didn't I *think*?

Does my father know Luc's uncle is involved as well? Or does he think they're fighting each other?

I realize suddenly that it doesn't matter—none of this matters, because my father doesn't care. Where I've spent days trying to uncover the truth, justice, he doesn't care about that. He only cares about revenge.

He'll use them, and then he'll kill them.

Just like he did to Anthony.

Whatever lingering need I have for my family's approval shatters, and in its place something burns.

Rises.

"I'll make them pay for that," I whisper, my voice distorting with rage. With violence.

The coin flips, and I know without a doubt which side is needed tonight. Which side my fire burns on.

The snake in me seeks to lunge, to bite. But the human pauses for just a moment. Together, we consider. Think. Realize.

The lights beneath the water outside reflect eerily on the surface of the pool. I watch the blue tinge ripple over the still faces of the Hunt, letting my mind go almost dormant as I put the pieces together.

"My father would never hand over a drug that could kill him," I say softly. "No matter how soon he planned to betray the user."

Something twist and reform within me, settling into place. I'm no longer afraid of losing. I can do this. Luc was right; I can control the drug.

A smile creeps onto my face, my reflection in the window glinting eerily in the light.

"I'll make them all pay."

The reshaped thing inside me burns, lighting a fire within my soul, sending golden light glinting off the glass as my eyes burn back at me.

Through our invisible bond, the energy anchors within our pack, connecting us, and I know then that the bond of fate is stronger than whatever drug my mates have been given. I'll pull them back from the edge.

We're going to win, and now I know why.

Okay, so maybe I'm not the final girl.

I'm the killer.

"Shift," I tell Luc, my eyes still burning. "Break down the walls. Leave the Hunt and the vipers to me."

He smiles, slow and feral. Then the shift takes over.

Scales ripple over his face, hot breath hitting my skin. His bones shift and pop, neck stretching as his shoulders break and reform, wider and wider. I grab hold of one shoulder and swing on top, crouching below his giant skull as it bursts through the roof and the walls of the poolhouse crumble around us.

There's that hat trick I predicted.

Casually, smugly, Luc puts his foot through the painting.

The Hunt gazes up at us, unnaturally still even as the vipers writhe and shift, preparing to attack.

"Don't even think about it," I bark, sliding down from Luc's back as he takes to the sky, following a second giant, reptilian shadow into the night.

As one, the vipers fall still. The ones in human form kneel.

The blood still calls to me.

Now I need to decide what I'll do with it.

Marcus stares up at me, his eyes brimming with anger.

"What are you waiting for?" he hisses, ignoring the sudden crumple of clothes beside him as a man turns into a rat.

I don't ignore it, but I'll let him think he's escaped, for now.

Watching the rat out of the corner of my eye as he scurries away, I shake my head. "They don't follow you, do they?" I tilt my head, using my brain for probably the first time in years, where it concerns my family. "You always had to make them follow you. They never did it by choice—why else would an alpha hoard a drug that controlled the powerful? It's so... weak." The word drops from my mouth into silence.

He's weak.

His face contorts into an ugly snarl, and I know what my younger self would have done. Cowered. Simpered. I would have been desperate to regain his lost favor, because the only people my father can control naturally are scared, traumatized little girls.

And I'm no longer one of them.

"You turned me into a monster, you know," I tell him conversationally. I turn my hands over, studying them. They're covered in real blood, this time. Mine. "You molded me into the worst parts of you, and when I fought back, you killed me."

That's where I've been, all these years. Not dormant. Not hidden. Not repressed.

Dead.

And now I'm coming back to life.

"You were a weak little bitch," my father snarls. "Are you going to stand here talking all day, or are you actually going to put your money where your mouth is?"

My eyes snap to his, fury welling up inside me. My soul guides me, soothing me, bringing me back from the edge so we can stay in control together. "Shut the fuck up, old man," I hiss.

I reach up to the stub of my ear, still leaking blood in slow, painful droplets. I pull a face, already disgusted by what I'm about to do.

I tear through the final flap of skin and throw the stub of my ear down onto the ritual table. It isn't the whole thing; just the tip.

That's what she said.

"Third tribute, gods," I call without taking my eyes off Marcus. "Any chance one of you wants to be my queen for the night? I forgot to bring one from home."

Silence. And then, a ripple of unfamiliar sound passes behind me, like a tittering, singing breeze. I think it might be laughter.

A familiar figure, with terrifying eyes and long flowing hair, appears from nowhere and settles to my right. With a smile, Fate gestures to me, holding her hand out with her palm facing up.

My heart stutters, but I place my hand above hers, barely touching. Her skin is ice-cold, like a glacier. I wonder if I've been tricked, and I'm about to be destroyed for daring to think a god would be my queen.

But then a heavy weight appears in my free hand, and I look down to see a horn.

My mouth curves into a smile. The horn is a little shimmery around the edges, like the gods themselves, and I'm pretty sure it will only last for one blow, rather than granting me whatever carnage this full ritual is supposed to bring.

That's fine. One blow is all I need.

I raise it to my lips and give it all I've got. The sound echoes over the water, and the shimmering edges of the gods become real. Fate winks at me, her own shimmering form turning to midnight as she vanishes, reappearing at the center of the Hunt.

My father turns and runs.

A great baying sound rings out in the night as the stillness erupts into chaos. A dozen creatures rush past me, snarling and snapping. Horned skulls and strange wolves leap across the water, giving chase to their prey.

I watch from a distance; I'm not finished here.

That's one Hunt freed, but the second is still in chains.

My jaw shifts enough to let my forked tongue free. It tastes the air, flicking back into my mouth so I can discern each subtle nuance. Each chemical.

I can taste the drug. What's more—I can taste its reach. Cameron may have caught the Hunt, but as I suspected, my father has owned the vipers for years. I close my eyes, letting my soul's curiosity and instinct take over as she sniffs the air and studies the strange magic. This thing is like an alpha command, coiling around the shifter souls it's corrupted and nudging them toward the commander's control. Powerful. Unbeatable.

But that's also its downfall. Cameron may have stolen a position at the top of the hierarchy, but alphas rule by that system. It's in our blood.

This is my family's drug. Whether the victims are the Hunt, controlled by a drug powered by my blood, or the vipers, controlled for years by a drug fueled by my fathers', it's my family bloodline. My lineage.

Mine to control.

I let instinct take over, rising, reaching. I wonder what the gods will see when they look at me. Will they see the blackened flame of my shifter soul snatching those warped tendrils from the air? Or is it all in the bark, in the command?

I call the drug to me with a hiss, as my father no doubt planned to do in the final moments of the ritual. Right before he sacrificed me.

And I let them all free.

The snakes twist distractedly, writhing into the space

created by their sudden freedom. A ripple spreads through them as understanding hits, as their minds and choices return to them for the first time in years. The ones at the top would have known about the drug. They just wouldn't have known it had been used on them.

Every alpha in Marcus's network was bought without their consent.

Every beta is a potential accomplice.

Chaos erupts. Furious vipers join the Hunt, while others use it as a cover to escape. I can barely see through the mass of bodies. I take a step onto the rubble of the poolhouse, testing it. It seems sturdy. I climb to the top. Beside me, a wolf and a tiger appear from the shadows, guarding my back as I rise.

From here, I have a better vantage point of the carnage. The tiger snarls, while the wolf beside me tips his head back and howls.

Marcus's head whips around at the noise, and our eyes lock. There's no pity and no apology between us.

Marcus transforms, but all I see is a writhing coil of scales before an entire pit of gigantic snakes descends on him, followed by the gods' Hunt, feral and wild. The knot twists and undulates, falling into the pool to disappear below the surface as the water churns above them, red with blood.

Meanwhile, the earthly Hunt rumbles. Wolves growl, long and low, until the sound is picked up and echoed from every corner.

For a handful of seconds, I command them all. The gods' Hunt and the earthly Hunt together; they're all mine.

Like I fucking want that.

I drop the horn into the pool and watch as it sizzles into vapor. The gods—their faces eerily still, turned upward to mine from below the water's surface—shimmer and vanish. One of the panthers looks at me, her body held so still. Then, she leaps over the pool and charges into the distance, toward the dragon who once controlled her.

One by one, the others turn to follow. With their noses to the sky, they sniff the air, following the stench of dragon flame that puffs and bursts in the sky to the North. A baying cry rings out over the water, steam rising as the Hunt assembles and takes off into the forest to chase the dragon, and after that, simply to run, free in the night.

I leave them to it.

I have a rat to hunt.

My mates guard my back, and it isn't long before a third set of footsteps joins them. I glance over my shoulder to find Luc, naked and covered in a dozen cuts. Golden claws gleam at the tips of his fingers, like they do at mine. He grins at me, blue eyes gleaming in triumph.

I return the smile and look away.

We make a different kind of Hunt, the four of us. In the stillness of what this night has become, I can't help but feel it's the closest thing to that first Hunt. The divine Hunt. Fate's blessing surrounds us, tying our pack together as we finally accept the mission that was given to us by the gods I unwittingly called to.

This Hunt is about justice—ten years in the making.

The music pounds eerily in the empty rooms as I wind slowly through the house, searching. Smelling. My footsteps barely make a sound, but a rat would be able to hear me.

I can hear him, too.

Slowly, I begin to hum. The same three, tuneless notes, over and over. My tongue flicks free, and I taste fear. Repulsion.

"Come out, little rat," I sing. "You and I have some catching up to do."

Movement skitters by the corner, and I pounce.

My hands skim fur, and he's gone. Grinning, I chase after him. We're running now, the sound of terrified, instinctive squeaking giving him away. It would almost be upsetting, except for the blood that streaks his furred body—blood he took.

He slips beneath the door to the basement. We've done this dance before, but not like this. He's never faced me as a predator. In the upstairs landing I was cautious. Assessing him, as I would a foe. But he's no foe, no matter what magic he's stolen or tricks he's used.

He's prey, and I'm done playing.

I corner him above the paint tins and snatch him into the air. After a moment of squirming, he shifts back. I slam him back into the wall, my fist around his throat.

My mates settle by the door to witness.

"Why did you kidnap me?" I hiss.

He blinks, confused for a moment, before he realizes what I'm asking. I never even suspected him, although he's at least ten years older than me. And I knew he was some kind of smaller shifter. He should have been a suspect.

They should all have been suspects.

He shrugs, arrogant even in the face of death. "You were the easiest target. If I'd realized you were an alpha at the time, I'd have saved a lot of years of hassle." His expression turns to muted fury. "Ten years building to this moment, and you decide at the last minute that being one of those brutes was worth the cost. You could have just walked away, Jel."

He shakes his head, and I don't know how I never saw the revulsion in his eyes before. Does he look at every alpha this way? With pure hatred?

"You know, you almost impressed me," he continues. "Blocking off your alpha side. Hiding it away. I knew you felt guilty that you never stopped the dragon carnage, and I even regretted that I had to bring your alpha soul back out to get your blood for the drug. But your brother's wasn't strong enough and I couldn't get your real Alpha's." He laughs bitterly. "I was going to let the queen live, this time. I would have let you live." His eyes narrow. "But then you started sticking your nose in."

I close my eyes, clenching my fist tighter around his neck, hearing him choke.

"I was the easiest target," I say slowly. "And those girls you killed. The blood you drained. Were they the easiest targets, too? Were they the easiest way to get to me and make me break free from my cage?"

I pull him back and slam him in again, sending paint tins rattling around our feet.

He begins to laugh hysterically, wincing away from the shuddering shelves. "It was for a good cause. I was so close to getting that horn." His eyes glaze over as he imagines some distant, lost future. "I would have turned them on each other, and they would have had no choice but to do it. To kill. They would have been destroyed by their own twisted power."

His little fantasy is as chilling as it is unsurprising. He hated us, hated the gods for choosing us, no matter that the gods had long been forgotten.

"You didn't have to do any of this," I tell him, exhaustion creeping into my voice. "We aren't your enemy."

He scoffs, and in his eyes I see the same anger and loathing I've felt toward alphas for years. Toward myself.

But I was wrong.

The alpha my dad chose to be, the one he tried to turn me into. That's no alpha. That's no warrior, no protector.

I'm no longer afraid that's what I'll become. And I'm done turning away and letting those alphas rule.

No one should have to be afraid of them.

"It's a choice," I tell him quietly, almost as though I'm

talking to myself. "It's always a choice. And buddy, you made the wrong one."

He moves suddenly, twisting my grip and clawing me across the face, his eyes wide with fear. It's enough to break free.

Cameron might be no match for me, but a cornered rat can still draw blood. There's been enough blood. It's time to end this.

"You're just like them," he snarls. "I was wrong about you; you're nothing but a brute."

I laugh, the sound echoing through the cold basement. I begin to shift, my fangs elongating, the taste of venom sliding down my throat.

"For the record," I hiss, sibilant but still human enough. "Alphas aren't brutes. We're the people you turn to for safety. For protection. Our passion turns to violence when it needs to, but the rest of the time..." My voice flares with heat at the memories—lips on skin, teeth claiming what's offered freely, the deliberate submission of kneeling before a lover. "It's devotion. It was never meant to be a hierarchy of control, and it won't be again," I finish softly, my lip curling in anticipation.

My soul wants this. She's wanted this for years.

Fortunately for her, my humanity is in perfect alignment with this moment of justice.

This is for the dragons he sent to the slaughter. For everyone he killed just to get his hands on the one drug that would allow him to share a moment of breath with the gods.

This is for Anthony.

This is for me.

"But I have nothing to prove to you." I stretch my jaw, yellow light glinting off his skull, highlighting his fear as his eyes dart and search for an exit. "Goodbye Cameron."

I lunge at the same time he tries to run, my teeth sinking into his neck. The tangy scent of his blood washes over me as my venom paralyzes him for the kill, seconds before I tear his throat free and spit it out on the concrete. He crumples to the floor.

I leave him there to rot.

44

JEL

MY MATES INSIST ON TAKING ME TO THE HOSPITAL, AND, I MEAN, FAIR enough. I am missing part of an ear.

I don't think Jace is going to let me live that down. Every time I look over at him, he mimes ripping off his own ear and throwing it like a grenade. I don't care; I'd do it again, if it meant making sure those killers didn't escape the consequences. All of them, my father included.

I don't know what will happen to the vipers now, though. I don't want them.

The doctors buzz around us, running back and forth between stretchers as guests of the party are wheeled in. Cameron wasn't gentle when he took over command of their bodies, and he was straight out violent when he turned them on everyone at that party who wasn't an alpha.

Which is basically the dictionary definition of hypocrite. I know why he hated alphas, and especially vipers, but those other people never did anything to him. They were innocent.

I was right, in some ways, when I ran away from my family and the role they wanted me to play. Power can corrupt, especially power like that.

But it's a choice; it's always a choice. Our beasts aren't without logic. They're our partners—our pack.

"Jel!"

My body stiffens, adrenaline flooding me, mixing with pain and grief. It can't be. I'm imagining it.

But then I look up and recognize a familiar face on the other side of the hospital room.

"Anthony!" My voice breaks, and then I'm running, sprinting across the hospital floor and pummeling into my brother.

His arms loop around my waist and he winces, holding his stomach bandages out of reach. "Careful, Jel, I was fucking stabbed," he mutters, but he's smiling, grinning as he holds me close like he'll never let me go again.

"How?!" I splutter. My mates walk up behind me, but I can't leave Anthony. I keep hugging him. "I saw you fall!" My mouth twists, shame and grief flooding me. "I didn't protect you."

His smile shifts, fangs emerging just enough for me to see what's changed. There's only one fang, now. He shifts back.

"I got back up," he says quietly.

"*How*?!" I repeat.

Someone else familiar steps up beside him. "Well," Greta smiles, looking over her shoulder and waving Amelie toward our group. "You stopped answering messages, and we knew your boys had been taken, so things were obviously getting spicy." She shrugs. "So we hacked your phone a little—sorry—and your GPS told us you were there. When we saw your brother go down, we figured you wouldn't mind a switch in priorities."

She laughs at my stunned expression. "You didn't think I'd be worried about you, did you?" Her expression turns fierce. "We look out for one another. It's what we do. You did it for me, didn't you?"

I don't know if she means alphas, or women, or friends. It doesn't matter. It's not about that.

I let go of Anthony to hug her instead.

"See, you sort of did protect me, after all," Anthony says, ruffling my hair. "Because the other alphas had your back. Why else do you think the Hunt is a thing? You can't do it all on your own."

"Yeah yeah," I mumble, finally pulling away.

Jace steadies me, while Luc presses his warm, solid weight against my back and Theo crosses his arms, guarding me.

Suddenly, I'm so very tired.

"Can we go?" I ask, looking over their heads at the doctors. "They've bandaged me up, so that's it, right?"

Anthony pulls a face. "Yeah, I think they're going to be at this for a while. Speak to that nurse, and she might be able to discharge you."

I want to go, but I don't want to leave him. He grins down at me, raw and exhausted, reading my thoughts as always.

"I'll stick around," I say, but he cuts me off by ruffling my hair and pushing it over my face.

"Go on, twerp. I want to get some sleep."

I ruffle his own hair and shove it in his eyes, but it doesn't take much more convincing before I give up. I'm wrecked. I need a bed.

We make our way over to the station. I'm so exhausted by this point I can barely stand, but honestly, the nurse seems glad to get rid of four extra bodies. With one last hug for Anthony and a promise that no one is going to do anything stupid, we escape out the front doors.

Then, finally, *finally*, we go home.

Luc and Theo start out on the couch, but somehow we all migrate backward onto the bed, ending up in a giant nest overnight. With the morning light shining in on us, it's cozy and safe, my head tucked into Theo's shoulder and Jace's arm around my waist.

Luc lies sideways across the foot of the bed, his face unusually peaceful in sleep while his arms dangle sideways, over the back of the couch.

Carefully, I extract myself from the center, laughing quietly as Jace immediately readjusts to spoon Theo. I wonder what these two rival alphas will think when they wake up to each other.

I guess they probably won't mind at all.

Lying here like this, I can almost forget about last night. About all of it, the murders, Cameron... my own family's role in everything. Almost, but not quite.

The memories sink into my bones, weighing me down. Even the room seems darker, like a cloud has crossed over the sun, and yet, I'm warm. The press of my mates' bodies against mine still lingers, as strong a memory as the rest of it. The threat has passed.

I look at my hands, and they're clean. No blood in sight.

I shake my head, turning my attention away from my memories and back to the present. There'll be time for grief—and boy, is there grief to be had. But I'm not ready for that yet. For now, I want a reminder that we lived. We won.

Which means food. And painting.

Soon, the apartment is full of the scent of coffee—which gets my three's noses twitching—heralded by a light knock on the door as our breakfast arrives.

"Hope you like McDonald's breakfast," I say when Luc sits up sharply.

Theo stirs, his eyes snapping open and growing wide at the sight of Jace snuggled around him.

"What the—"

"Stop moving, you bony sack of shit," Jace mumbles. "You'd think all those fucking bicep curls you do would give you better cushioning, but no, I should've known you were made up of protein and spite."

Theo gapes at him for a full second before hiking up his legs and kicking Jace straight out of bed.

"At least I don't skip leg day," he crows, and then leaps over the top of Jace to hide behind me.

His arm scoops around my waist, pulling me close as a human shield. For once, I don't object or pull away. I fall into him, laughing as Jace throws his hair out of his face and turns to us, eyes glowing.

He charges but skids to a halt at the sight of the McMuffins lining the counter.

"I figured you'd want more than one," I say dryly.

Theo straightens, still with his hand around my waist.

"Good morning, babe," he murmurs into my ear. "How did you sleep?"

I glance over my shoulder at him, my body naturally curling into his warmth. I still can't completely get a read on him, but I'm starting to.

I'm realizing I don't need to have all the answers. I don't need to be in control. With these three, I can just trust, and it will all work out.

He'll tell me about his past one day, and one day I'll tell him about mine, too. The details of it—the ones that no one ever knows.

"Like a log," I answer, smiling softly as he kisses me again, this time on the corner of the mouth. "You?"

He lingers before pulling back, lips curving into a grin. "Best

night's sleep I've had in a week." His grin widens when he looks
down at my pajamas and chicken feet.

What can I say? It was a puppy dog pajama kind of night.

I hum in agreement, my body melting as two more bodies
appear behind me, their hands soft against my sleep-warmed
skin. "I had an idea," I tell them, fighting back the urge to
surrender.

For now, at least.

"Mmm?"

"I thought you could join me for a painting session."

Luc's face perks up with interest, but he's the only artist of
the three, and Theo and Jace hesitate.

"Do we need to be good?" Theo asks, grimacing.

"You can go totally abstract," I assure him, giving him a wry
look. "Just throw the paints at the canvas."

"Oh, I can do that," he says with a grin.

Jace shrugs, flicking his hair back out of his face. "I'm up
for it."

"Alright, but you can't laugh at my painting overalls," I tell
them, fighting to keep my face still. Unable to resist, I add, "And
you can't let their ravishingly attractive style distract you. We're
painting, not fucking. Promise?"

My attempt at being casual must work, because three smug
mates grin back at me and promise not to get distracted, clearly
convinced I'm about to bring out the dorkiest overalls known to
man. I can't wait to wipe the looks off their faces.

I disappear to change while Luc sets up a couple of easels
for us. It doesn't take him long, and when I peek through the
gap in the door, I can see them huddled like a little pack, even
though they barely seem to realize what they're doing. Their
shoulders press together, bodies angled in toward each other.
Toward safety.

Jace's smile is eager with anticipation, but relaxed too. Luc is as unreadable as ever, but his eyes never leave the door, as if there's nothing more he wants than to see me.

"Go on," Theo says with a smirk, folding his arms and leaning back against the wall. "Let's see these overalls then."

"I'm going to rate them next to the pajamas," Jace says, tossing his hair out of his eyes and bumping his shoulder into Theo's. "Do you think they're better or worse?"

"Unless they come with duck feet, I don't know how they could compare," Luc says dryly, but there's an amusement in his tone that tells me he's expecting duck feet.

I force my expression into something neutral, swing the door open, and step into the room.

The smiles fall from their faces one by one, replaced instantly with heat.

"Jel," Theo growls, stepping forward.

"Ah ah." I hold up one finger, my eyes glinting golden. "We're painting, remember?"

I watch the instinct wash over them, filling them with the desire to reach for me, to hold their mate close and make sure no one else can claim her. It wars with their loyalty to their promise. A low rumble of desire echoes through the room, and I smile, baring all my teeth.

"Good boys."

The rumble becomes a growl.

Laughing, I cross the room to my canvas and let them all get a good look.

I chose these overalls years ago, thrifting them from a tiny little store downtown. They were one of the first things I bought when I left my family behind, and they've always held a special meaning for that alone.

When I rode my bike home, though, it poured with rain. I was soaked through, and the only dry clothing I had with me were the damn overalls.

So I threw them on and painted, the storm raging outside. Something about it transformed me. The paint falling on my bare skin, the gentle shift of the satin lining against my breasts, and the breeze against my skin each time the material moved and bared my tits to the room. It was freeing, daring—open.

It represented everything I wanted out of my new life, and I've never painted in anything else since. At least, not in private.

The three hungry stares fixed my way aren't exactly private, but life's about change, right?

I pretend to think it over. "Well I guess we have time for a little distraction."

They're on me in an instant.

We stumble into the easels, mouths devouring, hands clutching at each other. It's like a wall has broken down, broken apart, and all I want is them. Their touch. Their bodies against mine.

The warmth and safety they bring.

Theo kisses me, possessive and rough as he demands my attention every time I go to leave. He snarls, biting hard on my lower lip when Jace tries to kiss me.

Luc laughs, a low, gentle sound, right before he kisses Theo on the back of the neck. Theo stiffens, pulling away from me in shock, his eyes wide. I don't think they've kissed before.

He turns, opens his mouth to speak, and grunts in shock as Luc grabs him by the back of the head and pulls him into a brutal kiss. A low groan of desire spills from his lips, and then he's kissing Luc furiously, devouring him, tasting him.

Theo's hands drop to Luc's waist as he pulls their hips together, grinding them in an aching, rolling beat.

Eyes flashing shifter gold, Luc kicks his knee into the back of Theo's leg and drops them both to the ground. They land with a crash. Jace and I lurch into action, trying to stop the inevitable fallout as my trolley of paints wobbles, but it's too late.

Theo rolls into the trolley, and they spill all over the floor.

And us.

"They're going to evict me," I sputter, laughing as the paint leaks dangerously close to the edge of my tarp.

"Nah," Jace said. "They wouldn't dare. Besides. I'm good with a hammer; I'll fix it." He grabs me around the middle, spinning me into his arms and smearing paint all over my body as he does. "Now, let me see these overalls."

His eyes drop to my breasts, darkening with heat. He leans down, kissing the mound of my breast above the fabric, making me moan as my head tips back and hits the wall.

Then he takes my nipple into his mouth, sucking.

A similar wet sound comes from the ground, and my eyes snap open. I look down, but it isn't what I thought.

It is, however, about three seconds away from it.

Theo sucks Luc's nipple, his teeth marring the skin as he shoves Luc's shirt up higher and fumbles with his fly with the other hand. I don't think I've ever seen Luc so desperately on edge. His head tilts to the side, fringe falling across his eyes as his mouth falls open. Rough groans drop from his lips as Theo mouths at him.

"God," I breathe, as Jace very lightly runs his teeth over my skin. "I really do want to paint at some point, you know. *Fuck*."

"I could paint you," Jace murmurs, moving his attention to his other nipple. He pauses only long enough to push me down on the couch.

"Will you be kissing me while you do?" I pant, my head falling back again.

"Well... when I say paint you, I mean... you're the canvas. So, yeah probably."

I can't help laughing, the sound mixing with a rough gasp as he drops the straps of my overalls over my arms. The front falls, dangling over my legs.

The sounds from the floor stop. I look down to see both Theo and Luc watching us, their eyes dark, hair falling across their faces. Even Theo's is mussed, his usual styled gel completely ruined from Luc's hands threading through it.

Luc glances at Theo, and a wicked glint appears in his eye. He props himself up on his elbows and blows a slow stream of smoke into Theo's face.

Theo shakes his head, startled, and turns back.

"Sit next to Jel," Luc commands.

Theo's face darkens with desire, and he rises gracefully to his feet before dropping down beside me.

"I like the overalls," he murmurs, slinging an arm over my shoulder and taking in a good view of my tits.

"Thanks," I say dryly, looking between my mates in confusion. Even Jace has paused, his expression mirroring Luc's.

It's like they all know something I don't.

Then Luc reaches for Theo's fly, just as Jace slides his thumbs into the waist of my overalls and pulls them down.

"What the—" I breathe, swallowing thickly as Jace lets the overalls rest halfway down my thighs, trapping me.

Theo begins to laugh, a dark, sensual laugh that does things to my insides. His head drops back on the couch at the same time Luc takes out his cock and swallows him down.

"Is this really happening?" I ask, my voice pitched higher than I meant it to be. Then: "Oh my *God*."

Jace licks my pussy, and I can practically feel the smug grin on his face as I moan and collapse back into the cushions.

"I feel like a fucking frat boy," I groan, clutching the cushions while Theo's hand reflexively clenches the air over my left tit. "Getting eaten out next to his friend. What the hell is this?"

"Ssh," Theo murmurs, hooking his arm around my neck and bringing me into a kiss. "If you were a frat boy, you'd be getting blown. See? Totally different."

I laugh against him, but the laughter quickly vanishes as he kisses me slower, deeper. I moan into his mouth, arching my hips up into Jace's tongue as he pulls my overalls lower and spreads my legs wide.

Breathless, Theo and I break apart, and I glance down at Luc between Theo's legs. Theo follows my attention, sweeping his free hand through the damp strands of hair over Luc's forehead.

Luc looks up, not taking his mouth from Theo's cock. His eyes narrow in amusement, and he slows down his movements to a slick, wet slide that has Theo gasping and my stomach clenching with desire.

Then Jace does something clever with his tongue, and my eyes roll back in my head, low moans dropping from my mouth as I thrust against him.

"Told you he was good with his tongue," Theo rumbles, his voice pitched low with desire. He wets his lips, watching Jace's head bob up and down over me.

I turn around to stare at him, startled. "Are you seriously telling me... I thought you were enemies!"

Theo shrugs. "We were competitors," he says, a small smile on his lips. "We never said what the prizes were."

Fucking hell.

"You mean... you two idiots were trading blow jobs all this time, and you didn't once think it might mean something when Fate pulled us all together?" I ask, incredulous.

Theo looks startled, like he never even considered it.

I begin to laugh again, but then Jace flicks his tongue in light, fast movements, and I can't hold back anymore. I'm coming, my body shuddering with the strength of it, waves of pleasure flooding me.

Beside me, Theo follows with a shout, his fist clenching in Luc's hair, rough but tender as he thrusts up into his mouth and strokes the hair from his forehead.

"God," I breathe, staring up at the ceiling. "I suppose that was better than painting."

"Nah," Jace murmurs, planting a kiss on my thigh and then dropping back onto his hands. "That was just the entrée. You can paint now. I wanna see what you make."

"What about you?" I ask, lifting my head.

Luc grins, pulling off his shirt and using it to wipe himself clean. "We can be dessert."

We pull our clothing back together, although Luc stays shirtless, and settle into a strange, quiet rhythm. Theo and Jace seem fascinated just to watch us, toying with the colors, painting the backs of our necks when we aren't looking. And Luc and I drift into a pleasant trance, losing ourselves in the art.

It's a different kind of trance to the one Fate put me in, but I can feel her presence here anyway. The sensation of her isn't like the fire she used to bring us together; it's softer. A steady warmth, curling around each of us like fine golden threads. The threads pull us together, leading us to where we always wanted to be, even when we didn't know it.

Our pack has finally come home.

***

THE END

THANK YOU!

Thank you so much for reading Viper's Fate. If you enjoyed the book, it would mean the world to me if you could leave a review on your favourite retailer or book community. Reviews help indie authors out so much more than people know.

Desperate to know what's next? There are lots of wonderful projects in the works over here, and your best spot for updates is to sign up to my mailing list, or join me in my facebook group—both available through my website.

www.jadebonesauthor.com

I share everything about the books in the group, along with giveaways for signed paperbacks and swag that I won't run anywhere else. So it's the best place to be if you want to stay up to date and get all the goodies!

ACKNOWLEDGMENTS

Well, that took a bit longer than I thought. So, I began this book around when I finished the Hell's Fire Burning series, and it was meant to be a quick and easy standalone between trilogies.

It... was not that. But I'm glad it wasn't, because now these characters have grown on me, like a barnacle or a fungus, and I don't intend to spray any vinegar. By which I mean, I love them so much more than I meant to, and there will probably be bonus chapters for them in the future, which is fun for all of us.

Also, this is apparently the second book in like two years I've written with the Wild Hunt as a major inspiration (although the other one isn't under this name). I'm getting the feeling I'm not done with the Hunt themes, either... So, like, head's up on that front.

Anyway, major thanks go to Veronica Eden, as always, for your insightful beta thoughts and suggestions on the book. They always come out better with your advice. To Kat and Kathryn for the cheerleading and writing vibes, and finally to the Booktober 2022 authors, for being such an awesome group of humans to collaborate with this year. I learned a lot from you guys.

So, if you've finished the book, I truly hope you enjoyed the ride. If you haven't... what are you doing here?! There are spoilers, like people who died and came back to life, or maybe never died in the first place. I'm really sorry about that, by the way.

Happy reading, here and everywhere else! Hopefully I'll see you in the next project.

HELLCAT ESCAPING
HELL'S FIRE BURNING TRILOGY, BOOK ONE

Available on Amazon

Three demon princes and one tortured soul with no memory... we're a match made in Hell.

When my final escape attempt from Hell's cages is thwarted by three sinfully sexy demon princes, Lucifer decides to offer me a deal. All I have to do to win his esteem is guard these three on Earth and bring them back safely. Easy, right? Wrong.

These boys have no intention of returning to Hell, and as far as they're concerned, I'm standing in their way. But after a little unexpected hellfire, an assassination attempt, and an unfortunate spell that won't let us move more than ten feet from each other, it appears someone has other plans—for all of us.

There's a deeper secret here than my princes', and it's turning deadly.

Sticking together is our only option for now, but the more I get to know them, the harder it becomes to remember why I should run. They're vicious and mean, but there's a different kind of heat building between us than the flames I'm used to, and when a strange cord appears to bind us together, that fire becomes impossible to ignore.

If I'm not careful, I'll get burnt.

The problem is, this might be the one fire I'd gladly burn in.

Warning: Hellcat Escaping is a reverse harem novel with multiple love interests, and as the first in a trilogy ends on a cliffhanger. Intended for mature readers, it contains dark fantasy elements regarding violence and assault, along with sexual content that some readers may find offensive. Please proceed with caution.

ABOUT THE AUTHOR

Jade Bones is a paranormal romance writer who loves writing about delicious demons, magical worlds, and steamy romps.

She is the author of the Hell's Fire Burning trilogy, a dark fantasy RH series following an escaped hellsoul and the demons stuck by her side. When Jade isn't writing, you can find her drinking tea, cuddling her dog, or taking tarot far too seriously.

www.jadebonesauthor.com

ALSO BY JADE BONES

Reverse Harem

HELL'S FIRE BURNING

Hellcat Escaping

Hellcat Fighting

Hellcat Ascending

RITUAL BOUND

(available in the Booktober 2022

charity anthology)

One True Love Romance

MY DEMON BOUND

Lock & Portal

Heart & Soul

Rite & Fire

Dreams & Desires

MY DEMON BOUND SHORT

Infernal Fate